# Playing Her Cards Right

## JO LEIGH

First Published in Great Britain 2016
By Mills & Boon, an imprint of HarperCollins*Publishers*
1 London Bridge Street, London, SE1 9GF

ISBN: 978-0-263-92068-0

05-0616

Our policy is to use papers that are natural, renewable and recyclable products and made from wood grown in sustainable forests.The logging and manufacturing processes conform to the legal environmental regulations of the country of origin.

Printed and bound in Spain
by CPI, Barcelona

**Jo Leigh** is from Los Angeles and always thought she'd end up living in Manhattan. So how did she end up in Utah, in a tiny town with a terrible internet connection, being bossed around by a house full of rescued cats and dogs? What the heck, she says, predictability is boring. Jo has written more than forty novels and can be contacted at joleigh@joleigh.com.

# CHOOSE ME

BY
JO LEIGH

To Birgit, for her enthusiasm and support.
And to Debbi & Jill, who rock. Hard.

# 1

**Bree Kingston**
Assistant copywriter at *BBDA Manhattan*
Studied Advertising and Fashion at *Case Western University*
Lives in *Manhattan* ❤ Single From *Ohio*
Born on March 22

BREE KINGSTON HAD BEEN IN Manhattan for five months and twelve days. This was her third visit to the St. Mark's Church basement kitchen, where she and sixteen women she barely knew were exchanging ten days' worth of frozen lunches. She'd gotten invited by Lucy Prince, whom Bree had known for four days. Lucy wasn't part of the exchange. Not anymore. She'd moved to Buffalo with her fiancé, thereby freeing up the foldout ottoman bed that Bree slept on in the one-bedroom apartment she shared with three other girls. Bree's rent was a steal at seven hundred per month. The stove at the apartment had been nonfunctioning for as long as anyone there could remember.

Technically, this was her sixth visit to the kitchen.

She had gotten permission to come to the communal church basement the evenings before the exchanges to prepare her lunches. Sixteen portions of veggie lasagna and medium-heat chili this week packed in small freezer-to-microwave containers, all ready to be handed out during the semimonthly trade.

Although it had sounded odd when she'd first heard about the group, Bree suffered from both of the two major maladies that came with living the Manhattan dream: no decent single men to date and no money.

She'd anticipated both. Since she'd spent most of her twenty-five years planning her escape to The Big Apple, she'd read every article, blog and book about the subject, saved her money like Scrooge as she'd worked her way through college, and even had a decent savings account set aside for emergencies. Bree was in this for the long haul.

Finding the lunch exchange had been a brilliant stroke of luck. Fourteen of the sixteen were also single, worked in the East Village and all of them knew where to find the best happy hours, the cheapest dry cleaning, cell service that actually worked and where not to go on a date, assuming one ever had a date.

Even better, she'd actually made her first real New York friends.

"Attention ladies!" Shannon Fitzgerald, a natural redhead wearing a fantastic knockoff dress Bree had noticed first thing, had needed to shout to get everyone to listen. All of them were standing around a rectangle of tables, their lunches in front of them in neat little stacks. Everyone had brought their own cooler bag with ice packs on the bottom. In a moment, they'd move from pile to pile, an elegant assembly line of working women, all of them under thirty-ish, all of them wearing something dark on this December day. All of them except Bree. She had chosen a yellow-and-black plaid skirt and jacket, emphasis on the yellow, hand-made from her own copycat pattern. Which would have looked very nice on Shannon, now that Bree thought about it.

"Hush," Shannon said, and in a moment, the room fell silent. "Thank you. I have had an idea," she said.

It wasn't just a sentence. Not the way it was said. No, all the words were IN CAPS and **bold**, like a headline. The **IDEA** was going to be good. Exciting. Way more than just a new frozen lunch recipe.

"For those of you who are new—" Shannon nodded toward Bree "—my family owns a printing press. Fitzgerald & Sons on 10th Avenue and North 50th."

Bree had seen the place. It was huge.

"We do trading cards. Mostly sports, but now everybody and their uncle wants them. Artists use them as calling cards, Realtors do the same. They've got them for *Twilight, Harry Potter, The Hunger Games,* and we just finished a ginormous order of official Hip-Hop trading cards."

Shannon paused, looking around the room. Then she smiled. "No one, however, is using trading cards the way they *should* be used—*to trade men.*"

Bree blinked, shot a look at her closest friend, Rebecca Thorpe, only to find Rebecca staring back. They raised eyebrows at each other and Bree was grateful all over again that she and Rebecca had clicked at that very first lunch exchange, despite their obvious differences. Bree was from a little town in Ohio and had a huge middle-class family. Rebecca was an attorney, the only child of a snooty New York family and she ran a charity foundation, one of the biggest in the world. Still, within five minutes of meeting, they'd made plans, ex-changed digits and by that night they'd been friends on Facebook and LinkedIn and had already talked on the phone for over an hour.

"Intriguing," someone said, and Bree snapped back to the **IDEA** and the drama.

Someone else said, "Go on."

Shannon obliged. "Three weeks ago, I went out on a fix up. My cousin knew this guy who worked with this other guy, and you know the drill. He was great. Really. We met at Monterone—I know, risotto to die for—anyway, he was good-looking, his job was legit, he'd been with someone, but they'd broken up months ago. It was a really nice blind date, one of the best I've been on in ages. But *it* wasn't there." The redhead sighed. "Zero chemistry. I knew it, he knew it. However," she said, only it was **HOWEVER**, "I knew, straightaway, that he and Janice would hit it off like gangbusters."

Every eye turned to Janice. Bree had met her, of course, but she was one of the few Bree hadn't had drinks with. She was a cutie, too. Tall, brunette, great touch with makeup.

Janice grinned. "We've been out three times, and he's fantastic. I can't even believe it." Janice put her hands on the table in front of her and leaned over her frozen chicken enchiladas. "I'm going to meet his mother on Friday."

The whole room said, "Ohhh," in the same key.

"I know," Janice said, standing up again. Back straight, face glowing. As if she'd won not just the spelling bee but aced the math final, as well.

Shannon spoke. "We've all got them, you know. Men who are nice and cute and have steady jobs. Who aren't gay or taken or married and not telling. Combine that with my family's printing press and what you get is…"

This was like a Broadway show, Bree thought. Or the Home Shopping Network. She held her breath, waiting for the reveal, the **IDEA** in all its glory.

Shannon raised her hands. Holding in each one, a card. A beautiful, glossy card. A trading card fit for a Heisman trophy winner, for a Hall of Famer. "On the front," she said, "the picture. Of course." Then she flipped her hands around. "On the back are the important details. The stats that matter."

"Like…" Bree said, surprised she'd spoken aloud.

"First and foremost," Shannon said, "marry, date or one-night stand."

The women nodded. Hugely important. How much pain in life could be eliminated by knowing who was whom. Each had their place. Bree would never be interested in a marry. Probably not a date, although that would depend. But a one-night stand? God, yes. Someone prescreened? It would be perfection. A Manhattan girl's idea of heaven.

"His favorite restaurant," Shannon added, and again, there was a collective "Uh-huh." "Because while I'm a gal who likes the pub down the street, some of you might prefer a little Nobu action. Then there's his passion."

Silence followed this statement, but Shannon milked it, in no rush to explain, though even she had her limits. "You know as well as I do that all of them want to talk about themselves, and usually they want to talk about their thing. No, not *that* thing. I mean, their other main preoccupation. You know, the Yankees, or the stock market, or the iPad or foreign films. If you're into the Mets, you don't want to get stuck with a day trader. Or maybe you do, but, at least, you'll know going in. And finally," she said, taking yet another dramatic pause. "The bottom line. Full disclosure. Snoring might not bother me, but it might bother you. Chemistry is downright fickle. But we all deserve to hear the unmitigated truth. Google can only give you so much, am I right?"

Again, there was silence, but not because anyone was confused. The beauty of the **IDEA** was sinking in, was gelling, was blooming like a rose in winter. As one, the semimonthly St. Mark's frozen lunch exchange began to applaud.

Hot Guys New York Trading Cards was born.

WITH A QUICK GLANCE OUT the window at the snowplow spitting down West 72nd Street, Charlie Winslow pushed his chair across his office to computer number three, the Mac. There were six altogether, each running a different operating system, each rotating views of his *Naked New York* media group. There were setups like this, well not exactly like this, but similar enough, in an apartment in Queens, a bungalow in Los Angeles, a flat in London and an office in Sydney. Then there was the huge old mansion in Delaware where the bulk of his servers were housed.

*Naked New York* was a gluttonous bitch, needing constant attention. What had begun as a single blog about Manhattan in 2005 had become ten separate blogs generating at last count over two-hundred-million page hits per year, and far more importantly, roughly thirty million per annum in advertising revenue. *NNY* was just like any other conglomerate, only the products manufactured were ideas and opinions, words and tips, photographs and gossip. Ever changing to remain ever pertinent. The revenue stream was one hundred percent advertising, and while Charlie paid a small team of full-time employees and a very large team of contributors, each blog was his baby whether it focused on celebrities, finance, sports, technology, gaming or even the female perspective on life. He trusted his editors, but it was his name on every masthead.

Which had made Charlie a celebrity, at least in the important cities. He liked that part. Hadn't considered it when he wrote up the initial business plan, but there were worse things than getting invited to every major event and having stunning women eager to accompany him to each one. He wasn't in Clooney's league, but Charlie's determination to remain a bachelor had passed from joke to fact to legend in the span of six years.

His phone rang, a call, not a text, and he answered, his Bluetooth gear attached to his ear directly after his morning shower. "Naomi. How are you today, gorgeous?"

"Filled with wonder and delight, as usual," his assistant said, her voice a nasal Brooklynese, her tone as dry as extra brut champagne.

Charlie grinned. "Any changes?"

"Nope. Just don't forget that the tailor is coming by at eleven. Don't make him wait. You did last time, and while you're precious as diamonds to me, his client list would make you tremble."

"You're always so good for my ego." Charlie glanced at his handset to see who wanted to interrupt his call. It was his cousin Rebecca. Odd, she rarely texted on a workday. "Got to run."

Naomi hung up even before Charlie pulled out the phone's keypad.

What's wrong? Has someone died? CW

A moment later, his phone beeped as his screen re-freshed.

Everything's fine. I have a treat for you, though.

He sailed across his floor again, this time to check the stats on one of his latest clients. Their ads had been on rotation in five markets, and they were doing well in four.

What kind of treat? CW

A date.

He laughed. His thumbs flew.

Come on, Becca. CW

She was his favorite cousin, which was saying something because he had a ton of them. His parents each had five siblings and they'd all bred like rabbits. Charlie had three siblings of his own, but only one had climbed aboard the baby wagon.

Instead of the beep announcing a return text, his phone rang. Charlie switched to voice.

"Seriously," Rebecca said. "I think you'll get a kick out of her. She's...different. She's new. Brand-new. Still, wears colors, for God's sake. And she's bright, tiny, funny and completely starstruck. She'll swoon over you, and make that head of yours so large you won't be able to fit through your front door."

"Ah, Rebecca. I didn't know you cared. She sounds perfect."

"I'm betting you're not booked for Valentine's day."

He sighed. "Don't be silly. I never plan that far in advance."

"You will this time."

He looked away from his monitor at the sound of her voice. Teasing, as always, but he hadn't missed the dare. He liked a challenge, and Rebecca was clever. Really clever. "Fine."

"I'll be in touch."

"What's her name?"

"Does it matter?"

He inhaled as his hands went to his keyboard. "Nope." Charlie clicked off and two minutes later, he was lost in a conference call, Valentine's Day and intriguing puzzles forgotten.

BREE HAD MADE CHICKPEA veg curry and mac and cheese for her frozen meals, but like everyone else in the big kitchen, she wasn't here for the food.

Today was CARD DAY.

The past few lunch exchange meetings had been more focused on the trading cards than food. Everyone, with one notable exception, had offered up at least two men to the trading card list. They'd brought in pictures, supplied the back copy, agreed that *all* first dates were to be held in very public venues, with the submitter knowing the details and phone numbers involved. Then, Shannon had done mock-ups of the cards, changed them twice until they had a design that worked. The actual printing of the cards hadn't taken that long, but time had stretched like putty since that day in December. Finally, a month and a half later, here it was. There was actually a chance, remote as it might be, that Bree would find a card that had her dream man on the cover, and all he'd want was a night that would blow the lid off this town.

She didn't deserve to find Mr. Right Now, though. Because Bree had brought zero men to the table. Zilch. Nada. She knew some single men at the advertising agency, but she'd never gone out with any of them. Not that she hadn't been asked. But she was planning on moving up in the company as quickly as possible, and didn't want to make any alliances until she'd been there at least a year. She might be from Ohio, but she hadn't just fallen off the turnip truck.

Bree had plans. More specifically, she had a five-year plan. End goal: to become a fashion consultant, author and television personality. The plan was her guiding light, her pathway through the Manhattan madness. One cornerstone of the plan was that under no circumstances was she to get involved with a man. Yes, a girl had needs. She'd been on dates since she'd moved to New York, but only a couple of them had included sex. The earth hadn't moved either time, which meant that the idea of a selection of eligible, vetted, one-night men hadn't been far from her thoughts since December.

Scary thing, being mostly friendless in a city like Manhattan. Thrilling, too. But the men were different than the ones she'd known back home. The rules here seemed to be more…fluid. The stakes higher.

Thank goodness her friendless status had changed as a result of the lunch exchange. Enough, in fact, for her to have been included in the trading card deal even when she hadn't contributed.

Shannon entered the room, and chaos ensued. Frozen meals were abandoned without a backward glance as the women huddled around one empty table. Shannon's penchant for drama made her lift her cardboard box high in the air only to tip it over, covering the table in a cascade of beautiful, practical possibilities, all on 2.5 x 3.5 thick-coated stock, suitable for purse or wallet, as a handy reference, as a focal point for dreams and wishes.

Bree's gaze swept over the puddle of cards, her eyes wide, adrenaline pumping, hoping for someone nice, but not too nice. Someone easy.

Rebecca came up next to her and bumped into her shoulder. Bree glanced at her friend, but only to scowl. When she looked back down at the cards, her breath stilled and for a moment, her heart did, too. There was a single card away from the pile, directly in front of Bree. On it was a picture that sent Bree's heart racing.

It couldn't be. Not possible. The sounds of her friends dimmed behind the whoosh of blood in her ears as she reached with trembling fingers to pick up the card.

Charlie Winslow. *The* Charlie Winslow. It had to be a joke, a trick. He could have anyone. He'd already had practically everyone. Why would he be on offer in the basement at St. Mark's Church?

"I thought you might recognize him."

Bree tore her gaze from the card to look once more at Rebecca. Her friend's smile was as smug as if she'd gotten past the velvet rope at The Pink Elephant, but Bree couldn't hold out for long. She stared again at the trading card, double-checked. Still Charlie Winslow. "How?"

"He's my cousin," Rebecca said.

"Your cousin," Bree repeated.

"Yep. God knows he's single."

"He can have anyone."

Rebecca chuckled. "Yeah, but if all you're eating is

lobster and champagne every night, it's bound to get boring, don't you think?"

Bree shook her head. "Not even a little bit. Although now I understand why you're part of the lunch exchange. We're the tuna fish to your normal caviar, am I right?"

Rebecca dismissed the deduction with a roll of her eyes. "Trust me. He's bored. And he needs a date for Valentine's night."

Bree took a step back, just to keep her balance. "Me? I'm..." She blinked as she stared at the woman she'd thought she knew. They'd gone out for drinks more than a few times, and she and Rebecca had gotten along great. They'd laughed a lot. Rebecca was a couple of years older than Bree, smart as a whip, rich as Croesus, but grounded. Sweet, too. It was one of the mysteries of New York that a woman like her was wanting for dates, but Bree knew that was the truth of it.

"What do you say, Bree? Don't know where he'll take you, but it's bound to be glamorous as all hell."

"I'm from Ohio," Bree said. "I make all my own clothes. Taking the subway is glamorous. He'll get one look at me and fall over laughing."

Rebecca's hand landed on Bree's shoulder. "Don't do that. Come on. That's not you. I wouldn't suggest it if I thought you couldn't hold your own. I've known him my whole life. He's funny. He's smart. You'll like each other. And besides, neither one of you wants more than one night. So what have you got to lose?"

"He's like, the King of Manhattan. What'll I even say?"

"Call him the King of Manhattan. He'll love you forever."

"Don't want forever. But maybe, if people see me with him, even once, they'll remember."

"There'll be pictures," Rebecca said, her focus going back to the pile of cards. "There are always pictures with Charlie."

"What about you?" Bree asked. "See any possibilities in there?"

Rebecca lifted a card. The guy looked yummy, but when she flipped to the back, her expression fell. "One-night stand." She tossed the card back.

"Maybe not," Bree said. "Maybe he only thinks he wants a one-night stand." She kept hold of Charlie's card, knowing if anyone else wanted it, they'd have to pry it out of her cold, dead hand, but picked up the yummy guy's card, as well. "He's a musician. A violinist with the Philharmonic. That's impressive. And he hasn't met you."

Rebecca smiled as she flicked her long tawny hair behind her shoulder. "Are you going to change your mind? Suddenly want marriage and kids from one date with Charlie?"

Bree laughed. "No. Doesn't mean it couldn't happen to someone else."

"Don't worry about me, Kingston. I'll find someone. Let's get you all squared away first. Valentine's night. I'll set it up. Let you know the deets ASAP."

"Oh, God." Bree looked at her outfit. Made on the Singer that shared her closet-cum-bedroom. Hunter-green skirt, lined, with a mod patterned silk blouse, transformed from a thrift store bonanza. Black tights, black heels, a ribbon in her short, short hair. The only thing that had cost any real money were the shoes, and they were secondhand. What if he wanted to go to Pegu Club or 24 Ninth Avenue? Everyone would see instantly that she was a no one from nowhere, wearing nothing that mattered.

"You've got more style in your pinkie than anyone in this room. Than anyone on *Project Runway.* Come on, Bree. This is what you came to New York to do. It's your chance to grab the city by the short hairs. You can do it. I know you can."

Bree straightened her back. "All right. Worst that could happen, I make a complete idiot of myself. I've done that plenty of times. Get Charlie Winslow on the phone. Tell him he's about to meet someone new."

Rebecca laughed. Then she leaned forward just a bit. "You should probably take a breath now, Bree. In fact, maybe we should find a chair. Come on, hon. There's a paper bag right on the counter. That's a girl."

# 2

---

**Charlie Winslow**
Editor in Chief/CEO *Naked New York Media Group*
Studied Business/Marketing at *Harvard University*
Lives in *Manhattan* ❤ Single From *Manhattan*

BREE BLINKED UP AT THE forty-three-story tower at 15 Central Park West, the newest of the luxury, legendary co-op buildings that lined the street across from the park. Just several blocks up were The Dakota, The Majestic and The San Remo. This was quite like being in the center of a very realistic dream. Except that it was freezing. She'd splurged on a taxi even though she'd spent every spare cent on her outfit, using every moment of the trip to talk herself out of a panic attack. The affirmations hadn't been very effective evidently, because even though her date with Charlie Winslow was about to start, she couldn't make her legs move.

She still couldn't believe it. If she hadn't known better, she'd have sworn it was all an elaborate practical joke. Why on earth would Charlie Winslow want to go out with *her*? Of course, she'd asked Rebecca that very question approximately a million times. Bree had gotten a variety of answers, all boiling down to the fact that Rebecca thought the two of them would have a good time.

A good time.

Bree couldn't *move.* Except for her now chattering teeth. The forties era shawl she'd found in Park Slope may have been the perfect accessory, but it did nothing to protect her from the cold. She might as well have worn her gargantuan puffy coat, considering the fact that she was *rooted to the corner of Central Park West and West 72nd Street.*

For God's sake, the most amazing Cinderella night of her life was only moments and a few feet away. She had pictures of this very corner in her New York dream book, the one she'd been compiling for eight years. The only reason Charlie Winslow's photograph hadn't been clipped and pasted was that even her outlandish imagination hadn't been that optimistic.

She had to remember not to call him Charlie Winslow, as if he was a movie star or an historical figure. Bree had practiced. She'd said his first name a hundred times, sometimes laughing, sometimes looking shyly away, coy, sassy, demure, outraged. She was very good at saying *Charlie,* but she couldn't quite help the Winslow part. She'd read so many articles by him and about him, and none of them referred to him as Charlie, or even Mr. Winslow.

She pushed herself forward. If she waited any longer she'd be late, and he'd probably leave without her, which had its merits as then she wouldn't have to endure actually meeting him, but that would defeat the purpose, and dammit, she was brave. She was. She'd gotten on a plane all by herself, knowing absolutely no one in New York, let alone in Manhattan. That took guts.

So did tonight. But she could do it. Because, like her relocation, Charlie Winslow fit perfectly in her five-year plan.

1. Move to New York
2. Get a job in fashion advertising
3. Continue fashion education
4. Find a way into the Inner Circle
5. Become a regular at fashion events
6. ????
7. Publish
8. Success!!!!!!

Look how far she'd come already. She was flying past three directly into four and she'd only been in Manhattan six months! Meeting Charlie Winslow was a piece of cake. The easy part.

Okay, no. That was a total lie. As she headed for the doorman, complete with hat and epaulettes thank you very much, the truth settled like a stone in her stomach. Meeting Charlie Winslow was like meeting the President or Johnny Depp, or Dolce *and* Gabbana.

She would not throw up.

Somehow, the door was opened by the tall man in the cap and gloves, and he smiled at her as he gave her a tiny bow. Then she was inside where it was warm and unbelievably gorgeous. This building wasn't as famous as The Dakota, but it was right up there in the stratosphere of luxury. Her entire apartment could fit into the reception area where she had to sign in. Everyone smiled. The security guard, the other security guard, the woman by the elevator wearing a winter-white suit, whose huge honkin' diamond ring must make it an effort to lift her hand.

No Charlie Winslow in sight.

Bree let out a breath.

"May I announce your arrival?" The security guard sitting behind the beautiful burnished oak desk leaned forward so elegantly it made her think he was desperate to hear who she was going to see. Either that, or he'd almost lost his grip on the automatic weapon hidden above his lap. Just in case she didn't have the right name or something.

"Bree Kingston for Charlie Winslow," she said, and she only had to clear her throat once.

The way the uniformed man's left eyebrow rose meant something. Bree had no idea what. She glanced down to make sure she hadn't dribbled on her dress, but she appeared fine. If nervous. If very, *very* nervous.

The guard picked up a phone, but his hand stilled midway to his console. He nodded, looking past Bree's shoulder.

She turned, holding her breath, praying she wouldn't make a complete ass of herself. And there he was. Just like his pictures, only better.

Tall, though everyone was tall to her, considering that she barely reached five-one. His hair was as perfectly mussed as it was in his photos—dark, cut with such precision that she imagined he woke up looking camera-ready. He wore a black suit with a simple perfectly tailored white shirt beneath, no tie, slim cut, Yves Saint Laurent? Spencer Hart? Or maybe her beloved D&G?

As gorgeous as the trimmings were, it was his face that snagged and kept her staring. Much, much better than his pictures. Big eyes, brown. Very big. A generous mouth, too, but she kept getting snagged on the eyes, and how he looked as if he'd discovered something wonderful and interesting, except he was looking at her. Smiling big-time. At her.

His gaze let hers go as he took his time across the lobby. Not that it went far: a long slow trip down her body, pausing for a moment on her boobs. Not enough of a pause to make her self-conscious. Any more self-conscious.

She'd been scoped out before, sure. But this felt different. Like an audition. Her heart pounded, blood rushed to heat her cheeks, hell, her whole face. Then he was looking in her eyes again, and she exhaled when he seemed even more pleased. Maybe it was an act, probably was, in fact, but it didn't matter because it was only for one night and she'd imagined dozens of expressions on his face, but none of them had been quite this fantastic.

"Bree," he said, his voice low, a cello kind of baritone full of resonance and promise.

"Hi," she said. "Charlie."

He took her hand in his. The one not holding her clutch, the edge of her shawl. "Rebecca told me you were pretty," he said. "She's never in her life made such an understatement."

Bree's blush went four-alarm and she knew it was a crock, but a gorgeous crock, and if he wanted to say things like that to her for the rest of the night, she wouldn't mind in the least. "You're very kind."

"Not really," he said. Still holding on to her hand, he glanced behind her. "George, could you call for the car?"

"It's in place, Mr. Winslow."

"Thank you," he said, then Charlie looked at her again. "Did she tell you where we're going?"

"She wouldn't. She said I'd like it, though."

"I hope so." He led her out, his hand still holding hers until they got to the exit. When the door was pulled open, Charlie put his arm around her shoulders and picked up the pace. Before she knew it, she was sitting in the backseat of a black limousine driven by an honest-to-God chauffeur and Charlie was scooting in on her left.

How was this her life? Her high school graduating class had under two hundred kids. Seven years later, every one of her friends were married, and most of them had at least one kid. And here she was, being whisked off into a mysterious night with one of the most famous men in New York. On Valentine's Day. Holy mother of pearl.

CHARLIE NORMALLY DIDN'T have champagne chilling in the limo. It had only happened twice before, in fact. Once, when his guest had been a Queen. Not the kind from Asbury Park in New Jersey, but a real royal Queen. The other time had been for a friend who'd been crushed by a devastating loss in the love department. A night of drunken weeping and aimless driving had helped pass the time and given her the courage to face the sunrise.

In tonight's case, he'd ordered the Dom Pérignon Rosé Oenothèque for Rebecca's sake. He knew every detail of the evening would be reported to his cousin, and he was determined to impress Rebecca despite her opinion that he was still the same adolescent terror he'd been at thirteen.

But now that he'd actually met Bree, he wasn't sure

Rebecca deserved such an expensive champagne. Bree was pretty, all right. Petite and sweet-looking with an elfin haircut and a nice little body. But as his date? What was Rebecca thinking?

Clearly there was something more to Bree than his first impression would indicate. Rebecca was bright and she knew him very well. Which meant she knew that the women he went for had mile-long legs, wore nothing but the top labels, were on the cover of *Vogue,* never *Home Sewing Monthly.*

Bree was…tiny. She didn't look terrifically young, just compact. Everything diminutive. There was definitely something appealing in her almond-shaped eyes, heart-shaped face, her pale skin and slight overbite. She was Lula Mae before she became Holly Golightly, and where they were headed? She would be a guppy out of water.

He was almost afraid to speak to her, not having the first clue what to say. He was just a vain enough idiot to have loved the way her eyes had widened at meeting him, how she'd trembled, although that could have been from the cold. But that rush could only last so long. Some champagne would help both of them.

She turned from the window as he popped the cork. "I didn't know that was a real thing," she said. "Champagne in a limousine."

"It's decadent and foolish, but then this is Valentine's Day. Besides, we're not driving, so what the hell."

"No, we're not. I should warn you, I'm not much of a drinker."

"We'll have to be judicious with our ordering, then. But how about one drink, to christen the adventure ahead?"

She stared at the crystal flute in his hand. "Yes, thank you. I'd like that."

"There will always be tonic, soda or juice wherever we are, although you'll be surrounded by booze." He filled her glass, careful what with the stop-and-go traffic. "If you tell me what you prefer, I'll make sure you have it."

"I like pineapple juice the best," she said, taking the glass from him with her slender hand, her nails trim and shiny and pale.

"Pineapple it is." He poured himself a glass then sat back, lifting the flute to hers. "To blind dates."

Her smile did nice things to her face. Made it clear she hadn't learned to hold back yet, to equate cynicism with sophistication. He hadn't seen that in a long while. Not up close.

"To extraordinary things," she replied, clicking his glass gently.

The champagne was excellent, perfectly cold and just dry enough. "Tell me about yourself, Bree," he said, leaning back into his corner of the seat. He didn't want to crowd her or make her uncomfortable. They had a big night ahead of them, and as long as she was his date, he truly wanted to show her a good time. Nothing extravagant, naturally. Experience had taught him it was better to stay low-key with new people of any stripe. Since the success of *Naked New York,* he'd had to relearn public navigation.

His celebrity could still be an awkward fit, although nothing like it had been when the business had hit critical mass. He'd set out to make a name, but when he'd first put the blog plan together, he envisioned himself more like a Jason Weisberger of BoingBoing than an Arianna Huffington. Someone whose name would be recognized by people who mattered, but who was not easily recognized in person. Instead, he'd become part of a new phenomena. In Manhattan, more people recognized him than recognized the mayor. Financially, it was the best thing that could have happened. Personally, it had been…interesting and not terrifically pleasant.

Bree turned her lovely green eyes to her glass, watching the bubbles pop and fizz. "I'm a copywriter," she said. "At BBDA. A baby copywriter, which means I'm mostly a gofer and I take a lot of notes, type a lot of memos. But it's good. The people I work with are quick and creative and they aren't out for blood. Well, not more than you'd expect."

"BBDA is a big firm. A number of their clients advertise on my blogs."

Her eyes widened again. "Seventeen of them, at the moment. *Naked New York* is a major focus in the eighteen-to-thirty-four demographic."

The last word had been bitten off, and she pressed her lips together for a second. "Anyway," she said, her voice lower, slower. "I graduated last year with an MBA from Case Western. I'd always wanted to come to New York, so I did."

"Is New York what you thought it would be?"

"Much better. I loved it even before tonight."

He laughed.

"Come on, you have to know how much this evening is blowing the bell curve. You're Charlie Winslow and we're going on a mystery date, and even though I have no idea where, I'm sure it's going to be the most thrilling night of my life."

He couldn't help his wince, although he tried not to. "Most thrilling? That's a tall order."

She lowered her head, frowned a bit, then looked up at him through her long lashes. "Really? This—" she waved at the lush interior of the car, at, he imagined, the night in general "—is insane. It may be your day-to-day, but it's certainly not mine." Bree sat back, sipped the cold champagne. "Rebecca wouldn't tell me. Every time I asked why you'd want to go out with me on Valentine's night, for God's sake, she smiled in that smug way that made me want to pinch her."

He smiled. "You know, I find myself wanting to pinch Rebecca a lot."

"Then you'll understand my frustration when I ask you straight-out, why are we doing this? Why are *you* doing this with *me?* I can't help thinking it might be some awful mean-girl prank. That wherever we're going, there'll be a big spotlight on me when I'm covered in green slime or something. Which would be horrible by the way. In case you need to call ahead."

Okay. She made him laugh. Big point in the plus column. And now that she'd admitted her fear, she seemed more relaxed. Now that he'd noticed, he lingered on the way her simple sleeveless dress showed off the woman more than the garment. He liked that she wore no jewelry. It was a bold choice, but it brought his focus to her neck, which had more appeal than a neck had any right to. There was just something about her skin, the way her chin curved, her elegant clavicle. There was a thought he'd never expected to have.

"Rebecca isn't like that," Bree said, softer now, more to herself than him, and Charlie remembered she'd asked him why he'd pursued the date.

Before he could answer, she added, "I haven't known her for long, so maybe I'm wrong, but my instincts are pretty good, and she stood out right from the start."

Bree used her hand again, not a wave this time, but a flip of the wrist. A tiny wrist, delicate and feminine.

"We went for drinks this one night at Caracas, Rebecca and me and our friend Lilly, who teaches music at this amazingly exclusive prep school, and it started out a little weird, because the three of us only knew each other from the lunch exchange, but then we started talking and we clicked, especially Rebecca and me. When I mentioned how desperately I'd wanted to live in Manhattan, both of them completely got it. How I don't mind paying a fortune to live in the Black Hole of Calcutta with four girls I barely know, and how I can't even afford to go to a movie, let alone have popcorn. They grinned and we toasted each other with sidecars, and I felt as if I was home." Bree blinked and then for some reason her shoulders stiffened again. She cleared her throat. "That may have gotten away from me a little."

And…he liked her. Just like that. No, she wasn't his type, not even close, but he liked the cadence of her speech, the way she talked with her hands, how she was clearly nervous but not cowed. The night changed right then, between Columbus Avenue and West 61st.

Charlie touched her arm. She was warm and soft, and she flinched a bit at the contact, catching herself with a breath and a smile.

"No," he said, "it's not a prank or a trick. Rebecca thought we'd get along. She and I grew up together, were friends through private schools and first dates and proms and way too many horrific holiday celebrations." He shuddered thinking about some of the epic Christmases, the ones where half the family wasn't speaking to the other half, where feuds were conducted across air-kisses and designer wreaths. All that passive-aggressive power brokering over Beluga caviar and shaved truffles. "She knows me as well as anyone. And she's never wanted to set me up before."

"So what does that mean?"

He thought for a second. Excellent question. "I don't know."

Instead of pressing him for his best guess, Bree's head tilted fetchingly. "Where are we going?"

"You don't want to be surprised?"

The way she looked at him made him want to meet her expectations, even though there was no way he could. "I've been stunned since you took my hand."

Stunned? "What were you expecting?"

She shrugged. "Not sure. Something else. I mean, I'm not shocked about the doormen, the limousine or how amazing you smell, because I was secretly hoping for all that. I've never been around celebrities much. I've seen some since I've been here. The obligatory Woody Allen sighting, of course, but there've been others. Quite a few of them, now that I think about it, but they've all seemed, I don't know, extraordinary. In the truest sense of the word. As if the air around them was sparkly, or that even if they looked like they'd thrown on a potato sack and bowling shoes, it was on purpose, but I wasn't cool enough to get it. You're not like that."

"Is that a compliment?"

She nodded. "Yes. It would have been okay if you'd turned out to be a major hipster, although I definitely would have bored you to tears."

Charlie grinned. "Know how many hipsters it takes to screw in a lightbulb?"

She grinned back, leaning in for the punch line. "How many?"

He purposely rolled his eyes. "Some really obscure number you've never even heard of."

Bree laughed. It started out as delicate as her wrist, but ended in an unexpected snort. Her eyes widened and she held her hand up in front of her face, but then she did it again. The snort, not the laugh. And she added a blush that was the most honest thing he'd seen in years.

Okay, Rebecca might deserve more than a sparkling wine. The vote was still out if she'd end up with a '96 Krug Clos D'Ambonnay.

# 3

BREE KNEW SHE WAS BLUSHING, but there wasn't a single solitary thing she could do about it. From the way Charlie was smiling at her, the problem wasn't going to fix itself anytime soon.

She wished they'd get to wherever they were going. She needed some distance, just for a moment. A bathroom stall would work, a private place where she could squeal and jump and act like a fool and get it out of her system. Because *whoa*. Charlie Winslow plus limo plus champagne plus the fact that his dates always ended with more than a friendly peck on the cheek and she was practically levitating. The whole night, no matter where they ended up, was improbably perfect. Her once in a lifetime.

Someone had reached into her fantasies, reviewed those that were most outlandish and most frequent, decided they weren't grand enough then given her *this*. She wanted to lean over the front seat and ask the driver, a nice-looking guy she'd guess was in his fifties, if he had a video camera, and would he mind filming every second of the rest of the night so she could watch it until her eyes fell out.

She glanced out the window and all her thoughts stuttered to a halt. "This is Lincoln Center," she said, her voice high and tight.

"It is," Charlie said, and while she couldn't take her eyes off the scene in front of her, she could hear the amusement in his voice.

"It's Lincoln Center," she repeated, "and this is *Fashion Week*."

"Right again."

"It was in the blog. This morning. I read it. This is the Mercedes-Benz/Vogue party for Fashion Week."

She wanted to open the window, stick her head out like an overexcited puppy so she could see *everything*. But she might as well paint a sign on her forehead that said *hick*. Still, she couldn't help it if her hands shook, if her breath fogged the window, if she wanted to pinch herself to prove she was really, really here.

"I thought you might have guessed." His voice sounded smiley. Not smirky, though, and she would have thought…

"No." She grinned. "No, really. No. It's too much. Come on. It's…fashion Nirvana. The single event after which I could die happy." She turned, briefly, to gape at him, to verify the smile she'd guessed at. "I've been sewing since I was twelve."

Then she was staring again, at the klieg lights, at the people. Glittering, gorgeous, famous, glamorous people. Her heroes and heroines. In one small clump standing near a police barricade there were three, *THREE,* designers. Designers she adored, well, maybe not *her,* because she was kind of derivative, but still, Bree was going to be in the same room, at the same party as Tommy Hilfiger, as Vivienne Westwood!

She turned again to Charlie, almost spilling her drink. "We are going to the party, right?"

"Yeah, we're going to the party."

"Oh, thank God. That would have been really embarrassing. If we were going to a concert or something."

He laughed in a way that made her shiver and reminded her again that this wasn't a dream. The limo was in a long line of limos, and Bree guessed it would be a while until it was their turn. Which meant that she had a window of alone-time with Charlie. She leaned back in the luxurious leather seat so he was the center of her attention. "I remember reading about this last year. It sounded as if you had a good time."

He nodded. "I did, considering it's part of the job. I think this year will be better." He spoke casually, as if they were talking about stopping at the corner market. As if they knew each other. Casually, but not bored or above it all. This was a typical night for him. A night to look forward to but not to panic over.

Speaking of panic. "We're at Fashion Week, and I'm wearing a homemade dress. My shawl…" It had cost fifty cents at the thrift shop but he didn't have to know *that*. "Oh, God."

He studied her, grinning. She couldn't tell if it was because he thought she looked adorably out of her league or laughably ridiculous. When he leaned forward, Bree wasn't sure what to do until he crooked his finger for her to move in closer. Conspiratorially closer. "The whole point of fashion is originality and talent. Everyone will look at you, at your dress, and wonder who the new designer is. I suggest you milk that till the cow's dry."

She had to laugh, because well… "That's a very nice thing to say." She touched the back of his hand to make sure he knew she wasn't kidding, only the second her hand was on his, she realized how they were mere inches apart. She could feel his breath on her cheek, the warmth of his body sneaking into her own.

That he could think she was capable of pulling off something so outrageous was…awesome. "I'm not sure I could keep a straight face."

"Look bored," he said. "That's the key. Act as if you'd rather be anywhere else on earth, and they'll all think you're the next big thing."

"Bored. I can do bored." She had to lean back a bit because being this close to Charlie was making it hard not to hyperventilate. "Actually, no, I can't, not here. My God, no one's that good an actress. But I can be observant. Which almost looks like bored."

He moved back, too, his smile lingering in the way his eyes crinkled. "Observant can work. Remember, though, that there's no one here you need to be intimidated by. Well, almost. But you probably won't meet them, anyway."

Oh, he was good. This was effortless charm, the true heart of tact and perfect manners. To put her at ease as they inched their way to the Mount Everest of her aspirations? Wonderful, wonderful. But she'd better bring herself down a notch, because at this height, a fall could kill her. "I read an article once," she said, "by a woman whose passion was movies, and she went and got herself a job in the business. She said that in the end it was kind of sad. That what she'd loved were the illusions, the characters, the fantasy. Once she'd looked behind the curtain it was never the same again."

Charlie finished off his champagne and put his flute back in the space next to the ice bucket, slowly, as if he were giving deliberate thought to what she'd said. "I can see that. Most terribly brilliant people I've known are also terribly troubled. Not all of them, but a lot of them."

"I don't think I'll be disappointed. I know it's all illusion. And that's okay with me. I had normal. A whole hell of a lot of normal. It wasn't for me."

"Where was that?" he asked. "Your normal."

"Ohio," she said. "Little tiny town. Great big family. Happy. Well-adjusted. My folks had lots of siblings, I have lots of siblings, everyone else in my family wants to get married, if they aren't already, have a bunch of kids, live within driving distance of the family home. We're a Norman Rockwell relic, with small rebellions and modest dreams. I can't tell you how much I hated it. Not my family, they're great, but that life. Knowing what the day would bring. The Sunday dinners and the baby showers, knowing every person at the Cline's SuperValu and never having to look at the menu at Yoders. I wanted out."

She took in a deep breath of Manhattan limousine air. "I want unpredictability and crowds of people, all of them in a rush. I want to go to clubs and stay out till 4:00 a.m. when I have to be at work at eight and I want to eat things I can't pronounce and I want to have my heart broken by callous men who wear gorgeous suits."

She looked away, feeling foolish. Talk about TMI. It was all nerves, of course, but there was no way not to be nervous given the circumstances. The line of limos, hiding their secret passengers, was still impressive.

"I think you'll be great here," Charlie said, and it occurred to her that the timbre of his voice wasn't the biggest surprise, the kindness was. "They're all divas, and what do divas do best?"

"Get free swag?"

Charlie laughed as he shook his head. "They think about themselves. They'll be far too preoccupied to focus much attention on you. The only reason they'll notice me is because they can use me. So relax. Enjoy it. You'll have a great time."

She was already having the time of her life, and they hadn't left the car, so the possibility of enjoying herself for the rest of the night wasn't out of the question. She wouldn't necessarily trip or spill something down her dress. She'd already decided she would eat nothing that could possibly get stuck in her teeth. And she'd make sure she didn't get drunk.

Charlie leaned forward until he had his driver's attention. "We're going to be at least a few hours, Raymond," he said. "Feel free to leave. I'll give you some warning when it looks like we're ready to go."

"Will do, Mr. Winslow. Thanks."

Bree shook her head. When she'd first come to the city she'd been prepared for mass rudeness, cynicism and impatience from every corner. Hadn't happened. Not that there weren't more than a fair share of asshats in residence, but the proportions had been off. Mostly the people she'd met, whether it was asking for directions or standing on line at Starbucks, had been nice. Pleasant. They could be brusque but they were more than willing to help, even when she hadn't asked. Those were the regular folks, though, not people like Charlie. If television shows about rich New Yorkers were to be believed, he should have been a complete bastard.

Instead, he'd brought her to *Fashion Week*. She'd been a slave to fashion since seventh grade. Her walls had been covered with her collages, a perfect pair of shoes from *Vogue,* with a particular skirt from *W* and a top from *Seventeen.* Of course, there'd been photos of accessories included, affixed with Mod Podge and shellacked so they'd be permanent reminders that she had more than a daydream. She had a goal.

Her love of writing had come later, and the combination? That had been a match made in heaven. Her destiny was set—she'd be a style writer, a trendsetter, a goddess of form and function.

To be here with Charlie was...nope. No words came close to what this felt like.

The man himself shifted in the seat so he could watch her, but also have a clear view through her window. "It's a hell of a culture shock, moving to New York," he said. "A lot of people find nothing but trouble in Manhattan."

"I wouldn't mind finding a little trouble," she said, a blush stealing up her cheeks. She touched her purse, hyperaware of the thong, the toothbrush, the condom and the rest that made up her one-night stand kit. Rebecca hadn't said it outright, but she hadn't needed to. Charlie's bachelor ways were the stuff of legend.

The theme from *Mission Impossible* rang from her purse, scaring the crap out of her.

"I bet I know who that is," he said.

Bree opened her clutch, not wanting him to see her kit, or, heaven forbid, his trading card. She snatched her phone and saw she had a message from Rebecca.

U there yet?

Bree grinned.

!!!!!!!

Knew U 2 wld be gr8

*We'll talk tomrw I ❤ u for this!*

You're welcome. Knock m dead!

Charlie tried to sneak a peek, and she helped him by turning her screen.

He pulled his own phone out of his jacket pocket. Of course it was something amazing looking. Might have been a BlackBerry, she thought, latest gen at the very least, if not some exotic model not available to the public. Unlike her second-hand first-gen iPhone.

He was amazingly fast with his thumbs. Dexterous. But his texting couldn't hold a candle to how expressive his face was. He grinned in a whole different way than he had a moment ago. None of that sweet, reflective rumination. Now he was the very picture of high amusement, his head tilted to the side, his eyebrows raised in either surprise or delight, possibly both. Or maybe something completely different, but this was the night for believing the best, right?

Before she put her phone back, she turned it so she had his face framed for a quick photo. She'd be damned if she wasn't going home with some physical mementoes from tonight, and no, blisters from her incredibly high heels didn't count.

As she reached to put her cell in her bag, it hit her. Why she was here. Why Rebecca had given her Charlie's card. What the whole deal was.

*A favor.*

First night out with Rebecca, Bree had spilled her five-year plan all over the conversation. Her dreams, the steps, the obsession. Rebecca hadn't told her she

*Choose Me*

was related to Charlie. Hadn't seemed to be aware of Fashion Week at all. That sneaky…

Which meant Bree had better pull her expectations down another fifty notches. She wasn't really on a *date* with Charlie. She was on a favor. Those two things ended in completely different ways. Favors didn't extend to the bedroom.

Charlie put his phone back in his jacket pocket just as her phone beeped again. "It's going to be crowded in there. I've just sent you my number. If we get separated, text me, and I'll find you."

*She had Charlie Winslow's cell phone number.* She could be excited about that. It might be a one-off, but so what? Just because it was a favor didn't mean it wasn't the biggest kick of her life.

"You okay?" he asked.

"Fine. Great. Am I likely to lose you?"

"Not if I can help it—ah, we're here."

The door next to Bree opened as Charlie slipped her glass from between her fingers. In yet another spectacular fairy-tale moment, she stepped onto a red carpet. She hadn't flashed anyone, she hadn't tripped and she managed not to let her jaw drop even when flashbulbs popped all around, blinding and thrilling in equal measure.

Charlie took hold of her arm above her elbow, and that was good because she really couldn't see a thing. People around her were shouting, "Over here!" and "Look up!" over and over, and she hadn't anticipated so much noise. Whenever she watched this part on TV it was silent, a voice-over, then a cut to a commercial, but here it was loud and scary and intrusive.

Charlie's hand squeezed gently as he escorted her toward a towering white tent, which she knew was the

Fashion Week venue in Damrosch Park. The area was huge, with runway shows from morning till night, cocktail parties, dining areas, meeting rooms, press rooms.

She'd been here, to Lincoln Center, but on the other side, with the fountain and the Met and the magic staircase. To be here now, when the whole complex was dressed up in its fancy best, when to get inside the tents should have been impossible for a girl like her, was a lot to process.

Thank goodness for Charlie's steadying hand. What world was she in that the most comforting thing around her was Charlie Winslow? She honestly couldn't tell if she was trembling more from the freezing cold or the excitement.

There was so much to look at between flashes of light, she was shocked to step inside. There was a line, and because this was the real world, there were metal detectors to go through. No one seemed to mind, though. Security was tight, and the slower pace as they were herded forward gave her a chance to catch her breath, only to lose it again as she got a load of who she was standing near.

Charlie's breath warmed her neck as he leaned in close. Goose bumps. Everywhere. Down her spine and up her arms. When his voice followed, low and warm, her own breath hitched and her eyes may have rolled up in her head for just a second. Probably in a minute she'd get with the program. She wouldn't feel faint from his touch, or by standing one person away from her favorite designer on earth. The problem was, she couldn't decide what to stare at—the clothes or the designers themselves. Oh, God, there was the model who was on the cover of this month's issue of *Elle,* and good God almighty, that was the star of her favorite CSI, and Bree was so grateful for Charlie's arm.

"You'll never see more food go to waste than you will at this party," Charlie said in that same intimate whisper he'd used in the limo. "I don't think any of these people actually eat. They do chew a lot of gum, though. Ketosis. It's a breath thing, not that you'll ever hear about it in *Vogue* or *W*. People who don't eat may look fantastic on camera, but their breath could kill a buffalo. Be warned."

Bree giggled, and while it was true that everyone in the two long lines snaking into the tent was on the ridiculous side of thin, most of the people she saw were subtly chewing, or standing in such a way as to avoid being breathed upon.

Of course, she thought of her own breath now. She'd barely eaten today, too nervous.

"You're fine," he said, with a minty-scented chuckle. "Don't fret."

She smiled at him as they inched along. "I guess I'm not hiding my small-town roots very well, huh?"

"I don't know what you mean."

She gave him a knowing look. "I'll try harder to appear blasé."

"Don't do that for my sake." Charlie tugged her around even more, until they were facing each other. "I like that this is magical for you."

"I'm a real novelty, huh?"

"Truthfully, yes. But a good one. I want to hear much, much more about your life before New York. I'm a native, and the way I was raised, you'd think there wasn't anything between California and New York. I've never been to Ohio, although I'm reasonably sure

I could point to it on a map. It's at the bottom of Lake Erie, right?"

"Wow, I'm impressed. Yeah."

"And where in Ohio did you grow up?"

She waved her hand at him and turned to check on the line's progress. "You've never heard of it." When she looked back, his smile was a bit crooked. "So that food you mentioned. Passed around on little trays? Buffet? Sit down banquet?"

"The first two," he said. "There will be places to sit, tables all around, and here's a secret. You can completely tell the pecking order by who sits, who stands and where those two things happen."

Her eyes widened at yet another morsel of insider-y goodness. She felt as if he was giving her the ultimate backstage pass, and while she knew a lot of it had to do with manners and even more to do with Rebecca, there was a tiny flare of hope buried deep inside that perhaps he was letting her in because he liked her? A little?

Probably a good idea not to linger on that thought. She needed to be in the moment, enjoying the hell out of what she had. To ask for anything more was tempting fate.

## 4

CHARLIE COULDN'T TAKE his eyes off Bree. What had Rebecca seen that had made her believe this absurd blind date could work? That it was working was...bizarre. He never would have guessed he would find Bree enchanting.

Hell, that he found anything enchanting stretched credulity.

And yet, watching her reminded him what it was like when he'd had heroes. Though he'd never been as innocently enthralled by glamour as Bree. Given his background, how could he have been? His family was part of xenophobic wealthy New York, the inbred, insane inner circle that made disdain and dismissal an art form. So his heroes had been those outside the fold: sports stars, indie musicians who would never be mainstream, oddball scientists and computer hackers. The last, thank goodness, had actually set in motion key aspects of his life.

"Oh, God," Bree whispered, her hand clasping desperately at his lapel. "That's Mick Jagger."

Charlie followed her gaze a few feet away to where the old warhorse stood, surrounded by his all-but-invisible-to-him entourage. The Rolling Stone hadn't been there a few minutes ago, but there wasn't a person in the tent, hell in the city, that would call him out for cutting in line.

"Huh," Bree said, still staring curiously at the mega-star.

"Better get used to that," Charlie said, enjoying himself. The past couple of years, the novelty of his lifestyle had dulled. He rarely considered anything outside of the job. Who to interview, who to keep an eye on, who was ready for a career obit. Filling Bree in was fun. She'd been right. No way she could pass for bored. Not even close. "Almost everyone's shorter than you think," he continued, stepping closer to her. "The men, especially. Not the models, though, they're giraffes, but the actors, the musicians? Most of them are even shorter than I am."

"You're not," Bree said. She turned and laid a smile on him that made him feel like a giant. "*I'm* short. Ridiculously so. It's awful."

"Why awful?"

Her smile changed and the tips of her ears turned pink. "I'm twenty-five, not twelve. Everyone thinks I'm cute. And harmless. Like a baby bunny. I've had people pat me on the head. I mean, come on. Who does that?"

"Not me," he said, holding his hands up and away, mostly because now that she'd said it, he wanted to.

"I want to take his picture," she said, lowering her voice as she stole glances at Jagger.

"So? Take it."

She shook her head. "And that would advance my agenda of being a bored new designer how? I'm already an outsider. I'd like to at least pretend for a bit."

Charlie turned to the person in back of him, some

guy he didn't know, but who looked like he might be a reporter. "We'll be back in a sec, okay?"

The guy nodded, and Charlie kept his grip on Bree's arm as he crossed over to the other line, right smack in the middle of the rock stars' party. "Hey, Mick," he said, holding out his hand. "Charlie Winslow. I'd love to get a photograph with you and my lovely date. Do you mind?"

The man shook Charlie's hand, but only smiled once he set eyes on Bree. Then he couldn't have been nicer. In fact, before they'd been there two minutes, Jagger had his arm around Bree's shoulders and Charlie was taking the photo with her phone.

Bree looked thrilled to her toes even when Jagger copped a surreptitious feel during the photo op. Charlie wasted no time escorting her back to their saved place.

"I have to see," she whispered, pressing buttons on her cell. "My hands are shaking. I'm such a dork."

He took over the delicate operation, and she oohed and aahed at her fantastic luck. She was trembling with excitement and he would never have guessed. When she'd stood with one of the biggest celebrities on the planet, she'd appeared completely cool about the whole affair. Now her eyes hid nothing of her excitement. She grinned widely and clapped her hands together like a kid at the circus. Which, he supposed, she was.

Then they were at the security checkpoint, and there were wands and buckets and well-behaved guards. A short walk across a cold path, and they entered the main tent, the vast pavilion filled with music and chatter and laughter and a hundred different perfumes. Dresses that cost more than cars, faces that had been sculpted to the point of madness, lots of skin, lots of white teeth, and Bree looking like she'd arrived in Wonderland.

Charlie tried not to stare at her as they weaved through the crowd, as some chart topper sang her country tunes and photographs were taken. He sent a waiter for pineapple juice, and when he handed it to Bree, she blinked in utter bemusement.

It was too entertaining to last, because while he was on a date, he was also on assignment, and at least fifty percent of the guests at this shindig wanted their names on his blog tomorrow.

Normally this dance was one he could do in his sleep. Tonight, though, he wanted not just to include Bree, but feature her, make sure she met everyone she recognized. He wanted to see what she'd do, how she'd react. Unexpected. Completely out of character for him and puzzling, but nothing he cared to examine.

He felt drawn to Bree, which hadn't happened in so long he'd almost forgotten it could happen. What was more interesting was that he couldn't pinpoint why. If he had his way, he'd spend more time figuring out the deal with Bree than getting the dirt on the A-listers at the party.

"What's wrong?" After a tour of the immediate area, complete with air kisses, handshakes, posturing and pumped-up drama, they found a spot as far away from the speakers as they could get. Yet even next to the side exits to the powder rooms and private paths, Bree had to shout.

"Nothing. You having a good time?"

"Yes," she said. "Although I'm still in shock. It's overwhelming."

"It is. There are a lot of people wanting attention."

"I see what you mean about the seats," she said as she scooted closer to him.

He slipped his arm around her waist. Interest-

ing, holding someone who was so small. He felt...
protective.

"It's as if every chair is a throne, exclusively for the
most important kings and queens."

He nodded. "Some of them have a seat for a lifetime,
but not many. For most of them, it's a limited run."

"You could sit," she said. "You probably do, don't
you?"

"Nope. I work the room. I may be recognizable to
some, but my job here is to shine a light on the real celebrities. I'll have to blog this in the morning, and if I
don't get it right, I'll get dozens of calls and texts and
emails from furious PR people telling me I'm a disgrace
and I'll never work in this town again."

A waiter carrying champagne came by, and before
Charlie could say anything, Bree touched his hand. "I'd
like one, please."

"Sure?"

She nodded. "It's a champagne night."

"You must be starving. I haven't seen you eat a
thing."

"I'm too excited to eat. I shook hands with Tim
Gunn!"

"I know," he said. "He liked what you were wearing."

"He did not," Bree said, almost spilling her drink.
"Why, did he say something?" She closed her eyes.
"No, don't answer that. You're being sweet."

"Yeah, but if he'd had a minute to notice, he would
have liked your dress. You look stunning."

She sighed. "I didn't expect you," she said. "To be
honest, I'm not even sure what to make of you."

"What does that mean?"

"I know I'm not at all what you're used to. Yesterday, I saw a picture of you with Mia Cavendish. Then I saw her on the new Victoria's Secret billboard in Times Square. Rebecca went way above and beyond doing me this favor, but you've made tonight incredible. A dream come true. I don't even…"

He hadn't thought of it in the car, or in line, or after the Jagger incident, but right now, he couldn't think of anything in the world he wanted more than to pull this tiny person into his arms and kiss the daylights out of her.

So he did.

BREE SHOULDN'T HAVE BEEN shocked by his lips, but she froze, stunned more completely than she'd been at being bumped by Jean Paul Gaultier. *Charlie Winslow* was kissing *her*. Softly. Teasing her with the tip of his tongue, waiting for permission to enter.

She obliged.

He turned out to be a gentleman in this respect, as well. No thrusting, no swallowing her whole. Entering slowly, he gave her time to get used to him. To savor. She'd expected champagne but he tasted like mint, although come to think of it, she had no idea what the finish of champagne would taste like.

One flat palm touched her bare shoulder, his other hand pulled her closer, and the tentative portion of the kiss ended, as did all but the most basic of thoughts. He angled his head and settled in for a stay as they explored each other. It didn't take long for her shoulders to relax, to feel comfortable enough to pull back for a breath and a peek, then return for more.

That hand on her shoulder moved across her back warming her wherever it touched. It wasn't cold in the room, not with this many people, but Charlie's touch felt hot, not only his hand, either. The bass from the band made the room vibrate but she was already quivering. Kissing Prince Charming did that to a person.

As if the night wasn't spectacular enough.

She'd never forget this, the song that was playing, how she felt him moan even though she couldn't hear him. It was dizzying, every part of it, and her hope that this was more than just a favor went from not daring to think it to letting the idea take a seat.

He pulled back, not very far. "As much as I'd like to stay right here, I have to work. I'll warn you now, the people we're going to meet won't pay you enough attention. They're working the room, as well."

"I don't mind," she said truthfully. She expected nothing from this crowd. Which couldn't be said about Charlie. She had to stop herself from touching her mouth like a lovesick tween, but God, he had great lips. No matter how she looked at it, there'd been no reason to kiss her, none at all, except he'd wanted to. There went her breath, and any hope of walking on her wobbly knees.

"A room this size, it's going to take a couple of hours. Make sure at some point that you get something to eat. I won't be able to look after you as carefully as I'd like, and we can't have you keeling over from starvation. Grab things when you can, or duck out to the buffet. I'll be holding my cell, so I'll hear if you call, and we'll find each other."

She nodded. "Go. Work. Do your magic. I was always excited to read your Fashion Week blogs. You made me feel as if I was there."

"Really?"

"Well, now that I'm here, not exactly, but more than

enough. Don't tell, but I like your reports better than the ones in *W.*"

He grinned. "Now you're just being nice."

"Nope." She crossed her heart. "Mean every word."

"Come on, then. Let's go meet some famous people."

Bree was tempted to pull him in for one more kiss, to make sure it had been real, but didn't dare. Although it was hard not to imagine what it would feel like to walk across the lobby of his building, to go up in that elevator. Before her foolish notions got too carried away, she was reminded, quite spectacularly, of what she was doing now. A boatload of iconic symbols had come to life.

She felt like a Lilliputian in a world of Gullivers with Charlie as her guide. He led her through paths between tables, ice sculptures dripping and corks popping, and always, always the intrusion of cameras. Around the perimeter of the party, the different celebrity gossip shows had staked their territories, and their camera lighting bounced off the white of the tent making the entire arena glow.

They would walk two, maybe three steps, then stop as another celebrity, each one a surprise, approached Charlie. Interestingly, none of the familiar faces looked quite right. They were either better or shorter or skinnier or blonder than they looked in *People* or on TV.

Bree was good with makeup. Really. She'd made a point of learning the correct techniques at a beauty school near her college, but there was an element of magic to the faces that passed by. And the clothes…

She'd browsed through some of the high-end boutiques in Manhattan. D&G, of course, but a few couture houses, as well, showcasing their elegantly crafted suits and dresses, not daring to touch because each button or zip was worth more than everything she owned or would own for years to come. Now she saw those creations in motion, and it was poetry. No way to call it anything other than art. Each designer's style was as individual as a Picasso or a Rembrandt. She felt humbled. And grabby.

Instead of touching the fifty-thousand dollar gown, she snagged some hors d'oeuvres. Prawns and sushi and filet mignon, each with a little napkin and dabs of aioli. If she hadn't been an adult person standing next to famous people she wouldn't have stopped shoving them into her mouth because they were *fantastic*. The champagne was chilled, and she should switch back to pineapple juice because even with the food her edges were sliding toward fuzzy.

She turned to Charlie, only Charlie wasn't there. Not where she'd left him, but that had been before she'd followed the hamachi tray, dammit. She did a complete three-sixty, pausing as she saw clumps of celebrities, and that made her giggle, because certainly clumps wasn't the proper collective. What was? A cavalcade of celebs? A coterie? An ensemble? No, a *superficiality* of celebrities. Ha.

Bree pulled out her cell phone, pulled up Charlie's cell number and typed. *You're not here.*

He could be anywhere, so it wouldn't hurt to meander. Maybe get a small bottle of water. Her cell would vibrate when he texted back, so she could work on her Not From Hicksville Face as she gasped to herself.

Where are you? CW

*Standing next to 1 of the Olsen twins. Not sure which 1. Doesn't matter.*

Not able to find you via Olsen twin. Something more stationary please? CW

*Ah. Stella McCartney holding court.*

Perfect. But can't leave quite yet. Ten min. CW

*Who are you with? Nvr mind. Ur busy.*

Bree lowered her phone, but it dinged.

3 people who want in. 2 who'll get in. 0 fun as U. CW

She flushed with pleasure, even though it was a line, nothing more, and yet she'd never delete that text ever.

❤

The second she pressed Send, Bree panicked. It was a heart. She meant he was being sweet. Not— Oh, crap, he'd probably—

*Um. I meant thank U.*

☺ CW

She exhaled, still freaked out enough to barely glance at the second Olsen twin. She switched contacts, and texted.

*Rebecca, I screwed up.*

How?

*Sent him* ❤

???

*SENT HIM* ❤*!!!!!*

No worries. He won't mind.

*But—*

Hush. Trust me. & smile

The ding from a different text happened. Charlie.

Stay by Stella ETA 2 min CW

Bree decided to believe Rebecca and smile. Then she dialed the grin down from eleven to a reasonable five. Her heart, however, wasn't so cooperative. It was a silly mistake, that's all. Not even a mistake. A ❤ didn't have to mean anything significant. She used it with her friends all the time, and they didn't think she was declaring her undying love.

She was nervous, that's all. The atmosphere, the date itself. The *Olsens*.

And what came next. What *might* come next.

As a sneak peek, the kiss held great promise. She liked Charlie more than she'd expected to, and he'd kissed her, so he didn't find her repulsive or anything, so that was a point in her favor. Truthfully? She was equal parts good-anxious and insanely terrified-anxious about spending time alone with him. But first time—only time—sex with anyone was scary. So much potential for catastrophe. The ♥ was nothing compared to all the things that could go wrong.

She'd had her fair share of errors in the bedroom. The memories of which made her blush. But now was not the time to brood about mistakes made when learning the ins and outs, so to speak, of sex with relative strangers. It was the time to look for Charlie, to appreciate every single moment of being here, in this miraculous room, with a date that made her nipples take note, favor or not.

There were no twins at all around her now, but Ms. McCartney had a very large and enthusiastic crowd around her, and it was easy to see why. Although she couldn't hear the designer, or even see her face very well, the people within ear and eyeshot were smiling. Not the kind of smile that made a person shiver, the kind that erased years and made it fun to eavesdrop. But there was Charlie, and his smile....

God.

That was something. If it was fake, she'd take it, hands down over many other genuine things in life. Somehow, though, she didn't think it was fake. No matter, she grinned back, honest as the day was long. It wasn't that he was the most handsome man she'd ever seen. There were a number here tonight who would look better on a magazine cover. Of course, they were models, so that made sense. Charlie's charm was in the reality of his face. There were lines, small ones, that would have been airbrushed out on a cover, but she liked them. They gave him character and made him look as suave as he was. They were smile lines, which were always a good sign. Especially on the King of Manhattan.

She liked that he was thirty-one. Men in their twenties could have…issues. Fine, no problem, she was in her twenties and could make lists of all the things she wished were different, so no throwing stones, but guys were boys longer than women were girls, that was a fact. Charlie would be a wonderful lover, she imagined as she met him halfway to the dessert spread. That kiss had been an amuse-bouche. The meal would be like heaven.

"You look relatively unscathed," Charlie said. "I'm shocked."

"Why?"

"I'd have thought every straight man in the building would have been all over you."

"Stop."

"Not a line," he said. "I mean it. I'm stunned. I rushed. Although I figured you could take care of yourself."

"Based on?"

"Everything I've seen so far. You and Mick Jagger, for instance." Charlie slipped his hand across her lower back. "What would you like to see next?"

Bree met his gaze. "The view from here is fine."

He sighed, and because there was a momentary pause in the music, she heard it. The live music had stopped a while ago, and now there was recorded stuff—the mix excellent. Of course they'd have a great DJ at a party like this.

"Tell you what. Let's do one more circuit. I promise not to drag it out, no matter who we meet, but you're allowed to linger as long as you like, anywhere you like."

"Wow. That's very generous."

"I'm feeling magnanimous." He nodded toward a waiter. "Pineapple juice? Champagne? Pastry?"

She held up her water. "All set."

He hugged her closer and they began the procession, and she truly did feel like a princess. Her free hand ended up around his back, and somewhere around a very large ice sculpture of Michelangelo's *David* that was a bit worse for wear, her head came to rest on his shoulder. There were a number of places she thought about stopping, because the odds of her seeing these people again were nil, but not even Michael Kors himself was enough to pull her out of the spell of being with Charlie, her one-night-only prince.

# 5

THE LIMO ARRIVED, AND THANK goodness Charlie knew the driver because all of the limos looked identical, except for the radical fringe who liked their Hummers and their Bentleys stretched and bedazzled. Chivalry wasn't dead, Bree was glad to see, as Charlie stood in the safety position blocking her as she got into the backseat. When he climbed in after, he pulled her close, his arm around her shoulders.

"That was amazing," she said, rubbing her hands together in an attempt to get warmer.

"It was. Everyone came out to play tonight."

"I'm still trying to get it in my head that it happened, that it wasn't a dream."

"Nope. A hell of a lot of the pictures and videos coming out of tonight are for *Naked New York*. I'll make sure you get copies, how's that?"

Bree looked up at him, astonished. "Really? Of everything?"

"Yep. On disk, so you can Photoshop whomever. Just do me a favor and don't publish them. That could get tricky."

"I won't, I swear it. Not the Photoshop part—I'm to-

tally going to do that, and I'm going to save every last
nickel until I can get a color printer, but I swear I won't
publish. I wouldn't abuse the privilege."

"I'm not worried."

She couldn't stop staring at him. "How can you not
be? You don't know me at all. I could be anyone. A
competitor. I could work for Perez Hilton or Gawker,
and then where would you be?"

"You don't, though. Because Rebecca likes you."

"She barely knows me, either."

"Rebecca has excellent instincts about people. You'll
do well to stick with her. Don't tell her I said this, but
she's very, very smart. The smartest one in the family,
and we've got a couple of federal judges running
around, in addition to a bunch of politicians."

"Speaking of, lately I've been seeing all these bill-
boards for Andrew Winslow III. I didn't think of it
before, but are you guys related?"

Charlie's expression turned sour. "And so it begins.
He's a cousin. Not one I'm fond of. Although, I'm not
fond of most of them. Rebecca is the exception."

Interesting, his distaste for his family. So different
from her own experience. Sad, too. She didn't know
what she'd do without her family's support. Best to get
back to the relative he liked. "I'm enjoying the hell out
of our friendship so far. Rebecca's ridiculously funny.
And she knows the city the way I want to some day.
All the little places and the secrets."

"Why New York?" he asked.

"The Chrysler Building started it," she said. "I love
art deco, although when I first saw pictures of the
building I didn't know what art deco was. Then I discovered fashion, then theater and what was available
here, something incredible down every street. I fell for

the city long before I stepped foot in it. And yes, thanks to Woody Allen, it came with a score by George Gershwin. I think I must have lived here before in another life. Not that I necessarily believe in reincarnation, but if it's real, then I was here. This is home."

"There's a heartbeat to this place that's either in sync with your rhythm or not. I notice its absence every time I travel. If you're one of the chosen, Manhattan becomes home base and every time you come back, it's as if you can finally breathe again. That's how it is for me, at least."

She smiled at him, as if they shared a secret handshake. She supposed they did. Then she leaned over, her head resting gently on his shoulder. "Thank you, Charlie. Tonight's been one for the books."

Charlie closed his eyes as he pulled her closer. He agreed about the night. It hadn't been easy to leave her while he worked, and when had that happened at one of these things? He couldn't recall.

Not that he didn't like the women he asked out— he did. He liked women of *all* sorts, but he had some strong preferences, he wasn't going to deny it. He wasn't just dating for his own amusement, after all. His image was part of the *Naked New York* brand, and so were the women he was seen with. Some were better than others, some he could talk to, some couldn't string two coherent sentences together, but to a woman they were a type.

Bree wasn't even close.

So far she'd surprised him in almost every respect, though, and as he'd plowed through the glitter, he'd tried to remember the last time surprise had been in the mix. Scandals were par for the course these days, scripted or not. Hell, scandals were the point, whether they were caused by celebrities or of his own creation. Parties were only excuses to be seen or heard or photographed. Everything was grist, and he was both the wheat and the miller. Surprises? Once in a blue moon.

He wanted to know more about the woman warming his side, which was also rare, at least in this circumstance. He'd always been interested in people. That's why he started the blog in the first place. Well, that and wanting to shove his parents' plans for him where the sun didn't shine. He wanted Bree's details. The minutiae of the life she'd given up to come here, who she hoped to become. Something to do with fashion, obviously. Was that dress of hers a new design? Meant to stand out? Charlie might be around high fashion far more than a normal person should be, but that didn't mean he was a member of the inner circle. As far as he could tell, Bree's dress was nice. It showed her shape, the look of her skin, her curves and the soft skin of her thighs. He liked it. But was it fashion? No idea.

On the other hand, maybe he didn't want to know more. He'd hardly be seeing her again, even if she and Rebecca were friends. Charlie's social calendar was a function of necessity, not desire, and however much he liked Bree...what the hell was her last name...she wasn't on the agenda. Couldn't be. Whatever had motivated Rebecca to set up this date, it wasn't to fix him up. He'd known that the moment he'd set eyes on the girl from Ohio. But he wasn't sorry for the time spent with her. She'd made his night.

She'd fairly sparkled with how the event had dazzled her. He had to give her credit; she'd handled herself beautifully in the face of many challenges, but even so, there was no hiding her excitement. It was likely she didn't realize how she came off. He had the feeling it might bother her to know that she lit up like a marquee every time she saw someone famous. The ideal fan, in truth. No squealing or flailing or "Oh, my Gods." Just that inner light, the spark in her eyes, the coy and charming way she bit her lower lip when it got to be too much.

He breathed her in, glad the perfumes of the night hadn't swallowed her whole. Another surprise came when he noticed he'd been petting her all during the drive home. Running his hand over her arm. By the time the car stopped, Bree was practically purring and from the look in her eyes, exhausted. Adrenaline drop, probably.

She sat up, looked at the building, then back at him. "So, this is good-night?"

*Yes* sat on the tip of his tongue. What he said was, "Only if you want it to be."

Her eyebrows lifted, as did the corners of her mouth, but a second later she hesitated and concern took over. "You don't have to. I mean, this was—"

"Do you have to work tomorrow?"

She nodded sadly.

He paused for a single beat. "Do you want to come up, anyway?"

BREE WONDERED IF SHE WAS reading the situation correctly. She inhaled sharply as she remembered his kiss, the way he'd touched her. If this were Ohio, she'd have known exactly what he wanted. In New York? She'd have to take a risk. "I would," she said, hoping she sounded far more confident than she felt. She was going up to his apartment. To his bedroom! Maybe!

Charlie helped her out of the limo, and slid his arm around her shoulders as she thanked the driver. They both nodded at the doorman, but nothing was said as she and Charlie crossed the lobby, his arm draping across her back, his touch warm.

They were quiet during the ride up the elevator. She fit at his side, tucked in neatly. It felt amazing having his arm around her, warming her with gentle friction. She studied him in the mirrored cab, but only got as far as his eyes, staring at hers in return.

They got out on eighteen and the doors opened to a small atrium and the entrance to his home. He pushed open the door and stood aside to let Bree walk in first.

Even after reading *Architectural Digest* for years, watching rich people's lives on reality television, she wasn't prepared for the beauty and elegance of the room she entered. "This is…" she said, heading straight to the windows that made up most of the far wall. The view was spectacular, Central Park in its winter glory, the lights of the city sparkling.

Bree wanted to check out his furniture, the gorgeous art deco design work of the black-and-white floor, the magnificent marble fireplace and the sheer novelty of so much space. But she couldn't stop staring at the city. Eighteen floors up, the breathtaking view covered too much territory to take in, not when there were so many other things to think about. She might or might not have another shot at it, though. What the hell, she could go to any high-rise in Manhattan to see a view, but Charlie was one time only.

Charlie spoke behind her. "Would you like something to drink?"

She turned to him, not sure of much, but she knew she was thirsty. "Tea? If you have any."

His hesitation made her think her request wasn't one

he got often. "I think so," he said. "Give me a minute. Make yourself comfortable."

Charlie dropped his coat on the back of a chair before he disappeared into the kitchen. The tiny glimpse she'd gotten through the swinging door showed a lot of stainless steel and what might have been the edge of a teak cabinet. Strange how when she'd mentioned her love of art deco he hadn't told her they shared the passion. Or maybe the apartment hadn't been his design choice?

The weird thing about her mental tangent into decorating wasn't the coincidence of their taste, but her reaction to Charlie. She was fascinated by him, beyond the obvious. Which begged the question: Would she have agreed to come up if he had been anyone else? Was she honestly as attracted to him as her hormones would have her believe, or was it the *idea* of Charlie Winslow that had her aching to strip him naked and do every naughty thing she could think of to him?

She opened her clutch and sneaked out Charlie's trading card. After a quick check to make sure he wouldn't catch her in the act, she turned the card to the back side.

* His favorite restaurant: *Grand Central Oyster Bar*
* Marry, Date or One-Night Stand: *One Night is his max, but it'll be a fabulous night!*
* His secret passion: *Down deep he's old-fashioned. I know, surprise, huh?*
* Watch out for: *The idiot is obsessed with his work. He needs a break.*
* The bottom line: *Have fun! Just be yourself!*

Bree grinned at the personalized responses Rebecca had inserted. This was one card that wasn't going back into the pile, that was for sure. No, this was Rebecca's gift to Bree, and Bree wasn't going to let her insecurity get in the way of the rest of the magical night.

She flipped the card back to his photo. Objectively, he was a good-looking man. It was well documented, how good-looking Charlie was, in magazines, television and online. But she felt completely drawn to him in a way that wasn't exclusively about looks.

She knew what that felt like. There had been times in college and here in New York that she'd liked a man's looks and just gone for it. Those times had been okay in a hedonistic way, not something she did often. But she had to consider why she was staying, assuming it wasn't just for tea. Was the quick beat of her heart a groupie thing or common, everyday lust or… Did it matter?

The answer was as instantaneous as it was physical. She wanted him in a way that was neither common nor everyday. She'd have wanted him even if he wasn't the King of Manhattan. He'd been a surprise. Nice. Captivating. He'd purposefully shared insider nuggets so she would feel less like an impostor sneaking into the palace. He'd come looking for her, and he'd laughed at her jokes, and he'd kept her warm. That kiss had been…

Well, she'd need to be on her toes tonight, that's all. If they did end up in bed, which was not a sure thing as there seemed to be a whole different world of signals and innuendos she wasn't aware of in this rarefied air of his, but if they did, she'd have to be careful.

How Charlie made her feel, *that* could be dangerous. That was the difference. The other guys, both of them, had been fun in that risky sort of exciting manner when you've taken all the safety precautions so you're not precisely scared, but he was new, and what if he was terrible in bed, or his penis was teeny tiny or he wanted to wear her underpants?

Charlie might have all of those issues, but that wasn't dangerous. The real fear was that she could *like* him. The kind of like that meant nothing but trouble. Liking a guy was not part of the five-year plan. In fact, it was the antithesis of the five-year plan, the one thing that could turn even this unbelievable stroke of magnificent luck into a disaster of epic proportions.

After tucking the card back inside her slim wallet, Bree rested her butt on the arm of a gorgeous white leather couch. She continued to wait, wondering what was taking him so long. As her gaze wandered across the cityscape, she reminded herself about Susan. They'd been college roommates their freshmen year, and they'd hit it off from day one. Susan had decided to go into politics. She'd taken prelaw, had already picked out the three schools she would apply to; in fact, it was Susan who'd shown Bree the wisdom and power of the five-year plan. Susan had been brilliant. Formidable memory along with a quick mind and a powerful presence. It was easy to think of her as a potential senator or even president.

And then Nick had come along.

Susan had fallen slowly. Incrementally. But fallen she had, so hard that it had knocked the plan right out of her. She'd gone on to law school, yes, but at UCLA because of Nick. Yale and Harvard had both come calling, but she'd been in love. Bree had been a bridesmaid at her wedding, and the two of them kept in touch on Facebook, but Susan had a baby now, and she was a stay-at-home mom, which was fine. Of course it was fine. But it wasn't the dream.

If it had only been Susan, Bree wouldn't have given

it too much thought. It wasn't, though. Almost every friend she'd had in high school and the early years of college, every female friend that is, had somehow, someway subverted their dreams because of love. Her experience might be a statistical anomaly, but it was a damn scary one.

Bree had nothing against relationships, but that was for later. She wouldn't even entertain the thought of marriage before thirty, and quite possibly longer than that. Forget a child in her twenties. She wasn't even sure she wanted to have a child at all. Not something she had to worry about at the moment, thank goodness, but liking Charlie? That was a distinct possibility.

Of course, his liking her back was highly improbable. On the level of her winning the lottery. Which was worse in some ways, because even though it was one night, and she had a hint of a crush on him, there was every reason to believe there might be sparks in the bedroom. It would be so very Bree to find herself enamored with Charlie, only to crumble in a fit of pining and lovelorn paralysis for however long it would take to get over it. That would also not be good for the plan.

This having-sex decision was more complicated than she'd thought. Thank goodness she hadn't given in to more champagne.

She wasn't wearing a watch, but Charlie really had been gone a long time. She pushed off the couch and went toward the kitchen, hoping nothing had gone wrong. Two steps later, the door swung open and Charlie came in carrying a silver tray. On it, he'd put a pot, an actual teapot, made of fine china decorated with flowers and vines. There were matching cups, two, and saucers, also two. A little cream pourer, a bowl of sugar lumps, tongs, *TONGS,* lemon slices, a strainer, and she had to get closer to see that the tins were actually different varieties of tea. She looked up at Charlie, and he looked back. It was a…moment.

Part of her wanted to laugh, but a bigger part of her wanted to know *what the hell?*

"Seems I have a tea service," he said, his voice low and wickedly deadpan. "I never knew that. I don't do a lot of cooking, and someone else put my kitchen together. But I thought, why not? I may never be asked for tea again."

"I see—oh, that one isn't tea. That's biscuits?"

"English shortbread cookies," he said. "Fresh, according to the package." He put the tray on the coffee table after she'd scurried to clear off some magazines. "My guess is that my housekeeper is the tea aficionado. She comes in three times a week, and I don't pay attention to her snacking habits. Makes sense, though. She stocks the fridge. The tea set looks like something my mother would own, and expect me to own."

"And here I was thinking a mug and a Lipton's tea bag. But this will do."

"It will, huh?"

Bree nodded. "So many different kinds," she said, busy investigating. There was chamomile, Earl Grey, Darjeeling and one she had never heard of called British Blend. She pointed to it. "Shall I make a pot?"

"Go for it."

She was very glad she'd used loose tea before as she poured the leaves into the hot water, then left it to steep. In her cup, she used the tongs to put in two lumps of sugar, poured in a hint of milk and waited nervously as she realized how close together they were on the couch.

This wasn't like having his arm around her at the

party or even sitting pressed up to him in the limo. A bedroom was now involved, only steps away.

She could take one of two approaches to the next minute: she could bring up the decor and keep wondering what was going to happen until he did something obvious, or she could put on her big girl panties and ask if they were going to share more than tea. "So," she said, "you like art deco."

Charlie glanced up at her, his own sugar lump tonged and hovering above his cup. "Yes. I do."

She barely heard him over the cursing in her head, which was frankly not very nice. She wasn't a wimp and hated to think she was a chicken, but the only way to prove she had cajones was to act like it. "Is the whole place art deco?" she asked, trying to be sexily coy, not creepily stiff. "Your bedroom, for example?"

She winced. She couldn't help it. A fifteen-year-old could have done better.

The sugar fell into the cup with a soft plunk and Charlie smiled. "Perhaps, after tea, you'd like to see it?"

Bree nodded, then busied herself with straining the leaves and pouring. She decided she'd said enough already, but Charlie didn't pitch in to fill the silence. He might have been watching her or gazing out the window; she didn't know because she didn't dare look up. It was enough to will her hands steady and her thoughts calm and composed. Something had happened in the past few seconds; maybe it was how his voice had lowered and how the husky murmur slid over her skin like a warm vibrant promise—she had no idea.

No, he was definitely zeroed in on her, she decided, as the weight of his stare seemed to change the very air around them. She could actually feel him watching, waiting, missing nothing. She set down the pot, picked up her cup and took a sip, barely tasting more than the warmth as the quiet stretched between them. The element of surreality, what with silver tongs and it being two in the morning, made time shimmer and slow. She drank again, the delicate cup insisting she raise her pinkie.

She finally glanced over and saw that Charlie was, in fact, staring. He also lifted his cup to his lips, drank silently, his hand large and his fingers long, his eyes never leaving her, never wavering.

She was acutely aware that he could have glanced down to the tops of her pushed-up breasts, to her barely covered thighs. If he had he would have noticed the intermittent tremors, the pink skin she felt sure was not just on her cheeks but the tips of her ears.

It was unbearably sexy, that stare, his dark eyes so large, unblinking. As if he could see more than she wanted him to.

As every second ticked by, the heat intensified, until she couldn't take it any longer. She blinked. "The tea's good," she said, surprised her voice was steady.

He swiped his bottom lip with the edge of his tongue; barely a swipe really, only enough for the light to catch on the moisture.

"Although I have no idea what makes it a British blend. It tastes like…tea."

He lowered his cup. "I've got a window in my bedroom," he said, his voice—still low and rumbly—moving through her like distant thunder. "I want to take your dress off slowly. Let it fall down your body. I've been wondering for hours what's underneath. I'm guessing black, maybe lace, maybe silk, but definitely black. You'll look incredible standing by that window with the lights of the city as your backdrop."

Bree almost dropped her cup, clumsy and awkward as a surge of wet heat flowed through her. She'd been so together, too. All calm and reasonable and thinking things through. And then he had to go and say *that*.

She was officially in another plane of existence because there was no one in the world as she knew it who could have said those words in that tone with that look in his eyes. If she hadn't known better, she would have thought there was someone sitting behind her, some model or actress or virtually anyone who wasn't Bree Kingston.

"Bree?" His smile was slow, controlled, while she hesitated.

God, why *was* she hesitating? A few more seconds and maybe she could get her legs in working order.

He stood and held out his hand for her. Heart beating flamenco style, head swirling in a cloud of lust and weirdness, she rose without spilling, tripping or making any unfortunate sounds.

Instead of pulling her closer, Charlie stepped into her personal space, then into her. His body touched her from chest to thigh, and he was warm and big and he smelled as if he'd just walked in a forest. Looking up was nothing new, but meeting his gaze so near, feeling his tea-sweet breath caress her lips, that was stunning. As he bent down, her eyes closed at the last possible second, and then, and then...

# 6

CHARLIE SHIFTED HIS BODY as he kissed her. He'd been getting hard for a while now, since he'd put down that ludicrous tea tray. Bree wasn't his type; there was no question about that, but she was something—

Something.

So small. Not thin, thin was ubiquitous, a thing to get over, not to enjoy. At least the kind of thin he was used to. Bree was diminutive, delicate. How he wanted to hold her completely in his arms, lift her from the floor and carry her off to his bed. More absurd than the tea service because there wasn't a romantic bone in his body and also not enough booze to let his imagination get away from him, and yet, his hands moved down her black dress—which had to go—to cup her hips, her bottom.

Instead of giving in to his urge, he walked backward, pulling her with him. He didn't need to look, not yet. It was a straight line to the hallway, where he would have to make sure to turn them, then another straight shot to his bedroom.

They kissed and walked in their odd shuffling gait. He touched wherever he could, mostly the parts that were bare, and warm, and pebbled with goose bumps. He hoped those were from him, not the temperature. Decided not to ask.

The bedroom was obscenely large for Manhattan, but the building was prewar and the place had been re-modeled to make it expansive. He'd put in plush carpet for the pleasure of it, outrageously fine sheets, condoms and water bottles near the California king. Bree broke away from his kiss with a gasp. Not at the luxury of the room, she hadn't looked at it yet, but for breath. To give him a smile.

He nodded toward the wall, all windows, the elec-tronic shades up and hidden to capture the view. "There," he said. "I want you there."

She turned. This gasp wasn't for air. "Oh, it's beau-tiful."

"It pales." He took her hand and guided her closer to the windows and kissed her again, sneaking his tongue between her lips as his fingers found the zipper pull. He heard nothing but breathing and blood flow, but he followed the zipper with his left hand on her bare back until he reached the end. He touched the strip of elastic that was the line of her thong. The touch was enough to pull him away from the gorgeous heat of her mouth. He needed to see.

The dress fell, puddling at her feet, and it was better than he'd imagined. The thong wasn't black, but red. Dark red, tiny. Seeing it against her pale flesh made his cock harder, his desire intense.

Odd, so odd, this reaction of his. She was pretty, she really was, but she wasn't architecturally beautiful. Per-fectly proportioned, yet not so slender she didn't have curves and a little bit of a tummy that made him want to rest his head right there for a week. God, her breasts.

They were mouthwatering, with pale pink areolas and firm little nipples, puckered and waiting.

Bree stepped out of her dress, and oh, that was something. Her in nothing but a ruby thong and high heels. Stunning, delicious…for Christ's sake, the woman was two feet in front him, willing and eager.

He worked his clothes off in a controlled frenzy, flinging things away as he multitasked, toeing off his shoes and socks, moving closer to Bree as he unzipped, hissing as the silk of his boxer briefs brushed against the underside of his aching cock.

He kissed her again, but she was trembling and just chilly enough for him to bow to the nonsensical urge to scoop her up into his arms—she was a featherweight of soft flesh and hitching breaths—and dammit, he should have pulled the bedcovering down. She huffed a laugh as he stood her up, and together they got rid of the extra pillows and pulled down the duvet.

He waited, and when she sat and bent to take off her heels, he made a noise. It wasn't a squeak or a whimper, but it was close on both counts. Bree grinned, rose from the bed. There was a wicked sparkle in those lust-darkened eyes of hers, and when she turned around and went onto all fours on the mattress, Charlie made another noise, but this was a groan that came straight from his balls. She crawled across the bed, her hips swaying in invitation, giving him flashes of red between her thighs.

When she got to the second pillow, she made a show of lying down, grinning at him, flushed and breathing hard as she posed for him. Hands behind her, clutching the teak headboard slats, hair dark against the white pillowcase. Her legs came up, one canted over the other, like a pinup from the forties, like a siren, like a dream.

Miraculously, he didn't come right there and then. He made it onto the bed, took his time but he had to close his eyes before he touched her. Because, God.

When he licked a trail up the inside of her thigh, she trembled on his tongue.

BREE STOPPED BREATHING as Charlie's mouth inched up her thigh. The sexy pose wasn't like her, but then, she wasn't the same Bree tonight. Thank goodness her hands gripped the slats or she'd have floated straight up to the ceiling. She wanted to hurry him, his hot breath teasing her so near the creases where thigh met thong but not quite there.

He'd caught her left ankle in his hand, holding her leg aloft as his other hand smoothed up the front of her right thigh. She watched him, her excitement mounting, but the angle of her head was tricky to maintain with the firm pillow smooshed awkwardly under the top of her back. As much as she wanted to let her head loll back, her eyes close, let out the cry trapped in her throat, she couldn't do anything but stare at him, naked, crouched low on the bed between her knees. So she kept watching, urging him to move up, let that hot breath of his sneak under the silk, let his tongue follow.

Every inhale expanded her chest so her breasts, too small for her long erect nipples, came into her line of sight. When he looked up, he smiled at the same broken view, but from below. Okay, so maybe her breasts weren't *too* small. From how he groaned, never letting his tongue lift from her flesh, he seemed to like them. A lot.

Despite the groan, the stubborn man refused to *move*. "Charlie," she whined as she lifted her hips. What did he need, an engraved invitation?

His low chuckle dialed up her frustration.

"Patience," he whispered, his mouth moving closer to where she needed it. But instead of his tongue, he slipped his nose in that crease, nudging the thong over. He inhaled as if she were a bouquet of roses, and oh, God, he lowered her ankle as his teeth gripped silk. The tug was forceful, but not enough to snap the G-string panties, only to push things to the side, to let her feel a brush of cool air on her naked flesh.

When she let go of the slats, her hands ached. She was sure they were dented from the pressure, but she didn't care. It was necessary to touch him. She was shorter than any one of her friends, but the distance between the top of the bed and Charlie's body seemed to stretch on for miles. Yet she reached him with no strain, touched his dark, soft hair, her fingers tracing his temples.

He moaned, inches away from a different crease. Then that artful tongue of his started exploring and Bree's body arched with the shock of it.

The battle with the awkward pillow was lost in an instant. Her head lolled back, her eyes shut as he licked and sucked and flicked until she had one leg pressing down on his shoulder and a grip on his hair that had to hurt like a mother.

He didn't let up, not when she whimpered, not even when she turned his name into a pitiful plea.

She came with a jolt, another full-body arch and a cry that started low and ended so high only bats could hear it.

Charlie held her through the tremors, kissing his way up to her belly button, to her chest. Soft kisses, hard kisses, some wet and filthy, then chaste and sweet. His teeth scraped her skin, making her gasp, but the licks afterward soothed her into a sigh. When he reached her breasts, he settled in for a while. Bree quivered beneath him, every nibble and suck on her sensitive nipples sparking aftershocks.

She ran her hands across his shoulders as she whispered his name over and over, tugging him up, closer. But the obstinate bastard had other plans. He abandoned her nipple with a long swipe of his tongue and met her gaze, his eyes darker than ever. His lips were wet with her moisture, his smile three steps past sinful.

"You need to reach over there," he said, nodding at his bedside table. "Open that drawer."

"I do, huh?"

His smile widened and she felt his hand sneaking down her tummy. "If you wouldn't mind," he said, and she could have sworn his voice had lowered a full octave.

"Charlie, what are you doing?"

"I'm not finished being in you," he said. "So I'll just amuse myself until you think you might like more than fingers."

"Maybe I've got a thing for fingers."

"That's okay," he said. But he was pushing himself up to kneeling until she could see him. See his very hard, very ready cock.

The hand that wasn't petting her pussy, toying at the very edge of her lips, encircled his erection. It was a handful and he looked like he knew how to use it.

She swallowed and clenched her muscles as he squeezed up his length until just his glans peeked out, a drop of precome beading obscenely.

Bree hated to look away, but it couldn't be helped. She found the condom quickly, opened it with shaky fingers. He did the honors of putting on the rubber—

making a damn show of it—and then he laid himself over her, leaning on his elbow so she wouldn't be squished.

The kiss was salt and sex, his tongue giving her a preview of what was to come. Spreading her open, he rubbed up and down between her labia getting his bearings by feel. All the while, he watched her with dark, hooded eyes.

When he thrust, the cry she'd been holding in caromed off the walls, stole all her air.

Everything from then on was white heat and being filled. Raw and hard, every slap of flesh was followed by a desperate gasp from him, from her.

She came again. Squeezing him, pulling him closer, tighter. Then he froze, his face a mask of intense pleasure.

When he came back from the edge, he kissed her. More than the date, more than the tea, more than anything, the kiss turned everything sideways. Long, slow and deep, it wasn't a thank-you or showing off or like any other après-sex kiss she'd ever had. It was as real as the night sky, and it made her as dizzy as if she'd downed a magnum of champagne.

After, as she gathered in her stolen breath, he fell into a graceless heap beside her.

She still had her heels on.

When he forced himself out of the bed and into the bathroom, she closed her eyes, still dazed and confused. "Happy Valentine's Day, Bree," she said softly so he wouldn't hear. "Whoa."

It was six-forty. Charlie had looked at his alarm clock at six thirty-eight, then at Bree, still sleeping, still with him. All he'd been able to see was part of her bare shoulder and the back of her head. Now he was staring at the ceiling and having a panic attack.

He'd never had one before, but the way his heart was hammering in his chest had to be a sign. As a test, he turned his head to catch a glimpse of her. *Fuck*. What the hell had he done?

The last time he'd felt like this, not quite like this but the closest thing he could remember that had a similar vibe, was at fifteen. His first time. It was at Amy Johnson's house, in her twin canopy bed with her parents two doors down the hall. He'd been crazy about Amy, madly in whatever passes for love at fifteen. The sex had been horrible but he'd gotten off. He couldn't imagine how bad it had been for Amy. He'd felt like the stud king of the world, and even when he fell flat on his face escaping out her bedroom window, he'd considered the night a raging success.

He'd made sure his parents found one of the condoms from the box of Trojans. Their apoplectic fit at the inappropriateness of sex with a girl from that kind of family—she went to public school and her father was a dentist at a clinic—had been the most satisfying development in his life until age sixteen and a half, when he'd discovered the joys of older women and realized how much he had to learn.

Those lessons had been a downright pleasure.

But no one and nothing since Amy had recaptured the out-of-his-mind exhilaration of that maiden voyage. Until last night.

No matter what they'd done, Bree was definitely an innocent. Ah. Okay. Bree reminded him of Amy. Nothing to panic about. His breathing should return to normal soon. Last night had been a rerun of a great night. That's all. His reaction had nothing to do with the nice woman in his bed. He would give her coffee and cab fare, and that would be the end of it.

The sooner the better. She had to get to work, and so did he.

He stilled as she turned over and they touched. His hand, her thigh. It was warm, the place where they came together, and all the progress he'd made in the breathing department went to hell.

Why was he getting hard again? Shit.

He pictured her in that pose, her hands gripping the headboard, her nipples hard as little rocks and those heels. Jesus. She'd smelled like honey and tasted like the ocean, and he hadn't been that hard in years. He bit back a moan as he pictured her face when she'd come. And there was the problem in a nutshell. Or should he say in his nuts.

Forcing his mind to focus, he refused to acknowledge anything below the waist. If he'd been thinking with anything but his dick he would've sent her home last night. As soon as she'd asked for tea. Tea? Seriously? Then he'd made everything worse by getting down the goddamn silver. What was that about?

Screw his hard-on. This was ridiculous. He had work. Last night had been a favor for Rebecca, a nice surprise for him. No denying Bree was fantastic in bed, but that wasn't important. It didn't matter. He didn't need a great lay, he needed A-listers, women who would draw readers to the blogs, gossip fodder. He needed Mia Cavendish and her counterparts, the more photogenic and controversial, the better. He wanted to trend on Twitter, make the headlines on the *New York Post*'s Page Six. He needed ad revenue and infamy.

Bree could get him exactly none of that.

GOOD GOD ALMIGHTY, she was in *so much trouble*.

How was it possible that the best thing about her night as Cinderella had been a one-night stand with the King of Manhattan?

Not the limo, not Charlie's fame, not the stars or the dresses or meeting her design heroes. No. The best thing, the thing that would cripple her if she didn't get a grip *right this minute* was making…sex with Charlie.

She was no blushing virgin and she knew what happened between the sheets. She'd had bad sex and she'd had amazing sex and what had happened with Charlie wasn't even on the same scale.

Falling for Charlie was not acceptable.

She really needed to get out of bed because if he moved the hand against her thigh even a little bit, she couldn't be held accountable for her actions.

Where was her dress? By the window. Somehow, the room wasn't filled with light, which it should have been because the last time she'd looked, there'd been nothing but glass between them and Central Park. Yet, it wasn't dark, either. She hadn't opened her eyes, but there was some kind of pale gold thing happening behind her lids, so…

The lamp that had been on while they'd been…

She inhaled quietly, regrouping. It didn't matter what Charlie was doing. She was in control of her actions and her thoughts. She'd throw back the covers, get out of bed, pull up her dress, slip on her heels and go to the bathroom. She wouldn't have to look at him at all.

*Crap.* The back of his fingers brushed against her thigh. Just that quickly, her resolve vanished and her body tensed. Things were happening against her will. Nipples hardened. Kegel muscles contracted. Not to mention the thunder of her heart.

*It was one time, Kingston. One night. You had champagne. It was like being in a fairy tale. It's not real. Things like this don't happen in the real world. It's over. Stop being a moron and get out.*

After a silent count to three, she did it. Tossed covers, pulled up dress, screw the zipper, picked up shoes, darted to the bathroom, slammed the door, breathed.

Cursed herself from here to Sunday because while she was in the nice, safe bathroom, her purse with all her stuff was in the living room.

She sighed and leaned on the door, barely restraining herself from banging her head against the wood until she passed out. Her makeup was already a disaster so crying wasn't out of the question.

What were the odds he had a spare toothbrush in this humongous room? The shower alone was bigger than what she laughingly called a bedroom.

She could wash her face with whatever soap he had, and rinse her mouth with something that would at least hide the morning breath for a while. All she had to do was be somewhat presentable for a cab ride home, then she could start forgetting about Charlie as she hustled to get ready for work.

Coffee. Coffee would help everything. No, *aspirin* and coffee. That's what she needed, and her world would fit neatly back into place.

A knock on the bathroom door made her jump so hard her dress nearly slipped all the way down to the floor. "Um, busy," she said, yanking it up again.

"Yeah," Charlie said, and God, his voice rippled through her like a slow fire. "I thought you might want your pocketbook."

"Oh. Uh. Okay. Yes." She turned, holding up her

dress with one arm as she opened the door an inch. It wasn't quite enough. Another inch, then another, and finally her purse was inside. She snatched it as if it were connected to a mousetrap. "Thanks. Be out in a minute. Don't mind me."

Silence followed. Bree didn't know if he was there or not, but she didn't move. She pressed her ear against the door.

"Okay," he said, making her jump again. "I'll go make coffee."

"Great. Thanks. Sounds great." She winced at her stupid mouth, and reconsidered the whole banging her head against the door thing.

Finally, she turned around, resigned that there wasn't enough aspirin and coffee in the world.

*"WHAT'S THIS?"* BREE ASKED.

Charlie looked down at the hundred-dollar bill he was holding out to Bree. "Cab fare."

"A hundred? You think I live in Connecticut?"

"Wasn't sure. Look, I'm sorry I can't take you myself, but the blog..."

"It's fine. Really. I've got it," she said as she held up her to-go cup. "Thanks for the coffee."

"You're not going to be late for work?"

"Nope. Not if I get a move on."

She hadn't looked at him. Not once. At least, he didn't think so. He'd been avoiding looking at her, so there was no certainty, but it felt like she hadn't.

If nothing else had told him the night had been a colossal mistake, this morning's awkwardness would have. It was epic. Both of them stumbling, mumbling, embarrassed and basically acting like idiots. The problem was he couldn't tell why she was behaving like he had the plague. He'd thought the night had been great, and the sex had been fantastic. Too good.

Maybe that was just him, though.

Naw. It had been spectacular, and he knew what he was talking about. She was being weird for another reason. He'd like to blame the excessive cab fare move, but the weird dance had started when she'd first gotten out of bed.

She was making her way to the front door, although she didn't simply turn around and walk. She took a few steps back, checked behind her, then moved another couple of steps, and it made him want to kiss her.

Shit.

She had to go. Now.

He surged ahead of her to the door and opened it. "I'm sorry I can't see you—" He stopped before he repeated the whole sentence.

"Of course. And I have…" She was right in front of him now, looking up at him with those green eyes. "Thank you," she said. "It was the best night ever. I'll never forget you. It. The party. Doing…stuff."

Her cheeks had turned a really dark shade of pink, and yep, so did the tips of her ears. The urge to move a few inches, lower his lips to hers once more was stronger than he was prepared to admit.

"I had a great time, too," he said, his voice cracking on the end. "We should…" He stopped himself by biting his tongue. It hurt quite a bit. But he'd almost said they should do it again.

"Well, I'll be off. Down the elevator. To get a taxi." She stepped through the doorway sideways. Almost hiding behind her coffee, only spilling a little.

"Right. Bye."

"Bye."

He went to shut the door as she called for the elevator. Then stopped. It would be rude to shut the door. On the other hand, she looked desperate.

He split it down the middle. Left the door ajar, but walked away. To the kitchen. He didn't breathe until he heard the ding.

Holy crap.

# 7

BREE SAT IN HER CUBICLE, shuffling papers from one stack to the next. She'd been at the office for two hours and she hadn't accomplished a damn thing. Most of the morning had been spent rehashing last night, analyzing to death every single thing Charlie had done or said. Sneaking peeks at the picture she'd taken, of his trading card.

In the harsh fluorescent lights of BBDA, the events featuring Charlie seemed more like a dream than something that could have happened to her. But there was an ache in her body that wasn't a result of working out at the gym. She'd tensed her arms so hard gripping the headboard that her muscles had burned as she'd showered this morning, and there was that thumbprint bruise on her hip. Plus her memories, of course.

She had no business thinking about him. The night. Him. Really now. It was over. Done. A recollection that should bring her pleasure instead of this sense of loss. How could she have lost something she'd never had? Never could have?

God, the whole morning sucked. Her thoughts had been wild enough before she'd seen that he hadn't posted his blog yet. He should have. His routine was like Old Faithful, like atomic time. Instead, three other people had posted—one fashionista, one celeb tracker and one foodie.

So in addition to obsessing over the fact that sex had been no more than a part of the overall standard package rather than a romantically wonderful moment between the two of them, now she was pretty convinced that she had somehow jinxed Charlie. And she had a headache.

Surprisingly, Rebecca hadn't called yet, which was fine because Bree hadn't figured out how much she wanted to tell her and she wanted to be careful about that conversation, not dead on her feet. In fact, she seriously thought about sneaking in a nap today in place of lunch. She needed sleep more than food.

Her cell dinged and when she saw the name flash, she nearly choked. She clicked on the icon.

How are you feeling? CW

Bree stared at his initials, completely stunned. Why was he texting her? Good manners? Had she accidentally taken something from his apartment? She hit Reply then forced herself to think, not text, not yet.

This was silly. She shook her head as she used her thumbs.

*Fine. Thanks.*

You get to work okay? CW

*On time and everything.*

I'm glad. Also lunch? CW

*What?* Lunch? Was he asking her to lunch? Nope, no, that couldn't be right. Not after this morning. She stared at the gray panel of her cubicle for a moment, then looked once again at her message. She hadn't read it wrong. It simply made no sense.

Now her gaze lifted over the cubicle wall, but all she could see was the top of the heads passing by. There wasn't a single person at BBDA she could pull aside for advice. None of them knew about her date with Charlie. Or really anything about her except that she tended to keep to herself.

She quickly typed *BRB* letting him know she was away from her keyboard, and grabbed the landline. Screw not telling Rebecca about what happened. Bree needed help. Fast. She dialed, praying her friend would answer.

The second Bree heard "hello," she launched. "Last night was the most fabulous night in the history of earth, but this morning was completely weird and now he's…"

"Bree—"

"Oh, God, you're busy. Please don't be busy because I don't even— Wait. He's texting me now, and I don't know what to do."

"Texting you what?"

"He wants me to have lunch with him. Today."

Rebecca laughed. "Then go!"

"We both freaked out this morning. He offered me a hundred dollars."

*"What?"*

"For a taxi."

"Oh. Then I repeat. Go."

"But—"

"Trust me on this. I know him. Really well. Lunch is huge."

"Huge? Huge isn't good at all. It's over now, right? He doesn't do repeats, and I've got a plan, and it doesn't include liking anyone. Huge can't be the thing that comes next."

"Listen to me," Rebecca said, her tone one she surely must use when she was negotiating with billionaires or friends having panic attacks. "Go to lunch with Charlie. Eat food. Listen to what he has to say. You might be surprised. Then call me after."

Bree touched her hair and her face as her stomach flipped from excitement to dread and back again. Damn, she'd done almost nothing with her hair, and her makeup consisted of mascara. Period. She'd had barely enough time to shower and change, and then she'd had to scramble to make it to the office. "You'd better be right, Rebecca."

"I am. Good luck."

Bree hung up, then got her thumbs in position.

*Where? When?*

Bistro truck? CW

*Um...*

Mediterranean CW

*Okay.*

Sending map. U say when. CW

*1?*

C U there. CW

Her cell let her know the map had arrived, and the Bistro truck was only a block from her office. She typed the name into her search engine to check out the menu, wanting to be prepared and avoid anything messy. Figured she'd go with the phyllo-wrap veg and the Belgium fries, assuming she could eat anything. Even if meeting him turned out to be a horrible mistake, fries would soothe the wound.

After closing her phone, she stared at the paperwork she had to finish before noon, her vision blurring on the words. He wanted to see her again. Why? *Why?* And why was Rebecca so sure she should go?

New York was confusing.

CHARLIE STOOD ON A CEMENT bench on East 14th Street, searching the lunchtime crowds for Bree. Despite her little black dress last night, he remembered Rebecca's comment about Bree's affection for colors, so he zeroed in on anything that wasn't black clothes, which eliminated around seventy percent of the women. It helped that today was unseasonably warm, so that most of the coats were open.

He turned, not minding the stares he earned. This was Union Square at one in the afternoon. He did what worked. And work it did, because there she was. Her clothes hadn't caught his eye; her hair had, though. It was the same short pixie cut, but today she'd worn a slim pink ribbon complete with bow. It was ridiculous, and it made him grin like an idiot.

As she got closer, he forced his gaze down, not stopping on her face, not yet. No coat. Surprising, but not, because they were only a block from her office and she'd already proven she would rather freeze to death than ruin the ensemble. She'd need another winter in New York until she woke up and smelled the frostbite.

Today she had on a pink-and-green-checked long-sleeved button-down, which should have been ugly as sin, but wasn't. And a skirt, a little bitty one in a completely different shade of green. None of it had any business being on a single person at the same time. Even the flat matte gold shoes were wrong. And fantastic.

Her step faltered as he caught her eye. She smiled, one of those full-on middle American smiles that showed a whole lot of teeth. But as she started walking again that faltered, too. By the time he'd jumped down and met her on the sidewalk, she seemed worried. Or hungry. No. Worried.

"You all right?" he asked.

"Yes," she said, nodding. "Fine, thanks."

He wouldn't press now. First they needed to order. "Hungry?"

"Sure."

He grabbed her hand, and before they took a step toward the line at the big white truck, he kissed her cheek. He'd debated that move all the way over here. It seemed rude not to acknowledge their night together, yet he didn't want to emphasize that aspect of their acquaintance, despite the fact that the memory of her in his bed had been a constant low-grade fever since he'd opened his eyes this morning. It didn't surprise him that she stopped short and looked at him as if he were crazy. It didn't matter. He stood by the kiss decision.

Come on, how could he have resisted? One look at her with her pink bow and that small skirt…

Okay, shit, wrong turn. He breathed deeply the scent of fried foods and city buses, getting his bearings once more. They wouldn't be able to order for at least ten minutes, considering the length of the line, then there would be the food to deal with. Might as well dive in. He kept hold of her as he maneuvered himself close enough to talk without being overheard. "I have a proposition for you."

Her eyebrows rose.

"Last night, at the party, you were great."

"Thanks," she said, with just enough of a lift at the end to make it vaguely a question.

"I spent all morning trying to write the blog. So much time I ended up posting fillers from freelancers so people wouldn't get antsy."

"I know. I saw."

"Ah. Of course." He moved them up a half step in line. "Anyway, the thing was, you kept popping up in my first draft."

"I popped up?" She said it slowly, her forehead now furrowed in confusion.

He didn't normally confuse people. Piss them off, all the time, but clarity wasn't an issue. "I realized that I'd felt as if last night was my first time at Fashion Week. That didn't happen even when I did go for the first time. Seeing through your eyes was…different." He'd almost said exhilarating. True, but too much information. "That's what I wrote about. This morning."

"O…kay," she said.

He was not making his point. "I'm posting my blog late because I wanted to talk to you about it. I want to use your vision, for want of a better word, as the hook for the column. An innocent at Fashion Week. A new perspective."

"I'm not that innocent," she said, her tone brusque and bruised, as if he'd insulted her.

"You're new to the city. You're not jaded yet. Since *Naked New York* excels at jaded, I like the idea of approaching this series from another angle. I won't mock you. In fact, I won't use your name or image if you don't want me to. It'll be my impressions of your impressions. Which I've never done before, so you may or may not be fine with it."

"You already wrote the blog?"

He nodded. "Three different versions. One with you specifically, one with you obliquely, and one that focuses only on my impressions. I can send them to your phone now, if you want to read them."

"I would," she said. "Does it say that I…we…" She flinched briefly, then carried on. "You know, got together…at your place?"

"No. No, that's…no. This isn't about personal stuff. It's about the event. The party."

"Oh," she said, and this time it wasn't equivocal. "Send them, then."

He clicked the necessary buttons as a group of five in front of them suddenly dashed off, which moved him and Bree up to the food truck window. "What'll you have? I'll order while you read."

"Fries. Large."

"Nothing else?"

She thought for a moment, but couldn't imagine eating a whole sandwich. Not while her stomach was in knots. "Tea, two sugars."

He grinned. Couldn't help it. He still couldn't believe he'd actually served her tea on a silver platter. With tongs. Bizarre. But then, everything about last night had been.

He heard the sound of her receiving the documents on her phone, then he turned his attention to the guy behind the counter. He ordered, glanced at Bree, paid, looked again, then moved them to the waiting line where he out-and-out stared. He ignored everything but her body language, her expressions, the speed with which she read the screen. He learned absolutely nothing.

Turning so he could only see her in his peripheral vision, he reminded himself that whatever her response, it would be fine. Even if she went along with his whole scheme, it didn't mean anything. Not personally. This was a work thing. That's it. Maybe they'd have the opportunity to get together again, but that wasn't the point.

Even though the pink ribbon killed him. In fact, the pink ribbon *was* the point. None of the people he hung out with would have put that outfit on, not on a bet. It was an anti-Manhattan look. Those who attended Fashion Week were more afraid of not being cool than they were of being hit by a car. Bree's kind of unabashed adoration was straight from the heart with nothing expected in return.

Her point of view would ring true for the majority of his readers, many far more like her, young people who would never have a chance to go to a gala, never stand next to icons of fashion and film, never be able to afford a scarf from any of the designers, let alone a couture gown. The trick in this approach was the balance. There was a hint of sarcasm, because he was a sarcastic son of a bitch, but he didn't make fun of Bree. It was a fine line, a welcome challenge.

The whole concept could bomb, but he didn't think it would. He had good instincts about his readers, and this felt right.

She'd gripped an edge of her lower lip with a barely visible tooth, white and perfect. The urge to kiss her hit him again, only he didn't want her cheek, but her mouth. Ah, Christ, what was his problem? This was business.

"Hey, you. Blog guy. You gonna move up or what?"

The question had come from a beefy man with a pencil thin mustache. Charlie moved closer to the truck, gentling Bree along with a light touch to her forearm.

She looked at him as she closed her cell phone. Her cheeks blushed a pink that almost matched her ribbon. "Oh," she said.

That wasn't enough information. Out of an over-abundance of the need to appear cool at all times, he didn't push for more. He schooled his expression into one of disinterest, which was the only acceptable stance during a strictly business meeting.

Her head tilted a tad to the right. No blinks now, only a piercing gaze and "Why?"

"Why?" he repeated.

She nodded. "Your blog works perfectly as it is. Obviously. Your numbers are incredible. Why would you want to mess with the format?"

"Mixing things up isn't messing with the format. If it doesn't work, I'll find out quickly and drop the idea. It's not the first time I've tried something new, and it won't be the last."

BREE STARED AT CHARLIE. This lunch was even stranger than she'd expected. And not for any of the reasons she'd anticipated. It most definitely wasn't about the sex. Of course. Because that would have been crazy.

"Whatever your decision," he said. "I need to know quickly."

"Sure. Right. I understand." How could she have forgotten even for a second? From the moment Rebecca had shown her Charlie's trading card, she'd wondered what in the world a man like him would want with a girl like her. It had almost been a relief when she'd finally gotten last night that Rebecca had done her a favor, and in turn, he had done one for Rebecca. Why else would he have taken her out on Valentine's Day? Even so, it had not been a date. He'd been very clear about the fact that it was work. She doubted he was ever truly distracted from his business. That's how he'd become Charlie Winslow in the first place.

So he'd used her. Not maliciously, not at all. He'd found a way to parlay the favor, so good for him. He'd grabbed an opportunity, and by sheer luck, it might give her a spot on his blog. Other people would want to know who she was, how she'd scored a "date" with Charlie. She couldn't have asked for a better shot at her dreams. But she had to be smart about it. Especially smart, given that the girlie part of her brain seemed to want to turn this into a romance. Nothing wrong with romance, but there was a time and a place.

Now that she had leapfrogged into the big time, she had to be more clear than ever about what was in her best interest for the long term, and not be dazzled.

"Look—" he said.

"If you need to have an answer right this minute," she said, "it will have to be no."

Charlie stilled and that air of boredom he'd been wearing like a comfy jacket vanished. He seemed disappointed, but that undoubtedly had more to do with his plans being thwarted than not being able to work with her.

"Don't get me wrong," she said. "I liked it."

It occurred to her that she should have ordered more for lunch. She needed to appear as unaffected by Charlie as possible. "The approach is fresh for *NNY*. A good take on something done to death, and you managed to make me sound as if I'm not totally precious. Although…" She clicked on the most personal section of the blog he'd written and scrolled down a bit.

Here's what Bree said, but not in words:
1. Everyone is tall and beautiful and has better clothes than me. Anyone who looked in any way normal wasn't anyone. Example: Me.
2. People can be really rude, but at the same time, very lovely. Being with Charlie got me the last part. The first part was on the house.
3. Everyone has an iPhone/BlackBerry. And cameras are intrusive even if the whole point is getting your picture taken. Also? I'm really not in Ohio anymore.

"I'm really not in Ohio anymore?" Bree sighed. "Still. You did a nice job."

The way his lips parted, it was clear he hadn't expected her response, especially the way she'd said *nice*. Now if she could just keep it up. She'd imagined being the kind of woman who could go toe-to-toe with the biggest names in Manhattan, and now was her chance.

She'd been in Wonderland last night, and she wouldn't apologize for feeling like Alice. Charlie had captured that perfectly in his blog. But she was back on terra firma now. She knew the score, business was business, and if he was going to use her, then she wanted something in return.

Yes, he was *Charlie Winslow,* and her heart had been beating double time since his first text, but there was a larger picture here, and she'd be an idiot to let it slip through her fingers. Being linked to Charlie was cachet she couldn't ignore. "The blog would be better if you used my pictures. Used me."

"Would it?" A hint of a smile came and went. Good. They were both playing the same game. It was important for her to remember he had years of experience, whereas she had... She had chutzpah. It would have to be enough.

Charlie handed her a plate of fries and a cardboard cup of tea. He'd paid, which was appropriate. He'd called this meeting.

At the thought, she had a twinge of sadness, real regret, and dammit, she had to stop that. The sex had been sex. The two of them were about to talk turkey, and she couldn't afford to be sentimental, not for a moment. It had been great sex. The end. Her imagination could be a wonderful place, but it could hurt her, too.

Luckily, they scored most of a bench. The first Belgian fry was so good it made her moan, which made her blush, but only until she saw the spot of mayo on Charlie's chin. If she were the nice girl her parents had raised her to be, she'd tell him about it. But this was business, and him looking so very human helped.

"What's your concern?" Charlie asked.

"I'm really not as innocent as you've painted me. I understand that's the gimmick, which is fine, but I'd like to have some input. My bosses read *NNY,* our clients, too. It may only be one blog, but it'll have an impact on my career."

He took another bite of his burger, and instead of looking at his mouth, remembering what it had felt like against her own, she concentrated on the mayonnaise dotting his chin.

"I want more than one blog out of this," he said, after he'd swallowed.

Her gaze jumped to his eyes and for a sec she thought that maybe this wasn't *all* about business, but then she remembered.

# 8

"I'D LIKE TO MAKE THIS part one of a series," Charlie said, as if he was asking her for a fry. "Some of which would feature Fashion Week, but not all. Tonight there's a party at Chelsea Piers. I was hoping you would join me."

Bree didn't choke, but she did cough. Mostly to hide her astonishment, and get herself in check. "What do you mean by series?"

"Wednesday's open, but Thursday night is another Fashion Week party. Friday, there's a premiere. Have you heard about *Courtesan?*"

*Had she heard about* Courtesan? It was a major motion picture from a major studio starring major movie stars, and she'd wanted to see it since she'd caught the first ad. Inside, she jumped about five feet off the ground. For him, she nodded and took a sip of tea. "I have."

"I've got something else Saturday night but I'm not sure what. Either a perfume party or a book thing. Anyway, I'd need you, tentatively, through Saturday night. Maybe more, possibly less. It all depends on the number of hits, the comment activity. Could that work for you?"

To even pretend she had to think about it was useless. He'd know she was bluffing. "Scheduling wouldn't be the issue. I'd make it work, even if I have to get Rebecca to make my frozen lunches.

"That's the thing Rebecca does at St. Marks, right?"

"How we met."

"She's gonna love this." Now he didn't even try to hide his smile. It was the other Charlie, the charming cousin of her friend, the man who'd kissed her silly.

Bree cleared her throat before meeting his gaze. "What do you mean?"

"She's going to think the series was her idea. She'll be insufferable."

"Ah." Bree popped a fry as she fought against another pang. This one was even more foolish. She'd thought for a second there that Rebecca would love the fact that she and Charlie would continue seeing each other. Ridiculous.

But come on, this was better than dating. Sex for someone like Charlie lasted one night. He couldn't even fake interest the next morning. In the long run, what he was offering was more than her paltry dreams had imagined. He'd just shortened her five-year plan by half. "I still want input."

"It's my blog, Bree. People read it for my take."

"I don't want to come off looking like a fool."

"Is that how you read any of those articles?"

"No."

"We can draw something up, something we can both agree to. If the series works, it will be because people like my take on seeing my world through your eyes. It's in my best interest to make you relatable and sympathetic."

"Okay. But I think I would be even more relatable if I write some of the blogs myself."

He winced. "I don't know. My name brings the party to the yard. Sorry."

"Granted. Doesn't mean there can't be a sidebar. You've done that before."

Charlie used his napkin, wiping off the mayo by chance. After a longish pause, he nodded. "No guarantees. I'll read what you write, see how it works. I'll have my attorney draw up something to cover the rest of the week, but I'd like to post the blog I wrote today. What do you say?"

She knew she was taking a risk, not signing on the dotted line, but what the hell. Rebecca would have something to say if Charlie messed with her, but even more than that, Bree's gut told her to go for it. She held out her hand.

The shiver that ran through her body when they shook was strictly in response to the opportunity. Nothing more.

CHARLIE WALKED BREE TO HER office building, a giant among giants, blocking out most of the sky. It was windy in the street, and he put his arm around Bree's shoulders, pulling her close. He liked keeping her warm, liked the way her hair tickled his chin.

"Charlie?" She had to raise her voice as they walked, so he bent his head a little.

"Yes?"

"Assuming the paperwork is fine and we end up going to…things. What are we going as?"

"Uh, oh. Like last night. Together, but not a couple.

If someone asks, say we're friends. They'll all assume it's more, but that's not a bad thing. People like trying to figure things out, make connections, even if they're false. And gossip pays the bills."

She didn't speak, but she did slow her step.

"Bree?"

She stopped. Charlie turned to face her, not liking the troubled look she wore. "What's wrong?"

"Nothing. It's fine. I want to make sure we understand each other. If we do this, it's a business arrangement."

"Yeah." The way she stared at him didn't make sense. He was handing her a gift here. Sure, he was going to make money from the deal, but she would win, too. He should have asked her what she wanted. From her love of fashion, her work at the advertising agency, it wasn't hard to figure her area of interest, but it was sloppy of him not to get specific.

"I keep my business life and my personal life separate," she said.

It took him a beat too long to make the connection. Not because she was being unreasonable. On the contrary, she was being smart. He wasn't used to it, though. The women who came home with him didn't think of the sex as anything outside of the job. Neither had he, not since he'd started the blog, for God's sake. Bree was not from his world. That was the point.

In fact, she was a romantic. Not simply around the issue of sex, but about designers, New York, glamour, beauty, all of it. Too bad it wouldn't last.

Oddly, he didn't rush to agree with her. He'd assumed they'd sleep together. He'd wanted to. If the series got results, they were looking at a week, maybe two. That would be a long stretch to go without. Especially when she would be with him most every night. In the car, at his place.

"Charlie?"

"Right. No, you're right. Strictly professional. Good thinking."

Her smile wasn't very victorious. In fact, he was tempted to follow her as she backed away from him, just to see her better.

"I'm really late," she said, calling out now, against the wind. "Send me the contract, and I'll take a look at it. And the details about tonight. And, thanks," she said, but the word was carried away as she got swallowed by dozens of people all heading for the same entrance.

He lost her before she went inside. He knew BBDA took up four floors of the skyscraper, could picture where the copywriters sat. But he didn't go after her. He'd see her tonight. He pulled out his cell as he went to the corner to hail a cab. He needed to get the blog update done, call the attorney, make arrangements with the stylist.

After he told the cabbie his address, he looked back at Bree's building. No more nights like last night. Well, damn.

BETWEEN THE PHOTOGRAPHERS blinding her and the constant tweets, Bree barely had time to enjoy the party. It would have been overwhelming regardless. This event was much smaller. Maybe five hundred people?

Put on by one of the most sought-after design celebrities, it was being held at The Lighthouse in Chelsea Piers. The huge room had been decked out in Asian-themed splendor with floating lanterns, Zen gardens artfully placed between tables and paper dragons so large and beautifully decorated they were works of art.

Even the view of the Hudson River from the floor-to-ceiling windows stole her breath, and that was before she met a mind-boggling parade of fashion idols and A, B and C-list stars.

The good and bad news was that Charlie had been even more extraordinary, which she hadn't thought possible. He hadn't left her side, which was wonderful, but what got to her even more was how he'd introduced her to his people. And God, they really were *his people*. He made her sound as if she were the brightest new thing to hit the scene since Lady Gaga. It was totally over-the-top, but, and this went directly into the bad news category, it was totally to support the blog series. *She* wasn't important; the image was important, the mystique, the hip-by-association coupled with her "innocence" to make her a mini celebrity.

The plan was working though because after dinner—which was to die for, and God, how she'd wanted a doggie bag—she'd been approached, over and over.

Not that she hadn't realized before that celebrities were never what they appeared to be. They might feel as if they're old friends, having been on her favorite TV series, or in so many movies she knew. But who they were had no relationship to the person she'd created in her head.

She knew that, and she was fine with it. People had always had icons. It made them feel connected. Twitter, Facebook, *Naked New York,* Perez Hilton, E!, *People.* They were watercoolers, the center of invisible towns where neighbors gathered.

Being one of the chosen, knowing everyone she met, whether they were famous or seeking fame, had already made up a story about who she was, what Charlie saw in her, what would happen next, was bizarre in a way she couldn't have predicted. There was no preparation for this kind of exposure, and the strangeness of it was messing with her sense of time. One minute she was reeling from too many gazes centered on her, the next, she was standing beside a window staring out at the water without having any idea how she'd gotten there.

Charlie had helped. His hand on her arm was a steadying force, his presence, his introductions easing the way. But he was acclimated, and she was still gasping for oxygen.

It didn't help that each time, every time, his touch gave her a frisson of excitement that made her breathless once again. It was ridiculous. She should be over it by now. Knowing this was a business arrangement and nothing more didn't help. The disconnect between her brain and her desire worried her. It was as if she'd been given electric shocks all evening, each one immediately followed by a stab of regret.

"You ready?" he asked, his mouth so close to her ear she could feel his heat. It must have been a shout because the music was blaring all around them, but it felt like a caress.

She nodded, and he slipped his arm around her shoulders as they went from the steamy inside to the icy outdoors. Again, there were enough limos to fill a football field, but there were also dozens of valets, running off to find drivers in what must have been an underground madhouse.

"What did you think?" Charlie asked. "Better? Worse?"

"You tell me," she answered. "You were watching me like a hawk."

He studied her expression, and she was struck yet again by how much she liked his face. It really was absurd how outsize his eyes were. They weren't comic-book large or even unsettlingly out of proportion. They were definitely the first thing one noticed about him.

He raised one dramatic eyebrow. "You liked this one more, despite having to work. I think partly because you knew more about what to expect, and partly because you got to speak to some of your favorite designers."

She smiled even though his conclusion wasn't quite accurate. "You're dead-on. Is that a problem?"

"What do you mean?"

"I'm incrementally not as innocent. By Friday night, I'll be a stone-cold cynic."

Charlie laughed, and there were the lines on his face that made it impossible for her not to touch his jacket, touch him. Why lines? It's not as if they were deep grooves or anything close to it. He was in his early thirties, and they didn't make him look a minute older. Perhaps it was because lines of any kind, even laugh lines, were practically forbidden in this glamorous, youth-obsessed culture. She'd hate it if Charlie had Botoxed his out of existence. His lines made him seem genuine, made him seem attainable. *Seem* being the operative word.

"Trust me on this," he said. "While you're very savvy and not to be underestimated, you're nowhere close to jaded. It won't be as unbelievable to meet famous people in a week or two, but the thrill will still be there."

"Good." She wanted the thrill, at least as it pertained to celebrities. She could do with fewer thrills when it came to Charlie. "Sorry I'm making you leave so early. I imagine you close down these kinds of parties."

"Not at all. I stay until I have enough material, then

head home. I have to get up early to get the blog in on time."

"So the photographers send their pictures before they crash for the night?"

"Yep. I go through them in the morning. I also get the freelance pieces and gossip tidbits. I put together the blog, send everything to my assistant Naomi, and she does her thing until it's online by 10:00 a.m. If you've got a sidebar about tonight, I'll need it by nine."

She nodded, not wanting him to see how his mention of that aspect of the job terrified her. The words would be hers. Not an illusion, not a gimmick. She'd sink or swim based on talent. God, she needed to sit down.

"You okay?"

"I've been meaning to ask. The stylist? What are we aiming for here?" She looked down at the dress she'd worn, one she'd made back in college. It was a pretty green, a shade lighter than her eyes, and it was sleeveless with a purple-and-green bolero jacket. It would have been perfect for a night on the town with Rebecca and friends, but she was outclassed here by ten miles. She figured that was the point. Make her look like the hick she was.

"Ah. You're going to like this part. Glam to the max. Everything from shoes to gowns. The whole shebang, complete with makeup, hair, body airbrushing, everything."

"I don't understand," she said, unsure whether he was joking with her or not.

"Those sidebars? They should be about the entire experience. What it feels like to become a princess, to go to the ball. To be plucked out of obscurity and shot to the stars."

She blinked at him as people pushed forward to

get to their cars. Watched a smile bloom on his face. Wished like hell she could jump into his arms and hug him for yet another incredible surprise.

"And you get to keep all the swag."

She shoved him. Kind of hard. "Do not mess with me, Winslow. I will hurt you if you're lying."

"Not lying. Yours to keep."

Flashbulbs had been popping all night, but suddenly they were in her face, blinding her. Only for a moment, though, then they were gone, like a swarm of locusts with cameras. They'd done their job, however, and kept her from leaping into Charlie's arms.

It was the most diabolical torture. Give her all her dreams with one hand, steal her desire with the other. Rinse. Repeat.

"So, we discussed that you'll be meeting Sveta on Thursday, right? That you're off the hook for tomorrow?"

"Yep," she said, switching gears.

"You should sleep. You'll need it."

"I have to go make frozen lunches tomorrow night. Rebecca's going to be there."

"If I know her, she'll keep you up later than I have. The woman is a slave to details."

Before she hit the sack, she'd go through the pictures she'd taken. Those images were what she needed to focus on, not Charlie. Not his scent, not the resonance of his voice, not this wanting to be close to him.

By the time the series was finished, she'd be over her silly crush. Dammit, she would be.

# 9

"TASTE THIS AND TELL ME if you think it needs more salt."
Rebecca stood back so that Lilly could try the soup.

She obliged and faked a cough.

"Funny." After elbowing her aside, Rebecca saw her
cousin standing at the door of the St. Mark's basement
kitchen. He wasn't looking at her, or, she imagined, for
her. His gaze was on Bree.

Laughter still clung to the steam that swirled over
the industrial stove. Rebecca was making a giant pot
of split pea soup, Lilly was cooking a Texas chili and
even with those pots and the 350° oven, the basement
remained chilly. It wouldn't be for long, though, not if
what she thought was going to happen happened.

It was difficult to look away from Charlie. He was as
unguarded as she'd ever seen him. As an adult, at least.
There was a keen awareness in his eyes, a concentration that spoke of a hunger that had nothing to do with
pea soup.

One of his hands braced against the door frame, the
other held papers. He looked elegant in his bespoke
coat: dark navy, midcalf, styled perfectly. How Charlie it was.

The man knew what looked good on him, what he could get away with, and what would cause eyebrows to raise. Nothing was unintentional. Not online, in person, in a walk to the corner grocer. Seeing him blatantly wanting Bree was seeing him naked. Not that she had any personal experience with that, but she'd been with Charlie in family situations, private moments of grief, in trouble, in failure, in success, and this was new.

Rebecca grinned at her own brilliance. She was awesome. She'd known he would like Bree. And Bree would like him, but even Rebecca at her most conniving hadn't guessed they would have come so far so fast.

She'd have high-fived herself if she could have, for being just that clever. No one in the family believed Charlie would ever fall. He'd always have women, but never one woman. Not Charlie. His merry-go-round hadn't stopped spinning since puberty, and he got bored so quickly. Nothing could have suited her cousin quite as perfectly as this age of instant gratification. Charlie was born for it, breathed it, worked it. Everything lightning fast, and rest was for the weak and dull.

Bree wasn't dull in the least.

Rebecca turned to her friend. They'd played phone tag all day, then arrived at the kitchen as Lilly had come in, so all Rebecca knew was that Bree had gone with Charlie to a big fancy party last night, a heck of a second date, and she'd written a firsthand account of the party that had been in this morning's blog.

If that wasn't testimony to Rebecca's genius, she didn't know what was.

Things got really interesting when Bree shifted and sighted the man standing in the doorway.

If only the door had been closer to the prep area. It was difficult to know where to look. Bree now was a living demonstration of Modern Woman In Full Lust Mode. Her back straightened, her breath caught, showing off her chest in the most positive light possible. The thrift-store cashmere sweater she wore cupped her boobs perfectly, and Rebecca knew Charlie was having a little heart attack at the view.

Then there was the flush that swept across Bree's cheeks. Good lord, it couldn't have been more artfully painted by Renoir. Her eyes got wide and her lips parted and her pheromones were positively dripping.

The only sounds were the slow gurgle of thick simmering from the stove, the hiss of the radiator. Even Lilly, who'd come tonight for the company and the after-cooking drinks, had caught on that Something Was Happening.

Rebecca turned to Charlie again, and he'd dropped his hand, taking a single step inside the kitchen. He seemed to be fighting a smile. It would start to form at the corners of his lips, then flatten, but a second later the grin would start again.

Back to Bree, and it was like the slowest tennis match ever, the invisible ball staying well within the boundaries, the lobs back and forth languid and electric at the same time.

Rebecca's soup would burn in a minute if she didn't stir the pot. "Charlie," she said. "What's up?"

Rebecca almost laughed at how he jerked at her voice. And when she glanced at Bree, the blush had spread over her cheeks and down her neck, and there was a great deal of blinking.

"I came to show Bree her blog." He held up the papers as if proof had been required.

"Kind of hard for her to see it across the room."

Charlie's grin finally broke free as did his legs. He came inside, crossed the basement to Bree.

"That's Charlie Winslow," Lilly whispered, and Rebecca hadn't heard her approach. Luckily, no one saw Rebecca jump because everybody's gaze was on center stage. Even Lilly's.

"Yes, it is."

"Why is Charlie Winslow in the kitchen? With Bree?"

"Because she's seeing him."

"What?"

The word came out loud. Very loud. Loud enough that it halted the action.

Lilly smiled, gave a little wave. "Lilly Denton. Hey."

"Charlie Winslow," Charlie said. "Hey."

The moment passed. Rebecca dragged Lilly to the stove, Charlie went back to mooning at Bree.

"She's seeing him?" Lilly asked, her voice back down to a stage whisper. "Since when?"

"Not long."

"How do you know this?"

"Obviously you don't read his blog."

"I do, but I've been too busy the past few days." Lilly sneaked another peek. "That'll teach me for putting work first."

"Okay, it's not because of his blog, I know because Charlie's my cousin, and your chili is burning."

Both of them took up spoons, the industrial-size ones, and stirred like the witches in *Macbeth*. "Seriously, what the hell?" Lilly said.

"I set them up."

Lilly, who was something of a mystery to Rebecca, a friend in the making, but guarded, so very guarded, opened her mouth, then must have reconsidered. She did, however, step closer to Rebecca. "Explain. In detail, please. And remember, I have a large spoon in my hand, and I swear to God I'll use it if you keep being cryptic."

"I don't usually set people up," Rebecca replied. "Especially not Charlie because he's got hot-and-cold running women in his life, but he and Bree…they fit."

"Before the trading cards? During? Because if Charlie Winslow was a trading card then I want my money back."

"You didn't pay for anything."

"Rebecca."

"Right. He wasn't a card. Technically."

"I've been out with two trading cards. The first one was a wonderful guy, as long as you were willing to put up with his ardent love for his mother. The second guy's card said he wanted a relationship, but his actions were completely one-night stand."

"I know. My dates haven't been life shattering, either, although I hear Paulie met someone fantastic, and that Tess's one-night stand has turned into three."

"Which still doesn't explain Charlie Winslow," Lilly said, frowning.

"It's complicated, and we'll discuss it more when we go for drinks, but if I'm talking to you, my eavesdropping sucks, so let's keep stirring and shut the hell up."

CHARLIE SWALLOWED, WONDERING for the fiftieth time what he was doing in the basement of a church kitchen fumbling around like a teenager on his first date. Bree was reading the blog pages he'd printed out, and she was kind enough not to mention that he hadn't needed to come see her or print out the pages as the blog would be online first thing in the morning.

He'd asked her to do a little bio piece and tomorrow morning it would run. She'd already given a tease—her first sidebar about the Chelsea Piers party—and it could have ended right there. But blog hits had been up, and she'd gotten more than seven hundred comments on her column. Very encouraging.

So he'd moved forward. Tomorrow morning there would be more pictures of Bree, some from college days, one from here in New York in casual wear. He hoped it would start a dialogue.

His gaze went to Rebecca, whom he caught in mid-smirk, and he touched Bree's arm, interrupting her reading. "I'll be back in a few."

She nodded, and he went over to Rebecca. He smiled at her friend, then turned to his cousin. "A minute? Outside?"

Her eyes narrowed, but she put down her spoon and walked with him to the door. Once they were outside, she shivered at the cold, but didn't go back for her coat. "You can thank me now," she said. "And later. I accept gifts, too. The more expensive the better."

"We're not dating."

"I read *NNY,* you dope," she said.

"You read what I write on *NNY.* And evidently you haven't spoken to your friend since yesterday before lunch."

"That's true. We're going out after the meals are in the freezer."

As Charlie stuck his hands in his pockets, she grimaced. The bastard should have given her his coat. "Why did you set me up with her?" he asked.

"Why did you bring me out here to freeze to death?"

He rolled his eyes dramatically and took off his

coat with a sigh that would have done a Broadway diva proud.

She curled herself into the heavy wool coat, the lining as luxurious as the tailoring. "Because she's your type."

"No, she's not. She's not vaguely my type. Do you even know me?"

"Yeah. I do. And those skeletons you go out with every night are a joke. I imagine you can count the ones you actually like on one hand."

"It doesn't matter if I like them."

"You happen to be one of the only relatives I can stomach," she said, "but Charlie, it's time for you to move on. You're what, thirty-two?"

"Thirty-one."

"Over thirty. You've spent your entire working life giving your parents and our family the finger. It's enough. You need to start living for you, and stop giving them all the power."

He stared at her with his great big eyes, mouth open, as if the cold itself couldn't penetrate his shock. "What the fuck are you talking about, Rebecca?"

"*Naked New York.* Your blog. Not the others, not the legit blogs. Yours. The one that runs every aspect of your life. If you want to call it a life."

"I'm raking in millions."

"You already had millions. Look, I have to get back to the cooking. Do what you have to do, but think about it, okay? What it would be like if your evenings were full of things you actually wanted to do? If you went out with people you actually liked?"

"You're insane. The Winslow foundation has driven you around the bend."

"Yeah, well, maybe. Oh, and remember. Don't screw

with Bree, Charlie. She may want to play in the fashion big league, but she's a really decent person. She's not used to people like us. Tread lightly."

"I told you. We're not dating."

"The way you two look at each other? I give it three days. Four at the most."

"It's freezing, and I'm not listening to you anymore." He brushed past her, and she followed, wondering how such a smart, smart man could be such an idiot.

BREE LOOKED UP FROM the blog page as Charlie came toward her. He looked cold, and she saw why as Rebecca followed him. He'd offered his cousin his coat. Another nice thing, but not in the same league as what she had been reading. "You hardly changed anything," Bree said, when he stood in front of her.

"I didn't need to. You wrote a great piece."

"Wow." She flipped through the few pages, stopped at her New York picture. "Why didn't you say anything about my hair?"

"What?"

"It's all...wrong."

"You look gorgeous," he said. "It was difficult to choose which picture to use. Each one was great."

Okay, there was nice, and *too* nice.

Her suspicion must have shown because he touched her arm, making her look into his eyes. "I'm telling the truth."

She didn't speak for a while. Not that she didn't have a lot to say, but it sounded mushy in her head, inappropriate for what they were now. There were questions, too, about why he'd come in person, what it meant, and why on earth did she keep imagining longing in his gaze when longing couldn't be possible? "I have food in the oven," she said.

"Okay," he said, staring at her, waiting for…?

"After we put everything in containers and in the freezer, we're going for drinks."

"We?"

"Rebecca, Lilly, me. You?"

"That's a big crowd. Maybe we could whittle it down?"

It was tempting; of course she wanted to be alone with him, but that he'd even suggested it made her thoughts even more confused. "We've been missing each other, what with parties and appointments and things. I can understand if you'd rather not join us."

"No. I'd like to."

Well, damn. Why would he want to join them for drinks? Rebecca! That had to be the reason. "Good. You can help us put up the food. It'll go faster."

"Swell," he said, and she smiled at his put-upon tone. "Now that you know I make such great tea, you'll want me in the kitchen forever."

Bree's laugh stuttered, and a flush hit Charlie's face. She walked faster, so fast she had to look over her shoulder to say, "It won't kill you. I promise."

He'd come to a full stop. "I'm taking your word for it," he said, going for humorous, but not succeeding.

She made herself focus on food prep, and not the jumble in her head.

THE BAR WASN'T FLASHY. Most of the patrons were in business wear like Bree and her friends. She'd be willing to wager every last one of them was asking themselves what the hell Charlie Winslow was doing in a less-than-swanky pickup bar on a Wednesday night.

If she read him correctly, he didn't seem to mind. He had hailed their cab, insisted on paying for the short trip, then walked them inside as if this was the next stop on the Fashion Week tour.

The women in the place eyed him with undisguised hunger, the kind of looks that would make a statue blush, and all she could think was *I was with him the other night. Naked.*

She had to stop that *right now*.

They scored a booth in the back, and Charlie scooted in next to her, pressing against her from knee to shoulder. It would have been easier if he'd kept his coat on, but no, it was just him in his close-fitting white shirt, narrow black pants, and his hot body, clenching the muscles in his thighs and his biceps—

"Bree?"

"Hmm?"

"Drink?"

"Ah. Yes. Tequila Sunrise, please. Heavy on the sunrise."

"Got it." Charlie scooted out, and she instantly felt more relaxed. Jeez, didn't the man understand personal space?

Lilly leaned across the table the moment he walked away. The music wasn't deafening but it still made her have to shout. "Oh, my God, Bree, why didn't you tell me you were dating Charlie Winslow?"

"I'm not. Not really."

Lilly gave Rebecca a sharp look before she turned back to Bree. "I don't understand."

"The whole setup is a blog gimmick to get new readers. No big deal."

"Yeah," Lilly said slowly. "Tell it to someone who hasn't seen him look at you."

"Seriously, Lil? Come on. Would a guy like him honestly want to date a girl like me?"

"Yes!"

"Why wouldn't he?"

Bree blinked at her friends. Of course they would say that. What was the alternative? "Yeah, you're right. He could do so much better?" "Anyway," she said, waving off the both of them, "it's great. I get to go to Fashion Week parties, and he's publishing some of my pieces, which will make my bosses sit up and notice. I take a giant step up the ladder to success. Everybody wins, especially me."

Rebecca cleared her throat, and Bree reluctantly met her gaze. She did not seem pleased. "Why is Charlie here tonight?" she asked.

"Blog stuff."

"Since it's written for the internet, wouldn't it have been easier for him to, I don't know, send that stuff to you over the internet?"

Bree opened her mouth, but she had no answer.

EXCEPT FOR THAT WHOLE Psych 101 speech from Rebecca outside the church, Charlie had a great night. The food prep part he could have lived without, although no, that had been great, too. Rebecca was right about one thing—he hardly ever did normal stuff anymore. No grocery stores, no shopping in general, not when it was so easy to get everything delivered or picked up by his housekeeper.

He went to screenings or premieres, not movies. He was sent advance copies of books and films, invitations to parties from New York to Milan, Paris, London, Dubai, L.A. He didn't barhop, and tonight had been the first time in ages he'd had drinks with real people in a regular bar instead of with celebrities behind some form of velvet rope.

He'd liked everything from the music on the juke-box to the raucous laughter from the après-work crowd. He'd been reminded of the old days when he was just starting out with his first blog. The only part that wasn't great tonight had been at the end. Putting Bree in a taxi. Alone. And then hailing a cab for himself.

He consoled himself with the fact that tomorrow would be killer busy for his latest blog contributor. After a full eight hours at her day job, she'd be on the run with the stylist, then they had an art exhibit party to go to, which didn't begin until ten. She'd be lucky to get four hours sleep, and because he was a selfish bas-tard, he'd kept her out too late tonight.

He hadn't wanted it to end. But end it had, as all things did, and in a week, give or take, his time with Bree would be a memory. If it worked out, he'd use her for the odd column, and they'd run into each other at cocktail parties and openings. But he'd move on. That's what he did. What was for the best.

He thought again about what Rebecca had said. That his family felt slapped by what he did for a living was their problem, not his. He'd told them all the way back in high school that he wasn't going to fall into line. The idea of him going into politics had been ridiculous. They should have known that without him having to smear it in their faces. But they'd only seen what they wanted to see.

His answer might have appeared radical to anyone outside the family. Getting arrested in a public scandal his senior year in college was, he'd admit, a dramatic move. But Rebecca, of all people, should have under-stood. He'd done what was necessary. His success had been a matter of skill, planning and yes, luck. Why wouldn't he want to continue to thrive? It would have been nice to be with Bree. He couldn't deny the attraction. But she didn't fit. Not as anything except a temporary gimmick, a sidebar, a tweak on the blog.

And his bed. Good Christ, she'd fit there.

He stared at the window as the cab pulled up to his building. Life was about choices. Some tougher than others. Hell, she was just a girl. He'd learned long ago not to romanticize sex.

# 10

THE STYLIST, SVETA BREVDA, was tall and manic and thin as a whippet, and she wielded her opinions with an iron fist. The first stop—at *Dior!*—taught Bree to strip quickly, stand straight and keep her mouth shut.

She'd stopped being self-conscious about being naked by store seven. Didn't matter who was in the dressing room. Salespeople. Friends of salespeople, men, women.

For all she knew the pizza delivery guy was standing by the exit, nodding as he studied her slipping into a skintight dress with absolutely nothing beneath it as if he were picking out curtains. But the clothes were…

Bree had lost her adjectives. That's how fantastic the clothes were. And the accessories? Good Lord, she'd died and gone to heaven. Even though the shoes tortured her feet, she couldn't breathe in the two dresses that were honestly a size too small, and she was turned and bent and paraded around like a show pony, but the torture was totally worth it because she got to keep *everything*.

Even the bit where the silver-haired dresser from

Prada stuck his hand down her bodice and lifted her bare breasts. Now *there* was a blog entry.

All this done at the speed of a montage: cabs were hailed seconds before they stepped out doors, clothing selections were made preternaturally and perfectly, and she finally understood the worth of a good stylist.

The only thing missing was Charlie. She kept wanting to tell him things, to see his reaction, to feel his hand on the small of her back, but he was working, and she was, as well. Only this work made her feel like a model—despite the fact that every article of clothing had to be shortened—and like a prom queen. But mostly like someone had made a mistake that would be corrected momentarily.

Charlie wasn't the kind to make mistakes of this magnitude. Yet it would have been better if she could have talked to him. She'd texted in cabs—the only time she'd been able to—but he was in a meeting, so his response would have to wait.

CHARLIE HAD TO WORK TO KEEP his expression mild, to speak as if his parents dropping by wasn't something unwelcome and entirely too coincidental given his talk with Rebecca last night. He'd always liked Rebecca so much. She'd been his ally, his cover, his friend. Her betrayal hit hard and low. Shit.

"We're not here to take up much of your time, Charles," his father said, his gaze scrutinizing the living room. He—both his parents—were busy cataloging every change, the new lamps, the slate that had replaced the bricks around the fireplace. They'd only been to his place a few times over the years. He preferred meeting in neutral territory, although he went to family gatherings, typically one per year, wherever it was being held. He didn't shut his parents out completely.

"You've undoubtedly seen that Andrew is starting his campaign in earnest," his father said, his voice modulated and soft. That had been one of the earliest Winslow lessons. Speak softly. Make them *listen*. "We're very pleased with the endorsements he has now, but the committee is budgeting media advertising, and naturally, your blog group has come up."

So it hadn't been Rebecca. Charlie didn't acknowledge his father's remarks. Another lesson he'd learned at his father's knee. Never give anything away, not in expression, in tone, or in posture.

The Winslows were the quintessential image of subdued elegance. Nothing his parents wore was ostentatious, but everything was meticulously selected to evoke their status. The most expensive watches, Italian handcrafted shoes, tailoring from the finest hands in several countries.

His parents commanded respect, and made everyone who wasn't family feel small and insignificant. Polite to the extreme. They radiated power and privilege.

Christ, what they had tried to do to him. He was sure they wouldn't mention that it should have been his campaign, if only he'd not been so rebellious.

"We would very much like to utilize the family connection in the two most appropriate blogs, *Dollars* and *NYPolitic*."

"No," Charlie said. "I'm not going to promote the family agenda on my blogs. It's inappropriate, given I think Andrew would be a monumentally bad choice for the senate."

His phone buzzed again, and he took it out of his

pocket to find another text message from Bree. He couldn't read it now.

"We're not asking for a change of editorial direction or for you to give your personal endorsement," his mother said. "Simply space for featured ads. It would mean significant revenue."

He stared at his mother, knowing she was irked that he hadn't offered them drinks. It was only polite, the right thing to do, even for uninvited guests. In her home, nothing of the sort would have ever happened.

He smiled as he looked around. This was his home.

ON MADISON AVENUE, BREE and her posse stopped again, this time for shoes. Or maybe a bag, she wasn't quite sure. It didn't help that Sveta's accent—she was from Belarus—was nearly unintelligible. Bree mostly nodded and tried to keep up and not prostrate herself at the temples of fashion—Versace, Chanel, Anna Sui. Those were the kind of stores that only had a few items artfully displayed in minimalist snobbery. Where excellent champagne was served by stunning hostesses who knew every detail of the design and manufacture of the clothing on display. The music was always… interesting. Nothing you'd hear on Top Ten radio, because you could get *that* at the New Jersey malls.

The price tags made her hyperventilate. And even though the selections for her weren't the top-of-the-top-of-the-line, they were still extravagantly outlandish. Truly, she was in another world, someone else's life. Charlie's world. As she snapped another photograph of herself in a pair of heels that would likely cripple her after five steps, she reminded herself that she was a visitor. A tourist. Nothing more.

CHARLIE'S FATHER STOOD and even he couldn't control the way his rising blood pressure reddened his face. "Andrew is family, Charles. He's a Winslow. We've allowed you to set your own course, have your fun, but this is our legacy you're tampering with. I won't have it."

Charlie moved closer to the door, to the closet where he'd hung their coats. "Huh. It's good to know some things don't change. You continue to hold on to the ludicrous belief that you have any influence over me or my life. It's nice having our own traditions."

"Charles," his mother said, as affronted as his father, but less flushed. "That's enough. We are your parents."

He approached them and held out his mother's coat. "Thanks for dropping by. I hope you had a nice vacation in St. Barts."

She looked at his father who took both coats from Charlie. He didn't quite rip them out of his son's hands. But it was close.

"This will be remembered, Charles," his father said.

"I hope so." Charlie led them to the door. When it was closed behind them, he was still buzzing with anger. He needed to cool down, get Zen about the visit, about the message. He wished Bree were here.

He'd never mentioned his parents to Bree, hadn't asked about hers. They weren't friends. Yeah, he was comfortable with her. Okay, that didn't happen much anymore. But no. He wasn't going to talk to Bree about his parental issues. Jesus.

He pulled out his cell phone, and clicked on the earliest of her text messages. He was grinning by the time he got to his office.

FINALLY, THEY HAD MORE THAN enough clothing to get her through at least a week of parties. The most extravagant was the Marchesa gown for the Courtesan premiere. The evening dress, pinned to fit her body by a bevy of seamstresses, was so out of her league it hurt.

It was almost eight by the time the cab arrived at Charlie's. Sveta didn't need to announce herself. The staff at the front desk nodded respectfully as the door-men helped bring in bag upon bag upon box. Bree rested against the mirrored wall of the elevator, then took a few deep breaths before they entered Charlie's home. Her gaze went immediately to the hallway lead-ing to his bedroom, and the reality of their new ar-rangement made her ache. Then he stepped into the atrium, and everything else became background noise.

He smiled widely when their eyes met. She shivered as he came closer, knowing he would touch her, and that she was allowed to touch him back, even in front of Sveta and the doormen. Such a mixed blessing. She could touch, but not have.

Bree didn't regret her decision about keeping the re-lationship out of the bedroom. It was the right decision, the mature way to go. It also completely sucked. "This is too much," she said, as she looked into Charlie's dark eyes. His hands went to her upper arms, and his palms ghosted across her skin down to her wrists and back up again. He kissed her, on the lips, yes, but the moment there was a hint of heat, he backed off. She wondered whom he'd kissed her for. Sveta? The rest of the team? Had to be.

"It's not," he said. "It's part of the gig."

"Charlie, I saw the price tags."

He smiled. "Most everything was free."

"Nothing's free. I know it's barter, but I'm not even famous."

"You will be."

"In a week? I doubt it."

He walked her farther into his apartment as Sveta led the doormen down a hallway, her heels clicking so quickly Bree wondered if it would be rude to suggest a switch to decaf. "You won't be on the cover of *People*," Charlie said, "but you're going to be known in the city, where it matters."

He paused, his palm warm on her skin. When he spoke again, his voice tightened along with his fingers. "You're with a Winslow now, and the Winslows are the very heart of power in this city, didn't you know?"

Bree stopped. She wasn't sure what was going on, but she felt uncomfortable. What had happened during his meeting? He'd brushed aside her questions, told her everything was fine, but that clearly wasn't the case.

"Each item of clothing is going to get a lot of mileage in the blogs," he said, letting her go. His voice had changed back to something less strident, more like Charlie. "In addition to your sidebars, I've got some fashion insiders who'll be plugging them for weeks to come. I guarantee there will be ready-to-wear versions in Macy's by April."

Bree forced a smile even though she knew he was upset, that this last speech was him getting his bearings again. But she had no right to ask him to be honest with her, to tell her a single thing about his private life. "I've already worked up a quick first draft of what it was like to be fitted by a big-league design team."

"Can't wait to see it."

Sveta's clicking heels announced her entry into the living room. "You come dress now."

Bree checked with Charlie.

"It's a media room. Used for these kind of things."

"You style up all your women?"

His lips parted, but Bree hurried to follow Sveta, not wanting to know his answer.

The room itself gave it away, though. There were mirrors, hair and makeup stations, clothing racks. A lot of those racks held men's clothes, but there were women's, as well, all stunning. In a shocking nod to propriety, there was a changing screen in a corner. There were also people. Five people—one of them was a photographer she'd seen at the Mercedes party. His assistant was fussing with lights. Off to the side were giant rolls of backdrops, like bolts of material, ready to be swung into place for any kind of photograph.

There was even a sewing machine in one corner, which Bree longed to check out. It was most probably the Ferrari of sewing machines and would make her so jealous she would weep for a week.

"Change," Sveta said, holding up the purple jacquard V-neck dress they'd picked up from the Victoria Beckham collection.

Bree obeyed, as if she'd dare do anything else. It was a matter of moments to slip out of her office wear into the magnificent cocktail dress, especially because her only undergarment was her own bargain basement thong. Beige on purpose.

The moment she stepped from behind the screen, she was covered in a smock, sat in a chair and set upon by far too many hands touching her hair, her face, her fingernails. The lights made everything more intense, hotter, scarier, and when someone said *open,* she opened her mouth, and someone else tugged her hair so she would bend her neck just so.

Her personal space had never been so invaded. The scent of many breaths and colognes went from cloying to unpleasantly sticky, and if this didn't end soon, she was going to have to do something, stop them somehow.

"Hey."

Charlie's voice cut through, and in two, three heart-beats, those things that had been touching her, brushes, fingers, nail file, eyelash curler, pulled back. Bree sighed with relief, saw that she was gripping the armrests of the makeup chair so tightly with her unpolished hand her knuckles were white.

She watched him in the mirror, felt his hand on her shoulder.

"I didn't even ask," he said. "Have you eaten anything today?"

"I had lunch."

"That was what, eight, nine hours ago?"

"About."

His eyes narrowed in the mirror and he turned to face Sveta. "How long until she's ready?"

"Five minutes. Nails on her left hand. Mascara. Lipstick."

"Hold off on the lipstick. Finish the rest. I imagine you haven't eaten, either. No, don't look at me like that, you have to eat something. There's a spread in the kitchen. Enough for everyone."

Before he looked back at Bree, he squeezed her shoulder and smiled. "It's not drippy stuff, but I'd keep the smock on, anyway. Just in case. We can talk about tonight's shindig while we eat."

She nodded. Calmly. Touched by his consideration. She hadn't realized her panic was hunger. Mostly hunger.

Unable to turn, she was still able to watch him as he went to the men's suit rack, grabbed one from the middle and went out. At the doorway, he turned and winked at her.

Before she could even smile, her hand was grabbed and the camera clicked and clicked and clicked.

THE BEST PART OF THE evening postshow was Bree, but even she hadn't been distracting enough to prevent Charlie from thinking about his parents. He'd put a call in to Rebecca, but it hadn't been returned, and his thoughts just kept circling back to this afternoon. How dare they think he was so spineless he'd cross the line into promoting the Winslow agenda on his blogs. God damn, that pissed him off.

He looked up as a Pyramid Club waiter came by with vodka shots. He'd done it again, let his attention wander, although at this point, there wasn't much more to be seen. Bree was standing against the black brick wall, looking beautiful in her purple dress, in her impossible heels, surrounded by newshounds and fame seekers.

He'd warned her it would happen. This morning's blog insured that Bree was now on the B-list, which could stand for "by association." He had the feeling it wouldn't take her long to stand on her own, though.

Most of the real celebs were huddled outside in the smoking zone, freezing their asses off while they dished about everyone inside, and he should go join them, at least for the few minutes he could put up with the fumes. But Bree was far more enticing.

She held up her glass of pineapple juice, but it was her shining smile that told him he'd made the right choice.

"You enjoying yourself?" he asked after he'd dodged drinks and drunks to get to her.

"Dizzy with it," she said. Shouted. The noise level at these things was going to make him deaf before he was forty.

"It's late. We should go soon."

"Whenever you like."

It wasn't actually that late. Just past midnight. But she had work in the morning, her sidebar to write. And he wanted some time with her where they weren't talking about who to schmooze, who to avoid. He held out his hand.

Cameras flashed as they went toward the exit. It wasn't a surprise that they were stopped several times, but it didn't take long to get the limo.

Once inside, he slid to the corner and waited for her to scoot next to him. Instead, she pressed up against the other door. "You okay?"

"Fine."

"You look...chilly."

"No," she said, tugging down her skirt, avoiding his eyes. "I'm good. Maybe you could call ahead to your building, give them an ETA for a taxi?"

"We'll take you home."

"I have my clothes at your place."

"You're wearing your clothes."

She looked at him. "Right. I forgot."

He moved closer to her, concerned. "What's going on, Bree?"

She folded her hands tightly in her lap. "I was going to ask you the same thing."

"What?"

"You've been jumpy all evening. I admit I haven't seen you at many events, but when I have you've seemed like the most relaxed person in the room. Not tonight. Actually, I felt as though something was off at your place."

He shifted away from her, not one hundred percent comfortable that there was someone else who could read him. There weren't many. Naomi. Rebecca. His college roommate. Charlie liked it that way. It had taken him a long time to cultivate the image he needed for the job, and Bree from Somewhere, Ohio, had already pierced his carefully crafted exterior in more ways than he cared to think about. He considered changing the subject for the rest of the ride home, making it clear she'd crossed a firm boundary.

Instead, he met her gaze. "My folks came by today."

She certainly looked startled by his admission. She wasn't the only one. He barely knew this woman. And yet… "They've wanted me to go into politics," he said. "Ever since I was in high school."

"Really?"

"The Winslows have had political influence throughout the generations. It was time to prepare a new senator from New York. Long-term planners, my family."

"Obviously you weren't enthused about the prospect?"

"No. I wasn't. It didn't matter to them, though. I was taught from an early age that we had an obligation to do public service. That our privileged life meant we had to dedicate ourselves to a larger cause, that what we wanted was immaterial. Which sounds great in theory, noble and philanthropic. But it had more to do with keeping the family in the top tier of society than philanthropy. My destiny was supposed to include law school, the *Harvard Law Review,* a prestigious firm, municipal office, a seat in congress, then the Senate. Carrying the standard of the Winslow heritage."

"Wow, I can't see you as a lawyer. Forget a politician."

His smile was wry. "And what, you've known me for a week? What does that tell you about my family?" He stared out the window for a beat. This true confession business felt as awkward as wearing someone else's clothes. "Not that I don't believe in public service, I do. I take that seriously." He faced her again. "What I didn't want was to live a lie."

"So you decided to become an internet mogul?"

"Sort of," he said, aware his automatic half grin said more than most of his conversations with women he'd slept with. "I didn't expect the blogs would become this big. Not complaining. I was in the right place at the right time. I wanted to be independent."

"It's worked. You are. And quite successfully."

"Yes. It's worked. It'll continue to work." He studied his hands. He was the one who was supposed to unsettle his companions. He was very good at it, and Bree wasn't even trying, so whatever this was, it wasn't a power game. No, he had opened another door for her. Game changers, these exceptions. It made him nervous.

Allowing his parents to rattle him was frankly embarrassing. They didn't for the most part. He'd just been caught off guard, that's all. But telling Bree about it? Jesus.

"So their visit was uncomfortable?"

He reached over and took Bree's hand in his. She was cold, dammit. "It was brief," he said. "I made my point. Have I said how beautiful you look tonight?"

She stared at him, at their hands, then back at him. "Yes, several times. Thank you."

"Am I making you uncomfortable?"

She sighed as she tugged her hand free. "It's not that I don't want to…"

He nodded, leaned back. Incredibly tired all of a sudden. Maybe he was coming down with something.

# 11

FRIDAY NIGHT CAME ALONG with a tux for the *Courtesan* premiere, and the only reason it was bearable was that Bree was in the media room getting prepped. He would check on her after he was dressed, although this time he'd made sure she'd eaten before Sveta snatched her away.

As he worked on his tie, he thought about the night ahead, pleased that she'd get to walk down a legit red carpet. A dream literally coming true, she'd told him.

The less sleep she got, he'd discovered, the more she revealed about herself. How when she was a little girl she would practice her Academy Award acceptance speech in front of the bathroom mirror, holding a bottle of shampoo or a hairbrush. She would very purposefully *not* thank whoever happened to be annoying her at the moment, which would sometimes be one of her siblings, a teacher, a friend or one of her parents.

It had made him laugh when they were slouched in the backseat of a limo, and it made him grin now. He could picture it so easily. He wondered if she'd always had short hair. Probably, given that she was so small. You wouldn't want to hide any of that face, not with hair, not with too much makeup. Sveta had turned out to be the perfect stylist for Bree. People were taking note.

Her blogs were getting heavy traffic. Unique hits were much higher than with most of his new contributors, which made sense because this approach was fresh. Charlie had never asked one of his companions to post.

Much of the chatter was about the two of them, naturally. Were they? Weren't they? There had been reports of Bree leaving in separate transportation at the end of an evening, and his place had acquired a few more paparazzi hoping to catch her doing the walk of shame in the morning. Speculation without confirmation was exactly what he'd been hoping for.

Bree had turned up on TMZ, PopSugar, Page Six, on almost every single one of his gossip feeds, as well as in the newspaper tabloids.

He slipped on his jacket, glad he'd chosen something so traditional. Beautifully cut, nothing radical. He wanted Bree to shine tonight. He had no idea what Sveta had chosen for her to wear, and he wondered how the stylist was going to top last night's look. Bree had knocked his socks off when she'd made her entrance.

Come to think of it, every time he saw her she got to him. Having her so close, and so damned untouchable probably had something to do with it. Okay, a little interest from his cock, not good for the cut of his suit. Not good in a number of ways. She was off-limits. The statistics didn't lie, and this new deal had increased *NNY*'s unique hits remarkably. It might kill him, but he'd keep to the script. Unfortunately, that meant touching. So much damn touching.

He checked his watch, made sure he had what he

needed in his pockets and then went into the living room. He glanced at the open door in the atrium and wondered why he hadn't taken Bree across to his office. It wasn't that far to the other side of the elevator. Then again, they hadn't had much time for anything but work.

He heard Sveta in the hallway, and swung around in anticipation of Bree's entrance. Damn. She did it again. Like a slap on the back of his head.

She was a vision. So much for not getting excited tonight. He would have to put his cock in a straitjacket to pull that off, and yeah, he did not need to be thinking that when she was walking toward him with a smile that made him forget how to breathe.

Her white-and-purple dress was a structured strapless design that looked like origami. It drew his gaze to her face, then right to the bare stretch of skin from her long neck down to the top of her bust. Her waist looked tiny, her legs slim yet curvy, and with that smile and those smoky eyes, no one would be able to look away.

Jewelry would have been redundant.

"Well?" she said, her shoulders moving in an almost-but-not-quite shrug.

"You're gorgeous. You'll be the most beautiful woman on the red carpet."

Bree blushed, rolled her eyes. Charlie let her think he was talking her up.

He took her hands in his and kissed both cheeks. Very European. All business. Not close to what he wanted. He'd kissed her on the mouth that first night, when he'd barely known her, and now he ached to take her mouth again, to taste her, and not only her lips.

"We have a half hour before we go. Want a drink?"

"Just water," she said. "As excited as I am, I'm so

incredibly tired I'm afraid a sip of booze will have me passed out for the night."

"Can't have that." He nodded at the couch. "Sit. I'll bring you water, then take care of the rest of our group."

"Tell them again how wonderful they are, will you? I did, but I think they think I have to say it. I don't. They're magicians."

How could he not like her? She was the anticelebrity, the cure for New York cynicism, complete with authentic goose bumps and unabashed excitement. But even he could see she hadn't exaggerated about how tired she was. Not that anyone else would notice, but he'd been watching her for days, staring too frequently and too deeply. There was more makeup under her eyes tonight. He wondered if he should cancel tomorrow night's club opening. Bree had to work for a few hours tomorrow morning, but then she planned to sleep for the rest of the afternoon. He doubted that would be enough.

He fetched her water as she made herself comfortable, a feat in that dress, on the couch. Then he conveyed her compliments along with his own to the team and saw them to the door. The limo would be arriving any moment.

He could see Bree's dark hair over the edge of the couch, and he needed to remind her to bring her other shoes for when they got back in the limo. How women walked in those ridiculous heels...

Bree had rested on the leather sofa with one leg curled up under herself. The glass, now empty, tipped at a thirty-degree angle in her hand. She was sound asleep.

After carefully lifting the glass from her fingers, freezing for a moment when she made a little low-pitched sound, he touched her bare shoulder gently. "Bree? Bree, we have to leave now."

She mumbled something and adjusted the side of her face on the back cushion.

He hated that he had to disturb her. He brushed the back of his fingers across her cheek. "Bree," he said as he sat down next to her. He wanted to wake her, not scare her. "I know you're tired, but it's the premiere. Movie stars! Glamour! Lights, cameras, action!"

She tilted. Toward him. He repositioned himself quickly so she would land on the inside of his shoulder, not the bony edge. She slumped against him, the leg that had been tucked under now at a weird angle. While it looked ungainly and not very ladylike, it didn't seem uncomfortable.

It was too easy to shift himself, to wrap his arm around her back, to hold her close, to inhale the smell of her. Slumping turned to snuggling and he sighed as he gave his next move some consideration. Then, with his free hand he pulled out his cell. He had to call Naomi, as he wasn't adept at one-hand texting.

"You in the car?"

Ah, the voice. Car became cah, and he couldn't stop his grin. "No," he whispered.

"What?"

How she'd given that simple word such a swoop gave him equal parts joy and the willies. "We're not gonna make it. Danny can take my place. Catch him quickly, though, 'cause he's not going to be dressed for it."

"Why are you not going? Why are you whispering? Charlie, what have you done? It's something about the girl, isn't it?"

"Shhh," he said, although Naomi's voice over the cell

wasn't going to wake Bree. "She's under the weather. It'll be fine."

"How's it gonna be fine? You've got deadlines. You know how many comments you got today? Over twenty-five hundred. And you're taking sick leave? What the hell, Charlie?"

"It'll work out. Like always."

"Yeah, well, it's me you're talking to, sweetheart, and 'like always' my ass."

"Naomi. Call Danny. I'll send you the copy and photos in the morning."

He disconnected before she gave him additional grief, and put his cell down on the coffee table. Bree hadn't stirred an inch. She'd probably be mad at him for sending someone in their place, and he had no idea what he was going to do about tomorrow's blog pages, but there was no way in hell he was going to wake her. Not now.

She needed to rest. There would be other premieres. He'd spin the story to his advantage. In fact… He had the perfect angle. Take that, Naomi.

He'd have a story for tomorrow, but for tonight, he was keeping Bree to himself.

BREE HEARD A DOG BARK AND while it was a real dog barking, it was a dog once removed. A television dog. But she didn't open her eyes, not yet. She liked this place, the in-between where there was nothing at all unpleasant and no alarm was going to intrude. The subtle, woodsy scent of Charlie made her sigh and smile. He knew how to use cologne, not like some of the guys from work who showered in the stuff. There was always a hint of the man underneath with Charlie, and that was the best part.

She moved a bit, her head at a weird angle and it wasn't her pillow at all, and *oh*. It was dark, very dark. Charlie's window was right there, across from his coffee table and behind his big television. It was late. Wrong. All wrong.

"You're up."

She couldn't exactly see as some of her fake eyelashes were now sticking to her cheek, but she looked up in the general direction of Charlie's voice. "What's going on?" As nice as it felt to be pressed against his chest, she pushed off, up, until her feet were on the ground and she was sitting like a person. "What time is it?"

"A little past nine."

"Nine? p.m.? Oh, God, was the premiere called off? Did something bad happen? Is everyone okay?"

Charlie laughed as he rubbed his shoulder, the one she'd been nestled against. "Everything's fine."

"We were supposed to be at the theater at six."

"You were tired."

"I was…" She peeled the lashes off both eyes and settled them in her palm like two spiders. When she glanced back at Charlie he was still rubbing his arm, shaking it. She must have been sleeping on it the whole time. Hours. He'd undone his bow tie, the top button of his shirt, too. The apartment was darker than it had been because he hadn't turned on more lights. She'd slept through the red carpet. He'd let her. "I don't understand."

"I bet you're starving," he said, as he stood. "I know I am. How does Thai sound? Maybe some Tom Yum soup?"

"Wait." She raised her hand to stop him, but it was

the hand with the eyelashes. "Wait. Explain please. Why are we here? Why was I sleeping?"

"I told you." He turned to leave.

"No, you didn't." She stood up. She might be foggy headed and probably looked like hell, but she was going to get an answer. "Why didn't you wake me?"

He kept walking to the kitchen, his tux jacket swinging loose, and she thought of watching him take it off slowly, seeing those perfectly cut trousers fall.

Her heels clicked on the floor and made her wince with each step. Holy crap, these shoes were the instruments of the devil. Speaking of which, her dress, the architectural wonder of a dress, looked like a badly folded sheet. Sveta was going to kill her. "Charlie!"

He paused. Turned around. Smiled at her. "There'll be other premieres. I promise. I'll make it up to you."

"You don't skip things. You never do. I've read your blog every day forever, and you're always there. Even when you're not, you have a really good excuse. Like natural disasters. Not that your arm was trapped under a sleeping person. So what the hell?"

Charlie sighed. God, he really did look hot in that tux. "Take off your shoes. It hurts just looking at them." He kept walking to the kitchen, and she kept following, the pain in her feet making her blink.

"In fact," he said, not bothering to turn, "just get into something comfortable. We'll eat. You'll have a decent night's rest and so will I. We'll go back to the madness tomorrow."

They were in the kitchen proper and he'd flipped on the lights. It took her eyes a moment to adjust, to see he was holding a handful of delivery menus. Everything felt tilted sideways.

"Thai?" he asked. "Chinese? Pizza? Deli? There's

a terrific Indian place nearby that makes a hell of a chicken tikka masala."

Bree inhaled, noticed that she really needed to brush her teeth, and that she was still completely bewildered by everything that had happened since she woke up. "Whatever," she said, shrugging. "As long as it doesn't have cilantro, I'll like it. I'll be back."

She didn't make it to the media room before she took off the shoes. The dress came off in the hallway entrance. When she reached the racks of clothes, she'd already decided to wear one of the kimono robes because dammit, she wanted to be comfortable even if she did have to dress to go home later. Not a teeny short robe, either, because she didn't want him thinking she wanted *that*. They didn't do *that*. It had been decided.

Besides there was a particularly beautiful long black robe with a crane on the back that felt like heaven over her bare skin and covered her more than her dress had. She didn't even mind that it dragged on the floor. So what if she wasn't an Amazon? She was compact. Efficient. Far more comfortable in airplane seats.

The bathroom was next, and she debated keeping the makeup that had taken such time and effort to apply, but in the end it was just no. It took longer than it should have, but feeling clean and *herself* was worth it.

She looked once more in the mirror and stalled. It made no sense that Charlie hadn't shaken her awake. That they were here instead of Radio City Music Hall. The red carpet was long over now, of course, and that was the important part—not watching the movie. But there was an after party they could have attended.

It was highly unlikely that his excuse that she was "tired" was the real reason they'd stayed in. No, there had to be something bigger in play, but she was too fuzzy-headed to figure it out right now.

What she should do was get dressed, go home and go to sleep so that when she went into the office tomorrow to catch up on her real job, she might have an actual working brain cell or two.

On the other hand, a girl had to eat. That she got to eat with Charlie without a hundred people surrounding them was extraordinary. Unprecedented. They'd been on the run for what felt like months instead of days, seeing each other in snatches and in the blinding light of flashbulbs. The only truly personal moments had been in his bed on Valentine's night—which she wasn't allowed to think about—and last night in the back of the limo. She'd thought about that conversation all day. Not only about how different their worlds were, but how he'd opened up to her. It was as if she'd seen him naked again.

Screw it, she wanted to. Eat with him. Talk to him. Alone.

Her accelerated pulse and the rush of excitement that ran through her body merely thinking about what was next moved her out of the bathroom and into seeing dinner through. It was only her heart at risk, after all. And hadn't she admitted, to him of all people, that she *wanted* her heart broken by callous men who wore gorgeous suits?

# 12

CHARLIE GRINNED AGAIN. "So you're a black sheep, too?"

Bree swallowed her mouthful of noodles and took a sip of soda before she could answer him. "Oh, yeah. I was supposed to marry Eliot. My high school boyfriend. It was a thing. Big. Tons of teeth gnashing and hand wringing. Comfort food played a big role. In particular, fried chicken."

At the mention, they both ate for a bit in silence, which gave her time to go over what Charlie had told her about his struggles with his family. How was it possible for them not to be proud of his accomplishments? Maybe they were proud, but the family was crappy at communication. Rebecca had said that was an issue between her and her folks, and Charlie's parents were cut from the same cloth. But then again, Charlie was driven. He put the implementation of his goals above everything else. As did Bree. "You know what I can't figure?" she asked.

"What's that?"

"How come you're nice."

"Me? Nice?"

"Very much so. I expected you to be on the conceited side of horrible. You've been great."

He stared at her for a long moment. "Thanks. I'm glad you think so."

"Hmm," she said. "Interesting."

"What?"

"There was absolutely no agreement in that response. To be clear, I meant nice in an Ohio sense. It wasn't a dig."

"Well, then. I appreciate it even more. Nice can go either way around here."

"I gathered. How would you describe yourself?"

"Oh, that's a scary question."

"I'm not frightened."

"I'm not referring to you."

Bree grinned. "Come on. I'm already prejudiced in your favor."

"That's what's got me worried. I like that you think I'm nice."

"But…"

"I'm…focused. Extremely focused."

She ate a bit, trying on the word to see how it fit. "Is that all you are?"

His wince was extravagant for him. "Yeah, I'm pretty sure that's the whole deal."

"You're funny. That's not an opinion. That's fact. You make me laugh a lot."

"Hey, no fair talking about my looks."

"See? Cute. Very cute."

He put down the carton and picked up the beer, but he didn't drink. "What else?"

She almost teased him, but the look in his eyes stopped her. "You're thoughtful. You see who's around you and you don't take advantage of them. I'm not terribly experienced but I have the feeling that not everyone feeds the makeup and hair crew. Or even notices the building's security staff."

"That's manners."

Bree shook her head. "Nope. It goes beyond that. Most people in your position wouldn't give a damn about anyone around them. It would be easy to be horrible. Expected. But you don't need to be ruthless and evil to be a powerful presence because you're already a powerful presence. People get it. You don't have to shove their faces in it."

"I like that. Not sure I agree, but it's something to ponder. Of course, I don't want to completely disregard the whole ruthless and evil thing. That has a lot of appeal."

She gave a quick nod. "Yes. It does."

He drank some more, then reached for the rice container, but as he did so, he managed to move himself over until they were close enough to touch. The carton stayed in his hand as he leaned into her.

Bree held her breath. Warning bells went off in the distance, muted but not silent. "I should call for a taxi," she said. "Get home. Take advantage of the night off."

Charlie put the rice down, but his leg, his hip, his side were pressed warm against her. He smelled like spice and beer and her eyes closed as she inhaled. "I don't like beer. To drink. But I really like how it tastes when—"

He waited, not five inches between them, maybe not even three. "When…?"

"When I do this," she whispered right before their lips touched.

CHARLIE WANTED TO PULL her into his arms and kiss her until she cried uncle, but he held himself back, every muscle in his body on a hair trigger. Her lips were soft against his, brushing, teasing. Her breath came in gentle puffs, scented with galangal and heat, and no matter how fervently he thought *now, now, now,* he let her call it, let her make this decision. What the hell was wrong with him?

The whole night had been one bizarre thing after another. He didn't miss premieres. He didn't sit still for three goddamn hours just so he wouldn't disturb someone's sleep. He wasn't nice. Nice wasn't even a part of the equation, so what was happening? What was he doing?

A touch, fingers, small, cool, delicate on the back of his neck, and he became very aware of his cock. Not for the first time since they'd landed on the couch together. In another bid to make this the weirdest night ever, he'd found himself cycling through stages of hardness. From that first moment she'd leaned into him all sleepy and mumbling, he hadn't been completely soft. Not hard as a rock, either. Which was fine. He'd only touched himself the one time, and that was an adjustment. Even though this whole scenario was as close to an erotic dream as he'd ever had without sleeping.

She tugged his hair, pulled him closer, deepened the kiss. Little licks against his bottom lip, then the top, as if he were ice cream, a caramel apple. His cock filled, pressed against his fly. He should have taken off the tux, but it was too late to worry about that now. Not when she slipped her tongue inside and he tasted her for the first time since the party at Chelsea Piers.

Instantly he realized it was a mistake. A hormone driven error that would come back and bite him in the ass. He'd known better, but had he pulled away? Hell no.

He adjusted his head so they fit together better, then started his own exploration. He was not delicate or tentative. In fact, it was all he could do to stop himself from showing her just how ruthless he could be.

He opened his mouth and claimed her, sucked on her tongue, thrust with his own, and the sound she made, holy god…now he was getting the kind of hard that meant business. With determination and the endgame in sight, he pulled back. "Bedroom?" he asked. Hoped.

She blinked at him. Charlie realized he'd abandoned his beer and taken hold of her upper arms, the silk of the kimono warm beneath his fingers. She was virtually naked under that kimono; he knew that. He could see the push of her hard nipples against the silk. Maybe he'd been hit in the head or something, because this was not his style. This felt reckless, and he hadn't been reckless since his teens.

Her nod let him breathe again. He kissed her once more. It started out thankful and turned desperate with one slick of his tongue against hers.

They stood as they'd been sitting, his hands lifting her up, their mouths working together to remember, relearn, discover.

He had them halfway across the room before they had to take a real breath.

One of Bree's hands was in his hair, the other under his tuxedo jacket on the small of his back, as if they were doing some crazy waltz. "This is a bad idea," she said before she kissed his chin.

"Terrible. We decided." He captured her mouth again, amazed at how she let him guide her, backward, through the space. How, even with the height difference, the important parts matched, like her breasts against his chest and her lips within his reach. He only had to move a single muscle for her to react exactly as she needed to. It *was* a dance, not crazy, just theirs.

"Five years," she said, in a rush of air and half a moan.

"What's five years?" The hallway was coming, so they shifted slightly to the left.

"My plan." Her hand moved down right over his ass as they maneuvered the turn, and he pushed her back into the wall. Her "umph" made him swing her around as he stood straighter, the graceful equilibrium between them going down the drain.

"You okay?"

"Where's the damn bedroom?"

"Close," he said. Speeding them there would have been the smart move. He kissed her instead. The pull was too much, knowing he shouldn't, they shouldn't.

The hand that had been in his hair was now on his chest, rubbing in vague circles.

"What plan?" he said, his voice as husky as a pack-a-day smoker's. "To take over the world? To bring me to my knees? You don't need five years for either."

She laughed, stepped on his toe with her bare foot. It didn't hurt. "I'm going to be a cross between Tim Gunn and Tina Brown," she said, stumbling on the kimono.

If they didn't kill each other before they made it to the bedroom, it would be a miracle. "Good for you. You'll be great."

"Not if I can't say no to you."

He looked at her then, at her darkened eyes filled with a heat that could burn a house down. "You can."

She breathed in, then there was silence. Only his heartbeat loud in his ears.

"Please don't make me," she whispered.

A dark sound came out of his throat as he bent over

and lifted her into his arms. It was ridiculous, something he never did, would never do, but he'd had enough walking, enough of everything but stripping her bare, burying himself inside her for as long as he could, as deeply as he could.

"Charlie," she said, working her arm around his neck. "We're insane."

"I know." The door was there, right there, and it was open. He had her inside in a flash, over the bed in two, but he had to kiss her one more time before he let her go.

She pulled back from the kiss first, but she barely moved. Her breath brushed his face, soft panting, a faint-as-a-whisper tremor.

He lowered her slowly, head on the pillow, the shoulder of the kimono slipping down enough for him to see the crease where her arm pressed next to her side. It made his cock jerk and he wanted her so badly he didn't know what to do.

"It's my turn," she said.

"What?" He pulled his gaze from that patch of heretofore ordinary skin. "Your turn?"

Her normally very sweet smile and her big innocent eyes turned wicked as she looked him over. "Strip for me. Slowly."

He had to grin. She'd said the words like a crime boss, like a vixen. And then she shrugged that partially bared shoulder until the kimono... He could see the edge of her hardened nipple. Only the edge.

BREE BIT HER LOWER LIP hard as Charlie took off his jacket. He'd taken her at her word, so his movements were unhurried, but his technique? Bless his heart, he had no clue how to do a sexy striptease. He kept checking to make sure he wasn't going to trip and he tried to take both arms out of his sleeves at once and that made him cuss, and start again. She didn't want to laugh because, oh, God, he was trying so hard. Her whole body ached with how adorable he was, how the normally smooth, completely controlled internet mogul looked exactly like a seventeen-year-old virgin trying to impress the prom queen. They both relaxed when the jacket hit the floor. She wasn't about to put him through it again with his shirt and trousers.

"Come here," she said, patting the bed. "You needed a fedora for that move. Besides, you're too far away."

"Now look who's being nice," he said as he sat beside her.

Her fingers were working on his buttons. They looked fantastic—it was Armani, after all—but they were small and round and not easy with shaking fingers. By button three, she was tempted to rip the damn shirt open, but she could never abuse quality fashion like that. It would be like shooting Bambi.

Charlie ended up helping, and every time their fingers brushed she gasped. Couldn't help it. Now that he wasn't even trying, his unbuttoned shirt slid off his shoulders as if choreographed, and holy crap, he was half-naked, and so was she.

"This is going to be bad," she said, her perfectly painted fingernails trailing up his beautifully sculpted chest. Somehow, his muscles, his whole body, had been made to her specifications. Enough definition and muscle to be a gorgeous surprise, an ass to die for, and all of it belonging to the same Charlie who'd let her sleep, who made sure she ate, who'd given her a shot at her dreams. "It's everything I want," she went on, "and that never ends well." She finished the sentence with her lips on his chest.

His fingers smoothed through her hair, his inhalation loud in the quiet room. She kissed him again, moving over the warm flesh in front of her, sneaking her free hand to his slacks, only to realize she'd never get him naked like this. He couldn't have picked a more perfect tuxedo for the night. Stunning and sinfully elegant, and yet everything that kept the structure together—buttons, snaps, zippers—were as complicated as menswear could get. She wondered if somehow he'd found boxer briefs that needed a password to come off.

His fingers cupped her chin, and he lifted her up and away from his chest. "We can stop," he said. "I'll have to excuse myself for a few minutes, but we can stop right now."

She nodded, knowing it was the right thing to do, but when he sighed his disappointment, she grabbed for his hand to keep him from going. "There are too many things," she said.

"I'm not—"

"I keep thinking of all the things we didn't do that one time. How we wouldn't get another chance, and I'd never know…" She felt the blush and marveled at her absurd Midwestern shyness.

"Like what?" he asked, leaning over her more closely, his free hand moving to his difficult trousers.

She captured his index finger between her lips. Then she flicked the pad with her tongue before she sucked the digit into her mouth. She tasted him, fluttered her tongue against his flesh, made him understand.

His moan had her squeezing her legs together. She released his finger, but only so he could finish undressing. To say he was eager was an understatement, and he must have worn that tux often to be so adept, but she never blinked as the trousers hit the floor, followed by his sleek black blessedly uncomplicated briefs. Somewhere along the way, he'd toed off his socks, and there he stood. Oh, so hard. His cock painting a wet trail on his stomach as his chest rose and fell in harsh, quick pants.

"You thought about that?" he asked.

She nodded. Ran her hand up between the folds of the kimono, slowing as she traced her bared nipple. "I would really like it if you'd lie down. Soon."

His smile was as erotic as his erection, and both of them together made her squirm. He obliged, not without stealing a kiss that lasted a long, long time. Finally he was spread out next to her, and she could do whatever she liked. Taste, lick, nibble, tease.

She may have said it before, but this time she meant it. No more sex after this, because as she slipped off her panties on her way to straddling Charlie's hips, she realized that it wasn't exactly the smile or the erection or the meals or the clothes. It *was* everything she wanted. *He* was. Charlie. There was no use pretending, not anymore. This was no crush.

HE WAS GOING TO BURST into flames. There'd be nothing left but ash, and it would be worth it. Naked Bree straddling his waist was exactly the last view he wanted. The smile was a bonus, her bending over to kiss him more than a mortal man could take.

The kiss wasn't half as sweet as her grin. In fact, it was kind of a mess, full of tongue and teeth and saliva and his hips lifted her straight up off the bed it was so hot. Her hands on his chest steadied her, but before they had to break for the next breath, her fingers found his nipples. He loved nipple play, but the woman on top gave him two synchronized twitches that forced his head back, his eyes to widen then slam shut and he wasn't even going to try to explain the noise he made.

"This is fun," she said in the most wicked voice ever.

"You're killing me."

"Don't be such a baby. You can take it."

"I'm not used to this kind of insolence," he said, giving her his most imperious stare.

She raised her left eyebrow as she sat up. He only noticed she'd moved her hand around back when she gripped his cock.

He roared up again, thrusting his hips, her, everything, for more. Now. Please.

Then she pumped. Once.

He already knew she weighed next to nothing. He could simply lift her up, reseat her again in a more agreeable position. Because being inside her in the next ten seconds was the most important thing that would ever happen to him, ever, for his whole life, no exceptions.

When she let go he wanted to cry, and would have if he wasn't such a manly man.

Then she scooted back, lifting herself over his cock until she was settled on his thighs, and shit, the view, her bare-naked pussy spread obscenely exactly where he couldn't touch it.

One finger touched the base of his cock and she drew the finger up and up, and his back arched along with it. The crazy thing was, the whole time, he was looking at her, staring into her eyes, and she was laughing. Not out loud, not mean or taunting, just…delighted. Like a kid with the best toy ever. Jesus.

Her mouth opened in a big smile just before she bent over, and engulfed the head of his prick.

His shout came all the way from his balls, and it was everything he could do not to come right then and there.

*Game on,* he thought. Then he gave up thinking completely.

SHE HAD NO IDEA HOW LONG she'd been on the edge, but it had to have been hours. It was torture, how he'd bring her right there to that place where she held her breath, where she trembled and moaned and prayed, only to pull her over into a quivering mess, and then rev her up again until she couldn't think straight, until she'd pulled the fitted sheet off its corners, until she'd begged herself hoarse.

He came twice.

She lost count.

# 13

HE COULDN'T POSSIBLY be getting hard again this quickly, especially after a doubleheader, but his body was giving it a hell of a try. Charlie couldn't remember the last time sex had been this…intense. If it ever had.

He liked sex and he liked women, and he had liked some of the women he'd had sex with very much, but this, with Bree, felt different somehow.

He kept staring at her, his pulse quickening as her breasts, the nipples still hard and very pink, rose and fell. While the flush that infused her face and chest was slowly fading, her skin, like his, still glistened with sweat. He needed to get up, get clean. Offer her water, see if she wanted a shower, see if she wanted to go home, although he doubted that. It was crazy late.

His other hand reached over and touched her arm. She turned her head and grinned at him. "That was. Wow."

He grinned back. "Well said."

"I'm surprised I'm speaking English. With real words and stuff."

He laughed, squeezed her arm. "I have to do things," he said.

"Well, you're on your own. I can't move."

He nodded, or at least he thought he nodded.

"Here's what I don't understand," she said.

"Only one thing?"

"Ha. No. I don't understand a gazillion things. Starting with what we were thinking. Not that I'm complaining, mind you. But we did decide not to do this."

"Yeah, well. I blame you."

"What? You can't blame me. It wasn't even my fault."

"It was so. You kissed me."

"You ordered an entire Thai restaurant for dinner."

"You were naked under the robe."

"I had on a thong."

He looked at her again and found she was already staring. "You fell asleep."

"You didn't wake me," she said, only not as quickly. The gleam of laughter fading from her eyes.

"You needed rest," he said, his voice low, soft.

She swallowed, then turned over a little. She wasn't facing him full on, but her body leaned toward him. "You could have gone by yourself."

Whatever he'd thought she was going to say, that wasn't it. Because she was right. He could have. He should have. He could have gone alone. Called any number of women he knew who could have been red carpet ready in a heartbeat if he'd wanted company.

"Why didn't you go alone, Charlie?" she asked.

He pounced on the first answer that came to him. "I didn't want to wake you."

Bree's eyebrows lowered. If she was trying to figure out the hidden meaning in his words, she'd be at it for a long while because there was no meaning. No answer. No explanation. It hadn't occurred to him. Not once in three hours had he entertained the thought of leaving her to sleep so he could do his job.

Shit.

He let go of her arm, flung off his sheet then practically flew off the bed. Naked and really wishing he wasn't, he turned to Bree. "You want some water?"

She blinked, then nodded. "Sure. Thanks."

He got her a bottle from the mini fridge in his closet. When she took it, he headed for the bathroom. After he'd closed the door behind him, he realized he should have said something. Nothing important, just the typical, "Be back in a minute," or something equally mundane. According to Bree, he was supposed to be nice. What he was, in fact, was panicked.

He busied himself with cleaning up, but his thoughts were as scattered as shattered glass. He kept trolling for reasons, for a string of logic that would explain why he was standing in his bathroom washing the come off his dick when he should have been in his office finishing up his notes on the movie premiere and planning his morning blog. Alone. With no Bree in his bed or even in his apartment.

Nothing. It may not have been his idea to stop the sex when they agreed to work together, but he'd agreed. It only made sense. They'd had their one night, and even that had been questionable. It was completely out of character for him to change the rules like this. Something must be wrong with him.

He finished, barely remembering to turn off the spigot, as it occurred to him that because of the blog experiment, he'd been spending almost every night with Bree, which was unusual as hell, and not sleeping with anyone else, which was also bizarre, so, of course, he was off balance.

Okay, so he'd gone without having sex for longer than a week before and he hadn't done anything as stupid as ditch work, but the thing was, even during dry spells, he'd gone out with a variety of women. His batting average, despite the impression he cultivated, was nowhere near one hundred percent. There'd been extended stretches he'd gone without anything but his own hand. But he'd never gone any length of time accompanying the same woman to different events.

He snorted as he grabbed his towel. No cause for alarm. It was probably for the best if he didn't make a habit of this, of Bree, because that could get messy.

He could stop seeing her altogether. Fashion Week was moving on to London. He wasn't covering the show there, but neither was he covering the events at Lincoln Center. Tonight's premiere was only tangentially related, and after the club opening tomorrow night and the perfume party Monday, the town and the blog would move on. There was nothing in the contract that stipulated their working relationship would stop at the end of Fashion Week, although it had been mentioned. It would be simple, a nice, clean break.

Instead of the rush of relief he expected, Charlie paused again, his hand partway to the knob. He opened the door slowly, cautiously, unsure why.

She was in his bed. Sitting up, in fact, her side to him while she faced the window. If someone had been outside looking in, they would have seen her, backlit like a painting. They'd have seen him, too, which should have prompted him to shut the light, if not the door, because he was naked.

But so was Bree. She was naked and lit from behind, and he knew she could see his reflection in the window as he stared at her, as intrigued by the shadows as he was by what the light revealed. His gaze moved down the length of her back to the pillow at the base of her spine. He could see the proof of his fingers in her hair, the dark mark he'd made at the junction of her neck and shoulder. The soft roundness of her breast as it peeked out from under her arm—a suggestion, nothing more. It made him swallow, it made the base of his cock tighten and interest curl deep in his body.

He hated to do it, but he had to turn off the light behind him. The darkness wasn't complete because he'd thought of moments like these when this room had been redesigned. He was a visual man, and had no trouble sleeping when the space was less than inky black.

His image was still reflected, though not as clearly, but she could see him approach the bed, raise his arm, put his hand on her warm shoulder. "Stay?" he asked, his voice as low as the lights.

"I need to be up by eight. Well, eight-ish. I have to go to work in the morning."

"We can do that."

Finally, Bree turned to meet his gaze. "I was so sure you were going to ask me to leave."

"I thought about it."

She nodded.

"But it's late," he said. "And I want you here."

A barely there smile curved her lush lips. "Just this once."

He nodded. "Yeah."

"Good. Fine." She shifted, dislodging his hand. "I need to…" She nodded at the restroom.

He watched her small, perfect body as she climbed out of bed. She didn't reach for the robe, which was a surprise. But she was always surprising him.

The door closed before she turned on the light, and

he felt cheated. This was an irresponsible thing he was doing. Maybe that was the point.

IT WASN'T HER ALARM CLOCK that woke her at a quarter to seven. She wasn't sure what had. It took Bree a moment to remember where she was, and to see she was alone. She hadn't realized she'd wanted to wake up next to him.

The bathroom door was open, no sounds, no lights. She wondered if Charlie was in the apartment at all. It was only seven, so she could technically sleep for another hour or so, but that wasn't going to happen. A shower was, however, but first, she'd have to go fetch her bag, her clothes, shoes. Sadly, she hadn't packed her overnight kit. There weren't supposed to be any overnights. Lesson learned.

She grabbed the kimono and opened the bedroom door. It was quiet and chilly, or maybe the chilly was because she was hurrying across long sections of floor in bare feet. The sheer space of this apartment boggled the mind. She pictured her bedroom/closet and how doing anything was a logistical nightmare. The sewing machine couldn't be up while the bed was; the drawers had to be closed to get the sheets, to get anything on hangers. Most everything else was stored in her suitcases, which weren't particularly big or handy. And here she was darting the length of a football field to grab her bag before she rounded the couch to dash to the media room, never once hearing or seeing the master of the house.

She looked at her work dress and it made her sad. It was her own, of course. Not that it mattered. It was a Saturday morning, hardly anyone would be at her office and whoever was probably wouldn't remember she'd worn the same clothes two days in a row. She couldn't believe she had to go in at all, but between the shopping, the preparations, the parties and writing the blogs, she'd been neglecting her day job. God forbid she got fired. She was beyond lucky to have any kind of job, let alone a great one. At least she'd slept more last night than she had all last week. Which said volumes about how little sleep she'd been getting.

Tempted almost to the breaking point, she left the green DKNY dress that was calling her name on the hanger and fetched the blue shirtdress she'd made in college.

She debated using the en suite bathroom here, or going back to the bedroom. Staying here was too much like work, and she was off until tonight.

She kept her eyes peeled for him, surprised when he wasn't in the bedroom. Maybe not so much surprised as disappointed. Anyway, his shower was an otherworldly experience especially since the water pressure in her building was more or less random spitting. Even so, she didn't linger.

Fresh panties were an issue. She didn't have any, if there were some in the media room, she didn't want to know about it. She'd go without, but in this city? That wasn't a smart move.

What the hell. She went back into Charlie's empty bedroom. Second drawer in, she found what she was looking for. A nice pair of black silk boxer briefs. She'd replace them later.

Once dressed, she checked the mirror carefully, making sure no one would see her secret. It was kind of sexy, wearing something so personal of his. She might even tell him.

Then it was on to patching her makeup and fixing

her hair. It wasn't going to win her any beauty contests, but she'd pass. She left the kimono on the bed and went in search of her host. Or at the very least, a note.

She discovered that Charlie's apartment took up the entire floor. The elevator was situated in an atrium. His office took up most of the previously undiscovered country.

And there he was. Sitting in a giant room with enough computers to launch the shuttle. He wore jeans, which she hadn't even known he owned, and a scrumptious V-neck sweater. He made quite the picture, and not because he was so, so pretty—although that didn't hurt—but because he was in his element. The difference was written in his posture as he typed on his computer, as he sailed across the floor in his chair. She couldn't look away.

When he was at parties, even in the limo before parties, or when he was working with his crew inside the media room, there was never a moment when Bree wasn't aware that Charlie was watching. No. Overseeing. It wasn't super obvious, but she'd felt it, and on a couple of occasions she'd seen others notice. He was always one step removed, above it all.

That was one of the things that made even A-list celebs want his attention. He never gave too much of himself. He held back a small but vital part, the part that judged, evaluated. He was completely charming to everyone, so there was no hint, no clue. His real thoughts and opinions would show up in the next blog, or even worse, wouldn't show up at all.

But he was completely present in his big office. The difference in his attitude couldn't have been clearer. She'd been with this Charlie only twice before—in bed.

She shivered at the memories, still hardly believing any of it had been real.

He hadn't noticed her yet. She wasn't even in the room, just peeking in from the doorway. Bree wondered if it might be better to leave now. He was so wrapped up in the work, he wouldn't care. She shouldn't. Only an idiot would make more of last night than what it was. Tension relief. Nothing personal.

Except for the naked part and the kissing and how she'd felt when he was holding her.

Last night she'd had every ounce of Charlie. His body, his attention, his focus. It had felt like being plugged into the mainframe. Every touch electric and unique—

"You're being ridiculous," Charlie said.

Bree froze, held her breath. His back was to her, how could he—

"Naomi, stop. Just stop right there."

He was on the phone. Not a mind reader.

"Okay, okay. I'll bet you a week's pay there's more traffic today about me missing the premiere than any of the Fashion Week stuff." He laughed. "No, if I win, you have to be nice for a week." Another laugh. "Nice as in pretending to be someone else. Anyone else."

Bree turned to leave. She needed to go, and she could only excuse eavesdropping for so long.

"Naomi, for God's sake, it's the numbers," he said, pushing himself over to another computer. "It's always been the numbers. It's me, remember? When have I ever had another motive? The minute the Bree thing stops paying off, we'll end it. There's nothing else going on, so you can stop with your concern. It's unnecessary."

A spike of ice went through Bree's body, ripping

her heart. None of it had mattered, the conversations she'd had with herself, her determination to be realistic, to focus on business. She'd been an idiot. A fool. The soul-sucking pain told her she'd fallen for him, waltzed right into an illusion, knowing it was an illusion, and she hadn't even realized the fantasy had taken over.

She backed away from the door as quietly as she could on trembling legs. It was weird; she could feel her pupils dilating, feel a chill that had nothing to do with the air around her. But shock was an absurd over-reaction, wasn't it? No matter what was going on in her head, she'd never *believed* Charlie loved her. She hadn't. That he'd liked her, yes. That they clicked? That last night had been mutually extraordinary?

Wrong. Wrong as wrong could be. She was a gimmick. Nothing more. Nothing real. He'd told her up front, and she'd signed a legal document that confirmed it. None of this was Charlie's fault. Hell, she's the one who'd instigated the sex last night. She couldn't even blame him for that.

She had painted herself into this corner. And now that she was there, she had to get herself out. Now. She still had obligations, parties to attend as Charlie's date. He could walk out of his office any minute, and oh, God, if he suspected she had turned into one of *those women,* she'd die a thousand humiliated deaths.

It didn't hit her that she was in the living room until she saw the remains of their dinner on the coffee table. She needed to escape. Get her act together somewhere else. But she'd have to leave a note, something easy and quick.

There was the receipt from the Thai place. A pen in her purse. She scribbled "Thanks for the fun night. See you later!" It was all she could do not to run to the elevator, and even though it made no difference, she pushed the button over and over and over.

Finally, she flung herself into the small mirrored box, grasped the rail with both hands and held herself together. She would have to face the security people, the doorman, get a taxi.

Evidently, she'd learned a few things from Charlie. Like how to smile convincingly, and how to make idle conversation as if nothing whatsoever was wrong.

She even gave the cabdriver her address, and sat back for the ride.

Once she'd cleared Central Park West, she fell apart.

# 14

CHARLIE WAS ANGRY AFTER disconnecting from Naomi. He wasn't mad at her, not exactly, but she knew better than to keep pressing when he clearly didn't want to be pressed. That the woman kept his life together was an undisputed fact. He could probably survive her loss but even the idea bothered him. Nothing made him more aware of how important his routine was than the thought of his network splintering.

The inner circle—Naomi, the server techs that oversaw the equipment, his blog editors—were like his pulmonary system with Naomi at the heart. Which made it difficult to lie to her.

He'd done it before, mostly for the sake of ease. Trivial matters. That he'd missed the premiere, that he'd been with Bree over such an extended period of time, that he liked her, was not trivial at all.

He'd been staring at his monitor for several minutes without absorbing any data, but rather than getting back to business his eyes closed as the memory of Bree's body beneath him went straight from his brain to his cock.

She was probably still sleeping as it wasn't even eight, let alone eight-ish. The nice thing to do would be to leave her be. The girl was exhausted, and what they'd done last night hadn't helped. Yet he wanted to go to the bedroom right now and do it all over again. What the hell was up with that? They'd agreed, the sex might have been mind-blowing, but it wasn't smart. This was a rookie mistake, allowing his feelings into the mix. He'd end up as just another blogger if he wasn't careful. Someone who used to be someone.

He should wake her. Maybe with a cup of tea?

He pushed himself across the room, calling himself every kind of an idiot. Coffee was the polite thing to do. It was business as usual today. No screwing around. No goddamn tea.

This time, he'd give her a couple of twenties, make sure she took them. Explain to her how it was a write-off. That would get them both back on track.

She had work, they had the club opening tonight, and he had to put a spin on last night's premiere that would bump up the numbers.

As he went toward the kitchen to get her coffee, he saw her note. He picked it up, recognized her handwriting but didn't believe she'd left without saying anything to him. That she'd left a note instead. What the hell... that wasn't like Bree. Had last night been that bad?

Shit, missing the premiere hadn't been like him. Maybe Naomi was right. Maybe he was too messed up to see clearly. He glanced down at her note and the rush of disappointment churning in his gut made him more determined than ever. Bree was a bit player in a long-running play, and he'd better start thinking of her only that way.

THERE WERE SIX OTHER people on her floor at work, which was six too many. Unfortunately she was no longer the invisible new girl. Now she was Charlie Winslow's date. The one whose byline was on the front page of *Naked New York*. She'd wanted to be noticed, and she'd gotten her wish. If she could have, she would have turned around and gone straight back home. But she couldn't put her job at risk. More at risk.

As she sank into her chair, Bree was incredibly grateful for the cubicle walls. She knew she looked like crap with her swollen eyes and her red blotchy skin, but who cared? What difference did it make, now that she understood? The awakening had been inevitable. At least she'd gotten some really good sex out of it, right?

No, she would not cry again. Instead, she took out the preliminary copy for one of their lesser accounts. She blinked back tears and yet one dropped on the word *latte* and the letters in the middle lost their definition, spread and blurred into something that looked like failure.

The copy had been terrible, anyway. She crushed the sheet of paper into a ball and tossed it into the trash bin under her desk. Naturally, she missed. The carpet was a dark, wavy blue that was meant to disguise, meant to trick the eye into thinking it was clean when it wasn't. She didn't bother picking up her mistake.

Her phone buzzed before she could turn to her keyboard. Rebecca, sending a text.

Call me. SOON!

Bree ignored it; the prospect of speaking to Rebecca made her queasy. It wasn't her friend's fault; it wasn't. She had done Bree an unbelievable favor. It was nobody's fault but her own. She'd read the rules, entered the game with her eyes wide-open.

The task of rewriting the copy was too much for her to bear and she considered leaving, going back to her hole-in-the-wall bedroom, cowering under the covers for a while, but couldn't. She'd file now, give herself time to calm down, stop thinking that her life was some kind of tragedy when it wasn't. God, she could be a drama queen.

Poor Bree, getting a chance to meet famous designers and go to all the best parties in New York. How horrible.

Her sigh made the top few pages of her filing stack flutter up like little skirts. She grabbed a handful of reports. Boring as hell, maintenance stuff like expenses, inventory and billable hours, but they had to be sorted before they could be shoved into files, and what happened to the mythical paperless office? They were probably right there next to flying cars and silver unitards for all.

The image of Charlie swooshing across his office in his fancy chair froze her. She blinked it away, but the image lingered, filling her chest with pressure.

The phone, again, and this time it was Lilly.

Can U meet 4 dinner? Or is CW taking U somewhere fab?

The expense reports went on the far corner of her desk, setting the border of the assembly line. There were seven distinct piles, and she put every ounce of her concentration on each item, neatly squaring each stack as she went, the tap tap of the paper against her desk loud in the gray cubicle with the calendar next to the picture of her parents and the clips from newspapers and magazines, all precisely placed with only blue pushpins that matched the carpet and looked good against the gray.

The phone. A text. Again. Only this one...

Hey, Bree. Member me? UR SISTER???? Pick UP. PICKUPPICKUPPICKUPPICKUP. Call me. Beth. Who misses you. Brat.

Bree squeezed her eyes shut so tight she saw stars, little flashes of white that should have been beautiful, should have been fireworks. The pressure in her chest had turned to homesickness so deep it was the Grand Canyon of ache, the Mariana Trench of despair. She wanted to be sitting at the little kitchen table, the one that was for breakfast if all the kids and grandkids weren't there.

She wanted her mother's biscuits with honey from the Iverson's bees, and she wanted thick cut pepper bacon and scrambled eggs, and to hear her father humming tunelessly as he prepared his plate.

She wanted the music that was playing so loud from Beth's room it would shake the rafters, and Willow to be barking like a fiend outside because the chickens weren't behaving, and she wanted to be little again. Safe. Filled with dreams that didn't have thorns.

When Charlie texted, she dropped the papers in her hands.

Missed you this am. Re: tonight. 7 ok? Dinner 1st. Tea? CW

She went to text back, got a blank screen, her thumbs at the ready. But she couldn't do it. All she had to say was okay. Nothing else. Because, of course, she was going to go. She'd signed an agreement. She had a responsibility. It was her *goddamned dream come true*.

She turned off her phone. Just for a while. Until she finished the filing.

CHARLIE TOOK A DRINK FROM the glass of scotch he'd taken from the party and wondered why he hadn't asked for a bottle instead. He looked over at Bree and gave her a smile even though she'd decided, as she'd done on the way to the party, to sit as far away from him as was possible.

In turn, she gave him a pathetic excuse for a smile.

What was going on? She'd texted him once all day, only to tell him she wouldn't be able to make it to dinner. He'd barely seen her as she was getting ready in the media room. He'd wanted to keep things focused, not mention the note or the night before. Her aloof attitude should have played right into his hand, but he hated it. He was still pissed about the stupid note. She could have said something even if they had made a mistake. He didn't like being caught off guard.

Once they'd entered the club, Bree had perked up, charmed everyone she'd spoken to. Had her picture taken, danced with men, women, groups of men. Not him, though. He didn't dance. Everyone knew that.

Of course, people had asked about missing the premiere, and he hadn't answered. Neither had she. The two of them had touched and even kissed, although on the cheek. They'd made sure the crowd believed what he wanted them to. The only fly in that ointment was that the touching and even that nothing kiss had made him hard in his suit, and he'd had to wait outside with the smokers until he'd calmed down.

Whatever the consequences, this bullshit couldn't go on. She wasn't tired; tired was different. Even through the smiles and the gossip and the pictures and the pounding noise she'd seemed dulled, muted. The spark that made her light up a room had been muffled, and that had happened sometime between the best sex of his whole life, and a note on the back of a take-out receipt. Each time he looked at her, he both wanted her, and wanted to know what had happened.

"You're quiet," he said finally, heading into the breach.

She did that thing with her mouth that was supposed to reassure him, but accomplished the opposite. "I worked so much longer than I'd planned, I barely got a nap, and then I woke up in a panic…"

He nodded, but he didn't believe her. "I'm sorry I've been keeping you out so late. We don't have anything going on tomorrow. That's a plus."

"It is," she said, staring at her hands.

"Bree. Did I do something I shouldn't have? I can be an insensitive bastard, I know."

She met his gaze squarely. "No. You did nothing wrong. Not at all. Not one thing. You've been exactly who you said you'd be, and that's great. That's…great."

"Great," he echoed quietly, because that little speech made his gut clench.

"Sorry. You know what? I got a call from home today. Family and stuff. With so little sleep, I suppose I'm not very good company."

For the first time since 8:00 a.m. Charlie relaxed. Not completely, but family crap he understood. God knows, every time he interacted with his family he snapped at everything for hours if not longer. "Anything I can do?"

She shook her head. "Thanks, but no. Nothing anyone

can do, but accept what is. I'll be fine by Monday. We've got that perfume party, right?"

He nodded. "Yeah. I don't even know how a celebrity begins to find a scent. I sure as hell don't remind myself of exotic spices or citrus fruit, for God's sake. And they make millions. Do people really think if they smell like someone supposedly smells, it makes them sexier? More likely to become a famous person themselves?"

Bree laughed—the best sound of the night. Even with the buzzing still in his ears. Finally, it felt right in the car, if a little cold. She was still very far away.

"You, on the other hand," he said, slipping closer to her, "would make a wonderful perfume."

She eyed him, and instead of touching her as he'd planned, he simply lowered his voice. "You smell like honey and the ocean. The nearer I get, the more pronounced it becomes. It's there no matter what, so either it's the best perfume ever, or as I suspect, it's just you."

"I don't wear perfume," she said. "And there's no honey in any cosmetic I own. I'm not even sure what the ocean smells like."

He shut his eyes as he inhaled. There it was. He was not making it up. "It's gorgeous," he said. "Like you."

Bree whimpered softly, which made him open his eyes, smile. But she wasn't looking at him. She was staring out the window. The feeling of everything being right again vanished.

"Bree—"

"I'm sorry. It's not you. I promise."

"Okay," he said, uncomfortable that he didn't know what to do here. "Would you like to come up?"

She stilled, barely even breathed and then shook her head. "Not tonight, but thank you for the offer."

He shifted slightly, giving her space. Then he picked up his half-empty glass planning to polish it off before they reached his building.

BREE THREW CAUTION TO THE wind when she ordered eggs 'n' apples Benedict on French toast with maple syrup. The others, Rebecca, Shannon and Lilly, gave her approving nods, and even a lift of a Mimosa, then ordered eggs or oatmeal. They were having Sunday brunch at Elephant & Castle, and Bree should have been starving after an hour's wait to get seated. Her hand trembled as she lifted her coffee cup.

"He was nice," Shannon said, and Bree smiled as Shannon flipped her red hair behind her shoulder. Shannon communicated with her body. Her eyes lit up with joy, her disappointment showed in her shoulders and the wry arch of her brow, and when she was angry she jutted her right hip and put her hand on her waist.

In Shannon-speak, the hair lift was more about inevitability than disappointment. A forgone conclusion. Bree didn't have enough hair to copy the move, nor the acceptance. Not yet.

"We should have clicked," Shannon continued, after polishing off her first cocktail. "God knows he was hot. I almost went home with him, but it seemed unfair. To his card, you know? He wants something long-term. Sadly, there were no sparks." She looked around the restaurant, the buzz of the place not intrusive but definitely there. "Is it really only biology? A chemistry project? That doesn't seem fair."

"Well," Lilly said, pulling a trading card from her bag. "Here's mine. No matter what, you'll enjoy the evening. He's a sweet guy, and extremely bright. Money, too."

Shannon took the card, and gave hers to Lilly. "Here's to you and John clicking like crazy."

They both studied their new prospects. Bree sipped her coffee and when her gaze shifted to Rebecca, the woman didn't even pretend she wasn't staring, had obviously been staring.

"What?" Bree said, petulantly enough that she hoped Rebecca would get it.

"What's going on?"

"Nothing. Everything's fine."

Rebecca picked up her Mimosa, but Bree heard her whisper, "liar," before she took a sip.

"Rebecca, please."

"If he's done something horrible, you have to tell me."

"He hasn't."

"Then—"

"It's nothing. I'm telling you. We're fine. We're going to a perfume party tomorrow night. I haven't slept in what feels like years, and I would be in bed now if you horrible people hadn't dragged me out."

"You've been AWOL for too long," Shannon said, "and all we know is what we read on the internet. I have fifty big ones riding on what you and Charlie Winslow were doing instead of attending that premiere."

Bree's face went up in flames, at least that was what it felt like. She traded her coffee for ice water, and willed herself pale. "Nothing of consequence," she said.

The three of them exchanged disbelieving glances and in one more second Bree was going to get her purse and walk out of the restaurant. Quit the lunch exchange group, never look at a trading card again and start checking out airfares to Ohio.

She flushed again, but not because of Shannon's comment. She might have made a mistake allowing her feelings to get out of hand with Charlie, but she was not going to leave the table, or the state. She was not that person, and dammit, it didn't matter how many tears she needed to shed until she got over her heartache, she would not give up. She hadn't come this far only to slink home to Mommy.

"Seriously," she said, sitting up straighter in her chair. "Nothing much happened. Our scheduling was off. Charlie parlayed it into gossip and it worked. We were a blind item in the *Post* today, Page Six. It's all part of the master plan. *NNY* lives for unique hits. It's a whole big mathematical formula that determines how much he can charge for ad space. All relative to individual times a certain person clicks on the blog on any individual computer."

"That's it?" Lilly asked skeptically. "But, you guys are so cute together."

Bree turned from Lilly to Rebecca, meeting their gazes. "We're supposed to look cute together. I'm sorry I'm spoiling it for you guys, but I swear, it's business. In fact, as soon as the numbers dip and I'm no longer useful to the blog, I'll be raiding the trading cards myself."

"You gonna throw Charlie back into the ring?" Shannon asked.

"Believe me. He's not your type. Oh, he's nice and all, but he's not looking to date."

Rebecca tried to stare her down, as if she could make Bree take it back with telepathy. Bree touched her hand. "We'll talk, but not now," she said, low enough that the others couldn't hear, and then there was the food, and that was the distraction she'd needed. She relaxed, confident she'd crossed an important milestone.

Then her phone rang. She almost ignored it. When she did take it out of her purse, she knew before she hit a single button that it was Charlie. Only it wasn't about tomorrow night's perfume extravaganza.

Dinner tonight? Chef's table at Le Bernardin?

Bree saw the name of the top-rated restaurant in the city. The invitation was more than incredible. For her career, for her future, she shouldn't hesitate. There would be pictures and even more gossip when they went out to dinner without an event chaser. But for her sanity, she typed:

*Love to. Can't though. Other plans. See you tomorrow!*

## 15

CHARLIE PICKED UP THE PHONE, a smile on his face before he heard the words from the security downstairs. When his cousin's name was announced he flicked an invitation to some bullshit party to the floor as he gave his assent.

Maybe Rebecca dropping by wasn't so bad. It was weird, but not necessarily a terrible thing. She was friends with Bree. Since she rarely visited, she had to be here because of that friendship. Rebecca would know what the deal was, and that would help. Or maybe she'd heard he was going to cancel his reservation at Le Bernardin and she wanted him to take her? Well tough, because he wasn't hungry anymore.

He got up from the dining room table, not bothering to pick up the invite or any of the other accumulated mess. His housekeeper would be back tomorrow. It wasn't until he opened his door that he realized he hadn't put on shoes. Just socks. Black socks. He was in his jeans, and his Yankees T-shirt. He'd laid out clothes for his seven o'clock date, but screw that.

Rebecca, as always, looked as polished as a cultured

pearl. He took her coat and tossed it over the ottoman by the entrance. Heard her indignant huff and ignored it.

"You want coffee? Wine? Vodka?"

"It's two-thirty in the afternoon," she said, her heels clicking behind him as she followed.

"And?"

"Can you even make coffee?"

"You're a riot, Becca."

In the kitchen, she got out the milk while he poured beans into his coffee mill.

When the grinding finished, he put the grounds into the coffeemaker, and stood in front of the counter, with his arms crossed. "So?"

"What have you done, Charlie?"

"About?"

"Don't be obtuse. To Bree."

"I haven't done anything. She's the one who's been…"

"Been what?"

He shrugged, turned to watch as the coffeemaker gurgled. "Quiet. Off. I don't know."

"Want to tell me why you guys missed the red carpet?"

"No."

"Fine. Coffee to go, then. Oh, and congratulations for remaining fourteen no matter how old you actually get. Excellent job. You must be so proud."

"What are you talking about?" He swung around again, in no mood.

"Okay, let's deal with first things first. Do you honestly believe your family needs to advertise in your blogs in order for Andrew to win this election?"

"Yes."

"Then your ego has officially gone off the charts. Their visit to you, Charles, was their version of an olive branch."

"As if I'd endorse that idiot?"

"They weren't asking for an endorsement. You take ad money from all sorts of lunatics. During the presidential campaign, you had both parties shouting each other down constantly. And I know you didn't vote for both."

"So you did set them up. Hell, I gave you more credit than was due."

"What?" she said, taking two steps toward him.

"You actually told them to approach me, didn't you?"

"No. I didn't. I heard about it ex post facto. From Uncle Ford."

"Christ. This family."

"Is your family." She touched his arm. "I don't know what's happened between you and Bree, honestly, but I know she's different. And you—you don't go to your blog correspondents. They come to you. You don't pretend to have a lover for this long. And you sure as heck don't worry if one of your gimmicks is quiet."

He stepped back, dislodging her hand. He took out two mugs and poured for them both. "It's not personal. The numbers are up. They have been since that first night. I suppose I should thank you for that."

"I don't give a damn about your numbers."

He sipped his coffee and it was so hot he scalded the top of his mouth. "That's all I care about."

"Yeah. Right." She got one of his now-famous to-go cups from the cupboard and transferred her coffee, adding some milk before she put on the top. "It's not going to be easy to go back. After Bree, it's going to hit you hard. At least, let's hope so. I think there's a decent man inside you, Charlie. I've known you too long to give up hope."

"Who died and made you Yoda?"

She grinned. "I can dish it out. Probably because I've all but turned into a monk. But you know what? If and when I find someone you think is worth fighting for, I give you my full permission to take no prisoners. You got that?" She stepped right up into his face and looked him in the eyes. "You fight for me, Charlie. Fight dirty. Fight hard. Don't let me be right when I need to be happy." She kissed him on the cheek, took her drink and left him standing in his socks.

By the time he remembered his own mug, it was cold. But he'd made a decision.

CHARLIE CALLED HER at one-ten on Monday. Bree picked up after the second ring.

"Charlie? What's wrong?"

"Nothing. Why?"

"You're not texting."

"Oh," he said. "No, everything's fine. How are you?"

"I'm great. Great."

He winced at that. Two *greats* definitely made something wrong. "Good. Because, you know, there's the perfume gig tonight."

"Right. I was going to text. What time did you want me at your place?"

He swung his chair around and stared out his window. The whole city seemed gray. Despondent. "Seven? Six if you want to eat. We won't be staying late. It's perfume. I promised a friend, or I'd cancel." Charlie waited for her to say something, and when the silence stretched, he had Plan B ready. "You, on the other hand, promised no one. Tonight isn't really a big deal. If you want to pass, that's fine."

"Pass?"

"Yeah. You've had a busy week, and Monday-night parties are always second tier. I'll make something of it in the blog, something that'll keep them talking. If you want."

The silence was broken by her breathing, and he tried to picture where she was. Indoors, as there was no sound of traffic. In her cubicle? A restaurant? He wondered if she had a ribbon in her hair today, and he wished he'd gone to talk to her in person. Her voice wasn't enough.

"That would be great," she said.

"Okay, then. No problem. Get some rest. Catch up on that sleep, because there are a some big doin's going on starting Tuesday." He grimaced, remembering that Tuesday afternoon he'd agreed to walk down the runway for charity, but that wasn't Bree's problem. She'd be at work.

"Okay," she said, in a very small voice. "I'll get some rest. I… Thank you, Charlie. But if you change your mind. If you think it would be better…for the blog for me to be there…"

"Nope. Got it covered. You can read all about it in tomorrow's *NNY*."

She sighed. It sounded sad. He'd given her a lot of thought last night. Fine, he'd missed her. But there was no reason to think this mood was anything other than what she'd said, despite Rebecca's dramatics. Bree was far from home, on her own. She'd been slammed with brutal hours and tons of pressure. Tonight really was a lightweight affair, and while he'd rather be with Bree, he wanted her to take the time she needed to get herself back. He liked her happy. He liked her excited. He liked her.

IT WAS SIX-FIFTEEN ON MONDAY and Bree was in an elevator and it was possible that she'd actually lost her mind between the fifth and sixth floor.

Or maybe this trip was a direct result of not sleeping last night. She'd tried tea, yoga, meditation—that had been a laugh riot—a hot bath, warm milk. Instead of sleeping she'd read a year's worth of *Naked New York* blogs, every article she could find on Google about Charlie and every person he'd ever dated, started a new five-year plan a half-dozen times, and generally been insane. Work had been a circus. If she didn't get fired this week it would be because of divine intervention because she was not earning her salary. No matter what happened next, *that* was going to change. She would need BBDA more than ever after this ill-advised visit.

She hadn't called ahead. George at the front desk hadn't bothered to notify Charlie of her arrival, but he had asked if she'd been feeling okay because she hadn't been there on Sunday. George didn't work on Sunday. So he'd heard from other front desk personnel that she'd missed a night with Charlie. Which meant it wasn't just her—everyone thought Charlie and she were... something they weren't. She wasn't sure if that made her feel better or worse.

As the elevator approached his floor, she had to fight off utter panic because what was she even doing there? She had no idea what she was going to say. She honestly didn't want to go to the perfume party. Bree had never once imagined a world where that would be true.

Anyway, not going to the party felt worse. God help her, she missed him. Knowing everything she knew, she wanted him like an addict wanted crack. The break tonight was supposed to have been used for regaining her energy, refocusing on her goals, making that new five-year plan. Or sleep. Sleep would have been good.

The elevator stopped so smoothly it took her a second to get that she'd arrived. The second the doors

whooshed open she panicked, pressed the down button.
Twice.

As the doors were about to close, her arm shot out.
And wasn't this just the picture of her life. Stuck.
Unsure. Afraid to meet her own gaze in the mirror.
Terrified to walk forward, unwilling to go back.

She had no plan, and that was the scariest thing of
all. But she took those few steps out of the box, ready
to face whatever had compelled her to come.

Charlie opened the front door before she knocked.
When he saw her, his beautiful brown eyes widened
and his smile was so brilliant and so genuine that something inside her changed forever. "Bree," he said with
that damn voice of his.

"Hey."

"I thought—"

"I know. I wasn't—"

"Come in. The team isn't here, but we can do this.
We can figure this out." He stepped back, his gaze
and his smile steady and pleased. "I was just grabbing
dinner. Pizza. Cheese and mushroom. I can get something else if you don't like pizza. There's that curry
place I told you about—"

"I'm fine. It's fine. Pizza is great." They were standing inside. She was in her coat. Wearing a work dress,
boots, nothing special, just clothes because she never
imagined she'd get this far.

He was in jeans. A dark purple shirt with rolled-up
sleeves. Socks, no shoes. His hair was messy, but not
his usual cool messy. One important part was smooshed
against his scalp and it made tears bubble and her throat
tighten, which made no sense at all.

He came toward her, arms up, as she moved to shrug
off her coat but then he hugged her, trapping her arms at

her sides. Weird didn't come close to what was happening inside her. Tears on the edge of falling, a flurry of butterflies in her stomach, a blush of epic proportions and the smell of his skin both arousing and comforting.

She felt a little better when she caught him sniffing at her neck. Better still when the stiffness in his body and his stuttering breathing made it clear he felt as awkward as she did.

He stepped back, and oh, God, his blush. It was great. And awful. Because this wasn't what she wanted it to be. It *wasn't*. How could she not get that through her very thick skull?

She let her coat slide to the floor. It was all she could do not to follow it.

CHARLIE WATCHED HER WOBBLE, and he wasn't sure whether to grab her or what.

"Here's the thing," she said, her voice as shaky as her legs.

Charlie got caught by the pink of her cheeks and how she was trembling, and while she wore no ribbons, she did have a butterfly clip pulling back a small section of short, dark hair.

"I know not to mix things up." She tipped forward just a bit. "Business, pleasure. That kind of thing. I know that. You've been nothing but amazing, and you've completely changed my life. My five-year plan? It's fast-forwarded to two, maybe three now, but really, I'm rethinking the whole thing because I—it— I'm different. Because you let me write for you. You gave me carte blanche into the world I'd dreamed of, and dreams that come true become something else. Not bad, just not what I imagined. Which is okay."

She took a steadying breath, and man, she needed it because she'd pretty much said that all in one sentence.

Charlie understood her, though. Despite being swept up in her eyes, in her pink lips and how she flung her right hand to the side when she emphasized a word. He knew he was still smiling. Thought about stopping. Didn't.

"So the problem isn't you," she said. "It's that I broke the one rule. The big rule. The one that can ruin it all. I didn't know I was going to. I sure as hell didn't plan to. I'd made a promise. To myself. That I wouldn't get involved. I wouldn't let myself. Because my friends? My college roommate and all my BFFs from high school? Every one of them fell for a guy and then their dreams…diminished. And, yes, I know one doesn't have to lead to the other, but I know myself, and how I can be obsessive, and that's a great trait when I'm working toward my future, but not so great when it means I'm swallowed whole by love. It's not that I don't think love is good, 'cause it's fine—it's great—but my goals…they're important. I want to prove myself in the world before I settle down. Look at you! You went out and did exactly that. You haven't for a minute let anything or anyone get in your way, and wow, you've done it. You're the most successful man I know, and you didn't become a total sonofabitch doing it, and you have morals and you've been so nice to me, I don't even—"

*Good God.* Charlie blinked, and his smile cracked. Not completely, but enough. Love? Really? *Love?*

No. No, no, no. That wasn't what was happening here. He liked her. A lot. More than most people. A whole lot. Sex with her was off the charts, and as fantastic as that was, spending time with her was even better, but love?

Not happening. Not on the table. Not open for discussion, so what was she…

He was pretty sure a heart wasn't supposed to beat this fast.

"…but I think it's just because, you know, Cinderella and all," she said, her voice a little slower, her eyes not quite as vibrant. "Although I never expected that kind of happy ending. That's crazy talk. I mean, you're Charlie Winslow. You're the poster guy for living single. I'm the gimmick. Seriously, I know all that. It's fine with me. It's what I signed up for. I had it all planned out, see, how I was going to do this life, this part of my life, and then I went and did something stupid. Not that I'm exactly *in* love, but I'm heading there and if I'm not careful…" She swallowed. "It won't affect you at all. I mean that completely. If it makes you uncomfortable, well, then…"

She pressed her lips together for a second as a flash of hurt crossed her face. Or confusion? "Well, then, I'll just make myself scarce. That's cool. But if you still have the numbers, I'll live up to my agreement. I'll be the best damn gimmick I can be, and I won't embarrass you, I swear. I promise. It's my problem, not yours. Seriously. It's just that you've been so great, and I owed it to you to tell you what was really going on. You really have been great."

It was taking a long time for his brain to catch up to her words, and he might have missed a chunk in there somewhere. He thought she'd said she'd fallen in love? With him? Or maybe she was afraid of falling in love. With him. But she didn't want to because it was against the rules, and he was a poster child, and she was a gimmick. Or Cinderella.

He was pretty sure she'd mentioned it was her problem and not his, but there might be an argument in there about the veracity of that statement. If he gave it some thought, he'd be able to work it out, make sense of what she'd said, was still saying.

"You look terrified," she said. "I'm sorry. Don't be. I won't... I'm not... I'm not like a crazed fangirl or a stalker or anything like that."

She winced, and he'd seen that look before. It got to him, that scrunched-up face. Scrunched and beautiful, and oh, shit.

"Um," she said, softly. "That might have gotten away from me a little."

He had to clear his throat. "Bree, maybe we should go have a bite to eat. You know, slow down. Talk."

The knock on the door didn't register until Bree looked behind him. What the hell? Had the entire staff gone on vacation or something? "Just a sec," he said, then he went to the door.

It swung open and there was Mia Cavendish, in a massively huge faux fur coat, hair and makeup photo-ready and a look of such boredom on her face Charlie thought she might simply melt into a puddle in the atrium.

Mia glanced at Bree, then her wristwatch, then at Charlie. "Am I early? Naomi said to be here no later than six-thirty."

It was like being stabbed in the chest. Like an earthquake. Like a wake-up call. Bree tried to remember how to breathe as she prayed for the earth to swallow her whole, for the strength to move her damn feet before the elevator went back down to the lobby. She was *such* an *idiot*. And a liar, a total, complete liar.

"Naomi?" Charlie asked. "What?"

"For tonight's party," Mia said as she strode into his home as if she lived there. She smiled at Bree, although it was clear she couldn't be bothered. "I think this is what I'm going to wear, but I'm going to check the racks," she said, dropping her coat on an ottoman. "I'd kill for some champagne." She looked at Bree again. "Where's Anna? Oh, she's probably gone. Charlie?"

"Mia, when did you speak to Naomi?"

"This afternoon. Around one-thirty. Why?"

Bree heard them talking, but their voices were muffled. She needed to pick up her coat. Put it on. Get out. Now. Before Charlie noticed her again.

Although, why would he? One of the most beautiful women in the world was standing not five feet away. Tall, willowy, her face impossibly gorgeous—she was the kind of woman who should be with Charlie Winslow.

"Give us a minute, Mia. There's champagne in the fridge."

The model didn't look pleased about it, but she walked off, confident in her insanely high boots.

That got Bree moving. She bent at the knee, as her mother had taught her, to get her coat, and it was cold on her arms, heavy on her shoulders, but it was thick, and when she wrapped her arms around her waist it felt like protection. "I've got to go," she said, looking anywhere but at Charlie.

He came into her peripheral vision, and she stepped aside, quick as she could. "You know what's funny?" she asked while she backed up.

"Bree, wait."

"What's hysterical? I'm from Hicksville. That's the real town I'm from. Hicksville, Ohio. I went to Hicksville High, and nothing on earth has ever been more appropriate than that."

"What?" Charlie blinked at her, looked toward the kitchen, then back. "Wait, this is all going too fast. Don't go. Okay?"

She shook her head. "You've got to get ready. You made a promise, and you can't be skipping things. I've already knocked you out of your routine, and that's bad enough, but they're expecting you. And Mia Cavendish! That's going to raise some eyebrows, right? Wait till Page Six gets a load of you two together. Facebook is going to go nuts."

She hurried away from him, moving sideways, just as she'd done that first morning-after.

"Please," he said. "I don't—"

"It's okay. We'll decide what to do later. I really have to..." And she was out the door, hitting the damn elevator button, and why couldn't he have lived on the first floor? Would it have killed him? She would have been in a taxi already.

The elevator dinged, and she had never been so thankful. She stepped inside just as the door opened behind her, and Charlie walked out.

She found the close-now! button on the first try, and he didn't stick his arm out to stop the doors. Why should he? Charlie Winslow knew exactly where he belonged.

# 16

CHARLIE WANTED TO BE anywhere but at the Canal Room. The place was packed with the same people he'd seen Saturday night and Thursday night and Wednesday night. The same cameras and reporters and hangers-on made all the same noises. The play repeated endlessly and the only thing that changed was the costumes.

Mia was…somewhere. She'd seemed surprised when he hadn't cozied up after getting out of the car. It hadn't mattered that they'd not uttered a word during the drive, but when the cameras were rolling, there were expectations. Demands. He couldn't have cared less.

The press would say what they wanted to say, then it would be his move, and he'd make a more outrageous statement, and it would continue. Not even chess, but checkers. His thoughts, as he stood nursing a scotch near the rear exit, aside from debating making a run for it, were on the two women who had come to the center stage of his life. Rebecca, who had always been an ally, even when they'd been kids. There was no reason to believe, rationally, that she had changed her allegiance. He'd done nothing to hurt her or embarrass her. They weren't just relatives, they were friends.

Given that, perhaps it was time to consider what she'd been trying to tell him. She had nothing to gain by him reevaluating his relationship to his parents, to his business, to Bree. If he did a complete about-face in all three areas, he and Rebecca would continue on as before.

What was he afraid of? The idea of change? Change was always uncomfortable, and he'd made himself a very comfortable life. Say he was willing to step outside his patterns. Nothing written in stone, so what if he looked at it?

He was under no obligation to do anything his parents asked of him. He hadn't been for years. The life he led was his own. In return, nothing he did or said was going to influence his parents, unless they wanted to be influenced.

He sipped the scotch, felt the burn at the back of his throat. It occurred to him that the race had been over years ago, but Rebecca was right. He'd never stopped running. He'd been incredibly pleased with their horrified response to *Naked New York* and his notoriety. It represented everything they avoided like the plague: common interests, personal exposure, progressive views. Basically anything that wasn't them. He'd kept upping the stakes, they'd kept reacting with shock, with threats, with bribes. Huh. He'd made that little hamster wheel his life's work.

Why, of all the interesting things that were available to a man of his resources, was he still playing this ridiculous game? Movie stars? Fashion? Scandals? It wasn't that he thought all celebrity was nonsense—he didn't. Humans created celebrity culture because they were designed that way. There'd been gossip ever since there'd been speech. Technology only made it more immediate. It was part of the world, but only a tiny part, and when all was said and done, it wasn't a part he particularly valued, outside of the revenue it generated.

He took his glass with him and made his exit. He didn't have his coat, and dammit, it was freezing, but he wasn't willing to go back inside, not now.

He walked down the street, and even at twenty to eleven, there were people in the crosswalks, people talking, lights on, restaurants and bars filled to the rafters. God, he loved this city. The fantastic mess of it. Endlessly fascinating, and he was the luckiest son-ofabitch who lived there. Did he even know what to do with this world at his fingertips? If he walked away from *Naked New York* tomorrow, nothing significant would happen. He imagined he would still run the media group. That was fulfilling and he was damn proud of what he'd built. But if he never went to another party, never saw another premiere or opened another club, so what? Manhattan would find another king. He would have to figure out what he wanted to do with himself. His parents could stop being embarrassed by the women he went out with. Shit. He started laughing, out there on the sidewalk, and a couple walking behind him crossed the street in the middle of the road.

Oh, Rebecca was going to be unbearable. No one did smug like Rebecca. But what the hell. He owed her.

Not that he had decided to walk away. Not yet. It was too big a decision to make on a scotch and a confusing night. Besides, he had his team to think about. Transitions, changes, financial repercussions.

Which actually sounded like one hell of a good time.

Shivering, he circled back to the entrance to the club. He had no desire to go in, but he owed it to Mia to tell her she was on her own. So he braved the front door, ignored the strange looks at his reentry. Finding Mia was all he cared about at the moment. Because while leaving the spotlight of *NNY* was a big decision, it wasn't the most important one he needed to consider. Which brought him to the second woman.

If he was going to jump off the cliff without a safety net, he was pretty sure he didn't want to jump alone.

BREE WAS IN THE CLOSET. Her closet. On the ottoman mattress that pretended to be her bed. Her room might have been the size of a toaster oven, but it had a door and no one outside could hear her cry.

Although she wasn't crying at the moment. She was staring at her phone. She'd already decided she wouldn't be on the next plane to Ohio, but she wasn't back in Amazon warrior mode, either. She was sad. About as sad as a person who had so much could be.

That was the kicker. A full-on wallow wasn't possible, not when there were so many people with real problems. The only thing wrong with her life was that the boy didn't like her back. Not the end of the world, not unique, and who was to say Charlie was the great love of her life? Maybe he served a completely different purpose. What if her attraction to him was a test of her fortitude, her commitment to her future? Or a reminder that she had a functioning heart, and that she had to be far more careful with her emotions?

It could have nothing to do with love. He was a fairytale kind of guy, and she was human. She'd grown up on Disney movies and romantic notions. Charlie was magic. Of course she'd been swept away.

The problem was in pretending, fabricating, believing he'd been swept away, too.

She picked up her phone, clicked on Contacts and

went through her personal list. She liked Rebecca so much, but she was too close to the ache. Lilly was great, but they hadn't reached the heart-to-heart stage yet.

Bree was too embarrassed to call her Ohio crew. She'd felt so damn superior to them and their tragic mistakes. Talk about falling from the height of her own ego.

No, there was only one place to turn tonight, and that was family. Beth was two years older, and she'd been through a messy breakup before she'd found Max. She was also an amazing listener, and boy did Bree need to talk.

Beth answered after one ring. "Oh, thank God. I know something's wrong. Talk to me already, you insufferable brat."

Bree sniffed twice, and started from the beginning.

CHARLIE STARED INTO THE fireplace. It was late, or to be more accurate, early. He was dog-tired and he needed to sleep, but a lot had happened since he'd come home, and he was still reeling from it.

The moment he'd walked in, he'd headed for the office. The morning blog had been easy. He'd done the real work and built up the party and the fragrance—after all, they were spending big bucks to advertise the scent all over his blogs—and he'd kept the talk of Bree alive. It was surprisingly satisfying to call Mia an old friend. She'd hate that. Especially the old part. But she never stayed mad for long. Of course, he'd had to pump the next few days' worth of events, about the movers and shakers in Manhattan. Then he'd wrapped it up with something…personal.

With all that talk of Bree's goals and dreams, he'd gone back into his archives and reread his original business plan. It had been eye-opening. He'd come so damn far since those days, yet in some ways he'd hardly moved an inch. Right next to the archive file he'd kept copies of the scandal he'd created after being accepted into Harvard law to make sure his family would never consider him for anything of importance.

He'd purposefully gotten himself arrested for drugs. He'd planned it down to the last photograph—no one had been caught with drugs but him, and he'd made damn sure it was so circumstantial he'd never be taken to court. The damage was all in the gossip, in the inferences, in the pictures in the *Post* and the tabloids.

No matter how many attorneys tried to get his trust fund taken away, they hadn't been able to touch a penny.

Yeah. He could probably stop now. Give his folks and his whole family a break. Jesus, he could be an ass. On the other hand, he'd learned from the masters.

So, new plan. Bottom line? He was in a position where he could make a real difference in people's lives. He had money, access, some power. Politics was straight out. Not even a consideration. Creative problem solving? That held a lot of appeal, even if he wasn't sure what that would look like.

Bree by his side?

He stopped breathing as a picture formed, nothing noble or dramatic, just the two of them, lying in bed, in the dark. Naked. And yeah, okay, postcoital. But the fantasy was really about after. About talking. Soft talk in the middle of the night, about whatever. Touching her because he could, and her touching him back.

He thought about that last shot by Rebecca. The thing about fighting to be happy instead of right. Missing the premiere? That had been the easiest decision he'd made in ages. He could still feel the pleasure of having Bree sleeping against him, even with the tingling in his arms. He'd felt more relaxed, happier than he had any reason to be, and why? Not just because he'd put Bree first, but because he'd put himself first, too.

Holy…

Charlie turned away from the fireplace, and walked across the living room to the atrium, then into his office. His computer was still on. He never turned the damn thing off, so it was easy to sit back in his chair and pull up a blank screen.

As his fingers flew across the keyboard he found himself smiling. As the sky lightened over Manhattan, he got closer and closer to the cliff's edge, and there was no net in sight.

BREE HAD LEARNED A LOT in the past week about faking not only a smile, but an attitude, and she was putting her skills to the test as the doorman ushered her into Charlie's building.

"Nice to see you again, Ms. Kingston."

"Thank you, George." She nodded at the other staff in the lobby as she hurried to the elevator. She didn't really breathe until the doors had closed and she was alone. Pressing 18, her finger shook, which was unacceptable. This was business. Charlie already knew the worst about her, so tonight would be nothing but another party, another extraordinary opportunity to learn and network. That's what she'd told her sister, what she'd told herself over and over and over again.

Her shaking hand went back to the buttons and she pressed 17 in the nick of time. The elevator stopped with a whisper-soft bounce and Bree couldn't get out fast enough.

She stood in a hallway. Thank goodness. She hadn't even considered that other floors could be like Charlie's—private residences. No, this was a hall, although from where she stood she could only see two doors.

The carpet was incredibly thick, a rich aubergine, the walls a creamy yellow, and there were several wrought-iron plant stands along the wall with fantastic red gladiolus arrangements. Bree stared for a moment, not thinking about anything but how pretty and elegant it all looked and how in all her years she'd never imagined standing in a hallway like this one. Quiet, sophisticated, beyond classy. It made no sense. Nothing made sense anymore. Most of all the idea that Charlie Winslow could ever, ever want Bree Ellen Kingston, a daughter of Hicksville, Ohio, former member of 4-H, the Girl Scouts and the Aaron Carter fan club. It felt silly, ridiculous, that she'd entertained the notion for a single moment.

She pulled her cell out and clicked on the only text she'd received from Charlie all day.

6? CW

Her response had been the eloquent: K

She pulled up this morning's blog, Charlie's post about the perfume party. The bulk of it was just what it said on the box: who had been there, gossip, bands, more gossip. Barely a word about Mia Cavendish.

But the last paragraph…

Bree read the last paragraph again. Surely this time her heart wouldn't jump, her breath wouldn't catch.

The night could have been improved if the smokers had come inside, but that's nothing new. The upgrades at the Canal Room were minimal, but important. The men's room, the upstairs lounge and the new bartender were all worth a look. I imagine the ladies' bathroom was also better, but I have no confirmation. As for the reason for the party—Jazz and Cocktails perfume looks as sexy as the name, and it smells damn good. Not like the ocean and honey, but still, damn good.

The ocean and honey. God.

No. Nope, getting off at 17 hadn't worked. The hallway hadn't cured her; the moment of clarity hadn't been enough to make her see reason. She was still screwed. But she'd get through the night, because she wasn't thirteen. She'd put on her armor along with her makeup and she would be grateful and attentive and happy.

Okay, grateful and attentive.

She had to wait for the elevator and when she finally stepped inside it was empty. Which was good. She faced herself in the mirror. Back straight, eyes open and expressive, smile—careful, not too much. There. She was ready. Even the kick in the chest when she saw Charlie didn't knock her to her knees.

# 17

SEEING BREE STEP INTO the atrium stopped Charlie cold. He'd been saying something to Sveta, but he couldn't remember what. It didn't matter. "Hey," he said, holding out his hand to walk Bree into the house. "Rested?"

"Yeah," she said, although she glanced away when she spoke. "Thanks."

"I have some deli in the kitchen. You want to eat before you get ready?"

She made a beeline to the hallway that led to the media room. "No thanks. Not hungry."

Charlie followed, his mood on the downswing as he realized his master scheme for the evening was already going to hell. He could hear the team chattering away as they prepped the room, and he thought about the spread in the kitchen. He'd specifically gotten all the stuff Bree liked from the Carnegie Deli, including the Russian dressing and coleslaw for her corned beef sandwich.

Bree turned the corner, disappeared from view, and he staggered to a stop as it dawned on him that his "master scheme" to sweep Bree off her feet—a whole night that came complete with timetable, great mood lighting and a rather epic soundtrack—had left out only one thing. Bree herself.

Sveta swam in front of him, whipped her hair back in her usual dramatic style, then asked him three rapid-fire questions about tonight's book party.

He blinked at the woman and let her drag him down the hall to where the action was. As he entered the madhouse, he caught a glimpse of Bree in the big makeup mirror. She stared back and her gaze was so full of pain it nearly flattened him.

He'd realized last night that his decision to step away from the hands-on editing of his media group was a huge decision, but *this* leap he was about to make? It wasn't across a murmuring creek, it was across goddamn Niagara Falls. He'd sculpted himself a world that was made entirely of his rules, serving only himself, and every moment of every day was Charlie Winslow-shaped. The only thing he ever compromised on was the blog, but only when he had to, and only when it would serve the greater good—which was also all about his business, so no, he never really compromised at all.

It was good to be the king. And yet, how had he never noticed that it was also incredibly lonely?

Rebecca. She was good; he had to give her credit. She'd said this would happen. That being right only went so far. He wanted more now. More with Bree. With the woman sitting in the center of a whirlwind.

But could he do it? Could he change in the ways he'd need to, to actually be part of a couple? Put her first? A novel concept, and one he'd botched at the starting gate.

He'd been so caught up in the grand gesture that he'd

forgotten that he was about to ask a great deal of this woman. She had her own dreams, her own goals, her wondrous five-year plan. Would she even want what he was proposing? Maybe he should wait, think this through. Acting rashly wasn't in his nature. This was crazy.

He refocused on Bree. She hadn't turned away at all. But she'd done a very good job of masking her pain. Anyone else would have thought that smile was real, that her eyes were bright with excitement and anticipation. But he'd seen her when she was truly happy.

The hell with it. He was going in. "Can I have everyone's attention?"

It didn't take long for the group to settle. "Something's come up. We won't be going to tonight's event, so, if you guys could wrap up what you need to, that would be appreciated."

He knew the whole team would react, but his gaze stayed on Bree's image in the mirror. She looked completely confused, but he wouldn't keep her there long.

"Don't worry," he whispered, then cleared his throat and spoke to the team again. "Don't worry, you'll all get paid for the night's work. There's food in the kitchen. Take it with you. I'll never be able to finish it. Thank you, everyone. Sorry for the inconvenience."

Sveta barely blinked. She started putting the clothes back on the racks, boxing shoes, making sure everything would be in order for the next event. The team followed suit, and since they'd only begun it was a matter of minutes before they were clearing out.

Bree rose from the makeup chair. She grabbed her pocketbook, tugged the bottom of her very-Bree vintage sailor dress. God, she looked sweet. He couldn't help the ache that went from his chest on down. He wanted her to say yes as badly as he'd wanted anything in his life.

Charlie was aware that the team members were staring at him, at Bree, and that they were trying to clear out as quickly as they could. He didn't care.

Bree had her head bowed but her spine straight and tall as she followed the small group. At the door, he caught her hand in his. "I'd like you to stay," he said. "Please."

When they were alone, and they could no longer hear the footfalls of the others, she met his gaze. "What's going on?"

"I had it all planned out," he said. "Like I was writing a play. We'd go to the party, but we wouldn't stay late. I'd convince you to come back here with me. I had a couple of backup plans for that, just in case. It would have been great. Very dramatic." He stared at her, at those amazing green eyes. "But all that really matters right now is how very much I want to kiss you."

"We're not going to the book party because you want to kiss me?"

He smiled. "No," he said, then half winced. "Sort of."

"Oh," she said, as if everything made sense. A second later she shook her head. "I don't get this at all. Charlie, what—"

He kissed her. He couldn't wait another second. Honestly, he didn't want to keep her in suspense—that wouldn't be fair. As soon as he finished this kiss, he'd tell her everything.

Then she kissed him back.

His first response was *thank God*. This was what he'd needed. Bree in his arms, on his lips. The taste of her minty gum and the slide of her tongue made him ache.

"Charlie," she whispered, and it was like a match to kindling, the sound of his name on her lips. He stepped into her. He would have climbed inside her if he could have; instead he walked her back until he had pressed her against the wall, kissing her as if his life depended on it.

With a gasp, her head thunked back, her mouth swollen and damp and irresistible.

He forced himself to slow down. The first brush of his lips was soft, gentle. Tender. But it wasn't enough, and he hauled her up against him, his mouth hard, hungry, desperate, as the kiss deepened into an intense tangle of tongues and teeth that made him groan.

Tearing her mouth free, she gasped for breath as her small hands got busy on the buttons of his shirt. Her eyes were wide and wild as she fumbled and cursed.

"Bree—"

She gave up on his buttons and went for his belt. He groaned, but no.

"Not here," he said roughly, and wrapped his arms tight around her, lifting her straight up, bending slightly until she wrapped her legs above his hips. He wanted to just get them to the bedroom, but as always, he couldn't resist kissing her over and over. He swerved like a drunk, dizzy with the feel of her, with the promise of what was to come.

Somehow, they made it to his room and they stripped. No finesse, no teasing. Simply the need to be naked. Now.

As they stretched out on the bed, he took her hands

in his and guided them above her head as he balanced himself over her body. He looked down into her face and saw a new life.

THERE WAS SO MUCH IN HIS gaze that Bree went still. She was a lost cause, gone, any good sense she had swept away by passion and the awareness of his body. When he whispered her name, the world slowed, the air thrummed with heat and want.

His mouth spread hot, wet kisses down her jaw, along her collarbone. Her breast. His tongue curled around her nipple and he groaned when it beaded for him.

She bucked, and he did it again, reaching for the drawer, grabbing a condom. He protected them both with fingers that actually trembled, and then nestled between her legs. The moon bathed them in soft gray light, so luminous it was enough for her to see the details of his face, although she already knew each feature intimately, and could have sculpted each curve.

"Missed you," he whispered, but his words turned into a moan when he sank into her.

Her eyes closed as he filled her, and her pulse quickened when she pushed up to meet his slow thrust.

They stilled when he could go no farther, their panting breaths loud in the room, but soon it wasn't enough and she pushed up again.

"Move," she said, squeezing his arms, pressing her breasts into his chest.

"God, yes," he said, so softly she barely heard him past the pulse of her heartbeat.

"So good." He cupped her face as he pulled out

slowly, kissing her after a languid swipe of his tongue across her bottom lip.

Her breath stuttered with the shock of his tenderness. She'd been ready for frantic sex. Not this.

He slid his hands to her hips and rocked, going even deeper now, and thinking was all but impossible. Tossing back her head, she gasped his name, and he thrust as if each time would be his last. Again and again, his control driving her wild. She could hear her own heart thundering in her ears, their mingled murmurs and cries, raggedy gasps and low moans. Hers and his.

When his fingers slipped between them, he barely had to touch her. A long moment stretched like a tightrope in that unbearably sweet limbo just before the crash, and when it came, when her orgasm tore through her like a bolt of lightning, she cried out and clung to him as if he was the only real thing.

He didn't let her go, and he didn't stop. Between her trembling spasms he said her name again and again, and as the pace increased his voice got louder until he filled her so completely she felt him come from the inside.

Finally, he fell beside her, close, and she felt small and tender against his damp body as her gasps slowed. When thought returned as a trickle, everything was perfect and peaceful and nothing else. But the trickle turned into a stream and that brought panic along with clarity.

Oh, God, she'd done it now. Again. She'd made things a million times worse. She should have left while she could have, made a break for it and kept on running. Because they'd made love. The sound of her name in his low voice was imprinted forever. She was a goner.

She rolled away from him and out of the bed, grabbing her dress from the floor. If she was lucky, she could still make a quick getaway and salvage some part of her heart.

His hand on her wrist stopped her.

"I have to go," she said, her voice quivering and her heart pounding.

"No, please. Wait." He tugged. "Please."

She took in a big breath before she faced him. "I appreciate all you've done for me, Charlie, but this was a mistake. You and I both know it. I can't kid myself anymore. Not after this. I have to stop. Full stop. No working parties with you, no writing sidebars, nothing. I've stepped over the line and there's no road back except the one that takes me far away from you."

He sat up, never releasing her wrist. "Bree, please. I promise I won't stop you if you still feel this way after… Ten minutes. That's all I'm asking."

Bree's dress wasn't on, in fact, it just hung from her hand and for a moment she stared at it as if it was something she'd never seen before, but it wasn't her dress that had her blinking. Things were getting mixed-up again, and she was already so far past the line with Charlie she'd lost all her ground rules. There was no getting around it. She had fallen in love with him. Nothing would fix that except time and distance. But ten minutes? She could risk that, right? But only if she wasn't naked.

He let go of her, and then she slipped her dress on. Her panties were puddled by the door, but she could get those in a minute. Now, though, she needed to hear what he had to say.

She sat down on the bed, not close, either. If he touched her, there was a very good chance the tiny bit of backbone she'd found would vanish like smoke. "I'm listening."

He nodded, but then did some maneuvering under the sheet that had become a bundle at the foot of the bed. He dragged out his boxer briefs snagged by his toes, and he smiled with the achievement as he slipped them on.

That little grin didn't help. It was clear that ten minutes was nine minutes and fifty-nine seconds too long. She should have run when she had the chance.

NOW THAT CHARLIE WAS really going to tell Bree about the plan, there was more than a hint of panic involved. He sat up, bolstered his back with a hastily arranged pillow, then met her gaze. Might as well just dive into the deep end. "Okay. First, I need to ask you a question. Did you have a good time Friday night? When we missed the premiere?"

Still looking a little dumbstruck, she nodded. "Yeah. Yeah, I did."

"Were you happy?"

A flash of pain was there and gone in a breath. "Yes. Very."

"Me, too."

Bree looked at him as if he was nuts, and he supposed she was right.

"I was really happy that night," he said. "I didn't give a damn about the red carpet or the blog. I wanted to be exactly where I was. With you. I didn't expect that."

"That's…" She floundered for a moment, her hands rising, falling into her lap. "Amazing."

"You can say that again. I haven't felt this way about anyone, not for ages—actually, never. I like you so damn much." It was horrible not to touch her.

Wrong. He abandoned his pillow and swung his legs over, scooting inelegantly until they were sitting side by side, touching. Until he had her hand in his. "I haven't wanted to talk with anyone the way I want to talk with you. Going to parties this week has been a revelation. And working together, well, damn that's been…"

He lost his train of thought as she blinked up at him, her mouth open in what looked more like shock than confusion. Yet when she straightened her shoulders and leaned away from him, he was the one who was confused.

"I'm glad," she said. "I am. And maybe in a while I can come back on board, because what you've given me… But I have to focus on my goals. Especially now that they've changed. I'm not even sure what exactly I want, but I know it's important to keep my eye on the prize, and not let myself get distracted. And sorry, Charlie, but you're the biggest distraction ever."

"No, no. Wait, Bree. Don't decide yet. 'Cause I'm talking about change, too. For the better, I hope. Look, the last thing on earth I'd ever want is to sideline your dreams. I believe in you. You're a talented writer, and you have an eye for detail and fashion. You'll be successful no matter what you decide you want to do, and a big part of what I want to do is support you in any way I can."

She exhaled a big breath. "Okay…"

"I've decided to step down as editor of *NNY*."

"What?"

He grinned at how loudly the word echoed in the moonlit bedroom. "It's time to take on some new challenges. That don't involve celebrities or supermodels or fashion shows. I have no idea what that'll look like. Just that it won't be what it has been."

"Oh," she said again, and he could practically see her mind struggling to make sense of what he was telling her, rearranging everything she knew about him. Hell, throwing it all out the window.

He brushed her cheek with the tips of his fingers. He wanted her to say yes so badly. "We're good together. We are. We fit. I want to explore that. Together. While we both find out where we belong individually. Because I'm pretty sure I'm in love with you."

BREE THOUGHT ABOUT pinching herself. But when she looked at his eyes she believed him. He loved her.

"Oh, my goodness," she said.

He laughed. "Yeah."

"You love me? Me?"

Charlie nodded. "Not sure I'll be any good at it. You know, first time and all."

She swallowed as she struggled to appear as if she wasn't freaking out. "That's okay. You're pretty good at everything else. I imagine you'll pick it up quickly."

"Thanks," he said.

It was her turn to touch, to run her hand up his arm before she caressed his cheek. That helped a lot. She'd needed grounding and the feel of him was familiar and lovely. "Are you sure about this? Really sure?"

"Oh, yeah. I'm in."

"This is insane. This isn't even a life I could have imagined, and when I was seven I wanted to be a unicorn."

He laughed as he pulled her close, as his lips captured hers and she could taste his grin and his excitement. She was ten feet off the ground, in the arms of the soon-to-be-abdicating King of Manhattan, and the hell with a unicorn. She was Bree, and she wouldn't trade that for the world.

She thought about her friends at the St. Marks lunch exchange, and how they were all so hopeful and scared when they picked up a trading card. She couldn't wait to tell them not to give up. Ever. Anything was possible. Anything.

*The Next Day...*

*Huffpost Entertainment:* CHARLIE WINSLOW QUITS!

*New York Post:* Today in Page Six...No More *Naked New York?*

FACEBOOK

| edit profile |
|---|

**Charlie Winslow**
Editor in Chief/CEO *Naked New York Media Group*
Studied Business/Marketing at *Harvard University*
Lives in *Manhattan* ❤ In a Relationship

\* \* \* \* \*

# HAVE ME

### BY
### JO LEIGH

To Yael.
I strive to create heroines who are as terrific as you.

# 1

Where R U???

REBECCA THORPE DIDN'T bother returning her friend Bree's text because there was no need. She was already walking up the pathway to the St. Marks church basement, the ready-to-be-frozen lunches she'd prepared in a large tote in preparation for the bimonthly lunch exchange. That wasn't what had slowed her pace though. She took her hand out of her coat pocket and stared again at the trading card she'd been toying with for the past fifteen minutes.

Ever since Shannon Fitzgerald had introduced the idea of using trading cards for trading *men,* the lunch exchange group, now numbering a whopping seventeen women, had been in a dating frenzy. The concept was simplicity itself: everyone involved recommended men they knew who were eligible and in the market. Whether they were relatives, friends or even guys without that perfect chemistry—for them at least—there was suddenly a bounty of prescreened, fully vetted local men. None of whom knew that they were members of this very select group.

On paper Gerard had seemed ideal. He was gorgeous, not only on the front of the card, either. Tall, dark, handsome, he'd gotten his degree from Cambridge, then had come to New York to work for the United Nations. He was urbane, sophisticated, dressed like a dream. And he'd taken her to dinner at Babbo, which was never a bad thing.

Sadly, like the other three men Rebecca had gone out with, courtesy of the trading cards, there had been no sizzle. Maybe she'd see Gerard again because he was fascinating, and they had many common interests, but the man she was looking for wasn't him. She'd known ten minutes into the date that the magic was missing, and while she'd been disappointed, she hadn't been surprised.

She was too picky. Or something. She couldn't spell out her criteria for *the one* but she certainly knew when she hadn't found it. She'd never had luck with men, and that had as much to do with her being a Winslow as it did with her taste, but the end result was that she hadn't truly connected with a man, not for the long haul, and the trading cards hadn't changed her luck.

So, with all due respect to the trading cards and to the whole idea of dating, she was done. No more cards for her, no more setups, no more blind dates, no more searching and no more hoping.

If she met someone in the course of doing what she loved, then great. If she didn't, she was fine with that, too. At twenty-eight she wasn't willing to say she'd never try again. She wanted to have a partner, maybe even have kids. But for now? Work was enough. Work was almost too much. It barely left time for her to visit with friends, go to movies, the theater, read a book. She was taking herself out of the game.

Determined and damn cold, she walked into St. Marks. The sound of women, of her friends, greeted her the moment she stepped over the threshold. There was a lot of joy to be had in her world, and only a part of it depended on a man.

"There you are," Bree said, grinning as she met Rebecca at one of the long tables. "Charlie bet me you wouldn't make it today. He said the donor dinner is getting too close."

Rebecca started stacking the lunches she'd prepared. "What did you win?"

"Something juicy that would make you blush."

Rebecca was glad not to have to hear the details. Charlie Winslow was her cousin, and while he was her favorite cousin, and she'd played an integral role in getting him and Bree together, there were certain things she'd rather not have in her memory. "As long as you're happy, I'm happy. And he's right. The dinner is driving me insane. I hate this part. I despise having to ask for money."

"Hard to run a charitable foundation without funds," Bree said.

"I know. But it defeats the purpose if I have to wine and dine the donors to the tune of several hundred thousand dollars. That money should be used elsewhere."

Bree, who looked adorable in skinny jeans with a gorgeous camel cowl-neck sweater, patted Rebecca's arm. "You could always serve them dinner á la soup kitchen. As a statement."

"I've considered it. But I really do need their money. Besides, the Four Seasons isn't known for its soup-kitchen ambience."

"Keep thinking about how much good the Winslow Foundation does. Then suck it up."

Rebecca laughed, as Shannon, the most important member of the lunch exchange, came plowing through the door. The redhead didn't know how to make anything but a dramatic entrance.

"I have new cards!" she said, lifting up a box from her family's printing shop. "Brand-new delicious men. You guys have outdone yourselves this time. Truly."

Rebecca pulled out Gerard's card, which had been in the second batch of trading cards. The first exchange had happened in February, a couple of weeks before Valentine's Day. As this was only the group's third exchange, it was too early to say how successful the new venture would be overall, but none of the dates had been disasters, and that was something.

She headed toward the front table where the cards were spread out for the taking, indecisive about putting Gerard back into the mix. For a moment, she was tempted. Tempted to forget she'd decided only minutes ago that she was done with all this. Maybe one more try? But that thought was dismissed the moment she remembered what she had waiting for her back at the office. Even if she wanted to try again, now wasn't the time. The dinner, which was more of a banquet complete with orchestra and dancing, was in just over a week, and if she found time to sleep between now and then, it would be a miracle.

Someone—Bree?—pushed into her from behind into the long table. "Hey, jeez." What was this, sale day at Barneys? Rebecca dropped Gerard's card on top of the pile and was in the process of getting out of the way when a tiny little tap stopped her.

She picked up the trading card resting against her hip. Then she stared. The name on the top was Jake Donnelly. The picture made all her female parts stand up and take notice. So to speak. Because he was the single most attractive man she'd ever seen. Ever. He wasn't the handsomest, but handsome was easy, handsome was proportions and ratios and cultural biases. No, Jake Donnelly was the man who fit *her*. She hadn't realized until right now that she'd carried a blueprint in her brain, made of exacting specifications down to the texture of his eyebrows.

They were on the thick side, dark. As dark as his hair, which was parted, long on the collar, unstudied, and, oh, who was she kidding, it was his eyes. They were an astonishing blue. Not pale, but a vibrant, piercing cerulean. The rest of his face was great, fabulous, a perfect frame; rugged enough that the parts of her that weren't transfixed by his eyes were doing a happy dance about the rest.

A happy dance? Okay, so it wasn't a sale at Barneys, it was high school and she was swooning over the quarterback. Even when she'd been in high school she hadn't swooned. This was unprecedented in every way.

She blinked. Took in a much-needed breath. Looked around. Just like in the movies, sounds returned, the picture in her hand wasn't the only thing in focus and she was Rebecca once more.

Almost.

She turned the card over, found out Donnelly had been recommended by Katy Groft. Rebecca made her way through the tightly packed crowd and sidled up to Katy, an NYU postgrad studying physics.

"Oh, you found Jake."

"Please tell me he looks like this picture."

Katy grinned. "Oh, he's even better."

"Oh, God." Rebecca didn't dare look to see which

category he fell in…marrying kind, dating or one-night stand. Not until she asked "Is he already taken?"

"Nope. You're in luck."

"Thank God. Because wow. He is…"

Katy sighed. "It pains me, it truly does. Because he's a sweetheart and he's funny, decent and very discreet. But he doesn't want a relationship at all. He's extremely private, too, so if that's going to bother you—"

"Private's good. Private and discreet is even better. Can you call him? Oh, he's probably at work now."

"Did you not read the back of the card?"

Rebecca felt a little blush steal across her cheeks. "Um…" She turned it over.

* His favorite restaurant: *Luigi's Pizza in Windsor Terrace.*
* Marry, date or one-night stand: *One night.*
* His secret passion: *No idea. But he's renovating his father's house in Brooklyn between jobs.*
* Watch out for: *Nothing, actually. He was great. I found him through my uncle whom I trust beyond measure.*
* Why it didn't work out: *Nothing scary here. Hot and fun. He's not sure what he's going to do with his life.*

Katy laughed, which made Rebecca tear her eyes away from Jake's picture.

"What?" she asked.

"Nothing," Katy said. "I'll call him right now."

"That would be very, very good."

THE SINK WASN'T COOPERATING. It was a heavy sonofabitch, and he couldn't just drop it into the new vanity,

but the guy on the DIY DVD was talking too fast and
Jake needed to rewind to get that last bit. He shifted the
sink in his arms until it was balanced between him and
the wall, unfortunately on his bad leg, then reached for
his laptop. A second before his finger reached the touch
pad, his walkie-talkie squawked. "Jake?"

Jake swore, which he'd been doing a lot this morning.
This week. This month. It was his father. Again. About
to tell him another idiotic cop joke.

Jake would have preferred not to hear another joke.
Not while he was installing his old man's sink in the new
master bath. In fact, not while he was still able to hear.
But that's not how this gig worked.

He paused the DVD, lowered the sink to the floor and
pressed the transmit button. "Okay, let's hear it."

There was a muffled giggle, a hell of a sound coming
from a man who was sixty-three years old. "How many
Jersey cops does it take to screw in a lightbulb?"

Jake sighed. This particular joke seemed to be stuck
on repeat, as this was the third time he'd heard it in so
many days. "How many?"

Now the laughter wasn't subdued and it wasn't only
his old man laughing. The other two voices belonged
to Pete Baskin and Liam O'Hara, all old farts, retired
NYPD, bored out of their stinking minds and drunk on
nothing but coffee and dominoes. "Just one—" his dad
said.

"But he's never around when you need him," finished
Liam.

The three of them laughed like asthmatic hyenas.
The worst part about it? Someone had to be pushing the
transmit button the whole damn time in order for Jake
to hear it.

"Yo, Old Men?" he said, when he could finally get through.

"Who you calling old?" Pete yelled.

"You three. I'm trying to put in a sink. You know how much this sink weighs? I don't want to hear one more goddamn cop joke, you got it? No more. I swear to God."

"Yeah, yeah," Liam said. "Mikey always said you had no sense of humor."

"Well, I think he's damn funny looking, so I guess he's wrong about that, too."

"I can still whip your ass, Jacob Donnelly," his father said, "and don't you forget it."

Jake went back to the computer, replayed the section about the plumbing, then squared off against the sink. It hung off the wall, so the wheelchair wouldn't be an issue. In fact, the spigot was motion-controlled so his dad wouldn't have to touch anything if his hands were acting up.

Jake had already widened the door leading into the new master bath. It used to be a guest bathroom before his dad's rheumatoid arthritis started getting so bad. The wheelchair wasn't a hundred percent necessary yet, but soon his father wouldn't be able to make it up to his bedroom on the second floor, even with Jake's help.

He picked up the damn heavy sink and moved it over to the semipedestal, the plumbing all neatly tucked behind the white porcelain. It actually set easily, and since he'd been getting better with this plumbing business, he didn't find it necessary to curse the entire time he secured the top to the pedestal.

The problem wasn't the tools, but the pain. As soon as he could, he stood, stretching out the damaged thigh. The bullet had been a through and through, but what they don't say on TV is that it goes through muscle and tendon and veins and arteries on its quick voyage into, in his case, a factory wall. At least the thigh was less complicated than the shoulder wound.

Sometimes he felt as if it would have been better for everyone if the bastard had been a better shot. He rolled his left shoulder as his physiotherapist, Taye, taught him to do, then did a few stretches. This DIY crap had never been his bailiwick, but his dad needed the house to work for him, and the doctors had all thought it would be good for Jake to use his body to build something tangible.

Jake had realized when he was widening the wall that he actually liked remodeling. That was quite satisfying. The actual work itself though sucked like a Dyson.

But this was his life now. Crazy old men on the porch, fixing every problem the world had ever known. It didn't matter that it was March and as cold as hell outside; they kept on playing their bones, the space heater barely keeping them from hypothermia. Of course they had their cold-weather gear on. These men had been beat cops in so many New York winters the cold didn't stand a chance.

Thank Christ for electric blankets. 'Cause Mike Donnelly, for all his bluster, was getting on. It would be good when Jake had the new shower finished. Nothing to step over, nothing his crooked hands couldn't handle. Then he'd be able to jack up the heating bill to his heart's content, shower three times a day if he wanted.

In the meantime, there was plumbing to do. Jake limped over to the laptop and continued the how-to. Two minutes in, his cell rang. It was Katy Groft, which was weird. They'd gone out, it had been fine, but Jake had been pretty damn clear about his intentions. He wasn't one of those guys who said they'd call, then blew it off. None of that bullshit. "Hello?"

"Hey, Jake. Got a minute?"

"Sure."

"I'm sending you a picture."

"Okay." His phone beeped a second later. "Hold on." He clicked over to the photo, and what he saw surprised him even more than the phone call itself. It was... what's her name, the Winslow who wasn't called Winslow. Thorpe. That's right. Rebecca Thorpe. Ran some kind of big foundation or something, was always in the papers, especially the *Post*. What he didn't know was why Katy Groft would want him to see Thorpe's picture. "Okay," he said again.

"This is my friend Rebecca," Katy said. "Interested?"

"In what?"

"Her. Going out with her. You know, a date?"

He stared again at the phone, at the picture. Rebecca Thorpe was a beautiful woman. Interesting beautiful. Her face was too long, her nose too prominent, but there was something better than pretty about her. Every picture he'd seen of her, didn't matter who she was with, she seemed to be daring everyone to make something of it. Of her. Right now, looking at the overexposed camera phone photo, he had to smile. No choice. It didn't hurt that she had a body that struck all the right chords. Long, lean, like a Thoroughbred. "You do realize you called Jake Donnelly, right?"

Katy laughed. "Yes. I'm very aware of who you are. And who she is. And I happen to believe you two would hit it off well. I'm pretty clever about these things. And don't worry, she already understands you're not in the market for anything serious."

So this Thoroughbred wanted to go out with a quarter horse for a change of pace? "She knows I'm busted up, right?"

"Not a problem."

He gave it another minute's thought, then figured, "Sure. Why the hell not?"

"Great. How about the Upstairs bar at the Kimberly Hotel, tomorrow night at eight?"

It was his turn to laugh. "What is this, some kind of gag?"

"No. I swear. She's great. You'll like her. A lot."

He'd have to wear something nice to the Kimberly. But he hadn't worn anything nice in a long time. Before he got shot, that's for sure. "I'll get there a little early. Introduce myself."

"Excellent. You'll thank me."

"I'm already thanking you. For thinking of me. Although I'm still unclear why."

"You'll see," she said.

"Fair enough." He disconnected from Katy, but stared at the picture on his phone for a while. God damn, she was something else.

Katy had been only the second woman he'd been with since he'd been put out to pasture. She'd been great, and if his life had made any kind of sense, he might have pursued more than a onetime thing. But the only thing he knew for sure at the moment was that he was a broken ex-cop without a plan in the world except for rebuilding the house he was born in so his father could live out the rest of his days at home. After that was anybody's guess.

"Hey, Jake?"

He winced at the sound of his father's voice, tinny over the walkie. "Yeah, Dad," he said, his thumb finding the transmit button without his even having to look.

"How many cop jokes are there?"

He shoved his cell into his pocket. "Two," Jake said. "All the rest of them are true."

Laughter filled the mess of a bathroom, and Jake supposed that as far as problems went, having three lunatics telling him cop jokes all day was pretty far down the list.

## 2

REBECCA ARRIVED AT HER building just before 6:00 a.m. She needed coffee and lots of it. Facing her to-do list was not something she was looking forward to but there was no getting around it.

Her suite on 33rd was a behemoth. The size itself wasn't the issue—it was the fussy ostentation that got to her, the image that nearly outweighed their purpose. There was an enormous fresh-flower display next to the huge mahogany reception desk. Warren, the receptionist, wouldn't be in until eight-thirty, and Rebecca's personal assistant, Dani, had been coming in at eight lately, an hour earlier than she had to. It was very, very still with no one else on the floor, but then that wasn't unusual. The air of gravitas was nurtured like a living thing in this fortress.

Rebecca didn't make a sound on the plush burgundy carpeting in the long hallway that led to her office. She swiped her key card, put her briefcase on her desk, her purse in her credenza drawer, and went to the small private room—the truest symbol of how much the founders had prized their creature comforts. She headed straight for the coffeemaker.

Once she'd finished with the prep and pressed the button for the machine to start brewing, she turned and leaned on the counter. There was a huge LED television mounted on the wall across from the deep and supremely comfortable leather chairs, museum-worthy paintings on the muted walls and a couch with such deep bottom cushions that it was more suitable to napping than sitting. Fresh flowers were here as well, replaced weekly by a service that understood decorum while making a point that when it came to the details, no expense was spared. It was as ridiculous as it was sacrosanct.

She was the first woman to ever run the foundation, and her ideas about modeling their business plan after the great philanthropic organizations like the Rockefeller Trust or the Carnegie Group continued to be an uphill war. Picking her battles had been one of her first and most important lessons.

That's why she tried hard not to resent the time and money being spent on the donor dinner. The guest list included most of the *Forbes* top-fifty richest people in the world. They gave millions so that after all these years, their endowments were in the billions. She needed to remember that and just do the job.

Preparing her coffee in her favorite mug soothed her, letting her prioritize the next few unencumbered hours. It wasn't until she took her first sip that her thoughts turned to Jake. And there was a problem.

Not her excitement, that was a pleasure and a rush. It wasn't like her to want a man purely for sex. She was, in theory, at least to quote her mother, above that sort of thing.

*Guess not, Mom.*

When she returned to her desk, instead of clicking

on her email, she got her purse from the credenza and took out Jake's trading card.

Oh, yeah. She wasn't at all sure why, but looking at him made her clench all kinds of important muscles. She hadn't even met him and his face started a chemical spike inside her. The exact same reaction had occurred each time she'd sneaked a peek at his photograph. She refused to acknowledge how often that had been.

The problem was, with this level of excitement over the two-dimensional image, how on earth was the very three-dimensional living man going to measure up?

It was all about narrowing her expectations. She could do that. It wasn't as if she wanted to fall in love with Jake or for him to love her. She hoped to like him, though, because she knew from experience that if he was a complete jerk, her attraction would vanish in an instant.

They were going to meet for drinks and that was to her advantage. She didn't normally indulge to the point of feeling buzzed, but when she did, she became more forgiving. And, if it came down to it, she could probably get him to not talk at all.

She put his card away, determined not to look at it again until after work. Not only was she slammed for time, but she needed to get home early enough to go the extra mile with grooming. Oh, the joys and pains of getting naked with someone new.

She clicked on her email icon, and the sheer number of new messages was enough to chase away any thoughts of sweaty sex. Especially when the first of the emails was from her father. That never ended well.

THE MORNING COFFEE WAS already made by the time Jake limped his way down the stairs. It was freezing outside.

Sitting in the kitchen, his father was bundled up in a thick wool sweater and had a lap blanket tucked around his lower half as he warmed his hands on his old NYPD coffee mug.

"The weatherman says we're in for a cold one tonight."

Jake nodded as he fixed his mug. Two sugars, half and half. He didn't drink until he slid onto the banquette in the breakfast nook. He needed to do something about the cushion covers. They were almost as old as he was and the regular washings had made them threadbare and pale. "I'm going to the city."

"Yeah?" his dad asked.

"Yeah."

"Date?"

Jake drank some coffee, sighing in satisfaction as it warmed him. "Yeah."

"I'll get Liam to spend the night, then?"

"Already cleared it with him. He's bringing over DVDs."

"Ah, shit," his father said, putting his mug down on the counter, then turning his wheelchair a few degrees so he faced Jake. "That means another goddamn Bruce Willis festival. Swear to Christ, Liam has, a whatchamacallit, a bromance, going with that guy."

"What's it matter? Pete's got a hard-on for his car."

"Yeah." Mike picked up his cup again. "Everybody's got something. Except you. What do you got a hard-on for, Jake?"

"What the hell kind of a question is that?"

"Watch the tone. I'm still your father. I'm wondering, that's all. You spent a lot of time wanting to be in vice, then all those years doing undercover work. I'm thinking there's gotta be something else now. Something, please God, more interesting than Bruce Willis movies."

Jake drank some more coffee, not sure how to answer the question. If he should answer at all. But no, he would. He and his dad had spent a lot of years being distant. What with the work, then with Mom dying of cancer, and Jake having to be so hush-hush about everything. He'd decided to fix up the house by himself because he wanted to know his old man. Wanted someone to know him in return. Now was not the time to back off. "I don't know, Dad. I got nothing. Just the house."

"That's not gonna last forever."

"Nope. But it's something to do while I learn how to be a civilian."

"I hear that."

Jake nodded in tandem with his father. It wasn't easy, this talking thing. But dying alone in a warehouse filled with drug dealers wasn't easy, either. He could do this. The worst that would happen? He'd look like an idiot. He already did that without trying. "I've got a date tonight," he said. "She a looker."

"Good for you," Mike said. "Nice woman?"

"Never met her. Comes highly recommended, though."

"Yeah?"

"She's a Winslow."

"*Those* Winslows?" His dad settled his cup snugly on his lap as he wheeled over to the nook. "What the hell does one of those Winslows want with you?"

Jake laughed. "No idea. Looking forward to finding out."

"Probably heard who your old man was. Couldn't resist."

"You keep telling yourself that. See what happens."

Mike awkwardly put the cup on the table, and Jake

held back his wince. It was getting harder for his father to hold the damn mug at all, as his fingers twisted and bent. But there was no use crying about it. There wasn't a cure, and the medicines and physical therapy could do only so much. Retrofitting the house was what Jake could do, was doing.

"You know Sally Quayle? Three doors down, her husband was killed in Afghanistan last year?"

"Oh, no, Dad. Come on. We talked about this."

"We did, and we agreed."

"I'm not goddamn Santa and I'm not the neighborhood fixer. In case you haven't noticed, I'm also busy."

"There's always time to do right. She's worried about being alone. Thinking of buying a gun."

"Ah, crap. You want me to go talk to her."

"I do. We all do. She needs to know how dangerous that could be. Go over her house security. Make sure she's safe, yeah?"

Jake sighed. "Yeah, yeah. I'll go over this week. After I get a good start on the new shower." Why was it the only time Jake sounded like he was from Brooklyn was when he was home? He'd had the accent scared out of him at St. Francis Xavier high school, but it always came back the moment he was in the neighborhood.

"This week is fine. And don't start anything too big on the shower this afternoon. You need to look your best tonight."

"I what?"

Mike sniffed. "You're my only son. And a certified hero. She should know who she's dealing with, this Winslow woman."

What could Jake say? "Sure thing, Dad. I'll shave and everything."

REBECCA PAID THE CAB DRIVER, then got out on East 50th Street at the entrance to the Kimberly Hotel. She'd chosen it because the rooftop bar had spectacular views of Midtown. Also she liked the way they made their gimlets here with a very unique lime cordial. It didn't hurt that their luxury suites were gorgeous, the feather beds to die for. Even if magic didn't happen between her and Jake, she'd enjoy staying the night by herself, and if that happened, she already decided she'd be utterly decadent with room service.

With that in mind, she went inside, her gaze lingering on the lobby's beautiful grandfather clock as she went to the front desk. She handed them her overnight bag and her coat to put in her room. Registration took no time at all and once her key card was in her purse, she went to the lobby restroom. She had to remind herself that whatever happened would be fine, that if he was an ass, she'd lose nothing but a fantasy. Still, she wanted that fantasy, so she freshened her lipstick, fluffed her hair, checked her breath and let her heart pump and her hopes soar as she caught the next ride up.

It was the express to the roof, not giving her much time to think, which was good. There were only three men in business attire aboard, none of them speaking, although she had the feeling they'd been in the same meeting. They all looked as though they'd been to the battlefield and lost and that drinks at the penthouse bar would be a just reward.

Her nerves hit what she hoped was their peak as they reached the thirtieth floor. It was all she could do not to take Jake's trading card out of her purse and hold on to it like a talisman. Not that she wouldn't recognize him. She'd practically memorized his face. He'd look good on the roof with the blue and white fairy lights under the glass domed ceiling, with the city skyline behind him.

Frankly, he'd look good in a crumbling boiler room. But as long as she was making this into some kind of romantic one-night dream date, she might as well have the proper setting.

Another thing she liked about Upstairs at the Kimberly was that the music wasn't deafening. They catered to a more mature crowd and had some respect for eardrums. It was a bar made for getting to know a person.

The elevator opened at one minute past seven. There were several areas where Jake could be. On the main floor, at one of the tables, at the light-bedazzled bar itself or on one of the leather couches to either side of the bar. She ran her hands down her black sheath dress as she walked into the middle of the room. She glanced to her right, and there he was. He'd scored a hell of a table, one close to the window that looked out at the Chrysler building.

It was too dark to see the color of his eyes, but she could tell he looked pretty much as advertised. Dark scruffy hair, broad shoulders with a well-fitting jacket, a light button-down shirt tucked into dark trousers. He saw her and stood, and yep, he had slim hips and long legs. Even at this distance, he was hotter than hell, and *please, please, let this not crash and burn in the first five minutes.*

She hoped he would be equally impressed as she crossed over to him. He took a few steps himself, careful to keep close enough to the table to prevent poaching. It wasn't until the third step that she noticed his limp.

Katy hadn't said anything. Meaning she didn't deem it noteworthy. Rebecca had no problem with that. It was an interesting detail, something to discover by layers.

"Rebecca," he said, and goodness, yes, that was a great voice. Deep and mellow and she thought about one of her recent not-so-wonderful blind dates that hadn't been helped by Sam's unfortunately high and sadly nasal tone.

"Jake," she replied as she took his hand. It was warm and large, and the shake just firm enough. He also knew when to let go. Big plus. He almost touched the small of her back as he held her seat, giving her the best view.

He sat across from her. The candles on the table gave a hint of his eye color, but she'd need real lights for that. Later. Now was for talking. And drinking because her heart was pounding a bit too hard for her to ignore.

Before they had a chance to start the opening volley, a waitress came to the table. Rebecca ordered her vodka gimlet and Jake ordered a bourbon and water. Nice. Traditional. Masculine.

The second they were alone, he leaned a little toward her. "I'm never great with openings," he said. "I've always thought there should be rules, a standard pattern that all blind dates have to follow. Like school uniforms or meeting the queen. It would make things so much simpler."

She thought about her trading card, and how that had helped, and wondered if Jake knew he was on a card, if he'd approve. She thought, yes. "You're right. It's an excellent idea and should be implemented immediately. What say we start with the basics. The front page of the questionnaire. I'm Rebecca Thorpe, I live in Manhattan and work in the East Village. I'm an attorney although I don't practice, and I was born and raised here in the city. I've known Katy for over a year, and she's terrific, so I trusted her when she told me we might hit it off. I'm not looking for love, or for more than an interesting evening, which I hope is what you're after, and...well. That's about it."

His laughter suited her down to her toes. It was genuine, easy, relaxed. His smile was even more delicious than his picture had implied. So far, so good. But now, it was his turn.

"I'm Jake Donnelly, I'm currently living in Windsor Terrace in Brooklyn, in the house where I was born. I'm staying with my dad doing some remodeling work. I come from a long line of cops, all the way back to when the Donnellys crossed over from Ireland. I've been with the police department since I graduated college. Well, until earlier this year. I have no idea what I'm going to do after I finish the renovations."

He leaned back as their drinks were placed on the table, then sought her eyes again. "And it appears we're both looking for a night to remember. How'd I do?"

"Great," she said, then she lifted her glass and clicked it against his. Jake was totally unlike anyone she'd ever dated. He was from Brooklyn, but he'd given up the accent for something far easier on her admittedly snobbish ears. She knew absolutely nothing about being a cop, about Windsor Terrace, about renovations. She was incredibly curious to know if his limp and no longer being a policeman were connected. And she couldn't imagine, not for the life of her, staying with her own family for more than about three hours. She and Jake were worlds apart, completely unsuited in every way but one.

He was *perfect*.

JAKE DRANK A LITTLE AS HE tried not to look as if he was scoping her out from head to toe. But screw it, he was. At least, as much as he could, given she was sitting.

Rebecca Thorpe was, to put it bluntly, off the charts hot. Her hair was golden and shiny in the glitter of the bar, her eyes smoky and intense. She was tall and slender, but the way her dress hugged her breasts made him say a prayer this night would end with him learning a lot more.

No mention of the Winslow name or the foundation she headed. Why not? Being careful? Probably, although why she would assume he didn't recognize her was a little baffling. Everyone who lived in New York knew of her family. They were like the Kennedys. Politicians, judges, private jets, private clubs, more money than sense if you asked him, but nobody did, and that seemed fair. He wouldn't know what the hell to do in a room full of Winslows, but being right here, right now with this one? It was his lucky day.

"I don't know where to start with questions," Rebecca said. "Do you miss being a cop?"

He'd left himself open for whatever with that intro, but he still wished she'd begun somewhere else. He shouldn't complain. At least she hadn't opened with the limp.

He was still self-conscious about the scars. Odd how the shoulder looked so much worse. The leg was no picnic, either. But it hadn't made anyone run screaming. Yet. What the hell, if it freaked her out, there was nothing he could do about that. He'd just get on home and read up on shower installations. "Yeah, I miss it," he said. "Hard not to, when it's the only thing I've ever done. I could have taken a desk assignment, but that wasn't me."

"Ah, so you were hurt on the job?"

He nodded. "Yeah. Shot in the thigh and the shoulder. They're not pretty, but I was lucky. Either one could have killed me, so…"

"I can't imagine. God, shot twice?" She shuddered, winced. "That's horrible. I'm always astonished at how vulnerable the human body can be, while at the same time astoundingly strong. I had a friend once who slipped on a leaf. Fell. Hit her head. She was twenty-four, and she died that night. You were shot twice, and you not only survived, but it looks from here as if you're thriving."

"It is a mystery. I tell people it must not have been my time, but that's just something easy to say. I'm not a religious man, or one who believes in fate. Nothing mystical or predestined. I guess I'm a pragmatist. I was in a dangerous profession, in a risky situation. It's no big surprise I was wounded. I lived because they got to me in time, got me to the right doctors. Thriving? Well, I wouldn't go that far, but I'm learning to accept my limitations. Oddly, there are fewer than I expected, with the notable exception of losing my career."

She didn't respond immediately, but she did lean in. She didn't even try to pretend she wasn't staring, wasn't taking his measure. "A pragmatist," she said eventually. "That's helpful, living in this city. This world."

"It is. What about you?" he asked. "What do you believe in?"

She smiled, leaned back in her chair. Her bangs were a bit in her eyes and he wanted to push them back to see her better. Not complaining, just sorta wishing.

"Boy, you don't fool around, do you?"

"Guess not. We can always talk about this damn cold front, if you'd prefer."

"I'm good," she said. "I like the tough questions."

"I didn't even ask, would you like something to eat? I

haven't looked at the menu, but I know they serve food here. Or we could go somewhere else for dinner."

"Oh, food. I'm not starving, but I could eat something. How about you?"

"I could do with more than the bologna sandwich I had around four. Busy day."

"I happen to know the menu here is excellent. Why don't you see if anything suits your fancy. Meanwhile I'll consider my answer to your very provocative question and finish my drink."

He nodded, grabbed the menu from the center of the table. Not much he didn't like. When he looked up again, she was still staring at him. He should have been unsettled. He wasn't used to undisguised interest. In fact, his life had depended on his blending in, fading into the background. Even the dark wasn't enough to hide behind, but instead of getting that crawling itch to run, he wanted her to look her fill. And he wanted her to like what she saw.

He passed her the menu, then finished his bourbon, signaling the waitress when he caught her eye. "There's nothing on there I wouldn't eat," he said to Rebecca. "Could live without the foie gras, but I like the meat and the fish selections. I think you should pick us out a few, and we'll have ourselves a small buffet while we go at least one step beyond the surface. How does that sound?"

"Fantastic."

Their order was taken, fresh drinks requested, and they were alone once more. It was all he could do not to call back the lovely girl and ask her to add a room with a king-size bed to the tab.

"I'm a mutt," Rebecca said, folding her hands on the shiny table. "Philosophically. I lean toward Buddhism, but I've got some roots in the church from when I was a kid. I mostly try to make a difference. Walk the walk, not just talk about it. I tend to connect to people who do the same."

That could have been a crock of bull, but his instincts said no. She was telling him the truth. It fit with her job, but that wasn't what he thought she was talking about. Another skill from his vice days was how to listen for the truth. Of course, in this instance, he had to factor in how badly he wanted to take Rebecca Thorpe to bed.

Which was really damn bad.

# 3

REBECCA LICKED THE TIP OF her thumb as she finished the last of her salt cod fritter. She'd decided to play hardball with the ordering—all of it finger food. Zucchini fritters, lollipop lamb chops, decadent French fries, even the crisp baby artichokes. She'd picked up a lollipop first thing, watching him watch her bring the food to her mouth, take a bite. Gauntlet thrown, she sipped her second drink and waited to see what he'd do.

He started with a couple of fries. Slow moving, deliberate, and his gaze on hers never wavered. As he chewed, his jaw muscle flexed in a way that made her blush. He couldn't tell, not in this light, yet his thick right eyebrow rose along with the corners of his mouth.

She grinned back, pleased he'd decided to play. Somehow the music had become smoky jazz, and the heat from the temperature-controlled floor slipped up her dress all the way to her very pretty, very naughty La Perla panties.

Through it all, the ordering, the waiting, the cute young waitress flirting with Jake as she set down their plates, Jake hadn't once lost the thread of their conversation. Rebecca wasn't sure if they were at the third or fourth level now that they'd reached ex-lovers territory.

"She was great," he said, using his napkin. "And I like to think I'm a reasonably adventurous guy, but when she started talking plushies…" He shook his head, grabbed a tiny artichoke.

"Plushies. You mean dressing up like stuffed animals plushies?"

"I do. I hope that's not your thing, but I'd have to say right up front that nope, not gonna go there. I like my partners to be human. It's a radical stance, but one I'm not going to budge on."

"Where do you stand on aliens who look humanoid?"

He thought a minute. "Depends. Do they really look like humans, or are they lizard people in disguise?"

"I see your point. I always draw the line at shapeshifters. I include vampires in that, by the way."

"Damn. There goes my plans for the rest of the night."

She laughed again, charmed. Not so much at the obvious quip but at his delivery. Very dry. Very…sexy. "Nothing wrong with a little nip here and there," she said.

He cleared his throat and shifted in his chair. "I agree," he said, putting his napkin on the table. "Now, if you'll excuse me."

As he walked away, Rebecca let herself linger on the breadth of his shoulders, the length of his legs. He might have a limp, but there was still a swagger to him that had her crossing her legs.

When he got back, she would bring up the room. They hadn't eaten too much and had only two drinks each. If they wanted dessert later they could order from room service. Everything about the evening led her to believe he was amenable, even though they hadn't yet touched.

While she could, she retrieved her mirror from her purse. After a fresh coat of lipstick, she stuck a breath strip in her mouth, realizing too late that it didn't go with vodka gimlets. At all. A quick shudder, then she closed her purse, aware of the room itself for the first time since she'd stepped off the elevator.

There was a sizable crowd for a Tuesday night. Most everyone was in business attire, upscale. While she saw people on the prowl, the atmosphere was not that of a pickup bar. Here, the desperation wouldn't start until around 3:00 a.m.

She wondered what Charlie and Bree were doing and almost got out her cell to text, but no, Bree could wait on Rebecca's report. Tonight felt private, different. In other circumstances, she'd have felt this evening was a beginning. She liked him a lot. More than anyone she'd been out with in years.

On the other hand, maybe knowing this was a singular event had made this ease possible. They weren't at a relationship audition. Sex, yes, but she figured they'd nailed that about five minutes in.

The conversation had gone from philosophy to her explaining the intricacies of preparing lunches and trading them at a church basement, and then somehow they'd landed at exes. Hers, she realized, had all fizzled due to boredom. No, that wasn't fair. There had been reasons she'd gone out with those few men for longer than a handful of months, but there had been no grand passions. Weirdly, she'd felt perfectly comfortable telling Jake just that.

There he was. Smiling from across the room. She watched as he maneuvered through people and tables.

When he sat down, he covered her hand with his. "I took the liberty of booking a room here tonight. I won't lie and say I wouldn't be disappointed if you don't want to join me, but I'll also take it like a man."

She turned her hand over and squeezed his fingers. "The only problem with that is I already have a room here. And since I'm the one who instigated this evening, I win the coin toss."

He studied her for a long minute. "Wow. That's... Full disclosure, though. I lied about taking it like a man."

She grinned. God, he was adorable. "If you're finished, why don't I put this on the tab, and we go down to cancel your reservation?"

He fetched his wallet from his pocket. "I'll be taking care of this. But thanks for the offer."

They wrapped it up, he put on a dark knee-length coat she hadn't even noticed, then held the back of her chair while she stood. An old-fashioned move, but one she didn't mind. Especially because she was a little wobbly. Not from the booze; she hadn't had enough to faze her. From the touching. The "any second now, don't know where things are going to go" touching.

After she picked up her purse, he slipped his hand around hers. It wasn't like the handshake, not at all. It was just...wonderful.

WALKING WITH REBECCA TO the front desk reminded him of his prom. Not the dance, but afterward, going into the hotel in Brooklyn with Antoinette Fallucci on his arm. He'd been in a terrible borrowed tux that was too tight in the crotch even discounting the fact that he'd been seventeen, but Antoinette had looked like a princess in her strapless dress, and she'd been the homecoming queen, a cheerleader and without doubt the most beautiful and popular girl in his senior class. He'd strutted into that hotel. This time, he played it a little cooler, but he did feel that thrill, knowing he was with the best one, that every man in the place was jealous.

It had nothing to do with her being a Winslow. The subject hadn't come up and he didn't expect it to. Not when there were so many other interesting things to talk about.

He smiled as they waited for a desk clerk. She smiled in return and he wanted to kiss her. He'd stood close to her in the elevator, gotten a whiff of her perfume, and the effect still sizzled through his veins. He had no idea what the scent was, only that it made him want to spend a hell of a long time exploring that long, graceful neck of hers.

That they'd barely touched was both horrible and hot. He knew she'd be soft, but that was far too vague. How different soft was between the shell of an ear, the skin just under a belly button. His gaze drifted down as he realized there was no word for how it would feel to run his fingers across her inner thigh.

Shit, if he was going to be thinking like that, he should button his coat. Hide the evidence. Thankfully, the woman who'd made his reservation earlier called them to the desk.

"Is something wrong?" she asked.

"We double-booked. Miscommunication. I hope it's not too late to cancel."

"Mr. Donnelly, right?"

Surprised that she remembered his name, he nodded.

"I'll cancel that right now, sir. It'll be a moment."

Jake glanced at Rebecca. He liked that she was tall, five-eight, he'd guess? A six-inch difference was very doable. Not that anything couldn't be worked around.

He signed his name on the line, gave back the key card, and finally, they were free to leave.

"Thank you, Mr. Donnelly."

"Yeah, thanks," he said, tearing his gaze from Rebecca, but he barely gave the other woman a second because his date, this amazing woman in the sleek black dress, tossed her hair behind her shoulder and tugged him along and it was as if the flag had been lowered in a race he hadn't known he was running. It took him two steps to catch up, and when they looked at each other, side by side, gripping each other's hands, they grinned like idiots. Who were going to have sex. Really, really soon.

"Should we order drinks?" she asked as they walked, their speed increasing with each step. "Champagne? Wine? Soda?"

"Wine? Do you like red? Although white would probably be better after vodka. Maybe we should just get some vodka."

"I like red." She pushed the elevator button three times, leaning into her thumb every time. "Besides, you're a bourbon man. Bourbon men don't drink vodka."

"Who told you such obvious lies? Whoever it was should be banished from ever tasting another shot of Stoli. And he shouldn't be able to look at a bottle of Elit."

The elevator dinged and opened. Finally. A couple walked out, ignoring them completely. It was Jake's turn to pull Rebecca inside.

"Then why did you order bourbon?" she asked.

He shrugged, astonished they were speaking in sentences when his brain and his body were one hundred percent focused on getting inside the goddamn room. "I like it."

"Okay." She pushed the button for the fifteenth floor. "What booze don't you like?"

He couldn't stand it, he pulled her until she was flush against him and he was staring down into her dark, wide eyes. "Boone's Farm."

She laughed as she pressed her breasts to his chest. He inhaled sharply at the feel of her, the reality of her. Then her hand, her right hand, slipped under his arm, around his waist and up his back. Without his permission, his hips jerked forward, his quickly hardening cock meeting the perfect resistance of her hip. Each floor they ascended felt like foreplay.

"What about you?" he asked, straining to pick up the thread of their conversation, although he was pretty sure if he started talking about pork belly futures neither of them would care. "Is there anything respectable you don't like?"

"Tons of things. But I suppose you're talking about liquor." Her breath whispered against his jaw, and that hand on his back was moving in small circles, the hint of friction electric. "Oddly," she said, her voice maybe half an octave lower than it had been a minute ago, "single malt Scotch whiskey. I know, it's very girlie of me, but I hate it. What's worse, I get very cranky when people get in my face about how superior it is. The age and what kind of barrel it was kept in. Which is ridiculous because I do the exact same thing with wine and champagne, so who the hell do I think I am? But there you have it. Completely irrational."

"Good to know," he said, now a few millimeters away from brushing his lips against hers. "I was going to seduce you with my knowledge of Glenlivet, but I won't now. Pity. I know a lot about Glenlivet, and I'm incredibly charming when I add the personal anecdotes."

"That's okay," she said, as they came to a smooth halt. "I already find you incredibly charming."

He'd have kissed her right then, right as they stepped out of the elevator, but he wanted it private. Not that anyone was in the hall. It didn't matter. He wasn't going to do anything to this woman until he had her alone and there was a bed nearby. He checked the wall plaque and followed the arrows to room 1562, at the very end of the hall. They didn't run, but they moved as quickly as his leg allowed.

She got the green light with her key card on the second try and he shoved the door open. His first impression of the room was that it was big for a Manhattan hotel and that it was very full with a sofa and chairs and coffee table, but it could have been the size of a pencil box and bright chartreuse and he wouldn't have cared. It was theirs, and while there wasn't a bed in front of him, there had to be one close. Rebecca walked in, but she didn't get far.

As he slammed the door shut behind him, he gave her a spin, a sweet little twirl that set her back against the door with him blocking her path.

Her smile said she didn't mind, and her lips parting as she raked his face with her very large eyes told him they were on the same page. She huffed softly as he slipped his hand behind her nape and his tongue in her mouth.

It was hot slick tongues and broken moans as they tried to get his coat off, both of them reaching at the same time. She scratched his wrist then shoved the coat off his shoulder while he was trying to remove the other side of the damn thing, and he twisted his shoulder in all the wrong ways.

He hissed as he drew back, hating his body so fucking much because he could be kissing her right now instead of this.

"I hurt you."

"You didn't. We did. I just have to be careful." He threw his coat with force onto one of the big chairs, then took off his jacket, as well. He turned his head as he reached for his shirt buttons, but her fingers on top of his made him look.

"We can be careful."

"It's the scars. Left shoulder, right thigh. I can keep my T-shirt on, turn off the lights—"

She slipped the top button through the hole. "Don't worry about my delicate sensibilities. I'm fine. As long as we can hurry up and get back to where we're getting naked together."

Scooping her into his arms, trapping her hands, he kissed her. Not that panic sloppy kissing, which was good, damn fine, but this was something else. This was a preview, a warning. He liked this part, and he was good at it. So he'd take it slow for the next few minutes, because soon, the moment he had that dress off her in fact, it was going to get crazy again. Messy, wet and hot, and while he couldn't do everything he used to, he could do plenty.

Her moan was low as she tussled with his tongue. He moved his hands under her hair until he found the top of her dress, the zipper hidden inconveniently behind a fold of material, but he was using his dominant hand, not the one with the intermittent quaver, so no problem. His cock hardened as the zipper lowered until it hit bottom. The feel of her skin beneath his palms made him groan, but when she pushed her hips against his aching erection, he decided the lesson was over, and all bets were off.

He pulled back, not letting her have another chance with his shirt.

"Fine," she said, chuckling, "be that way." Then she took two steps away and lifted her dress over her head and let it flutter to the floor.

Jake choked. It took him a minute of coughing to get his act together, and when he did, and he looked at her again, he had to consciously remember how to breathe. "Holy God."

"So you're a La Perla fan?"

"I have no idea what a La Perla is, but I'm over the moon about your underwear."

Her grin let him know she'd planned to knock him off his feet with the stunning bra and panties. Jesus, she was still wearing her heels, and the combination was enough to make a weaker man come without a touch.

The garments were sheerest white. Barely there, except for a small triangle that covered her pussy so he couldn't tell what she was hiding. He didn't give a damn. She could be hairy, bald as a cue ball or anything in between, it all worked as far as he was concerned. That he didn't know even with all that flesh on display made him insane.

The opposite was true on top. There was nothing but that sheer, sheer white covering her stunning breasts. Hard little nipples in the center of pink areolas like iced cupcakes with cherries on top.

And while staring at her was a wet dream all its own, there was so much more to be done. He tugged his shirt out from his trousers, toed off his shoes, then his socks, and by the time he'd unbuttoned the shirt with his right hand, his left had undone his belt and was working on his zipper.

Rebecca was most definitely not helping. In fact, she

was making it ridiculously harder to do this circus trick because whether she realized it or not, every move she made turned up the heat a notch. The sway of her hips as she took a single step, the roll of her shoulder, the shake of her head so her hair fluffed around her face. There wasn't a thing about her that didn't make him want to beg.

"You're killing me," he said, his voice as rough as sandpaper. He let his button-down fall, leaving him in his undershirt, and then his pants dropped and he kicked those out of the way.

Her gaze moved down to his thigh even as she ran her fingers over her bare tummy. Jake tensed as he waited for her verdict. She winced, but her hand didn't stop moving. He relaxed. She wasn't freaked out. His first date after had been, and he could never bring himself to blame her, but his gratitude that this woman hadn't run for the hills knew no bounds.

"Are you going to just stand there staring?" she asked.

"I don't know what to do first," he said. "You're stunning."

For all that she was driving him wild, the hint of a blush that warmed her cheeks was almost more than he could bear. "That's a pretty good place to start," she said as she covered the distance between them. "But an even better place would be in the actual bedroom."

He swung his arm around her neck and pulled her into a punishing kiss. His free hand went to the low line of her panties, the covered spot, and he slipped his fingers inside the material.

Ah. Not a full Brazilian then, but a landing strip. They needed to get to the bed before he came standing in his boxer briefs.

# 4

JAKE KISSED HER AS IF HE'D read her diary. All the things she hadn't written down. How that exact pressure made her shiver. How one of her favorite things was when it wasn't only thrusting, but teasing and nipping and licking and just plain wanting to feel *everything*.

His fingers brushing the small trail of hair made her quiver, and God, they needed to stop screwing around. She stepped back from the glorious kiss and took his hand out of her panties. "Now?" she asked. "Please?"

He laughed, dipped somewhat inelegantly to grab his slacks then pushed her along with his hand conveniently placed on her ass.

Finally, there was the king-size feather bed. It wasn't merely a gorgeous thing to sleep on. The plush headboard, which was actually a built-in feature of the wall, made for comfy bracing, if it should be needed. She hoped it would be needed.

"What are you grinning about?" he asked as he spun her around to face him.

"Happy. Excited. Wishing you were very much more naked than you are."

"I can do that," he said. "Here goes—if it's too much

a turnoff—well, I won't need therapy over it." He yanked his V-neck undershirt up his chest, quick, like taking off a bandage.

Rebecca was caught by the view of his slim waist, the lines of his abdominal muscles, the almost-but-not-quite-perfect four pack and the fact that he had actual hair on his chest. She swallowed at the blatant masculinity.

She, in turn, felt, well, gooey. Feminine. Small, hungry, attracted, girlie. She moved closer to him, unable to stop her fingers from touching his dark, slender line of hair that rose from just below his ribs until it spread to lightly cover his chest.

He gasped at the brush of her hand, and she watched his muscles shudder. Then he pulled the shirt off the rest of the way, revealing the scar at the top of his left shoulder. "The bullet barely missed the subclavian artery," he said. "Came in smooth, came out rough, but I was lucky. The doctor says eventually I should regain almost all my mobility."

She appreciated the heads-up. The small wound was puckered, red, shiny, but nothing horrific. Whereas his back, when he turned, wasn't nearly as neat. She exhaled hard, not from disgust but from sympathy. His skin was mottled; that same shiny red here though making it look more like a fresh burn than what it was. She raised her hand again, but paused an inch from his poor flesh.

Her gaze moved down to his thigh. That was a deep gouge, something ripped away, not like the torn and battered scarring on his shoulder. "Will it hurt?"

"To touch? No. It's mostly numb. Not a hundred percent, and sometimes something will press the wrong nerve. But you don't need to worry. That is, if you still want to—"

She leaned in then, letting her fingers brush the

strange terrain as she pressed her lips to the edge of his wound. "I'm sorry you were hurt."

"Me, too." He turned around slowly. "Onward?"

She was the one to cup his face, to ravish him with tongue and teeth and urgency.

"Well, damn." He kissed her again, once, hard, then stepped away, carefully maneuvering the waistband of his briefs over his straining cock. She couldn't look anywhere else but at his darkly flushed erection. There was moisture at the tip, his foreskin barely visible. "I'm going to start begging in a minute," he whispered.

She forced her gaze up. "We wouldn't want that."

He groaned low and loud, his cock jerking against his taut stomach. His hands went to her shoulders, gripping her firmly as he walked her to the bed. He paused before the back of her legs touched the mattress. "Okay, I can't... I love the..." He indicated her outfit with a sweeping glance up, down and up again. "That bra... Amazing. You're amazing. But it's got to go, because there isn't a thing I don't want to see. All right?"

She nodded, not able to do much more because he still held her arms.

Releasing her, he reached around and undid the bra's clasp. Then he kissed the curve of her neck with warm lips as he slipped the straps off her shoulders. The bra fell between them, floated down, touching her skin, and his, too, if his sharp hiss was anything to go by.

His gaze on her breasts, he huffed a breath before he swallowed. "Jesus. Rebecca."

She blushed again. The heat filled her cheeks and where was all her bravado and determination to be in charge of the night? She felt...shy? A little bit. Pleased, definitely. Not that she didn't want his praise, but in a moment she was going to duck her chin and twirl her hair because in all her fantasies of how things would go, she hadn't considered that she'd see him as so much more than the man on the card. She liked him, and even though there wasn't going to be a second date, she wanted him to like her in return. Not only the sex, but *her*.

She sent her panties to rest on top of her bra. The only thing he couldn't see now were her feet but that would change in a minute. He grinned, like he had in the hallway, and fell into a cloud of white down, bringing her along for the ride.

They kissed, deeper now, possessive and exploring and hungry. He sucked the very tip of her tongue, showing her how good he was with small things.

There were hands at play as well, hers brushing over his arms, his sides, down to the tapered waist and slim hips. She loved hip bones with their curves and shapes, but more than that she loved the unlimited access. She suspected he'd let her do anything, feel him anywhere. She could paint his toenails blue and he'd stay hard to the last little piggy. And if he wanted to return the favor? She'd probably quiver so much she'd have nail polish up to her ankles.

She laughed while he was teasing her lips, and he pulled slightly away. "What?"

"I'm already having the best time ever. You're…" She sighed. "You're fantastic."

The sound he made wasn't a word, but when he turned them both so she fell back on the feather bed, she gathered he liked the compliment.

"Condoms," he said. "Pocket." Then he rolled off the bed to his feet, and she got a show of his extraordinary butt as he rifled his trouser pockets.

"My," she said, when he turned around. His cock

looked exceptionally eager. It was well proportioned, longer and thicker than average, and it was straining so that with every move it tapped his belly, leaving a trail of liquid excitement behind.

She rose to her knees, unable to lay back passively when she was as eager as he was to discover the next sensation, to taste and to touch and to let herself be carried away.

He got back on the bed, ripping open the condom as he shuffled to the center, then he brought his lips so close to her ear she shivered with the warmth of his breath. "I want you to ride me. The first time. So I won't miss a thing."

Rebecca nodded. She'd thought it might be easier for him with his injuries, but that wasn't her main consideration at the moment. She wanted to watch him, as well. See the expression on his face as he entered her. "You need to put that on," she said, touching the rubber.

Jake slung another pillow where his head was likely to land, then eased the condom on his cock, hissing the whole time. As he straightened his legs, he put his hand on the base of his prick, holding it steady, and he eased back, his head canted so he would have a perfect view.

Rebecca wasn't particularly showy in bed, always a little too self-conscious, but something about Jake... Still on her parted knees, she took hold of her right nipple with her fingers. Two fingers. Her nips were hard enough that when she squeezed them, the tip poked out, swollen and dark pink.

"God damn," he said, his voice an endearing combination of breathless and raspy.

Her free hand moved slowly down her chest to her

tummy. She circled her belly button, then walked two fingers down and down until they reached her landing strip. She hadn't stopped with the nipple play, so Jake's gaze was going up and down, his lips parted as his breathing became more ragged.

He couldn't seem to help moving the hand on his cock. He stroked himself and it must have felt dangerous because the muscles in his jaw tightened and so did the tendons in his neck. Then he closed his eyes, groaning as if she were killing him dead. "Rebecca. I'm already going to embarrass myself with how fast I'm going to come. Do you really want that to happen before I'm inside you?"

She removed her hands from her body and she felt flushed with more than anticipation. She liked driving him crazy. Which was only fair. She was feeling kind of nuts herself.

"Point taken," she said. She crawled close to his body so she could kiss him one more time. It started slow and sensual, but it turned into hot and burning in seconds. "Ready?" she asked, her voice a breathy whisper.

"Dying."

She got into position, took over for his steadying hand by reaching behind and lowered herself so slowly her thighs trembled. Watching him every second.

His pupils were huge, his nostrils flared, his lips were parted and he sounded as if he'd just finished a marathon. It was fantastic.

She didn't want to look away from his face, but movement down below forced the issue. It was his muscles. Pectorals, abdominals. Clenching, trembling. Chest rising and falling like a piston, and there was a sheen of sweat that made her feel like the Vixen Queen of Planet Earth.

As much fun as it had been to watch him unravel, now all her attention had switched to her own body. Because, whoa. He wasn't lying there anymore, he was thrusting. Up. His hands had somehow gripped her hips when she wasn't looking, and he was moving her to suit himself. She didn't mind. At all.

"God, you're gorgeous," he whispered, and that was the voice she'd remember. The wobbly, wrecked croak that was just this side of recognizable speech. "Hot and wet and, Christ, when you grip me like that. Dammit… warn me next time. No, don't warn me. Do anything you want. Just make sure I haven't passed out. I don't want to miss any…ahhh."

That made her tighten like a vise and she leaned forward enough to where his cock rubbed her perfectly. She'd been so close that all it took was a slight thrust with her hips and she was coming, her head thrown back, her mouth open and gasping, keening in a pitch she didn't recognize.

When she could see again, she realized he'd come, too, and she'd wanted to watch. Dammit.

She fell sideways, sprawling, gasping away. She managed to turn her head to find him looking at her. Grinning like a very satisfied kid at Christmas. "That was…"

He nodded.

"Again?"

His eyebrows rose and he blinked at her. "I'm thirty-four, not seventeen."

"How long?"

He breathed for a while. Then grinned. "Give me half an hour. I'm feeling inspired."

"I'll order drinks."

"See if they have Red Bull."
She laughed. "I'm sure they can oblige."

Well, how was it?????

OMG, Bree! Lunch? Here? 1:30?

Ur making me wait? I HATE u!

U do not. Bring caffine & IV.

LOL. C U later.

REBECCA CLICKED OFF HER phone as she stared at her open briefcase. It felt as if she was forgetting something, but given the lack of any sensible amount of sleep, she had no chance of remembering. She shut the damn thing, aware of how much work she'd skipped in order to indulge her libido last night, then put on her coat. She'd meant to have been at the office for hours by now.

It had been worth it, though. She grabbed her purse and briefcase. There was no one in the elevator, but that would change as she headed down. It was eight-thirty already; she wanted the espresso she hadn't had time or patience to make for herself. The elevator stopped two floors down from her twenty-eighth-floor condo, and she exchanged the traditional noncommittal, no-need-to-speak smile with the man who was exceedingly proud of his Swiss watch. She had at one time known the brand, but all she could remember now was that it cost over a million bucks, and that this guy with his salt-and-pepper hair and his cashmere coat took every opportunity to flash his prize possession. It reminded her of a girl with a new engagement ring.

The elevator stopped at almost every floor, and everyone got very chummy by the time they reached the lobby. She was, of course, stuck in the back, and Mr. Swiss Watch's back was squishing her boobs. Thank goodness for the layers of coat and clothes between them because she only wanted to think about her boobs in terms of last night and Jake.

She smiled as she crossed the lobby, nodding at the concierge and the doorman before hitting the street. It was freezing even though there was no snow left on Madison Avenue.

What she should have done was immediately get in line for a cab, but what she did was cross the street, swimming with the tide of dark coats and clicking heels, to Starbucks. Inevitably there was a long line, but she was desperate.

While she waited, she took out her cell phone and called Dani, her assistant, who would be wondering where the hell Rebecca was. Dani would have called her by nine, but not before.

"You okay?" Dani asked immediately.

"Headache. Late night. Everything okay there?"

"Except for your to-do list, everything's great. Mr. Turner called, of course."

Rebecca sighed. Turner was in charge of catering at the Four Seasons. "What now?"

"Something to do with the gift baskets for the guests, but he wouldn't tell me what because I'm either a spy for another hotel or an idiot, I'm not quite sure."

"I'll call him when I get in. Do me a favor?"

"I'll start the coffee in fifteen minutes. Are you getting something to eat?"

"Yes, thanks."

"See you soon."

Rebecca tried not to yawn, which made her yawn, and then she decided, the hell with it, she was going to think about Jake. To say he'd left an impression was… well, leaving him at the crack of dawn had been ridiculously difficult.

They'd been outside, on a very public street, and still she hadn't been able to stop kissing him. She'd blamed him, of course, said it was all his fault, but it hadn't been. She'd gotten all tingly the moment her lips met his. Tingly. God, who even said that. No one, that's who.

The one very good thing he'd done was not ask for her phone number. Because that would have been stepping over the line. Last night was a one-night deal. Okay, so they'd technically had sex this morning in the shower, but that went under the rubric of one-night stand, so there was no need to get picky about it. The essence of the agreement, from both sides, had been that it was to be a singular event. Nothing more. One incredible, fantastic, amazing, toe-curling night. The end. Anything else was out of the question.

It would have been different if she was the kind of woman who regularly practiced recreational sex. She knew a lot who did, but she wasn't one of them. First of all, she had too much on her plate as it was, and second, it never worked, not really. *Sex and the City* tried to glorify it, but in the end, all that fooling around didn't amount to much.

She'd rather do without, thanks.

But goodness, if there was ever a man who appealed in a *Sex and the City* way, it was Jake. She closed her eyes as she pictured the way he'd looked at her with so much hunger she'd forgotten how to breathe. His hands on her bottom in the shower, such big hands, and such a very hard cock—

"Hey, lady, move it. Some of us got jobs to go to."

Rebecca's eyes jerked open, her face flushed with heat, even though she knew no one could tell what she'd been thinking, but her voice was firm and in control as she ordered the biggest espresso they made. And a lemon bar.

"LEAVE IT ALONE, OLD MAN."

"I didn't say a word." Mike Donnelly rolled himself out of the path of the coffeemaker.

"I'm in no mood," Jake said, filling his cup for the third time since he'd gotten up.

His father looked at his watch again. Jake knew it was noon. So he'd gone to bed the minute he'd gotten home, what of it. He wasn't missing out on a day of work. And he'd already called to reschedule his physio appointment.

"You're not gonna tell me anything? Not you had a good time, the dinner was crap, nothing?"

"The dinner was great, I had a terrific time and I'm not seeing her again, so what difference does it make?"

"Oh. What happened? She say something?" He leaned forward, his eyes wide. "You say something?"

"No. Neither of us said anything. It was the deal. That's all. It was never going to be more than the one night."

"Oh. So you work these things out ahead of time, huh? Like something in your day planner or your Black-Berry appointment book."

"I don't have a day planner or a BlackBerry. Pa, it's no big deal. It was a setup, we had a nice night. She was…great. Really great. But no more than that."

"Huh."

Jake let out a hell of a sigh. "What?" He sat down at the nook, his thigh killing him. Worth it, though. Every ache and every pain. He'd do it again in a heartbeat. Which wasn't an option.

"You liked her."

"I just said that, yeah."

"No. You *liked* her."

"Dad, you have guests out on the patio. Go play dominoes."

"Pete and Liam, guests? That'll be the day."

"What are you trying to tell me? I've got a headache, and if I have to listen to you any longer, I'm gonna turn around and go right back to bed."

"I'm not trying to tell you anything, big shot. I know my boy, that's all."

Jake squinted at him over the rim of his mug. "Meaning?"

"Sometimes something prearranged can be rearranged. That's all I'm saying."

"You been watching those soap operas again? I'm not looking to rearrange my life."

"Okay, fine. Be that way. I'm going to have lunch with my friends."

"Knock yourself out." Jake sipped his coffee until he was alone in the kitchen. The stupid thing was he did want to see her again. Ridiculous. The two of them, they might have been great between the sheets, on top of the sheets and in the shower, but outside of that, what did they have in common?

Okay, except for film noir. That had been a hell of a surprise, Rebecca loving those old black-and-white movies. She knew a lot about them, too, and yet she hadn't even heard of *Stranger on the Third Floor*. It was the first film-noir thriller, and anybody who loved the genre as much as Rebecca should have that in her collection.

And yeah, she'd been completely interested when he'd told her about the secrets of Manhattan. Lived there her whole life, never knew what was right under her feet. He'd told her a few of the places, like the whispering gallery in Grand Central Terminal and she'd barely scratched the surface of Central Park, especially the Ramble, his favorite spot.

He could hardly believe they'd spent so much time talking last night. The in-betweens had been for refueling, but for two people who'd just met, they'd gotten on like a house on fire. Maybe being naked helped. He'd like to do more of that. Not instead of the sex, because Jesus, that had been spectacular, but he hadn't connected with a woman, with anybody, like that since college.

He finished off his coffee, then got out his phone. He didn't have Kenny on speed dial, but it was close.

"Jake, my man. What's up?"

"You still doing that motorcycle messenger thing?"

"Nah, I'm designing webpages for geeks now."

"You wouldn't want to make a delivery to Midtown for, say, a fifty?"

"When?"

"Now."

Kenny turned off whatever the hell noise had been in the background. "Sure. Why not? The business is just getting started."

Jake knew "the business" was housed in Kenny's grandmother's basement, and if Kenny had a client, it was a relative or someone who owed him money. "Great. See you in ten."

# 5

ALL THE CAFFEINE IN THE world might have been enough
to keep Rebecca from zoning out while she looked at
the spreadsheet for donations to date, but she didn't have
access. What she did have was about two minutes until
Bree would arrive, and that would help.

Bree had already been a friend when Rebecca had
decided to play matchmaker between Bree and Charlie,
and now that they'd been a couple for almost a month,
Bree and Rebecca had gotten even closer.

The best part of Bree was that she made Charlie so
very happy. Of all the relatives, and God knew the Winslows did like to procreate, Charlie was the best of them.
He was also the most notorious, being the editor in chief
of *Naked New York,* a blog that virtually everyone in
Manhattan depended on to find out what was happening in the city.

It was fascinating to watch the changes her cousin
continued to go through during his weird courtship with
Bree. He'd been an unswerving commitment-phobe,
ready to die on his sword before he'd succumb to a romantic attachment. Until Bree.

Which was one of the big reasons Rebecca had decided to stop actively putting herself out there for dates. It was a very Zen decision. The universe would provide, and in the meantime she'd relax about the whole life-partner thing and enjoy herself with Jake. With men like Jake.

She sneaked yet another glance at his trading card picture, and her sleep-deprived mind went directly to the memory of riding Jake like a rodeo queen. Holy—

"Incoming."

Rebecca jerked at her assistant's voice coming over the intercom. Good. Bree had brought them lunch, including a Red Bull, which would keep Rebecca going for another couple of hours. She had to be on her game today. Every day. Last night had been a horrible lapse in judgment as far as work was concerned. Personally, she had no regrets. It had been the best blind date in her life. One of the hottest dates, period. Just thinking about him made her want to pick up the phone right this—

"Wow, you look like crap," Bree said as she crossed the office. "You must have had an incredible date."

Rebecca ignored the dig because it was completely true and concentrated on her friend. Bree was a tiny thing, maybe five feet, but she carried herself with such panache, dressed herself with so much bravado and flair, that her short stature was always a surprise.

Today she had on superskinny black jeans, four-inch black heels, a white single-button jacket, which was all well and good, but the kicker was the sizzling chartreuse satchel purse and a matching wraparound belt. The outfit was one hundred percent Bree, as was the new do. "Hey, you did stuff to your bangs."

"I did," Bree said. "Little teeny tie-dye at the edges." She put her big purse on Rebecca's desk, then dragged over the wing chair so they could share the space as they shared their lunch. "Wanna see?"

Rebecca stood up and leaned over while Bree did the same. There were at least four colors teasing at the tips, including the brilliant chartreuse, cerise, blue and white. "Fantastic. How long did that take you?"

"Forever." She pulled two Zabar's bags from her purse, a Red Bull, a Dr. Brown's cream soda and a stack of napkins. The unveiling of the meal was done sitting down. Pastrami and Swiss on rye with spicy mustard, a half-dozen dill pickles, a container of potato salad with two plastic forks and, for dessert, four chocolate rugelach.

Rebecca was tempted to start with the cookies; instead, she opened the energy drink.

"So talk to me," Bree said, taking her half of the sandwich and two pickles. "And let me see the card again."

Since the card was already next to her computer keyboard, Rebecca obliged before she grabbed her own food.

"Holy mother of pearl, this guy is so gorgeous I can't stand it." Bree looked up. "Was he even close?"

"Better," Rebecca said, and the sigh that came out after the word made Bree laugh.

"Details, woman."

"He's a cop. Was a cop. Shot, in the line of duty, if you can believe that."

"You're kidding."

"Nope. He wouldn't tell me too much about it, but he was hurt so badly he had the choice of early retirement or a desk job. He retired."

"Where?"

"To the family home, which he's remodeling for his father, who has something. Uh, wait, oh. Rheumatoid arthritis. Poor guy. Nice, though, huh, that Jake's fixing up the house?"

"I meant where was he shot?"

"Oh." Rebecca took a bite of her sandwich before moving on. She was clearly buzzed from the gobs of coffee she'd downed all morning, and now she was giving herself another big dose of caffeine. Eating was no longer optional. She couldn't be flying around the room when her two-o'clock arrived. She ate for a bit, even though she could see Bree was impatient, but finally, she said, "In the shoulder and the thigh."

"Ouch, ouch."

"I'll say. Not that he let it slow him down. Jeez Louise, he's got some stamina. And a killer body."

"Have you ever dated someone like him before?"

"What do you mean?"

Bree took a sip of her soda, then tilted her head to the right. "A blue-collar guy."

Rebecca shook her head. "It made a nice change."

"Did you talk at all?"

"Yes, we talked. What, you think I'm such a snob I can't talk to anyone without an Ivy League degree?"

"It wasn't about you being a snob. I'm wondering if there was any common ground."

Putting down her sandwich for a moment, Rebecca smiled. "We not only had a lot in common, but he was really interesting. Even without discussing his work."

"For example?"

"Films, for one."

"He likes those old black-and-white movies you're so annoying about?"

"A lot, it was— Hey!"

"Sorry to bother," Dani interrupted via the intercom. "But you've got a package."

Rebecca frowned. "It can't wait?"

"It's personal," Dani said. "And I think you're going to want to see it."

"Okay, come on back."

Not a minute later, the office door opened, and there was Dani, looking sharp in her Chanel-inspired suit, her dark hair pinned up in a very sixties chignon. More noteworthy was the vase she held, filled with what looked like a dozen white calla lilies.

Rebecca realized instantly who they were from. That sneak. She hadn't given him her cell number or her work address, although she supposed she was incredibly easy to find. What did it matter? He'd remembered.

"Wow, those are gorgeous," Bree said, as they watched Dani set the glass vase on the end of Rebecca's credenza. "Are they from him?"

"Have to be." Rebecca went around the desk to look for a card.

Dani handed her an oversized envelope. "This came with it."

Suddenly flushed, Rebecca turned just enough that she could see the beautiful flowers and keep her reaction private as she opened the package. God, it would really be embarrassing now if it turned out Jake hadn't been the one to send it, but nope, the moment she saw the DVD cover, she knew. *Stranger on the Third Floor,* starring Peter Lorre.

Jake had been surprised that she didn't own it. With a collection of film noirs like hers, she should have what he referred to as the first "true" example of the genre. The conversation had been as enthusiastic as two punch-drunk disgustingly horny people could manage, especially when one of them was fingering the other blissfully as he spoke. What shocked her even more were the flowers.

"So?" Bree asked from directly behind Rebecca. "What is it? Where did he even find calla lilies? It's still winter."

Rebecca handed her the DVD. "It's from the film," she said, pulling out the note that was still in the envelope.

"Calla lilies are featured in a Peter Lorre picture?"

"*Stage Door.* Katharine Hepburn. They're my favorite flowers."

"Ah," Bree said even as Dani said, "Wow," but Bree went on. "Ten bucks says he wants an encore."

"I'm not taking that bet," Dani said. "Who the hell is this guy?"

Rebecca opened the plain note card.

Hey, Rebecca,
How about we go crazy and try this thing one more time. Dinner? You say when and where?
Jake.

His number followed. That was it. That was enough.

Bree was next to her now, and there was no way she hadn't seen Rebecca's grin or the way her cheeks must still be flushed with pink. "Oh, yeah. You owe me ten bucks," she said. "I like his style. You need to go out with him again."

Rebecca stuffed the note back in the envelope. "Not possible," she said, turning to face her friend. "We'd better finish up eating because I've got a fussy catering manager to deal with at two, and I need more sustenance. And more sugar." She went back to the desk, Bree following.

"No one's gonna tell me, huh?" Dani said. "Fine. No problem. I'm only the minion. I'll go clean the mirrors in the executive lounge or something. That'll be good."

Rebecca's first thought was to make sure Jake's trading card wasn't visible. Not because she didn't want Dani to know; their relationship was a good one, and while they didn't hang out together after work, they did their fair share of girl talk. But hot guys trading cards was like *Fight Club*. The first rule is that you don't talk about it. "He's a nice guy. A friend of a friend. Nothing serious. In fact, it's all in the past tense now."

"Those flowers seem pretty present to me," Bree said. "And a movie with Peter Lorre as The Stranger? That alone is worth at least one more round."

Rebecca took a large bite of sandwich as she sat down, purposefully ignoring the rolling eyes and shaking heads of her friends.

"Does Mr. Nothing Serious have a name at least?"

"Jake," Rebecca said, at the same time as Bree.

"Jake." Dani grinned as she went for the door. "Sounds hot."

That was the problem. He was too hot. And she had a banquet to coordinate and a foundation to run. There was a dinner at NYU she had to attend tonight, then tomorrow night she was going to have a preliminary crack at William West, her primary target for this year's new major donor at yet another fundraiser. The first night she'd even have free was Friday, and by then, if she lived that long, she'd have to pay through the nose to have her hairdresser come to her place so she could work while she was coifed.

It was impossible, that's all. Jake was a one-hit wonder. It was a damn shame, but there it was.

"WOULD YOU LIKE SOMETHING to drink? Coffee? I have some tea, I think, but I'd have to check. But coffee is already made and it's so nice of you to come over." Sally Quayle wrung her hands together. "I get so frightened, what with the news and the stories. Someone was robbed only three blocks away, did you hear? Albert Jester, he was robbed in broad daylight. Drug addicts. They're everywhere. They have no shame, no boundaries."

Jake hadn't had nearly enough sleep to be paying a house call, but he smiled as he gently herded his neighbor toward her kitchen. "Coffee would be nice, thanks. Then we can talk about security. How would that be?"

Sally pressed her hand to her chest as she nodded. "I'll fix you right up. It's freshly brewed, not even fifteen minutes ago."

"I'm sure it'll be great," he said, and he drew out a chair at the table and sat down. Everything still hurt this afternoon and he should have gone back to bed, but he'd never be able to sleep now that he'd sent the DVD to Rebecca. She would call. Why wouldn't she? Even if it was to tell him there wasn't a chance in hell, she wasn't the kind of woman to ignore him. Not after the night they'd had. Besides, she'd thank him for the flowers and the movie. At the very least.

He reached for his cell, twisting his bad shoulder in the process with a move that normally didn't hurt. He needed to make an appointment with Taye, who would read him the riot act while taking great joy in torturing Jake's poor muscles. He had to call soon, too, because lifting that new shower into place? Bending to fix the plaster and the pipes? Not gonna happen until he could move without wanting to punch a hole through a wall.

No calls. Which he already knew. He'd have heard the ring.

"Here you go, Jake." Sally put a big purple mug in front of him, then brought over a little plastic tray that had sugar and milk and a spoon. She took a seat, cradling her own mug in two slightly trembling hands. "My sister's brother-in-law says a Walther PPK pistol is the only way to go. It's what the secret agents use, and spies should know."

Jake put a couple of spoonfuls of sugar in his coffee, then added his milk, thinking about the best approach. She was scared right down to her toes, grieving a death that had happened thousands of miles away, that had to feel completely unreal, and there was no way he was going to let her get her hands on any kind of gun.

"Here's the thing about guns, Sally," he said. "Most people who own guns think they're safe…they figure they can handle anything that comes at them. So they don't bother with the extra dead bolt or the window blocks. And then, if someone does break in, because they've skipped over the houses that have obvious security, the gun owner is so scared, so terrified, either they end up shooting themselves or the perpetrator manages to take the gun from them."

"Oh, but—"

"Sally," he said, lowering his voice, making it as gentle as he could. "The very best way I know of, and remember, I've been a police officer for a long, long time, is to make sure no one ever gets into your house. Ever. We can do that, you and me. I have a friend who's an expert at putting together home security systems that are affordable, but most of all, they're reliable. What do you say we tackle this problem with the best information available, so that you can go to sleep knowing you're safe. Nothing is one hundred percent in this world, but this security system? It's got backups to the backups."

She stared at him for a long while, swallowing enough that he knew she was fighting off tears. Her husband had been a nice man. He shouldn't have died so young, left her on her own. At least she had family. And friends. Living on Howard Street, nobody was too alone, unless they made sure of it themselves, because this was a real neighborhood. As if it had been transported from another era, a time when checking up on one another was like getting groceries. Just something you did.

He took out his wallet, wincing as he moved his damn shoulder again, and brought out a card that had been sitting in there since he'd gotten out of the hospital. He pushed it across the table. "In case you feel the need to talk to someone. This guy? He's a grief counselor and he's supposed to be one of the best. He works with cops, and I've heard he also counsels spies."

Sally's smile told him she wasn't fooled by any of this. But maybe she'd make the call he hadn't been able to. "So what are window blocks?" she asked.

Jake took one last look at his phone, then put it aside as he started explaining the basics.

SHE WAS CRAZY. REBECCA WAS crazy and insane and she should have her head examined. She was also incredibly late, and Jake was going to be here in fifteen minutes, and she hadn't even showered yet.

Rebecca tossed her purse on her bed, kicked her shoes off then dashed to the bathroom, where she started the shower. In record time she'd stripped, put her hair up because there was no time and washed herself from the face down. She'd just shaved this morning, thank God. Shower off, she grabbed her towel and wrapped it around her body as she sat down at the vanity. She'd never done an elaborate job on her makeup except for special occasions and it took her a minute to decide whether tonight's encore presentation counted.

Nope. He'd clearly liked what he'd seen Tuesday night, so she went with the regular. As she smoothed on her blush, she went over what she had to do before he arrived. The plan had been to make dinner together. Homemade pasta with wild mushroom ragout, salad, dessert, the whole nine yards.

That plan had been ditched at four this afternoon, when the orchestra that was set to play for the donor banquet, which was only five days away, had canceled. The reasons were irrelevant, but her schedule, which had included setting out everything so that the actual cooking could be done quickly, had been replaced by her purchase of a very excellent pappardelle with wild mushroom sauce from Felidia in Midtown, and dessert was now a tiramisu agli agrumi. She and Jake would make the salad together. That could be cozy, right?

At the thought of his name, Rebecca shivered. A little frisson that raced from her brain straight down until it made her squeeze her legs together. It had been like that since he'd sent the flowers. No, that wasn't true. It had been like that since she'd sat down at the Kimberly Upstairs bar.

He was terribly distracting at the worst possible time. Every minute her mind wasn't engaged on a specific task, it was on Jake. His hands, the way he'd kissed her, his ass—oh God, that butt was to die for. Unless it was his laugh that stole her attention, or the way his speech quickened when he was talking about the things he loved, like secrets of New York, like films.

She had to get dressed. Now. She finished off her makeup with a couple of swipes of mascara, then a matte

lipstick that would stay put. She bent over and shook out
her oh-so-straight hair, then flipped it back and done.

Standing in front of the closet wasn't so simple.
There were too many choices. Sexy with an eye toward
a slower striptease? Something so low-cut the edge of
her red lace bra would peek out? Skinny jeans and a
loose sweater with mile-high heels?

She went with the loose-fitting but very low-cut pale
gray sweater over black skinny jeans with black heels
she wouldn't dare wear if she had to walk any real distance.

She had to suck it up to get the jeans zipped, but the
package came together well. None of the mirror views
were horrible, not even from the rear, and what was she
forgetting?

Food, check. Wine. Wine! She rushed to the kitchen
and got the bottle of cabernet from the rack. She un-
corked it, wishing she'd thought of this before she'd
showered, but she'd already planned on giving him some
icy-cold vodka for the prep stage. Only one small glass,
because neither of them needed to have a hangover, but
she knew the vodka would be a hit.

She twirled around her kitchen, the big butcher-block
island empty for the moment. Jake was probably minutes
away, so she went fast.

First, though, music. A wonderful collection of movie
soundtracks, themes from *Laura, Picnic, The Postman
Always Rings Twice* and more. Then, the kitchen. The
wooden salad bowl came out first, then the cutting board
and knife. He said he was bringing everything for the
salad, including the dressing. Then she got out plates,
bowls, dessert plates, including two trays so they could
eat and watch the movie at the same time. Wineglasses

came down, and she willed the cabernet to breathe faster because the clock was ticking.

The call from the lobby stopped her halfway between the island and the fridge, where she'd meant to get out the wedge of parmigiana cheese, kicking up her heartbeat. He was here, and she was more nervous than she'd been for the blind date, more nervous than she'd been for her very first date.

She picked up the phone and told the front desk that yes, Mr. Donnelly was expected. She hung up and debated sneaking a quick shot of vodka to calm the hell down. How ridiculous. She already knew the night was going to be great. She'd do her best not to stay up too late because she had to work tomorrow even though it was a Saturday. He already knew what she looked like naked, and he probably couldn't have cared less about her decor or the food or anything but the chemistry they'd already established.

It was one more night. A bonus. That's all. Just for fun.

The bell rang, and she grabbed on to the back of the couch to steady herself before she walked over to the door.

# 6

JAKE WIPED HIS FREE HAND down his jeans as he waited
for Rebecca to open the door. Jesus, the building was
incredible. He'd known it would be from the Madison
Avenue address, but he'd had no real idea until he'd
walked inside. It was a universe away from his old man's
house. This was a high-rise with all the bells and whis-
tles, and he couldn't imagine ever having enough money
to live there. Only two condos per floor, for God's sake.
A concierge. Museum-quality art in the lobby.

He hadn't thought about it much, her being a Winslow. She'd never known anything but luxury and ex-
travagance. He'd met people in her tax bracket before,
but they were mostly drug dealers, and there were typically a lot more automatic weapons involved. So his only
frame of reference for this kind of life was the movies.

She didn't seem like someone ultrarich. Especially
when she was naked and spread for him, pulling him
down as she pushed herself into his thrusts.

Maybe he'd try not to greet her with a hard-on, that
would be nice. Polite.

She opened the door and one look at her lost him that

battle. Christ, she was even more stunning than he remembered, and he had a great memory.

"Hey," she said, but she was grinning when she said it.

"Hey."

"Come on in."

He took a deep breath and went for it. God damn, but she was something in those heels, in that sweater. It wouldn't bother him at all if they skipped the dinner and went right to dessert.

"You can put that on the island," she said, nodding at the big grocery bag he'd brought. He was in charge of the salad, and he'd spared no expense. That thought made him chuckle as he put the bag down in a kitchen that would have looked at home on the cover of a magazine. With his hands free, he turned back to Rebecca and drew her close. "You're even more beautiful than I remember."

"It's only been three days."

"Extraordinarily more beautiful." He captured her lips in the act of smiling, knew without looking that her cheeks were flushed. She tasted clean and mint fresh, her tongue eager as they kissed as if they'd been apart for weeks.

Her hand moved to the back of his neck, her fingertips sneaking up his scalp, messing his hair and not helping the erection issue at all.

Sadly, she had on far too many clothes, and why were they making dinner when he could have brought a pizza with him? He didn't care about food, not when she was here and there was a bedroom so near.

She was the one to step back, although she paused before she did so. Her eyes were still closed as they breathed each other's breaths. It was all he could do not to close the distance, to take her mouth again and more, but this was her party. As she let go of him, a biting sharp pain shot through his shoulder.

Rebecca cleared her throat, looked over at the island and quickly back at him. "I can hang up your coat."

He obliged and while she went off to a closet in the foyer, he glanced around. The whole place was like something from *Architectural Digest*. Windows everywhere topped with white, scarlet-edged drapes that didn't block the view at all. He couldn't help stepping closer to the window past the dining room table. Spectacular. The Morgan Library was half a block away on 36th Street. When he turned his head to the right, there was the Empire State Building, its tower all lit up.

He then took in the living room. White furniture, white walls with that same brilliant red echoed in the pillows. The area rug was red and white geometric shapes that somehow made everything look cozier instead of just weird. On the wall over the couch was a giant painting, some abstract thing that was mostly deep blue. Not a drop of scarlet in it at all.

It was the kind of classy elegance he could appreciate from a distance. Up close, he had to admit it was intimidating. She was several galaxies outside of his orbit.

His gaze caught on a pair of sneakers half-hidden under a chair by the front door and he breathed easier.

"Vodka?" she asked, and he could tell she was a little nervous, too.

"Depends," he said, turning to face her. Again, it was like a body blow. A jolt made of desire and heat. "Is it the good stuff?"

"I'll let you decide," she said, opening the freezer door. She pulled out a bottle he recognized. Interestingly, it wasn't the very top of the line. Close, sure, but he had the feeling she was more concerned with liking the drink than impressing him. He hoped so.

She also took out two icy shot glasses, then a small bowl of lime wedges from the fridge. With a steady hand, she rimmed the glasses with the fruit, then poured them each a shot. He picked his up when she lifted hers, and they grinned at each other, which had become an actual thing. Between them. It wasn't something he did with many people, at least not since he'd been a kid.

He clicked her glass. "To second nights."

She nodded. "And calla lilies."

They drank and it went down smooth and cold, leaving him breathless and wanting to taste her again. "Put me to work," he said instead. The war between anticipation and action had moved from his head to his chest. She'd asked him to dinner. It wasn't the same thing as asking him to bed. "I'm good with a knife as long as there's enough room. Not so hot with measuring these days, but I can mix stuff."

"Confession time," she said. "We were going to make pasta. From scratch."

"You do that?"

"When I have time. Which I didn't tonight. So you're going to make me salad while I heat up the rest of dinner. If anyone gets to be the helper, it'll be me."

"It sounds like you've had a hell of a day. I'm decent with a microwave and takeout, unless there's something special about what you brought?"

She smiled at him as she shook her head. "Not a thing." Then she went to the fridge and brought out three different take-out containers. One was filled with pasta, one had a dark mushroom sauce and one she didn't open.

He located everything he'd need, particularly the wine, which he poured. He handed her a glass. "Sit down, relax, watch me tear lettuce to shreds. I like the music, by the way."

She inhaled deeply, let it out slowly, but rather than moving to the chair at the end of the island, she leaned in and kissed him. "Thank you. Work has been brutal."

When Rebecca turned, he could see a hint of red at the edge of the low-cut neckline. Like the edges of the curtains, the pillows on the couch. He was going to enjoy peeling away her layers.

He brought out his salad kit. Not that it was anything so studied or interesting. Four kinds of lettuce because according to his old friend Sal's mother only savages ate a salad with only romaine. Green onions were next, red peppers, cherry tomatoes, green olives, black olives and finally fresh basil from Sal's mother's kitchen window. Then came the grapeseed oil and balsamic vinegar he'd mixed up ahead of time, and finally, a lemon. He washed his hands, dried them on an incredibly soft kitchen towel, then went to work tearing lettuce as he stared at the gorgeous woman with the bared shoulder.

The sight was enough to make him thankful he hadn't picked up a knife yet. Her sweater had fallen to reveal one red bra strap across pale, perfect skin. Her legs in those tight black jeans were spread, one of her hands resting on the edge of her chair between her thighs. She raised a glass of dark wine to her lips and drank. When he was able to wrest his gaze from her lips, he found her staring at him, her pupils dark behind the fringe of bangs and eyelashes.

"How's the wine?" he asked, amazed his voice didn't break and that he'd said actual words.

"Good," she said. "Not as good as watching you manhandle that lettuce."

"The lettuce had it coming." He tore the last of the radicchio and picked up the escarole. "It must be demanding, running such a large foundation."

"It can be," she said, nodding as if the mere mention had reminded her again how exhausted she was. "Especially this week. I have no business doing this tonight."

"Why not? A girl's gotta eat."

She half smiled. "If that's all we're going to do tonight, then I think we need to have a talk."

"No, that's not all. But maybe we should postpone the movie."

She stilled, blinked at him.

Her reaction brought it home, what he'd suggested. This wasn't supposed to continue. Tonight was a one-off, a thank-you, he imagined, for the flowers and the DVD. "Or not."

She swallowed, even though she hadn't had any more wine. "No, that's a nice idea. The movie would be better if it happened after Wednesday night. After Thursday night, honestly, so I can finally get a decent night's sleep."

"What happens on Wednesday?"

"Big dinner. Huge dinner. It's where I flatter the hell out of our regular donors and woo the potentials. This year there's one very big fish I'm determined to land. He seems interested, but he's also playing coy. Teasing me along. But it'll be worth it. His contribution would end up in the tens of millions over the length of the endowment. That's game-changing money. That's schools and loans and medicine and lives saved. So many lives."

"No wonder you're exhausted. That's got to be a lot of pressure."

"Some things are worth it."

"I've always thought so."

"Hell, you were willing to put your life on the line. Talk about pressure."

He looked around the kitchen until he found the big chef's knife, then turned back to his salad and Rebecca. "Different kind, but yeah. Pressure was part of it. Not as much as deciding who gets what resources. That's tough. For everyone who gets, there are probably dozens, hundreds who don't."

She shifted on her chair, although thankfully she didn't adjust her sweater. He had to be careful because of the knife, but every chance he could, he'd look at that red strap, then her face. Holy shit.

"I don't have to make all those decisions," she said. "We have a board of directors. My job is to first make sure we're always refreshing our coffers and then to narrow down the choices of how we want to spend the money. So many need so much, it's not easy."

"I'll bet. I imagine you take into account what other groups are doing, try to spread the wealth?"

She nodded. "It's a triage system. Short- and long-term goals. Maximum benefit for the greatest number of people, things that hopefully turn out to be more than quick fixes. But I'd rather hear about your house and your father. You're doing a complete remodel?"

He grinned, thinking about what his dad would say walking into this joint. "Nope, just giving him living space on the ground floor. He has trouble with the stairs."

"You do a lot of that DIY stuff?"

"Nope. Learning as I go. Turns out the internet is a pretty useful thing. And DVDs. Lots of how-to DVDs." He finished the last of the chopping, put the salad together except for the dressing. He opened the containers of food, dividing the pasta and sauce between the two big plates.

Her hand on his shoulder made him jump. How had he not heard those heels click? Jesus, how rapidly his self-preservation instincts were devolving.

"I'll get this part," she said, so close to him that he felt the heat of her breath on his jaw.

Fast as that, he was all about Rebecca. The dinner could vanish for all he cared because her hand was still warm on his shoulder and her hip was pressing against him. He had his arms around her before he finished turning, his mouth on hers a second later.

Tasting her was better than anything on the menu. It was intimate and slow, their kiss, and maybe because he knew they were going to stop, that he wasn't going to drag her to the bedroom right this second, he paid attention to what was happening here, what he had.

She tasted like Rebecca. Jesus, how it compressed his chest to realize he knew that taste, could have picked her out of a crowd blindfolded. And while there were a dozen different places he wanted to memorize with his tongue, for now he slicked and slid against her in a slow back-and-forth, deep and shallow. Everything was what he wanted of this small, amazing part of her. Lips, tongue, teeth, breath, heat, wet.

He'd pushed his hips against her and it was the shock wave that brought him back to the room, to dinner. He pulled away, but only because he knew he would have her again soon.

SOMEHOW, REBECCA MANAGED to slow her heartbeat and stop her shaking long enough to heat up the entrée. Jake's salad was fantastic, and she ate more of that than the pasta. He did the reverse, so that worked out. The bottle of wine was almost finished and dessert waited, but Rebecca wasn't terribly interested in dessert.

"I could make coffee," he said. "There's that last box out on the counter."

She put down her wineglass and stood. "That's tiramisu, if you want some. Or we could just go back to my bedroom."

He looked up at her, and she almost laughed at the way his entire expression said there was no contest. "Where's the bedroom?" he asked, taking her hand in his, bringing it to his lips, where he kissed her palm.

"A hundred miles away."

He rose, pulled her into his body. "The couch isn't."

She shook her head, letting her lips brush his as she did. "Want you in my bed."

"Take me there."

It wasn't easy, letting go of him. So she didn't. She just slid her fingers into the waistband of his jeans and tugged him along, moving faster with each step and each thought of what came next.

The moment she crossed the threshold of her bedroom, her shoes were history. He was pulling up her sweater before she could get her hand out of his pants. They each worked on unbuttoning and unzipping, but he won the race by a mile. And then he tugged down, hard, pulling her jeans and her panties down to her knees.

"Oh, God," he said, and he ran his hands up the front of her thighs.

"Wait, wait. Do your shirt. I can't—"

"I don't care about my shirt. We have to get rid of your pants."

"I'm trying!"

"You suck at it." He batted her fumbling fingers away,

and they concentrated on divesting themselves of their own clothes. She shed her pants; his shirt had disappeared by the time she looked up, but when she reached behind her back to undo the clasp of her bra, he said, "Wait. Don't. Stop."

"Don't stop? Or Don't. Stop?"

"Leave it on." Then his trousers and boxer briefs hit the floor; his cock was as perfectly hard as she remembered. He whipped off his undershirt so swiftly he couldn't hide the wince as he stressed his shoulder.

He pressed up against her, his ability to control his hips apparently gone with his clothes, which she found extremely sexy.

After a kiss that nearly missed her mouth completely, he was pushing her backward toward the bed. "Sit," he said.

She did, wondering what he was up to.

It turned out he was going down on his knees. She worried for a moment, but he didn't seem to be in any pain, although she doubted he could kneel long. Then he had his hands on her knees, spreading her wide.

"Watch me," he said. His voice was unraveling. How much did she love that?"

He kept his gaze on hers as he bent forward. Her bed was high, and she had a nice view of the moment Jake switched his attention from her face to his new objective. Beginning with his lips on her inner thigh. Lips and tongue, a wicked combination. Hands and fingers, too, so that there was sensation all along the pathway to her pussy.

She wanted to press her legs together, but she couldn't, so she squeezed what was available. Jake must have noticed because he moaned low and long as he picked up the pace.

Finally, his hot breath painted her labia, and then, softly, he licked her from the bottom of her cleft to the top.

JAKE LOST HIMSELF IN THE taste of her, in the salt on his tongue, in the scent. His fingers spread her open, and he went to town. It was gorgeous, and she was amazing, and he'd loved every second of what she tasted like and the sounds she made when he pointed his tongue and fucked her with it.

Her hand was in his hair, and when he hit pay dirt, she let him know. His thigh hurt, but it was so worth it. The sad part was that he couldn't just move in, stay for the night. His cock was insistent, but his wound wouldn't leave him be, so he kept his tongue hard and pointed and worked fast on her full, hard clit.

That brought her other hand into his hair, and if he was half-bald at the end of this, well, hair grew back.

Her thighs pressed against his ears as her moans got louder, and when she started chanting his name, he went into fifth gear.

It was a race to see if he would suffocate or she would come first.

He lived.

It was a damn good thing she had the condom at the ready, because about one hot minute later, he was on the bed. He'd flipped her over so she was on her hands and knees, and he went to heaven as he thrust inside her.

She dropped to her elbows, her head on her pillow, and he'd never seen anything so erotic in his life. So proper on the outside, so cool and collected. In here, with him, wanton, abandoned and the sexiest thing alive. But dammit, he was going to come too fast. It's what she did to him.

He gripped her too tightly, his cock pistoned hard, hard, and he was swearing in his head because he couldn't even speak.

He meant to turn her over, to look her in the eyes, maybe kiss her as they came, but that would have to happen later because Rebecca stole a lot more than his composure. He came as if he'd never done it before, as if he'd do anything to be with her again.

# 7

THE ALARM WENT OFF AT the unholy hour of five, purposefully shrill. Rebecca threw her arm over to stop the beeping, but there was no way Jake could have slept through that. No one in a three-mile radius could have.

"That was…" Jake didn't finish the sentence.

"It's the only thing that gets me up. I just sleep through music or anything that doesn't make me want to rip out my ears."

"Next time, we're doing this on a weekend you don't have to work."

She turned over, kicking the duvet into something less restricting. They'd certainly been energetic last night. Despite her tiredness. At least they'd gotten five hours of sleep. "Next time?"

He turned to her, and while the draw was there, as urgent as it had been every time she got a look at him, they both played by morning-breath rules. "I keep doing that, don't I?"

She nodded. "Evidently, I don't mind."

"Excellent."

"I'm going to take a lot longer than you in the bathroom," she said. "Feel free to shower. There's a fresh toothbrush in the drawer under the rolled-up towels."

"I was kind of hoping for an in-home demo."

She brushed the back of her fingers across his cheekbone. "That would be a terribly risky thing to do."

"We're modern-day warriors," he said. "I have every faith."

Her laughter made her cover her mouth and start the day off better than she could have hoped. "Not when it comes to resisting you."

He hummed happily and planted his forehead against her chest above her breasts. His hand started petting her, long slow strokes that made what she had to do next very difficult.

"You have to get out of my bed."

"Harsh," he said, his sleep-roughened voice muffled.

"Vigilance is my only hope."

He sniffed. Moved himself back to the safe side of the bed. "Fine. I'll get out of your bed. I'll use your new toothbrush. But just know that I plan to make you a great omelet for when you've finished getting ready."

She laughed again. "Is that your idea of a threat?"

"Yeah, it's pretty weak. But it's all I've got. Too damn early in the morning." He threw back the covers and stood, his body still gorgeous, but she could see that some parts moved quicker than others. How much did those wounds hurt him every single day? She wished there was more to be done.

His cock certainly hadn't been affected. He was half-hard, and she knew it wouldn't take much to get him to attention. But work wasn't going anywhere. The thought of all she had to do today made her moan.

He walked to the end of the bed and collected his

clothes from the settee. "Anything you don't like in an omelet?"

She shook her head. "Everything in my fridge is fair game. Whatever you make will be wonderful. Oh, and the coffee should be ready in about five minutes."

He grinned and that quiver came back to her tummy. As she watched his butt while he walked to the bathroom, she wondered if she was being a complete idiot about all this. Letting him make her breakfast. Implying there'd be a next time. She was always careful about making friends too quickly, letting herself get too close. But kicking him out of her bed was hard enough. She just wasn't ready to kick him out of her life.

JAKE TOOK THE SUBWAY BACK to Brooklyn. It wasn't that crowded early on a Saturday morning so he was able to stretch out his leg. Of course, he did what he always did: scoped out the exits, every passenger who was in his car. Looked for signs of inebriation, of dilated pupils, of anything hinky. Then a sweep of the clothes, the hoodies in particular, the jeans. Possible weapon or cell phone? A loner paying too much attention to another passenger? It wasn't something he planned, it was the way he was. It didn't matter that he didn't have the badge, his brain had wired itself to the job. He never sat with his back to a wall, he always knew where the exits were, he was conscious of body language and facial ticks. A lot of good it did him now. Not only was he stuck with permanent injuries, he could also look forward to a lifetime of paranoia.

He was gonna have to get a little more serious about therapy if he wanted to keep up with Rebecca. And not just physical therapy.

He shook his head at his foolishness. Truth was, he

was playing with fire. Walking into that building last night had shown him everything he needed to know about him and Rebecca. Yeah, it was all fun and games and getting naked, but they'd also done a lot of other stuff. Stuff that didn't come with the normal one-night-stand package. Talked, for one thing. Talked a lot. Laughed. He'd cooked for her. She'd…opened wine.

He stared at the dark tunnel outside the subway window, everything speeding by. He would go home today, keep working on the downstairs bathroom. Listen to a ton of bad cop jokes. Watch his old man struggle to hold his fork, his mug, a domino. And parts of his body would burn angry at how he'd moved and strained and pushed too hard. But the other parts, the center of him, was glad he'd wrecked himself with Rebecca Thorpe, even if it never occurred to her that he might feel un-comfortable in a bed that cost more than he'd make in a year. Past tense. Made in a year.

Now, shit, disability. There was the house, eventually, but not for a long time, please God. And he had some savings. But he couldn't take her out to the type of places she was used to. Meals at some of those joints ran to the thousands. He could barely imagine what food could be worth that. Even with wine.

She was used to dealing in billions, he was looking for bargains at Greschlers' Hardware. He understood the part where they were naked, the sweaty part. He was having trouble with the talking. With liking her the way he did.

He rocked to the side at the curve, then settled. Being an undercover cop, being in with people who'd shoot him if he so much as looked at them funny, he'd learned to read people. It was survival, and it didn't go away once he was off the job. Rebecca liked him. She was comfort-able with him, and she wanted him to like her back.

The women he'd been involved with, they were all
people whose lives he understood. If they weren't from
his neighborhood, they were from one just like it. Pizza
from the corner was a fine meal, getting together for
some green beer and corned beef on St. Paddy's Day,
watching Notre Dame at the corner bar. That's what he
knew. Not that he was embarrassed by his home or his
life, not at all. But it had given him his perspective. His
frame of reference.

Rebecca didn't fit outside of the bedroom. No two
ways about it. He didn't understand her motives, and
that could be a problem. Motives were important.

Hell, he barely understood why he was pushing this
thing, asking for more when it should have ended. He
might have come from a long line of cops, but he wasn't
just some mook who didn't understand what was what.
Until her. Until Madison Avenue and fucking wild mushroom ragout, for Christ's sake. What were they trying to
prove? Was he her good deed for the year? Her attempt
to get to know the little people? Was she his last-ditch
attempt to prove he was still all man and not just an unemployed cripple?

The train slowed, and he looked up, saw he had four
stops to go. But he watched the doors as they opened,
scanned the small groups of people as they entered,
chose seats. A couple of gangbangers sat front and center, so Jake would keep his wits about him, but he didn't
expect anything to happen. Except a train ride back to
his real life.

He'd think about her, no question there. And he'd see
her again, if he could figure out how to meet on neutral territory. Not his place, because jeez, the old man?
Pete? Liam? They'd trip all over themselves trying to
impress her. But he didn't feel right about going back to

her place. Wouldn't, until he figured some things out. Like why he was already counting the minutes until he could be with her again.

REBECCA CLICKED THE TEXT function on her cell phone, clicked again on Bree's name and typed:

Donate my body to science

Not five seconds later, Bree responded:

Don't tell me you're still wrking

I will never not be wrking Bree. NEVER!

It'll get better. Tell me re BLUE EYES. Was 2nd as good as 1st?

He made me salad. Omelet this am. Yum. In every sense of the word.

Rebecca leaned back in her chair as she eyed the report spread out on her desk. She'd paused the demo that was currently on her screen and tried to get through the first page of the report three times, but she kept losing the thread. Thank God, the beep that told her Bree had texted her back saved her.

OMG. I can't stand it. U HAVE to invite him!

To what?

The donor dinner. Duh.

Rebecca blinked at the text, the message not fully computing for a full minute. She wasn't going to invite Jake to the donor dinner. He'd feel horribly out of place. Although she would certainly prefer sitting next to him rather than her cousin Reggie, not so affectionately known as Peckerhead, at least by Rebecca and Charlie. She took a sip of coffee before she set to typing again.

I can't invite him. Awkward.

For who?

Him!

Really? CW

Hey, who let you into this convo?

Sorry, he read over my shoulder. Stole my phone. I've slugged him.

Charlie, go away.

Is he a porn star? A gigolo? Missing teeth, perhaps? CW

Bite me.

Rebecca started typing instantly, before Charlie could get a text in edgewise.

It's not his kind of thing.

Says U. Ask.

Yeah, ask. I'm still betting missing teeth. Front uppers. CW

If I'd wanted a pain in the ass relative, I'd have had a brother. I have to go back to work.

Think about it. CW

Rebecca got out of her text screen and put her phone in her right-hand drawer. She glanced at the report, but didn't linger. Her mind was far too occupied by the notion of inviting Jake to the banquet. The idea had grown roots during that brief, weird conversation. Not all of them pleasant.

Jake in a tuxedo? That she could deal with. In fact, she wanted to see that very, very badly. Something tailored, fitting those broad shoulders and tapering to his waist. Black, almost traditional, but perhaps a hint of cerulean blue in his cuff links? It would have to be subtle, not even his pocket kerchief, a mere spot of blue. Maybe Burberry or Tom Ford, definitely single button and razor-sharp lapels.

She realized she was smiling when she reached for her coffee, but the grin faded quickly. What would an ex-policeman from Brooklyn do with a Tom Ford tux? The people she was hosting, these were men and women used to every luxury the world had to offer, and the most casual among them knew who was and wasn't one of them.

She'd grown up among the highest of the classes, and as much as their excesses bothered her, she had to be careful lest she not include herself. Just because she made it her mission to spread the wealth of the Winslow Foundation to a much broader and less-fashionable base, she didn't exactly live an ascetic's life. Her home was worth over three million dollars and that was just the space. She considered it a long-term investment, a clever buy at a time when the economy had taken a dive. But it was also what she was accustomed to.

She'd never lived in a building without a doorman. Never *had* to work. Her salary at the foundation was put right back into play as a donation, partly for the tax benefits, mostly to compensate for the guilt. It was convenient to think she was being generous when in truth, she could live extraordinarily well for the rest of her life on her trust fund. As it was, she barely touched the principal.

Her cup was almost empty, and she walked to the private lounge in a daze of sleep deprivation and hazy discomfort. Bree had come into her life, and therefore into Charlie's life, as a result of another pang of elitism. Rebecca had been invited to the lunch exchange by a professor she knew from NYU who no longer belonged to the group. They'd originally met in the park. Rebecca had never told Grace her last name, although she was fairly certain the English prof had recognized her. Grace had probably thought she was offering a chance for humility. Looking back, Rebecca agreed that she had.

Bree never spoke about it, about the disparity between their lifestyles. Rebecca imagined she and Charlie had talked. Knew they had, because he'd been so very famous as the creator and editor in chief of *Naked New York*. He was a celebrity in his own right, one who had used his wealth and influence to build his singular empire, one that had shouted clearly and loudly that he wasn't one of "those" Winslows.

As she poured a fresh cup of coffee, she thought about herself and Charlie, how they'd been so close growing up. Uncomfortable with the trappings of their heritage, but not enough to walk away, not completely. In Charlie's case, he'd replicated the success and influence, but in his own style. In hers, she'd decided to use her power for good. Going to law school had been hard, but worth it, as had learning everything she could about running a foundation and fundraising. Her sacrifices were tiny. Miniscule. Complaining about any of it unforgivable.

Which brought her in a roundabout way back to Jake and the question of his invitation. Once at her desk, she took out her purse and pulled out his trading card. God, he was ridiculously handsome, but his looks weren't what attracted her most now that she knew him. Maybe Charlie and Bree had been right to question her easy dismissal. Because it had been a knee-jerk reaction, that immediate no. Not, she realized, out of the goodness of her heart and concern for Jake.

She was honestly too tired to be having an existential crisis about her entire life. In another hour, she'd leave, go straight home to her mansion in the sky and put herself to bed. Tomorrow, when her brain wasn't packed with cotton, she'd think again.

"OKAY, HIT ME," JAKE SAID, taking a deep breath and letting his aggravation at being walkie-talkied to death wash over him like a passing breeze.

"What did the cop say to his belly button?"

"I don't know, Dad. What did the cop say to his belly button?"

"You're under a vest!"

Jake shook his head as he listened to the laughter coming from the front porch. After thirty or so seconds, he figured his old man was finished for the moment, and he could release the button. At least this joke hadn't made him groan. And where the hell they kept coming up with the vile things, Jake had no idea. He'd have guessed the internet, but not a one of them had a computer, or a cell phone with Wi-Fi. As for listening to anyone long enough to learn how to turn any internet-related device on, forgetaboutit. Stubborn old goats.

But, what the hell. He was something of a Luddite himself when it came right down to it. His needs were simple; he didn't have to have every new gadget that came down the pike. His laptop wasn't new, but it let him watch DVDs, get the scores, read the headlines and, from time to time, he'd even streamed a feature film. The screen was too small to make a habit of that last one, but it had come in handy when he'd been recuperating. Walking had been a real pain for quite some time, but as long as he had the laptop close, he didn't die of boredom. He was especially grateful for online books. They'd gotten him through some tough days.

Now, though, he wished like hell he'd never started this remodeling job. Putting up tile had to be the most tedious job in the world. It had all looked simple on paper but, as he couldn't escape learning, there was a great difference between remodeling and remodeling well. The bane of his existence wasn't the repetitive motions or the heavy lifting, even though those aggravated his wounds, it was the level. He could never tell when that water bubble was straight. He'd even sprung for one with a laser, and he still had trouble.

It made him long for the days of hiding in plain sight, hanging with drug dealers and fearing every breath would be his last.

The dreaded beep from the walkie-talkie interrupted his self-pity and he clicked on the button. "Got another one so soon?"

"Nope. Not quite."

It was Liam. Liam, who hardly ever used the walkie-talkie.

"We could use some help down here."

"What's wrong?" Jake dropped the trowel onto the tarp at his feet and hurried down the hallway, his senses on overdrive. He ignored the burn in his thigh as he raced through the living room to the front door. Throwing the door open, he saw the problem, and he had to stop himself from just lunging to his father, who was sprawled awkwardly on the sidewalk directly in front of the stairs that led up to the porch. He hadn't made the turn. It had happened once before, and Jake had promised to extend the porch but his dad had refused, insisted they would just move the damn card table they played on, move it back so he had more room.

"He's okay," Pete said. "I caught the chair before it hit his head."

Jake didn't see any blood. Liam was bent over, holding Mike's head in his big pale hands.

"I'm fine. Don't panic." Mike waved his crooked hand at Jake as if he was being a bother, and the way he glared at Liam it was clear the old moron hadn't wanted Jake to know.

Jake got down the steps faster than he had in weeks and squatted by his dad. "Anything hurt?"

"Yeah, my ego. Stupid ass wheelchair. I need to get me one of those sporty ones, the kind they race with."

"Yeah, that's exactly what you need." He put his arm behind his father's shoulders, the right arm because there was no way to use his left, not for this, not when a failure would matter so much. Screw it if the whole shower broke into a million pieces. Not this.

Liam helped, and together, they made one reasonably strong person able to lift Mike to his feet. The terrible claw of his hand grabbed on to Jake's upper arm, and while it hurt him, it had to be fiercely painful for his father.

"Come on. Let's get you in the chair you've got. See if it still works."

His dad nodded and took one unsteady step while Jake looked at him with every ounce of his attention. He didn't seem to be favoring anything more than usual, and he wasn't bleeding that Jake could see. But he'd still make an appointment with the doctor, get Mike checked over. So far, none of his spills had done anything too damaging, but it scared Jake to the bone each time it happened.

Whatever his own future held, it would include full-time care for his father. Maybe that would be Jake's job, and maybe it would last until he grew too old to get upstairs himself, but that was okay. He'd have plenty of breaks and time for himself, because they lived on Howard Street, in Windsor Terrace, and they were surrounded by a community who gave a shit when it counted.

Pete brought the wheelchair down the ramp, but not right up to Mike, which was good because Jake needed to watch him for a few more steps. Then they pushed him up. Pete and Liam did. The bastards slipped themselves into place, not giving Jake an option.

He could have made it up the ramp, goddammit, but it would have been a strain. He wasn't the man he used to be, not when it came to ramps or doing the job he was born to do or making love to a beautiful woman. He was a different Jake now, but the reality and his self-perception were still at war. Time, his physiotherapist had said. He had to give it time—

His cell rang, and as he limped up the steps after the old men, he put it to his ear. "Hello."

"Jake."

He paused, one foot on the porch. He felt a rush of heat down his back, settling low. "Rebecca."

"This is completely rude and please feel absolutely free to say no, but I'm actually in Brooklyn. Not far from your place, and I was wondering if you'd mind if I dropped by."

Every bit of his cop's instinct said it was a bad idea. Jake himself looked like a poor excuse for a day laborer. His father seemed to be okay now, but he'd be in a lot of discomfort and there was every possibility that seeing Rebecca Winslow Thorpe show up on his doorstep would be the final straw that did him in, and the house looked like shit. Not to mention Pete and Liam were about as tactful as three-year-olds. "Sure," he said, and with one word, he was doomed. "You know the address?"

"Well, yes. I know, creepy, but Google."

"It's okay. Come on over. Just be aware, you're gonna get what you get."

"That's all I want," she said. "I can be there in ten. Unless… I'm standing not five feet from Luigi's Pizza, which seems to be popular, given the crowd. I could bring one? Maybe some beer?"

Jake shook his head, more at the weird way this day was going than her offer. It was almost five, and he hadn't given a thought to dinner, knowing he'd either scrounge or they'd have something delivered. Rebecca didn't need to come with food, but as surreal as it was that she had called at all, it was also pretty brave, and she'd probably feel more comfortable if she came bearing gifts. "That'd be great, except there's four of us. My old man, his buddies, me. So how about you tell Gio behind the counter that the Donnellys need a couple pies and he can put it on our tab. Tell him to deliver 'cause it's gonna take him a little while if I know Sunday night at Luigi's. I got the beer covered, but if you want anything fancier than that, you're on your own."

She laughed. "I'll see you soon."

He clicked off, stared at his phone for a minute before he put it in his pocket. This was not his life.

# 8

REBECCA HAD ARRIVED IN picturesque Windsor Terrace, Brooklyn, at four-fifteen. Delivered by cab to what she guessed was the middle of town. It was certainly a busy street. Lots of people walking, businesses booming. Well, that was an exaggeration, if you didn't count Luigi's and the nearby bar.

But there were people on the streets moving at a pace that wasn't close to the speed of Manhattan, and there were families with strollers, dogs on leashes, dogs off leashes. Groups of teenagers, a startling number of whom were accessorized with not only tattoos, although those were plentiful, but metal. Industrial-looking rings embedded in earlobes, some stretching the skin so much it made her cringe. She couldn't help thinking of the long-term effects, but then that must be either a sign of her age, or that she was even more rigid and conservative than she'd thought.

The likelihood of her reaction coming from her class bias was mostly the reason she'd come to Brooklyn in the first place. After a long overdue excellent night's sleep, she'd continued to be bothered by the idea that she hadn't even considered asking Jake to be her date for the banquet.

After she'd run through all the reasonable issues—the fact that they didn't know each other that well outside of the bedroom, that they weren't technically dating and that he'd probably be bored out of his mind even if he did agree to go—she'd been left with a giant bundle of uncomfortable doubt. She honestly had no idea if she'd discounted him because she was being thoughtful or prejudiced.

It had taken her over an hour of walking up and down the big street to finally give in and call him, even though she was still confused and unsure. She could be calling him out of liberal guilt. She could be wanting him there because she liked him. What if it was both? What then?

No answers yet, but the deciding factor had been the pleasure she felt when she thought about him sitting next to her. Being able to look into his amazing blue eyes when she felt overwhelmed.

It was a novel sensation, liking him the way she did. Normally her turn-ons were more cerebral and practical. She liked brains, business acumen, elegance, good taste and a liberal bent. A sense of humor was a non-negotiable must-have, although difficult to find in combination with the rest of her requirements.

Jake was clever and he had a broad scope of interests. He made her laugh. She had no idea about the rest and hadn't cared that she hadn't known. Because he was for sex. Only, that wasn't how it was turning out.

She had arrived at the corner of Howard Street. One left turn, a few blocks, and she'd be there, at Jake's home. She'd meet his father. See the work Jake was doing on the house. There would be no sex involved. And while she was pretty sure she was going to ask him to be her date Wednesday night, she was leaving that option open.

The pizzas would arrive in the next ten or so minutes, according to Gio, who turned out to be the owner, so she should get a move on and stop stalling. Turning left, she looked at the row houses lining the wide street. The homes were virtually identical except for the front porches, which were wide and uniquely decorated, mostly with furniture that wouldn't be damaged by snow yet could be heavily used in more temperate months. She liked them, each of them, some with religious statues, some with art that gave a great deal away about the owners. The big old front porches were unheard of in Manhattan and she wondered what it would be like to grow up in a place like this.

The whole neighborhood felt as if it was from another era, and from what little she'd read about it in her Google searches, that was the point. The folks who lived here protected the ambience, and while they couldn't slow the gentrification of the main thoroughfares, they could maintain the residential streets in their old-fashioned glory.

She was nearing his place, and she hesitated again, her hands buried in the deep pockets of her thick wool coat, her boots clicking on the bumpy sidewalk and her nervous heart signaling her flight-or-fight response.

There were men on the porch, sitting at a card table. Old men, gray-headed and wrinkled, laughing at something. They weren't looking for her or even glancing in her direction. Jake hadn't told them? Okay. Fair enough, he knew the players.

She wasn't naive enough to think these men wouldn't know who she was. They would also have opinions about her family, and she would bet those opinions weren't favorable. The Winslows were not well-known for their charity and kindness despite the foundation.

She took another few steps and the laughing dimmed. The one with the most hair, the one facing her, had grown quiet. Seconds later, the two other men turned, making no effort whatsoever to hide their blatant curiosity.

She doubted they'd arrived at the Winslow part yet, but they would certainly know she was an outsider. "Hello," she said, smiling as she reached the front steps of the row house. "I'm here to see Jake."

"You are, huh?" The man who spoke was Jake's father. The one who'd spotted her first. This close, she could see he was in a wheelchair, see his gnarled hands. His accent, even with three small words, was epic.

"Yes, sir. He's expecting me."

"Then you'd better come on up," he said.

At the top of the steps, the appeal of the porch was made vividly clear. The large space heater did a terrific job of keeping out the bitter chill. She imagined only big storms would keep these troopers indoors. The card table was strewn with dominoes and coffee mugs, a couple of pens and a pad of paper. There were walkie-talkies, not cell phones, in front of each man, which must be their intercom system, a way to get Jake outside pronto.

The man sitting next to Jake's father raised his walkie-talkie to his mouth. "Jake."

"Yeah, Pete?" came the reply a few seconds later.

"Your friend is here."

"I'll be right out."

God, how they were staring. She felt a blush on her cheeks that made her even warmer. "I'm Rebecca

Thorpe," she said. "I was in the neighborhood, and Jake said it was all right if I came by."

"You come to this neighborhood often?" This from the biggest of the three, the one who had to twist around to see her. He had phenomenally bushy eyebrows.

"No. Never before today. It's a great street."

"We like it," Jake's father said, and it looked as if he was about to say more when the front door opened.

Jake wore jeans and a plaid flannel shirt, both looking as if they'd been with him a long time. She closed her hand into a fist to fight the urge to touch him, even though he was standing all the way across the porch. The tool belt hanging on his hips seemed a little newer than his clothes and the ensemble was surprisingly sexy. She couldn't hold back her grin, and neither, it seemed, could he. "You found it."

"I did."

"Gio give you any trouble?"

"Nope. But he also wouldn't tell me what kind of pizzas he was sending. I hope I didn't just get two pineapple and ham pies because that would be——"

"A travesty," he said, interrupting. "No. No pineapples have ever touched a pizza in this house."

"Okay, then. I guess I'll stay for a bit."

"Good."

Jake's father coughed. Loudly, and completely fake.

His son startled at the sound, as if he'd forgotten the old men were there. "Everybody, this is Rebecca. Thorpe."

"We know," his dad said.

"Ah. Recognized her, huh?"

"No, she had the manners God gave a child of five and introduced herself."

Jake, in the manner of kids from every walk of life,

rolled his eyes. "Rebecca, I'd like you to meet my father, Mike Donnelly, the emperor of Howard Street. To his left is family friend and classic car enthusiast Pete Baskin. The third gentleman is also an old family friend, Liam O'Hara. If you need any information about any of the *Die Hard* movies, he's your man."

"It's lovely to meet all of you, and I hope I haven't disturbed your game too much."

"Liam's cheating, anyway," Pete said at the exact same time Mike said, "Pete's cheating."

No one but Rebecca seemed to be surprised, but it made her laugh.

"Who's up for something to drink?" Jake asked. "The pizza should be arriving any minute."

Pete and Liam wanted beer, Mike coffee.

Jake held out his arm, inviting Rebecca into the house.

"Don't you hide her away in there, Jakey. We'll be wanting to talk to this beautiful young lady."

"Yes, Dad. I promise not to let her make a clean getaway."

"Hey, Rebecca," Pete said. "How many cops does it take to throw a man down the stairs?"

Jake groaned as all three men at the table smiled broadly, their wrinkles framing their grins like theater curtains.

"I don't know. How many?"

Pete laughed even before he said, "None. He fell."

The old men laughed. Hard. Full of wheezes and a couple of hiccups, it was impossible not to laugh with them. When she got a load of Jake's grimace, it all became funnier.

As she passed Jake and entered the house there was

no doubt she was not a native of this strange land, but a visitor on a guest pass.

The hallway was short, a little dark and had no photographs or flowers, only a place to hang coats and another to stash boots. Jake helped her off with her big wool monstrosity and hung it up, but he didn't ask her to remove her boots.

The front room was old-fashioned with a wooden fireplace, flowered wallpaper and a staircase leading to the second floor. There was a very nice hardwood floor. The furniture looked cozy with tables close at hand for cups or magazines. No TV though, but that mystery was cleared up when she was escorted into the living room. But before she could look around, Jake stepped close and pulled her into a kiss that went from welcome to "hi, there" in thirty seconds.

The flannel felt wonderful beneath her hands, or maybe that was knowing it was Jake she was touching. Unable to resist, she explored his manly tool belt and copped a grab of his ass for good measure.

He laughed as he kissed her, which was one heck of a nice thing.

When she drew back, she found his gaze, those blue eyes doing strange and wondrous things to her body. "I never just show up," she said. "Never. My entire family, including all my ancestors, are appalled. It's the height of rudeness."

"Boy, are you not from this neighborhood. No one calls ahead. They just barge the hell in, no matter what. It's a pain in the ass."

"It's a community."

"That, too."

"So it's all right that I'm here?" she asked even though she knew he would say yes no matter what.

"It's fantastic. And a surprise. I've been trying to figure out why since you called."

"Ah, that." She parted from him, took a look around. There was the big screen awkwardly hung half over very unique flowered wallpaper and half over the tallest wainscoting she'd ever seen. There was perhaps a foot of wallpaper showing, and the rest was green-and-white-striped wood with a small shelf thing running above the wainscoting across the length of the room. Here, too, were more comfy couches, two big recliners, more tables, but what really caught her interest were the photographs.

They were on every wall, on every tabletop. She started on the far wall over a console table. There was Jake as a kid, a little kid with a new bike complete with training wheels, smiling like he'd won the grandest prize of all. And there was his father, a young man standing proud in his NYPD uniform.

Her gaze stopped at an elegant picture of a woman with her dark hair in an updo, her makeup a little dated, but still tasteful, and Jake's eyes. That same blue, arresting, with dark, thick lashes Rebecca doubted were fake. She had a smile that was a little shy, but sweet, and there was a glow about her, as if she was looking at someone very special when the photographer had snapped the picture.

"She was a knockout," Jake said. "Oh, man, was my old man proud of her. He loved to take her dancing. There was a place in Park Slope that was an old-fashioned ballroom joint. No live orchestra, but they went there a lot. They were too young to be dancing like that, teased by all their friends, but they could dance. They won contests. Not a lot, nothing major. Didn't matter, that's not why they went."

"How long has she been gone?"

"Twelve years."

"I'm sorry."

Jake inhaled. "Me, too. She was a good mom. A little crazy. She liked to experiment with dinner. She sucked at that."

Rebecca laughed quietly as she put the picture back down. "Is there one of you in your uniform?"

He nodded, took her hand. They walked across the broad living room. It had the same hardwood flooring, but there was a big area rug in the center, deep green, which went with the wallpaper and the stripes. At the other end sat a bookcase, the lower shelves crammed with books. The upper two shelves had a few trinkets: a fancy candle, what looked like a music box, a set of those nesting dolls. And one large photograph in a silver frame of a much-younger Jake. His uniform was slightly different from his father's, but she couldn't have pinpointed how. The pride that came through in his posture and his eyes was identical.

"Oh, my," she said, "what is it about a man in uniform?"

"Depends on the man. I've known some butt-ugly cops."

She tugged him close. "Something tells me you had to fight them off with a stick wearing that NYPD blue."

"Hey, it wasn't the uniform."

"No." She looked at him squarely. "I'm sure it was your modesty."

"You're a riot."

She tilted her head toward the door. "If I'm not mistaken, dinner has arrived."

"I hope you like soy bacon and tofu and no tomato sauce."

"Ha."

The look he gave her made her worry that he wasn't kidding, but not for long. Not that he didn't try, but his eyes couldn't hide the smile that only teased his lips. Then he kissed her, slow and lush, until she forgot to be worried at all, and when he was through, he led her back to the Gang of Three.

THE PIZZA BOXES WERE EMPTY except for several discarded crusts courtesy of Liam, lying open on the coffee table in the living room. Jake's father was in his wheelchair, Liam and Pete were in the recliners and Rebecca sat on the couch next to Jake. They weren't pressed together, but they were close enough for their hands to brush. Every time that happened, a pulse of excitement surged through his body, particularly behind his fly. It wasn't critical—he wasn't seventeen any longer—but it made him hyperaware of her.

Even above the odor of pizza and pepperoni and garlic and onion, he had identified her scent. She wasn't one of those women who changed perfume as often as clothes, and for that he was grateful. This scent, something he couldn't name or even categorize, had made an impact. If he didn't see her for ten years, he'd still know it was her.

That was the good part. The bad part was that Mike had started telling stories. Embarrassing stories. Of Jake's childhood. Jake had given his father the glare of a lifetime, but no. Mike, the old bastard, was undaunted and unafraid. The first two had been uncomfortable, but they were kind of typical—peeing his pants at four, breaking an incredibly expensive vase at the police captain's house when Jake was seven. But this one...

"...he had one hell of a lisp," he father said, already

laughing. What's worse, Pete and Liam were laughing just as hard, and Rebecca, caught up in the moment, grinned at him as if it was all fun and games.

"Shut up, old man," Jake said. "It's not even funny."

"It's goddamn adorable, Jakey, so sit back and take it like a man."

Jake groaned, dropped his head in his hands. The only question was whether he should leave or stay. Staying meant utter humiliation. Running was cowardly, and he was still trying to impress the woman he wasn't supposed to be dating.

"So one day, my wife gets a call from his teacher. He's in second grade, mind you. Six." His dad had to pause for a minute to wipe his thumb under his eyes. "At first, see, my wife was worried. That his teacher was crying, she sounded so weird on the phone. But then, see, it turns out she was laughing."

"Oh, God," Liam said. "This kills me. Every fucking time." His eyes widened as he turned to Rebecca. "Excuse my language. I'm sorry."

"It's all right," she said. "I've heard the word before." Then she brushed Jake's hand as she leaned forward. "I've even said it a few times."

Liam nodded at her, then went back to staring at the storyteller, the father who had no concern whatsoever for his only child, the man who was single-handedly driving away any chance for a relationship with Rebecca.

"So she was laughing," his dad continued, "hard. Because my boy, my beautiful son, had been eaten alive by mosquitoes the night before. He was a mess, I gotta say, it wasn't pretty. But right in the middle of class, and remember this was a Catholic school and his teacher was a nun, so right in the middle, Jakey here stands up and yells, 'Thister, thethe methquito biteth are a pain in my ath.'" Mike had to stop and laugh for a while, and he wasn't alone. "So the sister says, 'What did you say?' and Jake just yells it again. The sister was calling my wife to tell her Jake had to go to the doctor because he had a pretty bad allergy, but damn, that story. It went all over the neighborhood like wildfire, and to this day, we can be walking down the block, and someone will yell out, 'Thethe methquito biteth are a pain in my ath!'"

Jake sighed, waiting for this hell to be over. Knowing that if he was really lucky, and he did get to see Rebecca again, she was going to bring up the lisp. No one could seem to help it.

Of course she laughed. Why wouldn't she? It was a riot. It wasn't his fault he hadn't had any front teeth. He was only in second grade, for God's sake, and weren't nuns supposed to be caring? Gentle? Twenty-nine years later, and he still kept hearing about the goddamn methquitoes.

Rebecca turned to Jake and held his face between her hands and kissed him, sitting right there on the living room couch. "It must have been awful," she said. "But so adorable I can't even…"

"Adorable. Just what a man wants to hear."

"You should want to," she said, keeping her voice low, as private as possible. "Because it's a wonderful thing. I'm so glad I came."

"Could have done without the show-and-tell."

She let him go, but didn't sit back. "That was the betht part."

Behind her, with laughter still lingering, Liam stood and started putting away the empty boxes. Rebecca noticed, then squeezed Jake's hand. "Walk me outside?"

"Walk you to 5th, you mean. Unless you want to call a cab from here."

"No, a walk would be good after all that pizza."

He stood back as she said her goodbyes, and he wasn't quite as bothered by the story being told. Of course, he'd get his revenge as soon as possible, but for tonight, it was fine. And wasn't she something as she spoke to his old man, touching his shoulder, getting personal. Jake didn't hear what she said, but he saw his father's face. Her visit made things more complicated, but that wasn't so horrible either. At least for now.

By the time he'd helped her on with her coat, Liam and Pete had helped Mike upstairs so Jake was able to leave comfortably. The two men would stick around until he got back. Now, though, he put on his own coat and went outside into the cold night.

They were quiet for a while, walking, her hand in his. It felt a little weird to have had such a domestic night when he'd never imagined her that way.

"I hope it wasn't too weird for you, me being there," she said.

"Interesting. Good interesting," he added, quickly. "I didn't expect..."

"I know. Me neither. I actually came here to ask you something."

"Okay."

"You know that dinner I've been bitching about?"

"Yep. Wednesday night, right?"

"Yes." She paused walking, faced him. "I wondered if you might like to come. As my date. But it's okay if you don't want to. It's black tie, and you know the kind of people who are going to be there, and it might turn out to be the most boring night of your life. Although my cousin Charlie and his girlfriend, Bree, will be there, and the food will be fantastic, but honestly, you don't have to say yes—"

"Yes," he said. "I'd love to come as your date."

"Really?"

Her wide dark eyes stared up at him with surprise, and he couldn't be sure but he thought she might be blushing.

"Really. It would be my honor. Where and when?"

She let out a big sigh, then grabbed the back of his neck and pulled him down into a kiss that should have waited for a much more private venue. He didn't mind.

# 9

OF ALL THE SKILLS REBECCA had learned from her parents, the ability to appear calm in virtually any circumstance was one of the most useful. It hadn't come easily, but over the years she'd found that she could separate her inner landscape from the outer facade. As she stood in the middle of the banquet room at the Four Seasons, those boundaries were being stretched to the limit.

It was early yet, with only staff in attendance, and the room buzzed with a controlled chaos. What had Rebecca sweating wasn't the catering or the orchestra or even the extravagant floral arrangements still being fussed with, but her own ability to let the people she'd hired do their jobs without her overseeing every last detail.

And Jake.

He hadn't arrived; it was two hours before anyone was expected. Dani was here, and the catering manager and one of the staff concierges and many, many hands to make sure every place setting was meticulous, that the food was superb in freshness, flavor and eye appeal. She had already checked into the room she'd booked for the night. If she had a lick of sense, she'd go upstairs immediately, lie down for at least twenty minutes, then begin her personal preparation. Dani was also going to use the room to change clothes so Rebecca's window of opportunity for a short nap was closing.

"Go. Everything's fine," Dani said, which illustrated perfectly the need for her to get the hell out of there.

Rebecca glanced around, still hesitating.

Dani, dressed in black pants, a striped shirt and low heels, crossed her arms over her chest. "You're making everyone nuts. If anything's going to crash and burn it'll be because we're all trying to impress you."

"Oh." Rebecca gave it a minute's thought and could see the point. "Fine. I'll rest. But I'm going to have my cell in my hand so call me if anything happens. I mean anything."

Dani's only response was to cross her heart, then stare pointedly at the door.

Rebecca took her leave and while she was certain she'd be unable to think of a thing besides the enormous checklist for the dinner, once she stepped into the elevator, it was Jake. All Jake.

She hadn't asked him about his tux, because that would have been unbearably awful, but she'd worried about it. Then she'd worried about worrying. He was altogether a difficult issue for her. Ever since her conversation with Bree and Charlie, Rebecca had played over every motive, every wish, every daydream she'd had in the short time she'd known Jake. Since she'd visited his home, her confusion had worsened. Yet hearing his voice instantly stifled her qualms, making it crystal clear how much she liked him. All the same, an hour later she was chock-full of self-doubt and second-guessing.

She entered the lovely deluxe hotel room. She was planning to spend the night there even though she lived quite close to the hotel, but she wasn't sure if Jake would stay. She hoped so now, but she might not later. A lot depended on the success of the evening, particularly her success with William West. When she'd met with him at the Gates Foundation dinner, he'd seemed interested, although she wasn't sure if his interest was in the Winslow Foundation or her.

He hadn't been overt, not at all, but the signs had all been there. Lingering eye contact, a kiss to the back of her hand that had made her uncomfortable. It was very likely that he was behaving the way he behaved with all women. He wouldn't be the first man she'd met who was like that. Under other circumstances, she wouldn't bother finding out the truth, but he had a substantial fortune he wanted to donate, and she was only one among many in line for it.

She just hoped she'd have a definitive read on him by the end of the evening. The last thing she wanted to do was waste time playing games.

She settled on the bed, her cell phone clutched in her right hand. She closed her eyes, but didn't expect to sleep. There would be dancing. The orchestra was fantastic, and they weren't going to go crazy with too modern a set because there wasn't a person attending who would know what to do to hip-hop. Well, maybe Bree and Charlie, but still. There would be slow numbers, mostly, and medium numbers, but nothing that would make anyone sweaty.

She had no idea how much of that, if any, Jake's leg could take. She'd prefer not to put him in an uncomfortable situation but that was unavoidable, wasn't it? And why was she even worried in the first place? If he had thought it was a bad idea, he'd have declined the invitation. He wasn't a child and he had nothing to prove to her.

God, they weren't even dating. Although they might as well be because there were going to be a hell of a lot of Winslows in The Cosmopolitan Suite. Her parents, to begin with. Her grandfather. Charlie. Andrew, her cousin on her mother's side, who was not terribly bright. He did, however, look great in photographs which was evidently all the family thought he needed to run for the New York senate. He'd be pressing the flesh, distracting and irritating everyone and taking the spotlight off the foundation.

She wouldn't think about that because there was nothing she could do about it. The Winslow family had her outvoted, and if she was honest with herself, she'd known keeping Andrew away was a lost cause before the discussion had come up.

She hated it, though. He was a jerk, and New York deserved so much better.

She moaned as she turned over. The nap was a farce, but maybe a shower would soothe her enough to deal with the rest of her night. She thought about asking her mother to bring one of her nice little calming pills with her, but rejected the notion immediately. If ever she needed to be sharp it was tonight.

She got her things together for her shower, made sure her dress and shoes were at the ready, then went into the bathroom, purposely leaving her cell phone on the bedside table.

JAKE ENTERED THE FOUR SEASONS from the East 57th Street entrance and walked into the elevator that would take him down one level to The Cosmopolitan Suite, unashamed to admit that he was nervous. He knew how to behave with high-end company, that wasn't it. He wanted to impress Rebecca. At the very least, he wanted to be what she needed, although it didn't help that he wasn't sure what that would be.

First thing, he'd find himself a drink. Okay, second thing, because as he entered the banquet room, there she was. And she was a stunner.

Man, she looked like a movie star. Like a forties glamour girl, and he had to wonder if her choice in gowns had anything to do with their recent discussions of film noir. No, that was a ridiculous thought especially when he took into account that the style fit her to a T.

The dress was floor-length, a rich red that showed off her creamy shoulders and amazing curves. Her hair was pinned up, her lips red, and when she caught sight of him, there was nothing and no one else in the room. The smile that lit up her face got him moving. By the time he reached her, she had turned, and while he wanted to kiss her until the sun came up tomorrow, he stopped himself in the nick of time. Instead he followed her lead. She took one hand and squeezed it and kissed his cheek, then whispered, "I'm so glad you're here."

He nodded slightly, then forced himself to cool it as he realized they were most definitely not alone. Not five feet away, Jake recognized a guy who had his arm around a really petite, pretty girl. On further inspection, she wasn't that young. Just small. And decked out in a dress that made him blink. Not that she didn't look great in it, she did. It was just odd with pastel colors in a weirdly geometric jacket on top of a black-and-white-striped skirt and shoes that seemed to be made solely of straps.

"Jake Donnelly, this is my cousin Charlie Winslow, and my friend Bree Kingston. They'll be sitting with you when I'm roaming around shaking hands, so it would be better if you liked each other."

"Sure, no pressure," Jake said, as he shook hands with first Bree, then Charlie. "You're the blog guy. I don't know why I didn't make the connection."

"I am the blog guy, but in this room, I'm just Rebecca's cousin," Charlie said. "Nice to meet you."

Bree said, "You know what? I could use a drink. How about you boys go fetch us some?"

"It's all equality until someone needs a drink or there's a spider in the bathtub," Charlie said. "You want pineapple juice or something for grown-ups?"

Bree gave Charlie a quick glare. "A Sea Breeze, please."

Jake turned to Rebecca. "And you?"

"I don't dare start drinking this early. I'll have a tonic and lime. That'll fool everyone, right?"

"No one's going to notice. They'll all be too dazzled by how beautiful you are."

"Oh," Bree said as if she'd just seen a kitten. "Okay, you can stay."

He laughed to hide the embarrassment of having been such a cliché, but the look on Rebecca's face told him he hadn't crossed the unforgivable line. "Be right back."

He and Charlie went toward the nearest bar and Jake finally took a look at the joint. It was huge; there was a stage with a full orchestra playing something soft and jazzy, enormous vases with huge flower arrangements all around the many tables, each set up with more glittering silver and crystal than he'd seen in Macy's. It was a massive affair, this party, and he slowed his pace as he watched a row of servers enter the ballroom. They were in black and white, wore gloves and held silver platters with tiny hors d'oeuvres on them. Jesus. She'd said there were billions at stake but he only believed her now. She was playing in the majors.

"You used to be a cop?" Charlie asked as they reached the bar.

"Yeah. Got in right after college. Planned on staying until retirement. Didn't work out that way."

Since there wasn't much of a line yet, they were able to order pretty quickly. Charlie went first, then Jake put in his requests. He glanced back to find Bree and Rebecca huddled, both staring directly at him. Great.

"Don't worry," Charlie said. "You already passed. Rebecca wouldn't have invited you if you were even marginal. Tonight is huge for her. It's like the Super Bowl of fundraisers."

"She's amazing."

"That she is," Charlie said. "The only relative I like, which is something because we've got relatives crawling out of the woodwork. I'll do my best to help you avoid as many as possible."

"She told me her folks would be here."

"Her father isn't a Winslow by birth, but he might as well have been. He's got the entitlement thing down to a science." Charlie got his drinks and waited for Jake. "We all do, honestly. We grew up on the milk of privilege, but Rebecca has always handled it like a responsibility, not a game. She could have done anything with her life. The foundation used to be more of a tax dodge than a charitable enterprise, but she's changing all that. It's not easy, considering who's on the board."

It was Jake's turn to get his drinks, and he took advantage of the moment to take a good sip of his bourbon and water. Although he'd have to grab some of those appetizers before long. He wasn't about to get drunk, not tonight. "We haven't talked all that much about our respective careers," he said. "Although I checked out the foundation online. Seems to be doing a lot of good work."

Charlie brought them to the women, drinks were exchanged, but he didn't stop looking at Jake. "You can tell me to go jump in a lake," Charlie said, "but I've gotta ask the guy question. You got shot? Twice?"

Jake had been expecting that since he and Rebecca had met, but not from her cousin. It didn't bother him. Charlie was right. Every guy he knew had hit him up for details. He wondered though if it had been a setup. If Rebecca had wanted to know and asked Charlie to front the question. From the look on her face, he didn't think that was the case. She probably did want to know so he plunged ahead.

"Undercover operation. Didn't go so well. We trusted someone who didn't deserve it. There was a shoot-out like you see on cop shows on TV. I'd never seen anything like it before, and I didn't see it for long.

"I was lucky, I would have bled out if there hadn't been paramedics right there. The getting shot part wasn't at all like on TV. It hurt like a sonofabitch, and it didn't heal up by the next commercial. I still go to rehab, my left hand shakes from time to time and I'll be living with this limp for the rest of my life."

Charlie held up his drink. "Thank you for your service. I'm sorry it cost such a high price."

Rebecca had lost her smile, but she held her drink up in salute, as did Bree.

Jake wasn't good at this, and did what he always did, which was to look at his shoes. "Thanks." When he looked up again, it was at Rebecca. "How about them Yankees?"

REBECCA IGNORED BREE AND Charlie completely. She kissed Jake on the lips. "I have to do things. I'll come back. I promise."

"Go," Jake said. "Knock 'em dead. As if you could help it."

A little "oh" let her know Bree had been listening, but Rebecca continued to ignore her friend. "I wish I didn't have to go. But duty calls." She pasted on a smile, went toward the entrance and began the fundraising portion of the evening.

While she welcomed guests that never failed to appear in *Time* magazine's 100 Most Influential People, some of them her own relatives, she couldn't resist sneaking glances back at Jake.

She wasn't sure of the designer of his tux, for all she knew it could be off the rack, but it didn't matter because the man wore the clothes, not the other way around. Did he ever.

It was traditional black, complete with bow tie and small pocket kerchief, white. The classic look was a fantastic frame for his face, his *eyes,* and she dared any woman in the room not to swoon over him after one sight.

"Rebecca." The strident voice couldn't be mistaken for any other.

Rebecca returned to her duties. "Hello, Mom. Dad." She bent for the air kisses and waited for the verdict. Both parents would have something to say about her, about the room, about the night, about every last little detail right down to the type of gloves worn by the waitstaff.

"You look very nice," her mother said. "Although you may want to rethink the strapless gowns when it comes to this particular event. You represent the entire family, and we wouldn't want anyone getting the wrong idea."

"I'm pretty certain everyone here would be able to tell I was a woman even if I wore a burka, Mother. And how's your hip, Dad? Better?"

Her father ignored the question. "The Bannerman Orchestra?" He sighed. It was all he needed to do.

"I like the way they rock the Hokey Pokey. Go get yourselves drinks. Have a good time. I made sure to have your favorite caviar to go with the Cristal Champagne. And don't annoy Charlie. He's in a mood."

Neither of them deigned to reply as they walked over to the bar. Rebecca had to admit they looked fantastic, but then the Winslows and the Thorpes had learned the art of presentation when they were toddlers.

And then she caught sight of Jake and he was looking at her, ignoring his companions, as far as she could tell. She smiled. He smiled back. When she held out her hand to Mr. and Mrs. Chandler, she knew she was blushing.

Time slipped by in a mixture of false bonhomie and genuine pleasure as she continued to schmooze the elite. The orchestra played old standards, reserving those best for dancing until later. Soon dinner would be served and while she couldn't wait for the seating, which would only come after she'd made her welcome speech, she was becoming concerned since William West hadn't arrived yet.

She'd felt sure he'd have come early, ready to continue the flirting he'd started last Thursday night. Well, she wouldn't really worry until halfway through dinner.

IT WASN'T A BIG SURPRISE that Charlie was great. He was Rebecca's favorite cousin, and made it to the list of things they both liked. So far he'd added good vodka, pizza crusts, his salad-making expertise, a deep appreciation for her underwear, film noir and the kind of sex that could start wars. Bree was cool, too. She made him laugh, and he appreciated the way she was with Charlie. Easy, but connected. They hadn't been together long, but he'd wager the relationship would take.

His folks used to look at each other like these two did. As if the words were nice, but unnecessary.

Rebecca's voice on the stage snapped his gaze back to her. Dammit, the woman knocked him out. Not just the way she was gorgeous, but the way she held the attention of every person in the room. Yeah, he wasn't such a Brooklyn yahoo that he didn't recognize half the people in attendance. Christ, he read the papers. Watched the news. What the hell he was doing here, he had no idea.

That question was becoming something of a problem. Anyone with half a brain would know he and Rebecca were a temporary item. There was zero chance that he was anything more than a passing whim. The issue was that he was starting to care about that. About after.

Who was going to measure up to a woman like Rebecca Thorpe? It wasn't about the money thing, the hell with the money. But the woman? The heat between them? How he felt when he was with her? Yeah, who would he ever meet that would begin to compare?

The crowd laughed at something Rebecca had said and he found her looking at him instead of her audience. For a minute, she lost the gleam in her eye, and that was all on him. He hadn't been paying attention, and, dammit, that was his job, his only job. To support her. To make her feel like a million. Well, in this group, a billion. He smiled and hoped like hell he could put her back on track.

The next words out of her mouth were confident,

smooth. Amusing. She was back, and he wasn't going to think about the unknowable future. He was here, now, and he'd be a moron not to enjoy every last second.

# 10

REBECCA BARELY TOUCHED her sole meunìere. Pity, because the food was unbelievably wonderful. She hated that her plate would go to waste.

If she could have she would have scooted her chair closer to Jake's until she could lean against him. She wanted his arm around her shoulders, his soft kiss in her hair. Instead, she contented herself with watching him enjoy his beef tenderloin, the sound of his laughter when Charlie or Bree said something amusing. It puzzled her, how much she enjoyed merely looking at him. At the funny and incredibly endearing way he would express himself with a quirk of his lips. He could transform from the essence of machismo to the picture of infinite kindness when he saw his father's hands.

She put another small bite into her mouth when Bree caught her eye. She pointedly glanced at Jake, then bit her lower lip as if Jake's pure awesomeness was too much to handle. Rebecca laughed, covering her mouth, trying not to choke.

"You okay?" Jake asked, his hand on her bare back above her dress.

She hissed at the contact even though his hand wasn't cold or a surprise.

He lifted it immediately at the sound, but she shook her head. "No, it's fine. I'm fine."

Jake was pulling away when her hand found his thigh. "It felt good," she said.

His smile unfolded slowly in all its slightly crooked glory as he touched her again. He kept his voice low, and she felt his breath on the shell of her ear. "You've nailed this," he said. "Listen. You can hear that people are enjoying themselves. I couldn't swear to it, but I bet for this crowd, that's unusual. Your fingerprints are all over this night. You should hit them hard as soon as the meal is over. They're pumped and primed."

She laughed again, but it was breathless at his compliments. She did as he'd suggested. She listened. The orchestra was on a break as she'd specified no music during dinner. She wanted people to talk. Above the clatter of silver, the clink of glasses, there was a steady mumble of voices, nothing distinct but the laughter.

She looked over her left shoulder to the nearest table. Not one of the guests was staring blankly while they ate. Everyone was engaged, participating. It was only one table, but indicative.

Her attention shifted to her immediate surroundings. Wine was being poured. Jake's hand rubbed a small circle on her back and her stomach tightened. Charlie asked Bree if she liked the amaranth; Bree told him she wasn't sure because she had no idea what amaranth was.

She hardly realized she had turned to face Jake, that she'd found his gaze and was staring, watching his pupils grow as his breathing quickened. "Thank you," she said. Then she kissed him on the lips. It was tempting to stay there, with his hand on her back and his words swimming in her head. But that would have to wait.

When she sat up, he drew away smoothly. He took up his fork and had another bite of the eggplant puree. His amaranth remained untouched. Perhaps it would have been wiser to go with a rice pilaf.

Rebecca was sidetracked by movement at the front door. William West had finally arrived. Although she couldn't make out the details, how he ripped off his coat told her everything about his mood. So much for getting him to commit to an endowment tonight.

Then again, maybe not. Once he'd turned back from getting his coat checked, all signs of tension had vanished and he appeared to be his usual confident self as his gaze swept the room. He found her quickly, giving her a courtly nod.

He wasn't much to look at. Average height, brown hair, a body that spoke of a golf hobby instead of a gym membership. He counted on his net worth to give him sex appeal.

Dani met him at the door, but West turned his back on her, which made Rebecca sit up damn straight. A woman Rebecca didn't recognize then entered, wearing what looked like a very politically incorrect full-length fur. She was tall and slim and beautiful, and she looked good as she smiled at Mr. West. She also looked very young, but that was par for the course in this crowd.

Interesting that while West had sent his RSVP in for two, he'd led her to believe that his CFO was going to join him. Well, perhaps the leggy brunette was the CFO.

West took the woman's arm and Dani led them to their table, making sure the waiter was on her heels with both wine and champagne.

Dani went from there directly to the kitchen. Rebecca

relaxed, knowing the next course would be delayed in order to give West and his guest time to catch up. Luckily, the fourth course was salad, and when it did arrive, the removal of plates would be handled perfectly. She may have begrudged spending the money on this particular ballroom, but the catering staff at the Four Seasons was impeccable, always.

For the first time that night, she lifted her wineglass. Part two of fundraising: the hard sell, would come all too soon, but she could handle it. Jake said so.

JAKE HAD LOST BOTH BREE and Charlie. Him to the bar in search of pineapple juice, and Bree to the ladies' room. Jake had watched in amazement as the banquet tables had been replaced by a dance floor and a number of cocktail tables had been set up on the periphery of the room. The entire operation hadn't taken ten minutes. Impressive.

He'd found a spot far enough away from the dancing to avoid being stepped on while leaving the tables for the more needful among the crowd. He normally didn't mind standing; he just wasn't sure how his leg was going to hold out.

A hand on his arm had him turning, expecting Bree. It was, in fact, a woman he'd noticed earlier. He'd place her age in her late fifties, mostly because of the obvious work she'd had done. He doubted very much lips that large had come direct from the factory, or that she'd been born looking so surprised. What had struck him before was that, according to the papers, she and her husband owned a large portion of Manhattan, so obviously the woman could have afforded the best in plastic surgeons. Hell, maybe she was actually in her eighties and the doctors had outdone themselves.

"I don't know you," she said, her words slurred with whiskey. He imagined she wore a very nice perfume, but it couldn't compete with the booze. "But you know Rebecca. Very well, I'm thinking."

"I'm glad to say she's a friend," he replied, smiling as pleasantly as he could.

"Friend, my ass. I'm Paulina."

"Nice to meet you," he said, holding out his hand. "Jake."

"You're the best-looking thing at this dinner. Did you know that?"

He bit back a laugh. "That's very kind of you."

"Oh, don't get excited," she said, waving her hand so that her jewels flashed against the lights. "I'm not going to do anything about it. My husband doesn't even mind. He knows I like to look."

"Paulina!"

Jake looked up at Charlie's voice, more grateful than he could say.

"We haven't seen each other in ages," Charlie said, taking her hand and spinning her away from Jake. "You get more beautiful every time I see you." He gave her two air kisses and a smile that looked one hundred percent real.

"Charlie. Honey. You're the best-looking thing at this dinner. Did you know that?"

"I did, Paulina, I did. There doesn't seem to be a damn thing I can do about it, though. I'm just that handsome."

She waved her hand again, laughing, and Charlie shoved a glass of juice at Jake before he guided the woman into the crowd.

"So he's thrown me over for another woman," Bree said, making Jake jump. The damn orchestra made it hard to know when people were approaching. "Is that my drink?"

He handed her the glass, then took a sip from his own. "He rescued me. Don't give him any grief."

"Well, damn, there goes my night."

"You're good together, you two."

She grinned happily. "I think so. It's weird though."

"What?"

"Him being Charlie Winslow. I'm from Ohio. Before I moved in with Charlie, I shared a tiny one-bedroom apartment with four people. Now we share a floor. A whole floor."

"It is kind of overwhelming," he said. "How really rich they are. But most of the time, I don't think about it."

"I ignored it when Charlie and I first started going out, but it's too big to ignore. It takes adjusting, on both our parts. He doesn't even get it half the time. What he has access to is insane. His normal is about fifty times grander than my wildest fantasies."

Jake thought about Rebecca's condo; the view alone let him know he was in over his head. "I don't think I'll be around long enough to have to adjust."

"Oh, no." Bree stepped in front of him, pouting. It was actually very cute. "Don't say that. Why did you say that? You guys are so great together."

"We're not even dating. Not for real. I have no idea why I'm here. We were a kind of setup thing. A mutual acquaintance. In theory, it was for one night only."

"Huh," Bree said, trying to hide her grin. "That's a familiar tale."

"Oh?"

"*Our* mutual acquaintance was Rebecca."

"Huh," he repeated.

Bree just wiggled her eyebrows.

Behind Bree, he caught sight of Rebecca, and the urge to join her was strong despite the fact that he knew she was working the room. She'd told him as much, apologetically, which he appreciated, but leaving no room for misinterpretation. Tonight was business, and he was... not.

On the other hand, her glass was empty. She kept bringing it up to her lips to drink, then lowering it as she recalled the tonic was gone.

"Charlie's on his way back," he said to Bree. "So if you'll excuse me."

"Sure," she said, glancing from him to Rebecca then back. "Go get her, tiger."

He ignored the crazy girl and went toward the bar. It took him longer than he'd like to get Rebecca's drink, but when he found her again, she was still talking to the same guy, and her glass was still empty. Jake's approach was stealthy, not wanting to disrupt the flow of her conversation, yet keeping the man's back to him so that Rebecca had a little warning.

Only, when he got close enough, he heard the guy laugh. The sound stopped Jake short. He'd heard that laugh before. One other time, twelve years ago. He'd never forgotten it, not a chance, because it had belonged to Vance Keegan.

"Lip" Keegan had been part of a very large drug bust. He'd escaped, along with about half a dozen others, when things had gone to hell. Unlike the other runners, Keegan had seemed to vanish into thin air.

Jake moved in slowly, trying to avoid Rebecca's attention until he could convince himself that he'd been mistaken. Even though the laugh was a dead ringer for Bender, a *Futurama* cartoon character, there had to be more than one person who sounded like that. Jake had been in charge of getting Keegan into the bus. He'd cuffed the guy, had him by the arm, and he'd let him get away. The piece of crap had laughed the whole way across the rooftop, a full block, right in Jake's ear. But that had happened a lifetime ago, when Jake had been a rookie.

The man with the uncanny laugh stepped closer to Rebecca. He reached over and touched her above the elbow. Jake moved in, right up between them, no excuses. Keegan stepped back, which was the point. Except it wasn't Keegan.

The face wasn't the same. The eyes were different, the shape of his jaw, his nose had been bigger. But shit, shit, under the mustache, this guy had been born with a cleft pallet. Same as Lip Keegan.

"Jake," Rebecca said. "Is everything all right?"

He forced himself to look at Rebecca. As soon as he did, the time and place came back to him with a jolt. He must have made a mistake, which was weird and embarrassing enough, but he'd intruded on what could have been a crucial moment. "I apologize. I lost my footing," he said, even more embarrassed that he was using his injuries to excuse himself. "I meant to refresh your drink."

His lame excuse, God, the pun made him wince, had done its job. Rebecca visibly relaxed and her smile wasn't at all forced.

"I'll leave you to it," he said, trading glasses with her.

"Wait," she said, touching his arm. "I'd like you to meet William West. The CEO of West Industries."

"Bill," he said. Dammit, that wasn't the same scar. Lip's scar had been jagged, a mess. "You are?"

Jake took the offered hand. "Jake Donnelly. A friend of Rebecca's." The handshake was tight, and Jake supposed he was fifty percent responsible, but all his instincts were telling him that West was not who he claimed to be. Jake thought about Paulina and her artificial face, and he wondered. With someone good on the end of a scalpel, it was possible.

"Thanks for the drink," Rebecca said, startling him again.

"My pleasure. I'll see you later." He nodded at West, then left, achingly aware of his limp and his confusion. He knew nothing about West Industries, but he did know that Keegan would have had twelve years to change his face, to reinvent himself.

On the other hand, the likelihood of Jake running into Vance Keegan at the Four Seasons was absurd. Still, he'd check it out, because even if the odds were he was as wrong as he could get, West was involved with Rebecca. If West did end up giving a grant or donation or whatever the hell people gave to foundations, Jake needed to be sure it wasn't blood money. Rebecca would never want that.

She would want him here. Thinking about her, instead of a long-shot hunch.

He ordered a bourbon at the bar, left a tip, then went straight back to Charlie and Bree, still standing near the dance floor. Charlie had his arms wrapped around her and they looked completely into each other. In love. Jake put aside his concerns and played his part as if his life depended on it.

THE ORCHESTRA CAME BACK from their break as Bill West kissed the back of Rebecca's hand. The gesture was creepy, but then the man was creepy, so what could she expect? It didn't matter whether she liked him or not, or that he'd flirted with her right in front of his girlfriend, companion, whatever she was. It wasn't difficult to see his *friend* hadn't been too thrilled. Rebecca wasn't either—not about the flirting, but how they'd ended the conversation. Even though West had said he was going to get involved with the foundation, no promise had been made, no dollar amount mentioned, and she'd needed both of those to happen tonight. On the plus side, they were going to meet privately later in the week. On the minus side, she'd have to see him privately.

Now the only pressing matter was finding Jake. She hadn't yet introduced him to her parents, and while that prospect wasn't thrilling, she figured she'd better. The last thing she'd want was for Jake to think she'd kept them apart. He'd never believe it was because she didn't want him to meet them, not the other way around.

She missed Jake, even though he was in the same room. She liked him. He'd brought her a tonic and lime because he'd noticed her glass was empty. Didn't sound like much, but in her experience it was almost unprecedented.

She spotted him on the other side of the dance floor. He'd been watching her. People kept blocking her line of sight, but only for seconds at a time as they danced by. He stayed where he was, watching, waiting. The room filled with the sound of strings, the violins romantic and dazzling, the cellos low and sexy.

They had to walk around the dance floor, but eventually, Jake was in front of her. She could reach out and touch him if she wanted.

She wanted.

Her hand went to the back of his neck and she drew him into a kiss. For a long moment there was nothing but his lips, the slide of his tongue, the warmth that spread through her body. He broke away, not far. She could still feel his breath on her chin.

"I'd sure like to do more of that," he said.

"Me, too. Will you stay the night? I have a room upstairs."

"Of course I will."

She brushed the back of his hand with hers. She wanted to steal him away, forget the party, the introductions, the good-nights.

"I know you have to go back to your duties," he said. "Dance with me first? Fair warning, it's not going to be pretty."

"Pretty is overrated."

They put their drinks on the nearest table and went to a corner of the dance floor, where Jake took her around her waist, drawing her close. Rebecca slipped her arms around his neck, rested her head on his shoulder. They didn't so much dance as sway, and even that was bumpy because Jake had to make adjustments.

It was altogether perfect.

The rest of the night would be so much more bearable knowing Jake would be there at the end.

# 11

AT ONE IN THE MORNING, there was absolutely nothing Jake wanted more than to get out of the ballroom, out of his tuxedo and into Rebecca. It didn't look like an escape was imminent, though.

He'd have figured the orchestra would have stopped playing by midnight, but nope. They kept on pumping out tunes, most of them a little peppier than the sleepy waltzes they'd featured when the crowd had been at its peak. Charlie and Bree had cut out over an hour ago, and William West had left an hour before them. Unfortunately, Rebecca was still being set upon by people who clearly didn't have work tomorrow. For God's sake, it was a Wednesday night.

Rebecca continued to look stunning. As if she'd just arrived. Not a hair out of place, her dress as beautiful and slinky as it had been when he'd first seen her. How did women do it? Stand up all night on tiptoe? High heels had to hurt like a sonofabitch.

He went over to the buffet table where they'd put out coffee and pastries a while ago. Since his leg was as tired as the rest of him, he was fingering one of his pain pills in his tux pocket. It didn't normally knock him out, but he didn't normally drink when he took the pill.

The coffee turned out to be a good idea. Sipping something hot and familiar made him feel more relaxed, let him give his obsessive mind a rest.

If he wasn't thinking about Rebecca, he was thinking about West. Keegan. That damn laugh, the lip. It was driving him crazy. That's what happened to a man when there wasn't a problem to solve that was more difficult than how to install bathroom tile. The mind turned to mush.

He was sinking into a really good sulk when he saw Rebecca coming toward him. He straightened, not giving a damn about his leg now, or his need for sleep. The nearer she got, the better his mood. Until he realized why the couple behind her looked so familiar. She'd said she was going to introduce him to her parents.

Fuck.

He put his coffee down on the buffet table and surreptitiously wiped his right hand on his slacks. Rebecca's smile would have put him at ease if her parents hadn't been right behind her.

"I'm sorry it's so late," she said, placing her hand on his arm and moving to his side. "I did want to introduce you to my parents before we left for the evening. Marjorie and Franklin, this is Jake Donnelly."

He shook their hands. He smiled, but only slightly, kept his cool because he had been trained by the best captain in the continental United States, and he did not give away the game under any kind of pressure. "Pleasure to meet you both."

"Rebecca hasn't told us much about you, Jake. What is it that you do?" Franklin's nonsmile reminded Jake of politicians and backstreet lawyers. He was unnaturally tan for March in New York, and he was fighting lean.

His wife was a beauty, and Rebecca favored her. Same honey-blond hair, same long face that sat right on the border of attractive in Marjorie's case.

"I'm unemployed at the moment," he said. "Doing some work on my father's house. Figuring out what comes next."

"Unemployed?" Franklin said.

"Yes, sir." Jake had been shot in the line of duty. He was under no obligation to explain himself. A glance at Rebecca told him she'd have no problem if he left it at that. But these were her folks. He didn't need to prove anything by being a dick, either. "I was in the NYPD. Major Case Squad detective. I was injured in the line of duty and took early retirement. I haven't decided yet where I'll land when I've healed up."

Franklin stopped looking at Jake as if he was infectious.

"That must have been terrible for you," Rebecca's mother said.

"It hasn't been a picnic, but I'm still here."

"And we're still *here*," Rebecca said, leaving his side to kiss her father on the cheek, then her mother. "It's late. Go home. I'm going to sleep soon."

"Tonight was very well done," Marjorie said.

"Thanks, Mom."

Franklin said nothing. He nodded, then took his wife's arm and went for the coat check.

Rebecca turned back to Jake. "Thank you. I probably should have prepared them."

"For what? That I'm so good-looking?"

She grinned. "That, too. They mean well. They're dinosaurs, you know? Stuck in time with very rigid boundaries. Charlie's parents, too. The whole family, actually. I think they stopped evolving when they got lucky during the thirties."

"Speaking of which," he said, sliding his hands around her waist. "That dress makes me think of smoky jazz clubs and men in fedoras."

"You'd look great in a hat."

"I have a hat."

"Really?"

"I'll wear it for you sometime."

"Do me a favor?" she asked.

"Whatever you want."

"Don't wear anything else when you show me."

He kissed her. Nothing too extravagant, not yet. Merely a preview of coming attractions.

Later, despite his best intentions and Rebecca's outstanding choice in underwear, she was so obviously exhausted when they finally climbed into the big hotel bed at two-twenty, that he couldn't do anything but hold her as she fell asleep.

By all rights, he should have been out like a light himself, but maybe it was the coffee, maybe how far out of his comfort zone he'd been all night, but he stared at the sliver of light coming in from the privacy drapes as his thoughts bounced around like a nine-ball off three rails.

If it wasn't about how much he wanted to see Rebecca again, it was about how stupid he was for wanting to see Rebecca again, and if neither of those made his gut tighten enough, he settled on the odds of William West being Vance Keegan 2.0, hiding his corrupt past with a fake identity and some excellent plastic surgery.

It took him a hell of a long time to get to sleep, but at least Rebecca was using his good shoulder for a pillow. That made up for a lot.

WAKING UP TO NO ALARM AND Jake wrapped around her like a warm blanket was everything a girl could want out of life. He must not have been up for too long if his fuzzy smile was anything to go by.

"Morning," she said, careful not to breathe in his direction.

He kissed her forehead. "Morning, gorgeous. I'm thinking about ordering up a lot of coffee. Maybe some French toast. You like French toast?"

She nodded, stifling a yawn. "I'll go do stuff," she said. "But save my shower for after."

"That's a hell of an idea."

"There are robes. In the bathroom. Big, thick white robes. I'll bring you one."

"Thanks. Anything else you want from room service?"

She shook her head, then felt him watch her ass as she walked away.

They lingered over food, teasing each other with cool feet sneaking up naked legs. Jake, aside from looking at her as if she was stunning despite her raccoon eyes and hair from her nightmares, continued to be amazing. Crazy amazing, like someone had built him to her exact specifications.

He did a recap of the evening that made her laugh and blush, showering her with kudos. Nothing would have pleased her more than spending the rest of the day in bed. And the night. Unfortunately, she did have to leave by two because as much as she deserved a day off, she wasn't going to get one. There were too many details to handle, her own notes and follow-up calls to enter on her calendar.

But it was only noon now. She put her cup down, then took his cup and put it on the room service tray. The edges of his lips curled up as she untied the robe's belt and pushed the thick terry cloth off his shoulders. She could only get so far, but Jake was quick, and he took over where she left off. She stripped herself bare, then rested once again on her knees.

Naked and mostly hard, Jake reached for her, cupping her cheek in his large hand. "You take my breath away," he said. "I want you all the time."

She turned her head to kiss his thumb. "Make love to me?"

"Yes." He shifted his hands to her shoulders and eased them both down on the bed until they were on their sides, inches apart, their gazes holding. "I never know where to start with you. If I go for the kiss, I can't see the rest of you. I don't have enough hands to touch every part of your body at once. I love being inside you, and believe me, I'm a big fan of coming, but then I have to rest, and that seems like such a waste."

It wasn't the same giddy shiver in her tummy. As strong, yes, but not the same. This was a warmth, deep down, that spread into her limbs and her chest and her throat and her hands. They met in a kiss, and he tasted like Jake beneath the maple and coffee.

As his hand ran down her arm, slowly, gently, tears built behind her closed lids. She liked him so much, she didn't know what to do with it. This was new. A part of herself hidden all these years. Triggered by his touch and how he saw her. So calm, so assured. He didn't care about her lineage or that she could be a snob or that she lived in a bubble of privilege. He had looked past all of it from that first night.

What surprised her even more was that she didn't care that he had no job, that his body was torn up, that he lived in a world she'd barely known existed.

His kiss deepened and she was on her back, with Jake settling between her legs. Everything felt slow as honey; even the light coming in from the terrace window steeped them in amber. She touched him, ran her palms down his back and over his shoulders and felt the muscles move beneath his skin. She breathed his breath and they rubbed against each other in a slow, easy dance that could have gone on forever. There was no rush to get to the finish line. This was enough. This was heaven.

She looked at his dark hair, mussed from sleep and her fingers, then down his strong back, so beautiful. Even the scar was a map of his character. He'd survived so much. He should have been bitter. Mad at the world. But that wasn't Jake.

He was a wonder. He'd expanded her world. He made her laugh and made her come and he was a terrible dancer. The way he talked to his father was something she'd dreamed of as a child. That she would wake up one day and her family would be close and they'd laugh together at silly things. That her dad would light up when she walked into a room. It was all so tempting.

Yet as much as Jake filled her with joy, she couldn't picture a future with him. But she wanted to. God, she wanted to.

She loved him. Oh, what had she done?

"You're trembling," he said.

Her fingers had gripped him so tightly, she had to be hurting him. She spread her thighs, lifted her hips with an urgency that hadn't been there a few moments ago. "Make love to me. Please."

He looked at her, his lips moist from her kisses, his eyes curious and a little worried. "Yes," he said again.

When he stretched to reach the condoms left on the bedside table, she clung to him even as she loosened her grip.

JAKE GOT HOME AT four-thirty that afternoon, still tired, leg and shoulder aching. The boys were on the porch, of course, giving him hell.

"My goodness, that was some party," Pete said, leaning back in his plastic chair. "I didn't think those fancy dress shindigs lasted all night."

"Maybe now he's been with hoi polloi," Liam added, "he doesn't want to hang out with us regular Joes."

Jake made it up the porch stairs and shook his head at the old busybodies. "Hoi polloi doesn't mean what you think it means," he said.

"Oh, so now we don't know English." Liam shifted. "Well, excuse me."

"I'm tired and cold and I need to get out of this damn monkey suit. But feel free to make fun of me in absentia."

The old men laughed, poking at each other as Jake hit the door. He gave his dad a grin, then went inside. Shower first, then he'd hit the computer. The downstairs unfinished bathroom made him groan with guilt. He'd get to it, but first, he had to see if there was any current record of Vance Keegan. Maybe the guy was in prison, maybe, more likely, he was long dead.

After another set of stairs, each step harder to climb, Jake started a hot bath, then went back to his room to put on some normal clothes. It wasn't as if he'd hated the party or felt overly uncomfortable. He just couldn't see making a habit of it.

That was the fundamental issue, wasn't it? Now that his uniform wasn't NYPD blue, it was worn jeans and comfortable shirts. He wore shoes he bought from the mall, he got his boxer briefs in a three-pack and his hair cut for five bucks at the local barber.

Rebecca and him? They were impossible. For a sprint, yeah, okay, but for the distance? No way.

He got into the tub even though there wasn't enough water yet and started massaging his thigh. Later he'd call about adding a therapy session. The muscles around the wound had gotten so damned tight it felt as if with the next step his whole thigh would tear in two. It was impossible to think when it got really bad, and according to the doctor, he was looking at a long rehab. Years. He'd never be the same, but if things went well, he eventually wouldn't have to depend on pain pills to get through a day.

Yet another reason he and Rebecca had a time limit. She could have anyone. The last thing she'd want to be saddled with was some broke ex-cop with no future.

He pressed down on his quadriceps with his thumb, digging into the worst of the pain. It hurt like a wildfire, spreading up, down, throughout his whole body. Why the hell was he even thinking about anything long-term? He had no clue what he was in for. What kind of life he could have, let alone what he wanted.

Rebecca was a slice of fantasy, that's all. He'd check on Keegan, make sure it was his imagination going off the deep end, and then, well, he'd see. She might not want to go out with him again, no matter how great this morning had been. He might wise up and end it before things got more complicated.

By the time he'd finished his soak and taken his damned pill, he'd changed his mind about hitting the computer. Instead, he went downstairs. His dad was in the kitchen, putting a piece of pumpkin pie on a paper plate.

"Did you eat dinner?"

"What are you, my mother?"

"Fine. Get rickets. See if I care. And cut me a piece, would ya?"

Jake reheated a cup of coffee then took both paper plates to the breakfast nook. Mike wheeled himself up to the table and managed his own cup.

"Where'd the boys go?"

He shrugged. "Liam wanted a lift to the mall. He needed some slippers or some damn thing."

Jake shoveled in some pie. "So I'm at this shindig, this party for millionaires, and I hear this guy laugh."

His father didn't look up. Ate. Drank.

"I recognize the laugh. Weird laugh, one you could ID easy, you know?"

The nod was noncommittal, but Jake hadn't gotten anywhere yet.

"The last time I heard it, I was on that joint task force. With the FBI and the ATF?"

"Your guy got away."

"Yeah. It was his laugh. That same weird fucking laugh."

His dad looked up at him. "That's what, a dozen years ago?"

Jake nodded. "I thought it was peculiar especially when I saw this guy from the front. He's got the same build, roughly, but the details are wrong. Hair, nose, eyes, jaw. But this guy, big shot, tons of money. Rebecca's trying to get him to donate a fortune. Anyway, he's got this cleft palate. Sewed up, but the scar is there. Like Stacy Keach."

"Yeah?"

"My guy had a cleft palate. It didn't look as good back then, but come on. The laugh and the lip?"

"Could be a coincidence."

"I know. It's more likely that it's nothing. That I got the laugh wrong. I mean, when's the last time you believed eyewitness testimony? It was years ago."

"He might have been in a fight. Been in a car wreck. Split his lip."

Jake nodded again. Ate some more pie.

"On the other hand," his father said, "you could have identified a fugitive. They had him on a murder charge, right?"

Jake sighed. Sat back and stretched out his leg. "Probably wouldn't hold up now. Evidence gone. Witnesses unreliable from the get-go."

"Might be worth a look."

"You think?" Jake asked, studying his old man's face. No way Mike Donnelly was going to toss him a bone. If Jake was full of crap, his father would say.

"What's your instinct tell you?"

"That he wasn't right."

"There's your answer."

"I could be completely wrong."

"That's true. So take your time. Be careful."

"I'm not a cop anymore."

"Jakey, you'll be a cop till the day you die."

REBECCA WALKED INTO HER condo just after nine-thirty, and she had enough energy to drag herself to her bedroom, strip, leaving her clothes in a heap, and fall into bed.

Things could have gone better at the office. She'd tried, she'd really tried to keep on task, but her thing with Jake had her tied up in knots.

Wasn't love supposed to be all rainbows and unicorns? All she felt was confused. It was supposed to have been a one-night stand. She hadn't meant to get involved with him. He was a wounded ex-cop from Brooklyn. She was...

She was exhausted. And scared. As unsure about what to do as she'd ever been. The idea of not seeing him again hurt. Physically hurt. But if she did see him again, what then? It would just exacerbate the problem. And if they wanted to take it to the next step?

He couldn't leave his father to come live with her. Besides, Jake was a proud man. He wouldn't want to live off her money. She wanted to believe she could become part of his life, but really? Commuting from Brooklyn? Living in a row house?

It was all too much, and her brains were scrambled from the banquet and Jake and the very real possibility that she'd become a person she didn't like very much. But she'd have to deal with it later. Maybe take a few days away from Jake, let things settle. She needed time. And some kind of miracle.

AT TEN-THIRTY, JAKE WAS AT the computer, his coffee fresh, and his leg had simmered down to bearable. There were a lot of hits when he typed in Vance Keegan's name in Google. But each link was about the past, the distant past. The biggest single subtopic was the missing money. They'd been expecting millions, and even the best forensic accountants hadn't been able to trace where all that loot had gone. The press had outdone themselves condemning the police, the FBI and the ATF. A separate task force had been put together to pinpoint the blame, and Jake's anger at reading about it was just as acute as it had been when it had happened.

But this wasn't about history, this was a mission of discovery. He wasn't having much luck. By the time the eleven o'clock news came on, he gave up on finding Keegan and started looking into West. Who was from Nevada. Henderson, born and raised.

The guy was worth a fortune. But he wasn't flashy with it and kept a relatively low profile. He was a venture capitalist who'd made some smart moves, including getting out of real estate before it had all come tumbling down. He was involved with a large number of limited partnerships that specialized in chains, everything from dry cleaning to mortuaries. There weren't a lot of articles about him.

According to the company bio, he was the same age as Keegan. Unmarried, no kids. He'd started his company with profits from a windfall, an inheritance from his uncle, his late father's brother. He'd invested the money, and the rest was a quiet success story.

Nothing hinted that West wasn't exactly who he said he was. But nothing eliminated the possibility either. What was really clear was that Jake didn't have near the access he needed. But he knew someone who could get deeper. A lot deeper.

Gary Summers was an old buddy, a guy Jake had known in college. Gary had been into computers, specifically hacking, since high school. He'd been approached by the government and decided that the good guys had the best toys so he'd signed up. He was an independent bastard, only taking on contract work that interested him. The two of them didn't talk about specifics, and that was probably why they were still friends.

Jake sent him a text. The answer came when he was downstairs helping his old man get ready for the stairs.

Come on up. Next week? Few days? U bring the beer. Send prelim info to 192.175.2.2.

Satisfied for the moment, Jake thought about calling Rebecca, just to hear her voice, but it was late, and he hoped she was sleeping. At the thought, his own exhaustion hit him like a truck. Waking up alone would be a bitch.

# *12*

THE OFFICE WAS QUIET AS A crypt; she should have finished her work hours ago. To make matters worse, it was Sunday, day three of her self-prescribed time-out.

Jake had wanted to see her. He'd asked her to the movies, offered to feed her, even suggested a trip to a real Irish pub. She'd begged off each time, and while her reasons were legitimate, they weren't the whole truth.

Sadly, it turned out time away hadn't made her situation any less confusing. She missed him. Thought of him so often it was absurd. Why was it that even though *she'd* chosen to keep her distance, it felt as if she was being punished? Yearning, it seemed, wasn't just in storybooks, and it had a specific shape and weight right in the center of her chest.

She rubbed her eyes, stretched her neck, then pulled out Jake's trading card to look at his gorgeous face. She thought about her last phone conversation with him. He'd seemed tense. Probably because he could sense she wasn't telling him everything. They'd made love on Thursday morning. They'd bonded intensely, well, she had at least. Based on their phone conversations Jake's world hadn't been rocked off its axis. The two of them hadn't discussed it. By now he probably assumed she was withdrawing since the banquet was over. After she'd seen him in her native environment and found him lacking.

It would be much simpler if that were true.

She should call him.

Rebecca glanced at the clock. Ten minutes had passed since her last check, which had been ten minutes after the glance before. Ridiculous. She picked up the phone and hit speed dial 1. He'd moved up from speed dial 17 on Thursday before her self-imposed exile.

He answered after the first ring. "Hey."

"The thing is," she began, "if I finish answering the emails and writing up the last two reports, I can start tomorrow with a clean slate. All the work from the banquet will be finished on my end."

He paused, then said, "I see. How long do you think that'll take?"

"Longer than it should. I'm in slow motion."

"Any chance you'll be up for a visit at the end?"

Now it was her turn to be quiet.

"Fair enough," he said. "How about this? How about you and me and your clean slate go out to dinner tomorrow night? Early, so that you can get to sleep at a decent hour."

She thought for a second. Seeing him was all she wanted. Also dangerous. Screw it. "That's very doable. In fact, I think it's a great idea. Although, we could eat dinner at home, thereby eliminating a step."

"Tempting," he said, and she could picture him leaning against the wall in the bathroom. The one he was fixing up. She could tell he was in there from the echo. He did like to lean, but that probably had more to do with his bad leg than posing. He'd be wearing his tool belt, too. And jeans. Soft, worn jeans that curved around his most excellent behind.

"Okay," he said. "I'll bring dinner. No cooking. No movie watching. Dinner, then bed."

"Well, that's not going to help me sleep."

"Don't be silly," he said. "We'll have just finished eating. We'll work off dinner. Then you'll collapse in my arms and sleep the sleep of the just."

"Bible quotes?"

"Really?" he asked. "I thought that was from an Elvis Costello song."

She grinned, wanting him with her, right there in the office. Just sitting there so she could look over and see him. He'd smile at her, and she'd get wiggly. Of course then she'd have to go kiss him and her grand plan would bite the dust. "Right. Dinner, my place—"

Another call came on her line, which she would most likely ignore. "Hang on. I'll be right back. It could be work."

She clicked to the second call, a New York number she didn't recognize. "Hello?"

"Rebecca."

William West. She recognized his voice. "Mr. West."

"I thought we agreed on Bill."

"Bill. Can you hold on a moment? I'm on another call."

"I'll wait."

She clicked again, hating that she'd have to put off Jake. If it had been anyone else... "Crap, it is work," she said. "I won't be long. I hope. If it is, we'll talk tomorrow and settle times and stuff, okay?"

"Don't stay up too late. I don't want you falling asleep in the soup."

She smiled and almost blew him a kiss, which...jeez. She was overtired. "Later."

She clicked back to West. "What can I do for you, Bill?"

"I think it's a question of what I can do for you. I'd like to take you to dinner tomorrow evening. We can start the ball rolling on the endowment."

Holy... "Absolutely. Where and when?"

"I'll meet you in front of your office building at eight. The chef at Per Se owes me. We'll have a window seat."

Per Se was one of the most exclusive restaurants in Manhattan, and getting a table there in anything less than six months took an act of congress. "I'll meet you at the car."

Rebecca hung up, looked at her long list of emails, thought about all her options and quickly redialed Jake. "Yeah?"

"Can you meet me tonight instead? In two hours?"

He was quiet for a minute. "Uh, sure. What changed?"

"William West. He's finally agreed to meet with me tomorrow night to talk actual money. It's not attorneys yet, but it's a major step closer. So I made the executive decision to scrap my noble plans for a clean slate Monday in favor of a delicious Sunday night."

Oddly there was silence again. She'd thought he'd be pleased. "Oh, wait. Is this about your father? We could make it Tuesday night. Give you time to set things up."

"No. No, my dad's fine. He's got friends on standby. Hell, half the neighborhood would volunteer to stay with him if I asked. So, no. It's no problem. I'll bring dinner?"

"That would be excellent."

"You like Chinese?"

"Love it. Especially dim sum. But brunch is probably over, so never mind."

"Never mind? I can get dim sum."

"Really? You're a magician. Oh, that would be… Maybe some extra char siu bao. And har gau. Oh, and spareribs."

Jake laughed. "Is that all? I can just order a couple of everything on the menu."

"I skipped lunch."

"I can't leave you alone for five minutes, can I?" he asked.

The tenderness in his voice made her sit back in her chair. It took her a second to respond, what with swallowing past the lump. "No, I guess you can't. I'll see you in two."

"Don't be late. Your concierge looked hungry the last time I was there."

JAKE WAS THE ONE WHO WAS almost late. Not because of dinner. Gary had called him while he'd been in the cab on the way to the Great Wall restaurant. It wasn't a long conversation, just enough to ruin Jake's mood. He ended up ordering all the dim sum appetizers, even though it was going to cost him a fortune, and he'd have to wait a hell of a long time for it. The wait was fine, and the money, well, he was pretty sure he was trying to prove something by draining his savings, but he couldn't worry about that now. Not when Gary had found something. It didn't necessarily make West a bad guy, but it didn't help.

Rebecca was meeting West tomorrow night. Getting ready to make a deal. What Jake had wouldn't prove anything. The man's laugh reminded Jake of a particular cartoon character. A lot of people were born with cleft palates. If the two things hadn't been combined, he'd have dismissed the notion with barely a second thought. But the two things had been connected.

He had to decide, before he got the food, before he got to Manhattan, whether he was going to ask her to postpone the meeting with West or not.

Dammit, he didn't want this thing with her to be over. Not yet. Yeah, yeah, it was inevitable, like death, like taxes, like his father driving him crazy, but not yet. He might not have a choice about that, though. Something had been off between them the past few days. Ever since Thursday afternoon. It wasn't her workload, that he got completely. She was her job, the way he'd been his, so he had no complaints about the hours she spent at the office. It was more subtle. Pauses when there shouldn't have been. An edginess to her voice.

She'd undoubtedly come to the same conclusion he had, that they were on borrowed time. That the more they saw each other, the more difficult the break would be.

She was the best thing that had happened to Jake in a long time. Even before he'd been shot, his life hadn't been all that spectacular. When he'd been working his way up the ranks, he hadn't wanted a relationship. When he'd gone under, he couldn't have one. And now? With no job, no idea what he was going to do? Even if she wasn't Rebecca Thorpe he'd have no chance in hell.

God, how he'd wanted deep cover assignments. It was always a choice, those, because of what they meant. It was dangerous as hell, obviously, but more than the prospect of being killed, the real long-term danger was getting lost.

He'd been on the edge of doing just that. He'd become Steve "Papo" Carniglia. A wannabe drug lord who'd worked his way up the ranks in the Far Rockaway Gang of Apes, getting close and tight with the man in charge because while he'd acted like a card-carrying member of the Queens' gang, he never played dumb.

As he sat on the really uncomfortable bench waiting for the food, he leaned his head back against the window and cursed his instincts. She had so much riding on West's money. Not just her, but all the people his money could help. The smart thing to do would be to let it go. Forget he'd ever heard that damn laugh. There were a lot of reasons it made sense to put the brakes on, but the one that had him tied up in knots was that she might be walking into something that could put her foundation in jeopardy.

Rebecca was doing everything in her power to elevate the image of the Winslow Foundation, to give it integrity and transparency. If he had a little more time, he could make sure who she was getting involved with. Then they could both rest easy. All he needed was a short reprieve.

He wanted to show her so much. Now that the banquet was over, she'd have time. First thing, he'd take her to the New York she'd never seen. The hidden city he'd spent so long exploring. He wanted to watch her face when she saw where she really lived.

He could have it, too. If she postponed that meeting. Or if he didn't bring up the subject of Keegan at all.

The host called Jake's name, and he shook his head at how overboard he'd gone in buying dinner for two. But he wanted Rebecca to have everything. Food, success, pride, honor, *everything*. How long he had before she came to her senses and showed him the door didn't matter in the end. Nothing mattered except Rebecca.

Well, there was his answer.

SHE OPENED THE DOOR AND laughed out loud when she saw the enormous bags he was carrying. "You dope," she said, taking one of the heavy bags. "You bought the whole restaurant?"

"You skipped lunch."

"Yeah, well, you're taking the leftovers home. That'll feed your dad and his buddies for a couple of weeks."

"Boy, do you not know my dad and his buddies. They may be old, but they eat like beat cops."

She watched him as he hung up his coat. He looked great, as always. No tool belt, dammit, but nice jeans, not quite as worn in, a little darker than the ones she'd declared her favorite, with a white oxford shirt tucked into them. She took another moment to admire his shoulder-to-waist ratio. She was a lucky, lucky woman.

"What's that goofy grin about?"

"You're very attractive," she said.

"That's it? Attractive?"

"That's a lot."

He shrugged.

"I'm not saying that's all you are."

He put his bag on the island, then took the one she was holding and dumped that, too. "What else am I?" he asked as he pulled her into his arms.

"Wow. Fish much?"

"From time to time. Come on." He kissed her, quick, teasing. "Give me something other than looks."

"As if you've never thought hot wasn't reason enough."

"I have, I'll admit it. But you're so much more than that," he said and then he really kissed her. It was as if he'd been starving, but for her. She felt his desperation in his hands and his lips and the way he thrummed with energy. She was helpless to do anything but kiss him back, to give as good as she got. When he finally drew back, she had to blink herself into the present, into the fact that the ache she'd felt for days had dissipated the moment she was in his arms. That she'd never felt like this before, not even dared to dream she could be madly, deeply in love, and that maybe, possibly, he felt… No, he was just being Jake. She'd know if he loved her.

She put some distance between them and the loss of his touch was like a slap. "Let's put out everything on the coffee table and grab whatever. Want a Sapporo?"

He didn't answer for a long minute, and she couldn't read him. Hesitance, and then a smile. His regular smile. "Sure. I'll start unpacking."

Rebecca got the beers, the plates and the good chopsticks. She also brought along her bottle of soy sauce because she had a tendency to squirt the packets all over herself and the furniture.

It looked like a modern sculpture, all the white boxes covering her coffee table. He'd had to put the magazines on the floor and the flowers on the side table.

"I'm going to have one of everything." she said, determined to keep things light. She handed him his beer. "Then decide about seconds."

"You'd better get a move on, because there's only three of each thing."

They sat next to each other on the couch. She had one leg curled under her butt; his legs were spread in that manly way that always amused. After he opened both beers, they grabbed their chopsticks, and it was on.

"Hey," she said, as she opened the third box. You cheated. This is the second box of char siu."

"Actually, I got three orders of those. And two each of the har gau and the ribs."

Before she could even think about it, she kissed him. "Thank you."

He kissed her back, lingering, until he came away with a sigh. "You're welcome. Don't eat them all."

"I wouldn't think of it," she said, deciding right then that the plan to keep her distance was ridiculous. She wasn't going to send him home after they ate. And she wasn't going to kick him out of her bed. Fighting it was a lost cause. Maybe the lesson here was to not be so damn logical about everything. So what if she didn't know where this would lead? That might turn out to be the best part. He'd already taught her so much. Who could say where he would take her next?

They didn't speak for the next while, but she managed to communicate quite well. Mostly by moaning. Taking a bite of the lobster after dipping it into a delicate sauce that was clearly made by the tears of angels, she made loud yummy noises as she chewed.

He laughed at her, looking at her as if she was extraordinary. It was the best dinner she'd had in ages. He stopped eating surprisingly quickly. Probably because he hadn't skipped lunch. Then he got himself another beer, and instead of sitting down again, he stood at the edge of the kitchen, watching her.

She smiled, but it faded after a minute. "I'm sorry about tomorrow night. I can't let this guy slip through my fingers. It's too important."

The words hadn't even finished coming out of her mouth when she saw Jake's demeanor change. His whole body tensed and he frowned, actively frowned.

"What?" she asked. "Are you okay?"

"Yeah. I'm fine," he said, but he burst into motion, leaning over to close the food cartons, avoiding her eyes.

"Jake, what just happened?"

He paused.

"You can't possibly think I have any interest in Bill West outside of his money."

"No. I don't." He stood, abandoning the boxes.

"So?"

"I'd like to ask you to postpone that meeting. With West."

"What? Why?"

He ran his hand through his hair, picked up his empty beer bottle and stared at it for a moment. "I have a bad feeling about him."

"I know. He's not my favorite person either. He flirted with me right in front of his girlfriend, or whoever she was. It was creepy. But I can handle myself."

"That's not it." Jake moved from behind the coffee table and walked over to the window. "Dammit, I wasn't ready to get into this yet."

Rebecca's stomach tightened and it wasn't pleasant. "What are you talking about, Jake? Tell me already."

He stared down into the street for too long before he turned to face her again. "I can't swear to it, but I'm pretty sure I've met West before."

The way he spoke, the way his voice lowered and his eyes grew cold made her very uncomfortable. "And?"

"It was a while ago. Before I did deep cover work. I think I met him at a drug bust."

"He was a junkie?"

"If he's who I think he is, he was a lot worse than that."

"Okay," she said, standing, walking toward him so she could see his face clearly. "I am so not understanding this."

"I have no proof, so this is going to sound crazy. And

I might be wrong. Really wrong. My gut, though. My gut is telling me there's something—"

She shook her head, waiting. Becoming more uneasy by the second.

"I recognized his laugh."

His laugh? She huffed her impatience and gave Jake a look. "Well, okay. It is…unique."

"Yeah. Not easy to forget. But that's not all. The guy I'm thinking of, Vance Keegan, he also had a scar from lip surgery."

"Am I supposed to understand?" she asked.

"No reason you should. He worked for a drug dealer named Luis Packard. A major drug trafficker who ran most of the East Coast for over ten years. Everything from heroin to coke to prescriptions. This guy Keegan was part of the organization, an office guy. Something with the money, although no one ever told me exactly what his role was. They killed a lot of people, sold a lot of drugs to a lot of kids.

"I was in on the bust. It was all over the news because when we were just about to lock it down, Packard's people hit us, hard. Smoke bombs, machine-gun fire. Packard was killed, and so were some of the good guys. The gun that killed Packard had Keegan's prints, among others. Keegan got away. Disappeared. Vanished. They looked for him, but he wasn't on the top-ten most wanted. They were more concerned with where the drug money had gone, all the millions of dollars that were supposedly in a panic room."

He kept talking, and Rebecca stared at him, barely comprehending what was happening. The whole thing was surreal. Jake sounded different, looked different… it was as if she'd stepped into one of their film noirs.

"I always believed Keegan's disappearance and the

missing money were connected. But that whole deal was way above my pay grade. Thing is, I was standing right next to Keegan, and he was laughing that weird laugh as we walked across the roof of the warehouse. He was laughing like he knew something, even though he was cuffed and surrounded by dozens of officers. Then he was gone."

Rebecca took a step back. "You think William West is really Vance Keegan? Wouldn't someone have noticed?"

"He hasn't been in New York in years. He claims to be from Nevada, has a home office there. He travels to Europe, to California, even to Africa and Asia, but he'd never been to New York until a few weeks ago. From everything I read, he's kept himself under the radar until last year. More importantly, he doesn't look the same. I think he had a bunch of surgery, reworked everything from his hairline to the shape of his jaw."

"Wait a minute—you've been investigating him?"

Jake moved a shoulder, his gaze unwavering. "I wouldn't say investigating," he said slowly. "Just searching online."

She had no idea what to do. Jake seemed dead serious. But West had a multimillion-dollar company. There was nothing shady about him, and her people had checked. "Jake, that's really a stretch, not to mention a serious accusation."

"I know. I told you it sounds crazy. And I'm not making an accusation. It's a hunch, but one that needs checking. That's why I'm asking for a postponement. Some time."

She needed some time herself. This was crazy information here, and if it had been anyone but Jake, she'd have laughed and dismissed the whole thing as some weird con. But it wasn't someone else. "I'm pretty certain there is a large percentage of people born with cleft palates."

"They called him Lip," Jake said, nodding. "That must have pissed him off. To be called that by Packard, who was a real piece of work. He was a vicious bastard, ran over anyone trying to get in on his territory. Didn't care who he took out in the process."

"Jake…"

"I know. That's why I decided to do some checking. I couldn't find anything, but my friend… This guy is a genius hacker. Works for Homeland Security. He told me tonight on my way to the restaurant that there's something fishy about the death of West's uncle. That's supposedly how West got his start-up funds. His uncle's estate. But the uncle was murdered. They never found out who did it. There are no other living relatives, and the uncle was a recluse. Lived way out in the desert with the scrub brush and the heat. His body wasn't discovered for almost two months."

Her stomach tightened; she wasn't liking the fact that someone else was involved. If West got wind of any of this… "I'm sorry, I don't see a connection between Keegan and a desert recluse."

"I wasn't gonna say anything. Because I know there are other explanations. I was undercover a long time, Rebecca. I survived by my instincts and training, but trust me, the instincts were more critical. Something clicked for me at the party. Something I can't ignore."

"I see," she said. But she didn't. Jake was wonderful, nearly perfect. But she hadn't even known him two weeks. This? This was kind of scary.

"I only need a week. That's all. Maybe less," Jake mumbled. He turned back to the window and his bad leg wobbled so much his hand shot to the wall for balance.

"But you're right. I'm probably going stir-crazy being stuck at home."

"I didn't say that. Honestly, the thought hadn't even crossed my mind." Unfortunately, it did now. She looked at his taut back, at his image in the mirror. She had the terrible feeling the next few minutes were going to have far-reaching repercussions.

So much for time to think things through. It was all down to *her* instincts now, and while there were many perfectly valid reasons to throw in the towel, and only one for sticking with Jake, she had to bet on the long shot. They might have been together only a short time, but she'd never had a connection like this with anyone. He wasn't crazy. In fact, he was the most down-to-earth, balanced man she'd ever met. Even as she knew her decision was final, she could barely believe it.

She stood behind him, placed her hand on his shoulder. "You're concerned for me," she said.

He faced her, all the ice gone from his gaze. Now his eyes were filled with doubt and fear, a very accurate echo of her own feelings. She couldn't picture a future for them, but she understood what was important to Jake now. Honor. Responsibility. All the things she'd fallen in love with.

"I am concerned for you," he said. "Very much."

"I could postpone, but I won't. Not because I don't believe there's a possibility you might be right. Admittedly, I think it's a very small chance, but anyway, I don't need to postpone because first of all, I'm not in any danger. Second, nothing is going to be signed tomorrow night. This type of deal takes time. The next step is only the negotiation to negotiate."

He nodded, but she doubted he was happy.

"The instant you have any proof, I'll stand with you

and we'll see him put away, but I need to tell you that every person who donates or participates in any meaningful way with the foundation is vetted by our security company. They have remarkable access, which is why they're astronomically expensive. They saw nothing wrong with West's background."

"I'm not surprised. If he did create himself on paper, he would have to have done a remarkably thorough job. I honestly do know how insane this sounds. It would be smarter to let it alone. But I don't think I can."

"Okay. Go with your gut. From what I know about you, I can't imagine you're taking any of this lightly."

He huffed a sad laugh. "So it's not a deal breaker?"

Rebecca ran her hand through his hair. "Nope. And that's why you need to see it through. Because nobody would give this up on a whim."

"Did I hear that right? Did you just tell me you're the hottest woman in New York?"

She laughed. "Now, that would be insane. No," she whispered, then kissed him. "But together, we're pretty incendiary, don't you think?"

His hands were on her now, confident, strong. Running down her back until they curved over her bottom. "Smokin'," he said and he bent to kiss her.

She put up a hand, stopping him. "Please, do not let West get wind of any of this. You have to promise me, Jake. He can't know."

Jake gave her his crooked smile. "You probably won't believe me, but I want to be wrong. I want you to win." Then his mouth was on hers, and she let herself relax against him, let herself trust him. There was an ache inside her and she wanted him badly. The way he'd looked at her, it made her heart hurt. No one had ever looked at her that way before. There'd been lust and hurt and greed and impatience. Even caring and concern and, yes, several kinds of love.

But his gaze had held more than she had words for. This man would slay dragons for her. There was no doubt at all about it. He would put her first over everything.

God, how she wanted him in her bed, in her arms. She wanted to be as close as two people could possibly get. When she tugged his hand, he followed after her, but this time, when they stood by her bed, it wasn't a race. They undressed slowly, one garment at a time, their gazes locked until the last possible second.

When they crawled into bed together, it was quiet. As they gathered each other, wrapping themselves in legs and arms and heat, she felt as safe as she'd ever been.

They kissed. No rush, just kissing. Slow, long touches and rubbing back and forth until the sounds of his breath and her own were only drowned out by the blood rushing in her head, by the beating of her heart.

When he entered her, she stilled him with a cry.

"Rebecca?" he whispered.

"It's good," she said, her lips against his. "Perfect."

# 13

STANDING OUTSIDE REBECCA'S building at seven-fifteen in the morning, Jake decided to hit a deli a few blocks down, have himself another coffee and try to put his head around what he was getting into.

That she'd made love to him last night, that they'd fooled around in the shower this morning was remarkable, considering, but not nearly as confusing as the fact that she'd made plans with him for Wednesday night. Future plans. When he'd told her his suspicions about West, Jake had seen the growing alarm on her face. He didn't blame her. It would have made so much more sense for her to cut her losses and be done with him.

As if he needed her to be even more incredible. Jesus. Not perfect though. He grinned as he crossed the street, letting the crowd swallow him and set the pace. She'd been cranky as hell this morning. Evidently, all this very fine dining was starting to get to her, and she'd been putting off yoga and the gym because of the donor thing, and she'd declared herself a disgusting slug this morning when her gray wool slacks were harder to zip than they should have been.

His repeated and heartfelt compliments about her

body, complete with kisses and petting, had been dismissed as irrelevant. Because he was a man. So, perfect? No. Which made her even better.

He walked over to 33rd to the 2nd Ave Deli and got himself a booth. He wished he had a notebook or something, but it was more important to have the coffee.

As he waited for the waitress, he tried like hell to organize his thoughts. The first option was to forget about Keegan. Leave it, ignore it. He had the feeling that's the option Rebecca would vote for, despite her support. She'd tell him he was doing the sensible thing. But he rarely did the sensible thing, and this was no exception. It would bother him to the end of his days if he didn't check it out to the best of his ability.

Second option, wait to see what Gary came up with. He knew his friend wasn't infallible, the internet did not have every answer in the world, and the man had a very demanding job. If Gary was discovered looking into anything suspicious, such as the background of William West, it could be bad for Gary.

Jake got his coffee, but before he did anything, he took out his phone. It rang once.

"I don't have anything else for you yet," Gary said.

"Not why I called. How much trouble can you get in for doing this stuff?"

"A lot. If I'm caught. But I won't be. And hell, now that I think of it, not that much trouble. I can always say I found something hinky and was doing my bit for the safety of our great nation."

"Do not bullshit me about this, dude. It's probably nothing. I'd really hate it if you were sent to prison."

Gary laughed. "I don't like you enough to go to prison. Stop worrying about it. I'll call you."

And that was that. Jake fixed up his coffee and as

he stirred, it occurred to him that he had another friend who might be helpful. Well, *friend* was stretching it, but the breakup hadn't been bad...hadn't been terrible at least. Crystal was great, but it was tricky, her being a lawyer and then becoming an assistant district attorney. Thing was, she worked in the Investigative Division of the D.A.'s office. Writing briefs, but still she was inside.

He didn't have her number any longer, but it would be better if he showed up in person, anyway. The one thing Jake had going for him was that he'd never been able to tell Crystal he was an undercover cop. Maybe now that he could, she'd understand why he'd been such a flake. If not, he'd play the sympathy card. She was a nice woman. It would bother her that he'd been shot, even if she had no desire to see him again.

So he'd go to her office. Ask to find out what she could about T-Mac, who was currently serving a life sentence in Sing Sing. He'd been part of the bust, took most of the heat after Keegan vanished and Luis Packard died. There was a chance T-Mac had some information on Keegan's whereabouts, although it was a slim chance.

At least Jake was already in the city. But first, he called his old man.

"You still shacking up with that gorgeous woman?" his father asked.

"Doesn't anybody say hello anymore?"

"Hello. You still shacking up with that gorgeous woman?"

"You're a riot. No. She's gone to work. But I'm gonna be a while. You doing okay?"

"I'm doing fine. The two domino cheaters are here with me, and everything's just peachy."

"Oh, God." Jake lowered his head, not in the least ready to hear about how Pete and Liam were conspiring against Mike to ruin his game. This happened at least once every couple of months and had more to do with the wheelchair knocking over the card table than duplicity and revenge. "You can tell me about it later. You need something for when I come home?"

"No. Yeah. Cookies."

"Chocolate chip or those oatmeal things?"

"Both."

"Maybe you should learn another game. I hear mahjongg is fun."

"Hey, Jakey? Go—"

Jake hung up. Then he got the number for the D.A.'s office and made sure Crystal was there. The odds weren't great that she'd speak to him, but he had nothing to lose. Story of his life.

THE LIMO WAS DIRECTLY IN front of the building, in the red zone; a female chauffeur wearing a traditional uniform opened the back door long before Rebecca reached the sidewalk, and William West stepped out of the car.

He was in a suit; she was sure it cost a bundle, but it wasn't anything special. Didn't particularly flatter him, but that didn't matter. He wasn't on display in this dance. She was.

She smiled and took his hand, then slid onto the seat. A few moments later, he got in on the other side. She'd had just enough time to remember why she was going to this dinner. No matter what ultimately happened, the best information she had right now was that West was a perfectly legitimate businessman who might be willing to donate a significant amount of money to her foundation. Many, many lives depended on those donations, and it was her job to help those people. She would use whatever tactics she believed would get the job done.

That meant manipulating West's attention. She'd be competing with the restaurant, the chef's tasting menu, the unbelievably fine service and the wine. She had to be more fascinating than all of that, and she had to make him feel as if he'd win something big by moving on to the next stage.

Not her. That was never, would never, be on the table, and they both knew that. This parlay was more subtle. It was a conversation. A tease. All about timing. She couldn't afford to think about Jake, about his instincts, about her feelings. Tonight she was fighting for inoculations, for clean water, for medical care, for food, for women and children.

"It's great to see you again so soon," West said. "I enjoyed the banquet, but this is even nicer, don't you think? A chance to get to know one another."

"It will be nice. I've been looking forward to it all day."

"Good. I called ahead. The chef's tasting menu tonight sounds fantastic."

"You know him?"

He nodded. "We've crossed paths."

"I didn't think you got to the city very often."

"Chef Keller travels to Las Vegas frequently."

"Ah, of course."

It was quiet for the rest of the drive, which wasn't long. Then they were at The Time Warner Center at Columbus Circle, and she was being escorted to the fourth-floor restaurant.

As soon as they were inside, the maître d' greeted them both by name. West walked behind her to take her coat. As it came away, she heard his soft gasp as he realized her dress was backless. Very backless. She allowed herself a tiny smile.

They were led to a window table with a gorgeous view of Central Park. She liked the restaurant, who wouldn't, as it was owned and run by the chef of the French Laundry, but the nine-course meal, even with tiny portions, was almost more than she could deal with after the week she'd had. It would have been so much better to be at Jake's place in Brooklyn, listening to his dad and friends, watching something on TV and eating a simple salad.

But she followed the rules of engagement. Nods at the wine, smiles and questions, letting him do most of the talking until the sixth course. She'd been judicious whereas West had been quick to refill his glasses of wine, different kinds, perfectly paired with each delicacy.

She excused herself, sure his gaze never left her back as she went to the ladies' room. Once there, she relaxed. It was just as elegant as one would expect. Spacious, beautiful, quiet. When she returned to the table, she'd get down to business, and she would get him to commit to a dollar amount.

So far she'd seen nothing suspicious about the man. He wasn't the most refined person she'd ever met but he wasn't in any way vulgar. He had no accent, not even a trace of New York. His laugh gave her chills, though she hadn't reacted, but she'd had to force her gaze away from his mouth more than once.

He rose as she approached the table on her return, then held her chair for her. As she was sitting, he bent in such a way that the light hit the edge of his hairline. That was when she saw it. A scar at his hairline, artfully masked by his dark hair. She'd seen enough face-lifts to know what she was looking at, and while it could be a remnant of his vanity, it might be something else completely.

As they continued on with little plates of perfect food, and talk swung to the endowment itself, she watched his face. Jake had said his jaw was different. Those scars were tricky, and not all could be hidden.

By course nine, she had him talking about five million a year for ten years. And she'd identified scar tissue just below his right ear.

That still meant nothing; half of her parents' friends had had work done. Although she'd apparently been giving him the wrong signals by watching him so carefully. The way he looked at her now spoke of a deal that had nothing to do with charity.

JAKE HADN'T EVEN TRIED TO sleep. It was eleven-thirty and he was bone tired but he was pacing the house like a caged animal. He hadn't asked her to call. But he couldn't imagine she wouldn't. She knew he was worried. The dinner probably wasn't over yet, so he should calm the hell down.

What he needed to do now was prepare himself. She had a lot riding on this deal. No reason for her to believe everything wasn't completely kosher, and if West had offered to give the foundation a ton of money, Rebecca would be pleased. And he'd be pleased for her.

Until proven guilty, West was nothing more than a victory for her and her foundation, and Jake could damn well keep anything else out of the conversation.

The TV was off, his old man was in bed, the place was quiet and Jake debated going to Midtown, waiting for her at her place. He dismissed the idea as beyond stupid, but man, he wished like hell she'd call.

He could call her. She'd know why. She was smart,

she was amazing, she'd be onto him in seconds. And she'd think he'd gone from being slightly nuts to tin-hat crazy.

He thought again about his afternoon at the D.A.'s office. He had no idea if it was going to pay off or not, but in the end it didn't matter what Crystal found out. He had already made arrangements with Pete to borrow his 1970 Barracuda. The car was the only thing, aside from dominoes and his friends, that Pete gave a crap about, and that he had given Jake the keys with no hesitation said a lot. That was one part of being home that had been great to relearn.

Of course cops watched out for each other, but when you're in deep cover, it was different. Any association with other law-enforcement personnel was dangerous for everyone involved. Jake hadn't realized just how empty his life had been for far too long. Filling it again was a privilege. He'd done pretty well with home and family. But that still left a lot of room.

Although it would play hell on his leg, he limped down the hall and grabbed his jacket. He wouldn't be gone long. He didn't like leaving his father alone, but Mike rarely woke up once he conked out. There was no reason for his father to go downstairs even if he did.

Soon, if Jake could ever get his life back on track, Mike wouldn't have to worry about stairs. Yet another reason this thing with Rebecca wasn't the best of ideas. Jake had his responsibilities at home and until he could figure out another way, that meant sticking close to Brooklyn.

He walked toward Fifth, taking his time, trying not to focus on his thigh but on his destination. There was a bar where a man could buy a beer. One beer, then he'd come back, get himself ready for bed.

When his cell rang in the middle of Howard and 4th, he jumped and grabbed for it so fast he almost dropped the damn thing. "Hello?"

"Did I wake you?"

Jake relaxed. Rebecca sounded good. Tired, but good. "I'm up. You okay?"

"He has some scars."

"What?"

"Scar tissue. One could have been from a face-lift, but there were several more, hard to see, and I might be wrong. I tried to dismiss it. I know a lot of people who've had work done, but I'll admit it's bothered me because it was a lot of scar tissue. It was behind his ear, but it wasn't like a face-lift scar. You said his jaw had been altered."

"Yeah, that's what I thought. The jaw, the nose, the hairline and his eyes."

"They weren't easy to spot. He had an amazingly good surgeon. And God knows a cosmetic scar isn't proof, or half my relatives would be arrested."

"No, they're not proof. But I may be able to get something more tomorrow. I'm taking Pete's car up to Sing Sing."

"Where's that?"

"Ossining. About an hour and a half drive. I'm going to visit one of the men who was working with Keegan. See what he can tell me."

"You're not a cop anymore," she said, and he could hear the soft movements of cloth against cloth. "Can you just show up like that?"

"I know a guy who knows a guy. Professional courtesy and all that. It shouldn't take too long. He'll either talk or not, but I figure he might be pretty unhappy to be sitting in jail while Keegan's out and about making so much money he can afford to give it away."

"If it's Keegan." She sounded tense.

"Right. If." He didn't feel much like getting that beer now so he turned around. "And if he's William West, how did your meeting go?"

"Look, Jake, you can't mention West's name tomorrow. Ask all you want about Keegan, but promise me you won't try linking him to West."

"I won't. I never planned to. You have my word."

She sighed with relief. "Jesus, you've got me all crazy and paranoid now."

He winced. Her words took a chunk out of him but he sucked it up. He couldn't blame her for not blindly jumping on the bandwagon. "Okay, for now we're assuming everything's copacetic with West. Tell me about dinner."

"It went well. There's the chance we'll be getting five million a year for ten years."

Jake whistled. "That's not chump change."

"I'm not holding my breath about it. There's a lot that could still fall apart on this deal. The foundation will go on, one way or another."

"I'm just glad you're okay."

"I am," she said. "Oh, and Jake?"

"Yeah?"

"You're considerate. Charming. Sexy. Funny. Decent. Dedicated. Heroic. Did I mention sexy?"

He laughed. "What's that about?"

"Last night you asked me what I liked about you. Aside from you being so very, very good-looking."

"I see," he said, flushing under the cold light from the streetlamp, glad she hadn't thrown in that he was nuts. "That was quite a list."

"All true."

"Sure you haven't mistaken me for an Eagle Scout?"

"Positive."

"Damn, woman. I wish you were a whole lot closer."

"Be glad I'm not. I'm so tired I can barely see. Do me a favor, check in with me tomorrow. I don't want to worry that you've been trapped in some prison riot or something."

"Okay. I will. And Rebecca? You're pretty goddamn fantastic yourself."

For a minute, he listened to her breath. "Good night, Jake. Drive safely. Be careful. Come back in one piece."

"I promise."

# 14

THE BARRACUDA WAS A BEAST in terms of power, but one hell of a beauty to drive. Now that Jake was almost at the prison, he turned down the factory-installed AM radio and went over his plan of action.

Crystal had come through, thankfully. She'd called him this morning with T-Mac's prison records and more importantly an overview of his phone records. Some of his calls had been from and to lawyers, but he had family. A mother and sister in Georgia. They didn't come by, only called. No calls to or from Nevada. As for T-Mac's life inside, he'd gone with the Bloods, which wasn't a surprise considering, and he wasn't classified as a high-risk inmate. He'd been there eleven years, time enough to get established, but not quite time enough for a chance at parole. They'd never been able to pin a murder on T-Mac.

His real name was Lantrel Wilson, and Jake had no idea where T-Mac had come from or what it meant. He'd been associated with Packard as a kid. Been arrested for selling drugs to other kids and sent to a juvenile facility three times before he was seventeen. He'd been thirty-four when he was busted in that raid, and according to testimony, which was highly suspect as it was given by other members of Packard's operation, T-Mac was not just an office guy, he was one of only three or four people who had access to the panic room safe.

The signs warning against picking up hitchhikers popped up frequently as he continued on toward Hunter St., the icy-blue Hudson to his left.

Then there was the rigmarole about getting inside. Crystal had come through on that, too, and he owed her now. Flowers. Expensive flowers. He kept his eyes and ears open as he went through check after check until he was finally admitted into one of the cubicles they used for attorney visits. It took fifteen minutes for the door to open, and T-Mac was led inside.

First eye contact was definitely a challenge, but this wasn't Jake's first rodeo so he ignored it, using the silence to note the changes eleven years had wrought. The man had some serious muscle now. Enough tattoos to decorate the cubicle walls a couple times over. And that was only what Jake could see. T-Mac wore his long hair in cornrows that looked greasy, had a Van Dyke beard and squinty little eyes.

"Who the fuck are you?" he asked, finally.

"You can't guess?"

"Cop?"

Jake smiled. "Ex-cop."

"So? What you want?"

"What can you tell me about Lip?"

T-Mac didn't blink. He looked uncomfortable, but that might have been because his chair was too small for his bulk. He could barely cross his arms. "Who?"

"Hey, you're the one that ended up taking the fall for Packard, for Lip, for everything. I would imagine

Lip getting away scot-free would be something to think about over the years."

"You don't know what I think about."

"I do not. You're correct. But I would like to find out what you know about Vance Keegan."

"For all I know, he's dead and gone. I got no word about him from nobody. Not for all the time I been here."

"Nothing? Not a sighting? Say, from someone in Nevada?"

That got Jake a wince and a look. "You think I got pen pals or somethin'? How'd you even get in here, ex-cop? What are you looking for?"

"I'm writing a book."

"Yeah, and I'm singing in a choir. That all?"

"I don't know. I have to wonder, though, if it turned out that Lip wasn't dead. That he was, say, living it up on the money that was supposed to be in the panic room. Making more money off that. Spending money. A lot of it. Would that clear up your memory some?"

"What the hell you talking about? Lip was nothing. Nobody. He got coffee and set up hookers."

"Yeah. That sounds about right. Packard. He was a real sonofabitch, wasn't he? Charging his own people twenty-percent interest? That had to sting."

That got a reaction. It had been a rumor, a note on a piece of paper that Crystal had found.

"It's time you left, ex-cop. I got nothing to say to you."

"Nothing to pass on if I should miraculously discover Lip is alive and well?"

T-Mac gave him a contemptuous look, then stood up. Jake found it was a lot faster to get out of the prison than in. Just as well…the trip had been nothing but a big waste of time.

IT FELT AS IF REBECCA hadn't been to the St. Marks church kitchen in months. Although they would meet next Monday to exchange lunches, today was a special gathering, a birthday party. Two women, an account rep for MetLife and a personal assistant of a famous author, were turning thirty. Rebecca couldn't always make it to the group get-togethers, but she'd been delighted to come to this one. Not only did she like Ally and Tricia, but left to her own devices while Jake was at the prison, she would have been a wreck.

It was too soon to expect a call, but she'd been on tenterhooks the whole morning. Her day, in fact, had been terrifically normal. Flowers delivered from Bill West, thanking her for the dinner. No meaning to it, just something men tended to do when they wanted to get into someone's pants. Or just to be polite, but that's not what West's gesture had been about. He wanted more. The way he'd looked at her at the end of the evening? It was as if he was doing everything in his power to figure her out, right down to how she liked her coffee in the morning. It had been an uncomfortable ride home, but maybe that was just her. What she knew about him, suspected about him, colored her perspective once the business of the evening had ended.

There was no proof. It was highly unlikely that he was a wanted man, a killer. If she eliminated that possibility entirely, what she was left with was a guy from Henderson, Nevada, who'd made a bundle and felt he wasn't getting enough attention. Or not enough attention from the right people. Why else come to New York to contribute his millions? He could have easily found worthy causes in Vegas or California.

No, he was looking for validation. He'd taken her to Per Se to impress her. That's why he'd brought a date to the banquet. He was preening, and that should have been her only consideration until there was more to go on than a couple of scars and an odd laugh.

"Well?"

Katy Groft stood in front of Rebecca. She'd changed her hair color to a softer brown with caramel highlights. It really suited her.

"You mean Jake."

"Yes, I mean Jake. How was it?"

"Great," she said, catching herself in the nick of time. Katy had gone out with Jake, too, and what was the proper etiquette for disclosure in the trading card world? She didn't know Katy that well. It might hurt her feelings that Jake and Rebecca had hit it off. Or she might be delighted. "He's a really nice guy."

"Nice guy, hell. He's gorgeous and funny and smart. He's the best date I've had this year. Wish it could've lasted longer with him, but *c'est la vie*."

Rebecca gave it up as a lost cause and told the truth. "You know what? Me, too. Best date in years. He's pretty amazing."

Katy stepped back two paces. "Oh," she said. "Why do I get the feeling it wasn't only one night with you two?"

Rebecca felt the warmth of her blush and was thrilled when she saw Bree approach. The lunch brigade were filing in now, and things would get moving soon. The cake was here, along with all the accoutrements. Instead of gifts, everyone was donating to the St. Marks kitchen, which, in addition to letting them cook, also served weekend meals to people in need. "It's been several more," she admitted. "And we're getting together tomorrow night."

"No," Katy said, her voice dropping low and loud. "You are kidding me."

"What?" Bree asked, not the least abashed by nosing in on the conversation. "Are we talking about Jake?"

"You know about Jake?" Katy asked.

"Met him. He's a dream. I swear, if I wasn't with Charlie—"

"You're still with Charlie Winslow?"

All three women turned at that voice. It was Shannon, of Hot Guys New York trading card fame, making her entrance with her usual flair, red hair flying, high heels clicking across the floor. "I should have charged money for these cards. The hits keep on coming."

"It was a stroke of genius," Bree said. "You should call the *Times*. Have them do an article."

Shannon gasped, her eyes wide and shocked. "No one is calling anyone, especially not the media. God, can you imagine? Men would be climbing all over themselves to get on the cards. And they'd all want to show off their *assets,* if you know what I mean." She held up her hand, index finger and thumb about two inches apart.

"Either that or they'd be lining up to sue you," Lacy said with a laugh.

Shannon shook her head. "For a dating circle? No one has that much free time."

"Besides," Katy said, "men are too vain. None of them would complain about using their pics without permission, especially if it got them on a date with one of us."

"Your lips to God's ears," Shannon said, with a glance toward the ceiling. "I want to keep playing with the deck. I'm certain I'm going to meet my Mr. Right through this plan. It's fated." She flipped her hair over her shoulder. "So let's all remember to keep this our little secret."

Rebecca grinned, but she agreed with Shannon in principle. The whole reason the trading cards worked was because it was a controlled environment. "Well, I'm thrilled that I'm part of it," she said. If Shannon couldn't get accolades from the press, she certainly deserved them from her. "I'm seeing someone really special."

"I didn't think we had any more gazillionaires in the stack," Shannon said. "Or was he posing as a regular guy?"

That stung. A lot. "No, he is a regular guy."

"Oh." Shannon frowned. "I'm sorry. I didn't mean—"

"Yes, you did. But it's okay. No reason not to. I was as surprised as anyone."

"Come on," Bree said, bumping her shoulder. "You're not like that. I'd know."

"No, I'm not looking for an escape clause," Rebecca said, touching Bree's hand. "I've had to do some real soul-searching over this. I never realized how accustomed I'd become to men of a certain class. It's been a real wake-up call. Yet another reason to be grateful for the trading cards."

Shannon wasn't frowning now. Her face softened, and her very pink lips curved into a smile. "That's good," she said. "Thank you for telling me that."

"I can't believe I let him get away," Katy said. "I had him first."

"You said it was all right."

Katy grinned at Rebecca. "Of course it's all right. I'm kidding. Jealous, but kidding. Now, return the favor and set me up with someone wonderful."

"I'll do my best," she said. She would, too. But there

wasn't a single man in her life, now that Charlie was taken, that she'd want to share with the women here. Her friends deserved better.

HE PULLED INTO A GAS STATION in Englewood to fill up the Barracuda. It took premium gas, for God's sake, and it drank like a lush. But, oh, how Pete loved this car.

Jake wasn't sure why—maybe he hadn't gotten the car gene—but he'd never been into them. Not even when he'd gotten his driver's license. He'd bought an old Toyota when he had enough money, learned enough to change the oil, change plugs and points, the basics, and that was fine. It was lucky he'd been a decent quarterback because he'd been harassed about that old bucket of bolts from day one.

Instead he'd become obsessed with guns. Not rifles, although he could handle one. Not hunting, he had no interest. He'd learned about guns at the shooting range, on a Smith & Wesson 36 revolver. He and his father had been like most teenagers and their dads, arguing, pissing each other off about everything, his hormones in charge, his father's patience stretched beyond the limit, but not at the range. There, Mike had been an extraordinary teacher, and Jake, an obedient and helpful son. That had lasted until Jake got two more bull's-eyes than his old man.

After he'd spent an ungodly amount on gasoline, Jake pulled the car into an empty space at the little food market, far from where anyone else would park. He was more afraid of wrecking Pete's car than he was of that prison riot Rebecca had warned him about.

He got himself a soda, found a seat on a bench where he could watch the Barracuda, which was worth a lot of money, not to mention Pete's well-being, and called Rebecca.

"Hi," she said. She sounded relieved, and that made him feel better than he'd expected, considering. "How did it go?"

"As far as concrete information? It sucked. But if you count inferences that could lead directly to the next step in the process, it also sucked."

"Oh, no," she said, but he could hear the relief in her tone. She probably assumed the poking around was over. That West was exactly who he said he was. She might be right.

"T-Mac wasn't forthcoming," he said. "The only undertone I got from him was his distinct wish that I would die. Soon."

"But I thought he was the one who got slammed with the whole deal." Rebecca sighed, and he could hear a murmur of voices in the background. "Wasn't he angry?"

"I couldn't tell. Probably. But then, the man's in prison for a hell of a long time. I don't think he has a lot of up days."

"No, I mean, shouldn't he have been more angry? Considering?"

It was Jake's turn to sigh. "I thought of that. But even if that's the case, there's nothing to do with the information. For all I know, Keegan's dead, T-Mac is just a guy in the joint and Packard had spent every last penny on a massive comic-book collection. I've got nothing."

"But you tried."

"Is that laughter I hear? Are you having fun while I'm moping?"

She giggled. "I'm at St. Marks. It's a birthday party, and it's almost over. I have to get back to the office."

"Ah, the frozen lunches. Put those together with the leftover dim sum, and you won't need to shop for a month."

"Ugh, food is the last thing I'm interested in. No lunches today though, only cake and ice cream. You want to come over tonight? Though it can't be too early because I have a meeting."

He was flat out grinning now. Had been since she'd said hello, for that matter, but that last question? That had been something else altogether. "I do," he said, tempted. No, he wasn't going to risk ruining his plan for tomorrow night. His leg had to be in full working order. "But I don't think I should."

"Oh?"

"I know it's very unmanly, but the truth is I'm exhausted. I need to do some work on my poor wounded body then get myself a full night's sleep. I won't do that if I'm with you."

"I give a pretty good massage."

Shit, her persistence was killing him, but did he want her to see how bad his leg was today? "Sweetheart, there is no way in the world I'm going to be in a bed with you and not keep us both up. Besides, you need to rest, too. I'm taking you somewhere special tomorrow evening."

"Where?"

"It's a surprise."

"No fair," she said, almost whining, which was pretty damn adorable. "Tell me."

"Nope. Wear something warm and comfortable. None of those lethal high heels."

"You like it when I wear high heels."

"Only when you're not wearing anything but your fancy underwear."

She didn't say anything for a minute. He could tell

she'd gone somewhere more private, quieter. "I'm sorry things didn't pan out about West. I'm happy for the foundation… You know what I mean."

"Yeah, I do. Although I'm not totally ready to throw in the towel. Unless that's what you want."

"How about we keep thinking it through," she said, her voice warm and sexy. "Who knows, together, we might come up with something that'll not only uncover the truth, but find all that missing money. Then I can negotiate a reward for the foundation."

He laughed. She really was good. "Yeah. Okay. We'll keep thinking. And if we don't uncover squat, we'll have given it a hell of a shot, right?"

"So tomorrow?" she asked.

"I'll pick you up at seven. Does that work?"

"Seven's great. Hey, Jake?"

"Yeah?"

"Sleep well. Take care of yourself."

"I…"

"Yeah?"

"Nothing. Thanks. You sleep well, too." He hung up his phone and stared at it as he took another big swig of soda. By the time he put the cell back in his pocket and climbed back into the car, he knew exactly how much trouble he was in.

He'd fallen for her. Fallen like a kid off a bicycle. Shit, he was in for a world of hurt.

# 15

WHOEVER THE HELL HAD invented full-length mirrors deserved to be sent to the same level of hell as shoe designers. The jeans Rebecca had on now were tight and made her look thinner, yet when she took them off they left a red indent around her waist, which Jake would see. Unless she wore a teddy under and didn't take that off until the lights were out and, oh, hell. Why was she so nervous?

She sucked it up to unzip, then traded the jeans for a different, looser pair. The solution to the whole problem turned out to be not looking in the mirror. Simple.

As per his instructions, she'd put on comfy boots that had virtually no heels at all, and a wonderful thick sweater she'd gotten for skiing. She had no idea where he planned to take her that would require walking in the cold March air, but for his sake she hoped there were plentiful rests and a nice place to snuggle when they got there.

The buzzer from the front desk caught her finishing her lipstick and speeded up her heart. She didn't even know how it could be more exciting to see him now than it had that first night. But it was. He made her pulse race, her insides tighten and her nipples get hard. What a fantastic superpower.

She couldn't even wait for the elevator to bring him up. Instead she stood outside by her open door, impatient and grinning.

At the sound of the ding she rose up on her toes, but settled before he stepped clear of his ride. His grin matched hers in intensity, and they sort of rushed at each other. It would have been ridiculous except for the kiss. That trumped everything. His hand cupped the back of her neck and she sneaked inside his coat to take hold of his hips. She pulled him in close so they were smooshed together thigh to chest and she filled herself up with his scent.

He went on kissing her, tasting her, the two of them greedy and eager as teenagers. When he moaned low and pushed his budding erection against her, she wondered if maybe they should skip the surprise and stay in bed for the next ten hours or so.

When he broke the kiss, he didn't go far. His forehead touched hers as he slowly exhaled, fingers still rubbing soft circles on her nape. "That was some welcome."

"Yeah, well, I love surprises."

"So it's the idea that's important, huh?" he asked. "For all you know I could be taking you for a pushcart falafel in the Village."

"It would depend on the cart." She needed to look at him. Still, she was disappointed when his hand fell away from her nape. "Come on, where are we going?"

"Get your coat. I'll show you."

She took hold of Jake's hand and led him into the house. Her coat and purse were ready. "You need to make a pit stop? Grab something to drink?"

He shook his head, his crooked smile melting her into a puddle of goo. "You continue to amaze me," he said.

She stopped short. "What? Why?"

"You surprise me every time we get together. Every time."

"How am I surprising you now?"

"You're like a kid on Christmas. I don't want to disappoint you. We're not going to Paris or anything."

She put her stuff back down on the table and walked to him. Hands on his shoulders made him look her straight in the eyes. "I don't care where we're going. Pushcart, Paris. Doesn't matter. I just want to hang out with you. And then screw like bunnies when we get back."

"Ah. I see. I hadn't thought of the screwing like bunnies part. I think I can change the itinerary. Anything for a friend."

"So, I'm a sacrifice now?"

He shook his head slowly. "You're the best thing that's ever happened to me." His voice had deepened and she heard him swallow, as if he hadn't meant to say that out loud.

She had to kiss him. Had to. She tried to make him see it was okay what he'd said. It was more than okay. Without scaring the pants off him. Or herself.

She was his best thing. She'd never been anyone's best thing before.

Wow.

JAKE TOOK HER HAND AS HE scooted into the cab beside her. "Brooklyn Bridge Station, please."

The cab took off, making its winding way to Broadway. Rebecca leaned against the window, the neck of her wool coat turned up, framing her face perfectly. "Brooklyn Bridge Station? Hmm."

"You won't guess."

"Let me think. What's around there?" She closed her eyes, and he wanted to kiss her. "It's the Financial District, so Bridge Café?"

"Naturally, you're going to think of restaurants. We're not going to a restaurant."

"Simply narrowing down the field." She grinned and fluttered her lashes at him, as if that had been her plan all along. "The Woolworth Building? South Street Seaport?"

"You're getting warm, but no. Not where we're going."

"New York Academy of Art?"

"How do you even know that?" he asked.

"Went to a fundraiser there. Oh, City Hall. Municipal buildings. Courts and things, right?"

"Yes. That's it. I'm taking you to courts and things."

She sighed as they waited in the crushing traffic. "I give up."

"Good. I bet you were hell on Christmas. Did you always find where your folks had hidden your gifts?"

Her smile faded a little. "No. Christmas wasn't like that at our house. My grandparents were taught to keep a rein on their emotions. That was a point of pride, and it was passed on. Drummed in. The trees were decorated by professionals. Christmas dinner was catered. I got mostly sensible gifts. Clothes, books. Charitable donations were made in my name."

"Wait. When you were a kid?"

She nodded. "Not only me. My cousins, too. It wasn't a horrible message. We'd been born into privilege and with that came responsibilities. When we were very young, we had chores around the house, and as soon as we were able, we were expected to do volunteer work in one form or another. It wasn't optional."

"But what about being a child? What happened to that part?"

"That was where Charlie came in. He was, just so you know, the devil incarnate. A rebel even in kindergarten. He gave me my first cigarette at eleven. Let's see. He helped me steal my first candy bar from a Duane Reade drugstore. We used to sneak into the liquor cabinets during the parties our parents would host and get absolutely smashed. I'm not sure why the nannies never busted us. I think they were glad to see us letting off steam. My family and his were really close, did everything together, until they caught us ditching school. We'd gone to Atlantic City when we were in seventh grade. I only saw him a couple of times a year after that. Well, officially. Unofficially, he remained my hero and we sneaked out all the time."

"I knew I liked him right off the bat."

"His parents were at the donor dinner."

"I didn't meet them."

"That's okay," she said. "They're…rigid. And the honest and horrible truth is, I don't think they like Charlie. Which is a shame because he's really something."

"I'm glad you had each other."

"Me, too. But when it came down to choosing what I was going to do with my life, the lessons of my parents had the most impact. I set my sights on the Winslow Foundation. We're doing good things."

He leaned over, helpless not to kiss her. "I was brought up the same way. Kind of."

"Yeah, I got that," she said, brushing her fingers over his cheek.

They swayed together with the stops and starts of the taxi. Rush-hour traffic was never easy. But that was okay. He was fine where he was. Jake brushed her lips with his one more time. "I never wanted to be anything but a cop. My family was full of heroes. I grew up believing that I could make a difference. I still do. My father, he was a tough sonofabitch. He didn't let me get away with much. But he worked like a dog to make sure I got into college, got my degree before I joined the force. I think he was hoping I'd grow up to be chief of police or something. I never wanted that. I needed to be on the street."

"You're pretty tough yourself."

"I was. I helped put away some bad people. I never took kindly to those bastards preying on the weak and the helpless. They destroyed families, kids. It was frustrating, because we'd get rid of one operation and another would take its place in a heartbeat. But you can't let that stop you. You do what's in front of you."

Rebecca's face was half in shadow, but he could see that she was staring at him, not grinning now, not moving. Just looking at him. "I admire you, Jake Donnelly. I admire your values and your courage and your willingness to take a stand."

He was pretty sure she couldn't see his blush. "I honored the job. Like my father did, and his father."

"Did you know you have a Brooklyn accent when you talk about your dad?"

"Is that so?"

"Yep." She leaned in, but the cab veered to the left and came to a jarring stop. "Brooklyn Bridge Station."

Jake had gone to the ATM before he'd picked up Rebecca, and even though he had to quit this crazy spending, he'd taken out a few hundred bucks. Just in case.

He paid the cabbie, then helped her out of the taxi. Now came the good part. It was brisk out, but not freezing. The air smelled clean for New York, and once they got free of the subway entrance, the street traffic thinned. "You ready to go on an adventure?"

"Oh, God, yes. Lead on, Macduff."

He grinned wide. "It's actually 'Lay on, Macduff.' But don't feel bad. It's misquoted all the time."

"I stand corrected," she said with a little bow.

He tried to leave it at that, but he couldn't. "That was on *Jeopardy* the other night."

She laughed and shook her head. "It still counts."

"Good." He took her hand again. "Follow me." He could have asked the cabbie to drop them closer to their ultimate destination, but he wanted it to be a surprise until the last minute. There was no rush. He'd accomplished what he'd needed to last night. Soaked for a long time, done the massage work, then he'd seen his physiotherapist for a session this morning. He'd needed it. Because tonight the pain was under control and his limp wasn't as noticeable. He figured he could get through the next couple of hours, no sweat.

Finally, in City Hall Park they came to another subway entrance: City Hall Station. When he pulled her to a halt, she gave him a sidelong glance. "Why did we go to the Brooklyn Bridge Station when we were coming here?"

"Because the subway doesn't stop here anymore. Well, that's not completely true. A train does come here, but only to turn around and leave again."

"Explain, please?"

"Let's explore the park. Do you mind?"

"Never. Adventure. Surprise. What could be better?"

She got closer to him, switched from holding his hand to putting her arm through his.

"In 1904, this was one of the first terminals of the IRT. This particular station was built as a showpiece. The city elders went all out. It was gorgeous, but it had two things that didn't work so well. One, not many people needed this stop when the Brooklyn Bridge platform was so close. Two, the trains back then were shorter than they are now, and the tracks here were configured in a pretty tight loop."

He led her to the park fountain, circled by flickering gas oil lamps, which made the water look magical. He pointed. "These are reconditioned lamps from the late nineteenth century, although some of them have been updated a little."

Jake watched Rebecca, her chin up, eyes wide as she took in the details of the old lighting fixtures. It was remarkably quiet around them, the swooping and falling of bursts of water onto the granite base of the fountain masking the traffic noise. He'd seen only a couple of people rushing across City Hall Park.

He was excited; he could feel his blood pumping and his adrenaline spike. He loved New York, especially Manhattan, and he'd become an urban explorer when he had time off, although he hadn't been able to do a lot of that since the shooting. He wanted her to see the hidden treasures all around her, and of course, it had to begin with City Hall Station.

He tugged at her arm and walked her around some greenery toward a circular tablet embedded in the sidewalk in the south end of the park. Most people never noticed it as it wasn't well lit at night. But he'd prepared for that. He pulled out a flashlight to better illuminate it. There were carvings in the center, a time line of the history of City Hall, including the abandoned subway station.

"There used to be a big post office building here. They called it Mullet's Monstrosity. It was on Mail Street, which didn't survive."

He moved the flashlight to the right. "That's where it used to be. There's more than one street that vanished," he said. "Tyron Row disappeared, too. Park Row, where we are, is the only street in New York City called a row."

She crouched down, staring at the careful workmanship. "I love this. How many times have you been here?"

"More than I can count. I started exploring the old places when I was in college. A friend of mine who works for the IRT calls himself an urban historian. He's got a great blog. And something far more important."

She rose again and looked at him instead of the view. "What's that?"

"Keys to the kingdom."

"Where are you taking me, Jake?"

"Back in time," he said, then pulled her along, anxious now to retrace their steps to the subway entrance. They were still in City Hall Park though, and he didn't rush her because this part was good. It was great to have her outside, not at a restaurant, no parties, no pressure. From what he could tell, she was enjoying herself. Interested. There was so much to tell her, too. But tonight was something extraordinary. He was taking her for a private tour of the old City Hall subway station, refurbished for the 2004 centenary, but closed to the public. Tours were available, and they were fun, but he wanted the two of them to be alone for this.

"Huh," Rebecca said. "I don't even know what IRT stands for. I've lived here all my life, and I don't know that. I mean, obviously Rapid Transit."

"Interborough," he said. "Right around here was the start of subways in New York. The groundbreaking ceremony was held in 1900 and this platform opened in 1904."

She turned to face him. "I think this calls for a moment, don't you? Something to celebrate?"

"What did you have in mind?"

She looked up at him, her lips already parted. The kiss started slow. More breath than lips at first, then a brush, a tease. Jake let her run the show. Standing in the shadows, she was the tour guide now, and she seemed to know every important stop along the way, mapping his mouth with deliberate care, then begging entrance with a moist nudge. Of course he obliged. He wasn't a fool. And God, she tasted like everything he wanted.

He ran his hands underneath her coat, wanting to pull her blouse out of her pants so he could touch her skin, but if he did that, the tour would be over. She compelled him like that, made him want too much. But that had been true from the moment he'd set eyes on her. He couldn't get enough.

Her fingers slid up the back of his scalp and he gripped her tighter. The pressure kept building inside him, but he couldn't break away, not completely. Not yet. His mouth went to her jaw, her neck, and he kissed her there where he could breathe her scent and trail his tongue up to the shell of her ear.

"Wait," she said, stepping away. "Whoa. I'm getting a little carried away here."

He nodded, catching his breath, willing his heartbeat to slow.

"I really want to see the surprise," she said. "So here's the rule. No more fooling around until later. Okay?"

He was about to agree when he heard a sound that

triggered every internal red flag he had. Two pops, one then another, and he grabbed Rebecca and yanked her down to a crouch, then ran as fast as his gimp leg could take him until they'd reached the restraining wall that kept pedestrians from the City Hall building.

"What the—"

"Shh," he said, knowing he was freaking her out, but he had to get the message across fast and hard.

Rebecca froze as if he'd slapped her, which was good. He listened. For footsteps, for voices. There. To his left. Footsteps, heavy, moving slowly, coming right at them. He reached back and pulled Rebecca closer, put his coat across her face, then he tucked his head down, in case there were lights.

The footsteps got damn close, then continued on, still slow, still careful. Jake held steady until he could no longer hear them, then waited some more. Finally, he let her up.

"What the hell, Jake?" she whispered.

"Someone shot at us."

"What? I didn't hear anything."

"You didn't recognize the sound. It was suppressed. They used a silencer."

"Are you sure?"

He turned to face her. "I'd bet my life on it."

# 16

REBECCA HAD NO IDEA WHAT to make of any of this. She tried to remember the seconds before he'd pulled her down, but she couldn't recall any sounds at all. Jake seemed completely certain about the gunfire, but *gunfire?* Wasn't it more likely there were fireworks somewhere, or a car backfiring?

"Come on," he said, stepping over the barrier once again, holding her hand tight. "We have to get out of here now."

"Jake, wait. Just stop. I'm sure it sounded like a gunshot to you, but I swear, I didn't hear anything. We're in the middle of a park on a Wednesday night. Who would be shooting at us?"

He met her gaze, but only for a second. He was still scouring the shadows and the sidewalks, so focused she could feel the tremors in his hand. "You may be right, and I may be nuts, but I'm not willing to chance it, not with you here. We have to leave. Now. And we have to be quiet and quick."

She nodded. There was no point arguing. He kept them away from the lights, right against the barrier as they walked fast toward Broadway. Rebecca was the one who saw someone crouching by a fir tree. She yanked on Jake's hand, and when he glanced back, she pointed her chin.

He looked. "Shit," he said, then he was sprinting back from where they came, and this time, she heard it. A pop like a cork flying from a champagne bottle.

There was another pop, and this time, cement from the barricade in front of her splintered, making her gasp and cover her face as they ran. Jake pushed her over the barrier; his grunt when he landed next to her was a painful reminder of his limp and his pain.

"Keep down," he said. "I'll come get you in a second."

His hand disappeared and she panicked. "Jake." She remembered to whisper, but it didn't matter. He'd moved into an even deeper shadow between buildings. She covered her head with her arms, so afraid she could hardly breathe. Every second felt like her last, and she kept chanting his name over and over, trying to speed up time.

"Rebecca."

She jerked her head up. "Come on. Keep low."

Crouched over double, it was difficult as hell to walk, and it must have been ten times harder for Jake. He led her to the dark spot, and then he took her hand and brought it up against the wall.

The darkness was so complete she couldn't see spit, but she felt the edge of a doorway. Then nothing. A breeze. Startled, she jerked when he leaned in close to her head so he could whisper.

"I'm going to help you find the ladder that leads down from this doorway. You're not going to be able to see much when you start. In a minute though, you'll see blue. Those are the lights of the station below, and they'll stay on. They never go off. You'll adjust quickly to those lights, so don't be scared. I'll be right behind you, okay?"

She nodded. Then said, "Yes, okay."

It wasn't a simple thing, this maneuver. Because of the dark. Because she was shaking so badly. There was someone out there and he wasn't some random mugger. That gun had been aiming for her. For Jake. For both of them, either of them, it didn't matter. It was a real gun and real danger, and he was still out there.

The worst of it was the first step. It was as if nothing existed past the doorway. No staircase, no subway station, no earth at all. Nothing but a void, and all that was holding her from an endless fall was Jake, his hand steady, his voice so calm. "That's it. Easy does it. Just reach down with your right foot until you feel the step."

"I can't feel anything."

"Okay, okay. It's all right," he said, squeezing her hand. "Move your leg to the right. Swing it over nice and easy."

She obeyed him, but only because she was too petrified to do anything else. Then her foot hit against something metal. The thunk sounded thunderous.

"That's the ladder. That should help you get your bearings. Now you know where the side is, you can find the rung. Try again."

She did. She blinked trying to figure out if her eyes were open and maybe that was the scariest part. Not being able to tell. When her boot heel touched metal, she almost cried out, holding back the noise at the last second.

"Good, great. Firm your grip. The rest is simple, easy as can be. Really soon, there's going to be a blue light, and it'll come on gradually, but you'll see it, and you'll know you're halfway to the ground. Take your time, don't rush. You let me know when you're ready to let go, okay?"

She didn't think she'd ever be ready to let go of his hand, but this was no time to be a coward. He had to climb down, too. He must be terrified up there. And he knew what it felt like to get shot.

Oh, bad thought. She couldn't think about that now or she'd freeze. "Okay," she said and lowered herself until her left hand found the ladder. She'd never held on to anything so tightly.

"I'm right behind. I won't let anything happen to you. I swear."

"I know," she said, even though it felt as if her heart would beat straight out of her chest. But Jake had promised. He wasn't abandoning her; he was leading her to safety.

She stepped down with her other foot. Found the rung. Shifted her right hand. No turning back now, just down, just one step and another and the next and there. Blue. She didn't turn to find the source, just let the light filter into her field of vision. One step after another, and then she was seeing the wall, the ladder, her own hands. Miraculous. Weird. Real.

Looking up, she could make Jake out, too. Mostly his legs and his butt. By the time she got to the ground level, she felt more in control. She stepped away easily, even if she was more scared than she'd ever been in her life

Not thirty seconds later, Jake was beside her. "You okay?"

She nodded.

"Come on. I don't know how much they know about this station. But they're going to realize we came down at some point, so we'll head for the exit. I left the door open up there. If they try to get down the same way we did, it'll give us time to get out." He found her hand and turned.

"Wait," she said. "They?"

"Yeah. Two of them that I saw. I don't know if there are more."

She and Jake were speaking in whispers, but their voices echoed. In the distance, she heard a rumble. It was indistinct, more a feeling than a sound.

"But—"

"No time. We'll talk when we're safe. Stay close to me. The trains come through here. There are tracks, which means we have to be careful of the third rail, so no moving without me, got it? I can't use the flashlight. It's too dangerous. So stick close."

"Like glue," she said. She hadn't thought about the third rail. Despite not knowing what IRT stood for, she had taken the subway. She was a New Yorker, of course she had. So she'd known what the third rail was from the time she was a kid: Death. Big old nasty frying death.

So. Two gunmen. At least. Aiming for them. And now a third rail. Next time Jake asked her if she was ready for an adventure, she was going to say no. In the meantime, she slipped her free hand into his back pocket. That ought to keep her close enough.

JAKE IGNORED THE BURN IN his thigh and cursed himself for every kind of fool there'd ever been. He'd walked right into this. Shit. He'd been such an idiot.

T-Mac hadn't just taken the fall. He wasn't left there by accident. He'd made a deal with Keegan. He'd do the time for money. Had to be. That family in Georgia who called all the time? Jake had put out some feelers to find out about them, but hadn't gotten any return calls yet. He imagined they were living quite well.

Gary hadn't been able to dig up much of anything that wasn't on the official records about West, but he hadn't had a lot of free time to dedicate to the search. Why should he?

But Jake should have known better than to waltz into Sing Sing and announce his presence like a rank amateur. It hadn't even occurred to him that T-Mac and Keegan could have been in cahoots. Why not? Life with Packard and life in prison weren't that different except with prison there was a chance of parole. And when he got out, he'd be set. His family would be set. There was a money trail somewhere, and if Jake lived through this night, he was going to make it his business to find that trail and make sure both T-Mac and Keegan were tried for attempted murder.

First, though, he had to get Rebecca out of here in one piece. That's what made him the angriest. Not that he'd been an idiot—he'd been a dope plenty of times before. Never when it cost so much, and never, never when he had something so precious in his care.

He should have kept his suspicions to himself. He should have kept his mouth shut and done his digging on his own time.

The train that had been way the hell down the line was now coming on fast. There were still work lights up, so he could get them safely behind the concrete wall that kept the maintenance crews from accidentally getting run over.

He released her hand and covered her ears with his palms; the trains made an ungodly screech as they took the curve of this loop of track. The squeal of metal against metal echoed back on itself, bouncing off the tile walls of the station. Under that was the noise of the train itself, which sounded like an earthquake this close. He surrounded Rebecca as much as he could with his body and his hands as the train rumbled and screamed, and he felt her press in, gripping his back for all she was worth.

Jesus, she had to be okay. Whoever these guys were, they weren't sharpshooters, but he'd wager a great deal that they weren't willing to turn up empty-handed at the end of the night. West's whole world was being threatened, and he wasn't going to hire muscle on the cheap.

Jake would have to be smarter, that's all. Whoever they were, they didn't know this station. He did. Every nook and cranny, and that was what would save them. He already knew there was no cell phone reception in the station. But there were call boxes, if he could get to one.

He winced as the sound assaulted his ears, knowing it would take some time before they'd be able to hear each other. The worst of it passed and he slowly stepped back from Rebecca, checking to make sure she was all right.

She gave him a smile. Not a big one, but a brave one, and he kissed her, then guided her hand to his back pocket and they were on the move.

They got across the tracks fine, and then they followed the curve of the platform, hugging the walls. Halfway to the exit stairs, he saw one of the gunmen on the right edge of the stairs coming down, his gun held in both hands, his head moving so he could sweep the area. No flashlight, but then he didn't need one yet.

Quietly and smoothly, Jake moved backward about fifteen feet, guiding Rebecca. He felt his way to the alcove, a niche built into the wall that had been his favorite place to hide while showing his friends around, the better to scare the crap out of them when he jumped out. He'd been such an ass.

It was a tight fit for two, but that was okay. He turned her sideways, then pushed in himself. Face-to-face. He could look out beyond her to see where the gunmen were. If they weren't both down here, they would be soon. Now, Jake would listen. Wait. After a quick check to make sure he was in the clear, he bent and got a couple of good stones for throwing. Maybe he could get one of them to step on the tracks. Maybe he could get them close enough and push one of them himself.

In the meantime, he had to protect her as best he could. She was trembling like a leaf. He wasn't much better. No weapon, no way of reaching help. Her life depending on his wits and his speed. Standing here without much range of motion was about the worst thing he could do as far as his leg went.

He leaned in close to Rebecca's ear until his lips brushed the silky lobe. "We wait now," he whispered as softly as he could. "We have home turf advantage. We're going to be fine. I'm sorry I can't show you where you are. It's so beautiful, sweetheart. Colored glass, tiles of green, tan and white up to the ceiling in the four corners of the vault over the mezzanine. The skylights are amazing. Imagine great pools of natural light from up above, and when they're not enough, they brought in brass chandeliers," he said, trying to distract her but she was still shaking. "The architect who designed the arches was famous back then. A showman. His name was Rafael Guastavino."

Jake looked out again, hating the vulnerability of sticking his neck out, but he did it, and it was a damn good thing, because both men were down the stairs, and one of them was walking toward their alcove.

Jake ducked back, then pressed them both, hard, against the back of the cubbyhole. It was dark, very dark, and as long as the man didn't flash a light directly at them, he'd never know the alcove existed, let alone that they were hiding in it.

His footsteps seemed as loud as the train had been at its worst. Slow, taking his time. But then a real rumble started behind him. Another train. The man needed to hurry. Step up his pace. Get past them, well past them to the walkway leading down to the dark end of the tunnel.

He needed the man to be far enough that when the train came, he and Rebecca could make a break for the stairs. It would be so loud the gunmen would never hear them. Jake knew exactly where to go, where to hide, but he needed a few minutes' grace. It didn't seem like too much to ask for, so he did, until the sound of the train ground in his chest. He took hold of Rebecca's hand, squeezed it tight. Prayed he could move fast enough.

When the conductor's car was twenty feet away, Jake broke out, pulling her behind him. Not too fast, even though he wanted to sprint. Not until she caught up to him, and then they hauled ass. Fuck the leg, screw the pain, they were running up the stairs, the screech of the train filling the platform to the rafters. They were soundless, they were panting and then they were past the curve and up the second shorter set of stairs and he could see where those bastards had broken in. No locks to mess with meant he could get her out more quickly. Good. The final steps, leading up to the sidewalk, and she surged in front of him, pulling him with her, and thank God for that because his leg was about ready to quit.

He yanked his phone out of his pocket, but she

wouldn't stop. Not until they got to the street and she'd waved down a cab and shoved him inside.

While he called the 1st Precinct, she gave the cabbie an address. Jake told the desk who he was, including his old badge number, that there were armed men in the City Hall Station and that they'd be gone damn soon, so get there fast.

He hung up after giving his callback number, pulled her into a fierce kiss, squeezing her too tightly, and, shit, he couldn't breathe, but he didn't care. But *she* needed to breathe so he backed off and met her gaze. "You okay?"

"Scared out of my mind. I can hardly believe what just happened. It's insane."

"But you're okay. You're not hurt."

"Yes. Yes, I'm fine. We're going to Charlie's and we'll figure it all out there."

"Good," he said, then he bent over and pressed down on his thigh as he tried like hell not to scream. Her hand was on his back and she was talking.

"It's okay, honey. You were fantastic. You're going to be fine. You got us out. We're safe now. It's okay. Please, be okay."

JAKE DIDN'T RECOGNIZE THE building they were dropped at, but it didn't surprise him that it was where her cousin Charlie lived, considering it was directly across the street from the park on Central Park West.

Getting out of the cab and into the elevator was something he could have lived his whole life without, but Rebecca was a champ. She did all of the heavy lifting. He tried not to make any sounds, but then he'd step down and a muscle would spasm and it was like being shot all over again.

The elevator opened to Charlie and Bree looking worried. And confused.

"What's going on? You were pretty damn cryptic," Charlie said, but Bree shoved him to the side so she could put Jake's other arm around her shoulder and help him into the house. Apartment. Palace.

"Maybe we should call an ambulance," Bree said, trying to help him to the couch, but not succeeding very well.

"No. I don't need an ambulance. I need to take my pain medication. It's muscle and nerve damage from doing too much. It'll settle down."

Charlie left. Rebecca and Bree hovered. It was sweet, but what he needed was a few minutes alone. He was about to do some major cussing and there might even be some crying involved, and he'd prefer not to have any witnesses for that. Especially not Rebecca.

He got his pill bottle out of his pocket and winced at how his hand shook as he opened it. He wanted to take two, but that would make him groggy, and he couldn't afford that now. One wasn't going to kick this. Not without some serious muscle work, but it would help. Charlie came back with a glass. Jake didn't spill much, only on his jeans. Someone took the glass and he breathed as deeply as he could, trying to remember what Taye said about letting the pain in, not fighting it.

There were too many people, too many thoughts. He couldn't stop and he wasn't going to hold it together much longer.

Rebecca took a couple of steps back. "I need a drink," she said. "You two, come with me, and I'll catch you up."

"I'll be right there," Charlie said.

There might have been a struggle, but it was silent and Jake gave up trying to figure it out. When he opened his eyes again, Charlie was still there. "Do I need to call an attorney? My man on retainer is excellent."

Jake shook his head. "You need to get Rebecca somewhere safe. William West is an ex-drug trafficker I ran into a dozen years ago. It's too long a story to go into. But I recognized him. He sent a couple of guys to kill me. Rebecca was collateral damage." He looked up at Charlie. "I put her life in danger. I almost got her killed. You have to get her away, understand? Out of town. Out of the state."

Jake forced himself to his feet even though the pain threatened to shut him down for good. But he took hold of Charlie's shirt and looked him square in the eyes. "Goddammit, *I almost got her killed.*" Charlie nodded. His face narrowed to a pinprick of light, then nothing.

# 17

REBECCA WAS SITTING NEXT to him on the couch. She looked pale and shaken as she held his hand. Shit. He must have blacked out for a minute. "What are you still doing here? You have to go."

She gently pushed him back down when he tried to get up. "It's okay. Calm down. Your pill hasn't kicked in yet."

"You don't get it. Keegan didn't just steal the money from Packard, he made a deal with T-Mac. The guy in Sing Sing. He paid T-Mac to take the fall. They've been working together all this time. I went in and spilled everything to T-Mac. He called West, and that's why those men were trying to kill us. Kill me. I'm sorry. I never should have said anything to you. I know, it's all my fault, but it doesn't matter now because Keegan knows you're with me so you're in danger. You have to leave. Now."

"Sweetie, it wasn't your fault," she said. "It wasn't you. It was me. The way I was staring at West over dinner. He knew I was looking for scars."

Jake sat up straighter and turned his hand so he was holding hers. He didn't think he'd been out long. Charlie was where he'd left him, but Bree was in his arms now. Fine. Good, but no one seemed to be getting the big picture. The danger wasn't over.

He turned back to Rebecca, mulling over what she'd said. "No way he would have made that connection," he murmured, knowing she wasn't necessarily wrong. Of course it wasn't her fault, but Keegan had to be paranoid returning to New York and anything could've set him off.

She shook her head. "But he did. I thought it was something else, I thought he was trying to figure out how to get in my pants. The way he stared at me. He knew something was wrong. I thought I was being subtle, but I wasn't. I was practically painting him a picture."

"It sounds like it was a combination of both those things," Charlie said, echoing Jake's thoughts. "The guy's been on the run for, what, twelve years? Anything could have tipped him off. Blame isn't the point. What do we do next?"

"We can't do anything until Jake can think without pain," Rebecca said. "Isn't there anything we can do for you?"

Jake shook his head, tried again to get up. How Keegan had put two and two together wasn't important now. Rebecca's safety was. "The only thing that will help me is for you to get the hell out of here. I mean it, Rebecca." He looked at Charlie. "What the fuck is wrong with you? I told you to get her out of the city."

Rebecca grabbed his chin and turned his head so he was facing her. "They're after you, too, goddammit, and I'm not leaving without you."

He'd never heard her swear like that and it stopped him. He glanced at Charlie, who had a faint smile tug-

ging at his mouth. What the hell was wrong with these
rich people? Did they think they were immune from
danger? "Those were real guns, with real ammo. They
meant you to die. They aren't finished. Your home isn't
safe. You're not safe. Do me a favor and go. Hire a car.
Don't go back to your place. Just get to the airport. Not
LaGuardia, go to Newark. Go anywhere. Pay cash.
And do it now please. I'm begging you. I have things
to do, and I can't even think straight while you're still
here."

"Ah," she said, nodding. "I get it now."

"Thank God," he said, putting his hand on his leg,
feeling instantly that it was way too soon to even try to
work on the muscle.

"But," Rebecca said, "I'm not leaving without you."

Jake stilled. What was it going to take? He ignored
her and looked to Charlie and Bree. "A little help would
be good here, people. I know you care about her. I can't
imagine any of you want to go to her funeral."

"Rebecca," Charlie said, releasing Bree from his hold.
"You're with me. Bree? Find out what this madman
needs, and let's get this show on the road. I don't want
to go to anyone's funeral."

Rebecca glared at him, then Charlie gave her a look
that spoke of years of collusion. She wasn't happy about
it, but she got up from the couch, squeezing Jake's hand
before she walked away with Charlie.

Jake leaned back on the couch. Now that he had an
ally, he could think clearly. At least that was his goal.

"What can I do?" Bree asked.

"I need to find out if the police got to those shooters.
And how we can connect the shooters to either T-Mac or
West, preferably both. I need to call Crystal Farrington.
She's an assistant D.A. who knows all about this." He

dug into his pocket for his wallet, the small movement making him wince. But there was her phone number. He'd call as soon as the spasm that was clawing through his quad let him go.

REBECCA TURNED ON HER cousin the minute the kitchen door swung shut. "I'm not leaving without him, Charlie. I don't know what you expect to accomplish, but changing my mind is not going to happen."

"Yeah, I got that," he said, smiling so smugly she wanted to slap him.

"Then what's with the 'Rebecca, you're with me' bullcrap?"

"Your cop needs to get his act together, and you being in his face wasn't helpful. The danger here is real, so we'd better figure out a way to get his goals accomplished while you're still in the house. Frankly, I don't like the idea that killers could be after you. You're the only relative I like. You're not checking out until we're old and decrepit."

"Oh. I thought you were going to argue with me."

"Nope. Before your little declaration there, I was going to tell you to fight for Jake. That he's the keeper you're always harping about. But you obviously have that covered, so now we can move on to practical matters. Like staying out of his way. At least for a while."

She hugged Charlie, real quick because they weren't the hugging type, and then she settled. "The way I see it, he only has a limited amount of focus at the moment. I'll keep back. Not away, because if something happens I need to be close, but I won't be obvious. I'll listen. So you'll have to be his sounding board. He'll know what to do, Charlie. He may not have his badge, but he's a damn good cop."

"Fine. You hang, I'll distract, and we'll get you both safe."

"Thanks, Crystal. Keep me in the loop, and I'll do the same." Jake hung up the phone and looked at Charlie, who'd suddenly appeared in front of the couch.

"Who was in charge of the original operation?" Charlie asked.

"Wait your turn," Bree said before she addressed Jake. "I have a wet/dry heating pad. I'm thinking moist heat. Would that help?"

Jake looked at her, and he couldn't help smiling. She was wearing an obnoxiously bright orange sweater over a green skirt. "Yeah. Thanks. That would help." She hustled off, and he faced Charlie again. "She's not gone. I would know if she was gone."

"She's making the arrangements. Right now. So, tell me what you need to get West behind bars."

Jake had brought Crystal up to speed, and she was going to work on getting T-Mac's phone records, this time through legit channels because this time, they would need it in court. Dammit, how long did it take to get a car here to Central Park West? It wasn't like Brook— "Shit, I have to call my old man."

Blessedly, Charlie and Bree left him alone while he dialed his father. Jake had already asked the department to send a couple of uniforms to watch the house, but he wouldn't tell his father. That would just piss him off. He switched on the speaker since he thought he could work on his leg now. Besides, his dad knew about the Keegan/West connection, so there wasn't much to say, except that Jake might have put him in danger. Him and Pete and Liam.

"Don't you worry about us, Jakey," his father said, and it was like they were on the walkie-talkies. "We have about a hundred years of experience between us. And a goddamn arsenal. I hope those bastards do come here. We'll teach 'em what NYPD cops are made of."

"Don't take any chances, Dad." Jake used both thumbs on the peripheral muscles, working his way inward. "Please. Just, see if you can go stay with Liam, huh? Get out of there, at least until we know what to do."

"I'll tell you exactly what I'm going to do, son. I'm going to call Dan Reaves is what. He'll get a judge to sign the warrants to get into West's business, and the prison phone records, and damn near anything else he can once I tell him what's what. He's tried to live that bust down all his career. He wants Keegan. More than you do."

"He tried to kill Rebecca, old man. No one wants Keegan more than I do."

His father was quiet for a long moment, long enough for Jake to remember how she'd trembled in his arms, how brave she'd been. How he'd move heaven and earth for her if he could, but he was useless like this.

"You're right, Jake. Your job now is to keep her safe. I'll call Dan—we go way back. I'll keep you informed. He'll probably want to talk to you so make sure you have that phone on. And take a goddamn pill, I can hear the pain in your voice."

"Tell Reaves to get in touch with Crystal Farrington at the D.A.'s office. She's working on the phone records from Sing Sing, but she could use some backup."

"Farrington. Got it."

"Thanks, Dad," Jake said.

"No sweat."

"Hey, Pop, how many cops does it take to screw in a lightbulb?"

"How many?"

Jake smiled. "None. It turned itself in."

His father laughed as Jake hung up. Then he felt Rebecca's hand on his shoulder as she leaned over the couch and kissed him like she'd never let him go.

IT TOOK TWO HOURS, BUT Rebecca and Jake finally made it into the Town Car that Charlie had hired. Jake had walked without assistance, but his limp was awful and he still looked too pale. She'd packed some food for the ride. Nothing much, just some protein bars and juice; they'd grab something better at the airport.

She pressed herself against him, hardly believing everything that had happened in such a short period of time. The shooting, the trip down the ladder, the terrifying sound of echoing footsteps all felt more like something she'd read than something that she'd lived through.

But he'd brought her out safely. This amazing man. Listening as he'd talked to the two policeman who'd come to Charlie's had been an education in itself. Of course she'd known Jake was a cop; he'd demonstrated that in his every action tonight, in his instincts that had ferreted out a killer. But she'd been utterly captivated and impressed with his logic, his approach to finding the critical proof that would connect T-Mac to West.

"You're an incredible policeman," she said. "Not only were you right about everything—"

He opened his mouth in what she knew would be a protest, but she stopped him with two fingers on his lips.

"—but you saved my life."

"Your life shouldn't have been in danger in the first place," he said.

"Hmm. The correct response should have been 'You're welcome, Rebecca.'"

Jake ran his knuckles down her jaw. "The thought of losing you…"

"We're both here, and we're relatively fine. We'll be better once we're wherever we're going. Any thoughts on that?"

"I have no idea," he said. "Vegas is out."

She grinned. "No passports, so we can't leave the country. But those can be sent to us so our first destination doesn't have to be our last. We had talked about Paris."

"We probably won't be gone that long. Phone calls were made tonight, or an email, or whatever, which gives us a window of time to focus the search on how West and T-Mac connected. How West contacted the shooter. T-Mac is in Sing Sing. Somewhere, there's a record. As soon as they can latch on to anything concrete, then they'll go after Keegan with both barrels. That'll be our cue to come back. We could have that connection by morning."

"We wouldn't have to come back right away, would we?"

He smiled. "What did you have in mind?"

"Time. Alone with you. You know, to begin."

"Begin?"

She shifted in her seat until she was facing him. "You do realize that when I said I wasn't leaving without you, I meant forever."

Jake's smile vanished and his jaw slackened as he leaned toward her. "Rebecca."

"Oh, God. You don't want— I'm sorry, I thought—"

"No, no." He took both her hands and squeezed them. "I do. I...I didn't know you wanted—"

"I did. I do."

"How?" he asked, and it was so earnest and hopeful she teared up again.

"I couldn't see it before either," she said. "Even though I'd fallen totally in love with you, I couldn't see how we could make it work. And then tonight, I got it. All the things I was worried about were just logistics. Everything important is you. That we're together."

"But I don't have a job, I've got my Dad—"

"You've got disability, so that's fine. Look, if you'd cared about the money, this never would have happened. So we make it work. Oh."

"What?"

"We can't be gone for too long. Imagine what the boys are going to do to your place? It'll look like an armored frat house."

Jake smiled. "Yeah, pizza boxes to the ceiling." He touched her hair. "What about the foundation?"

"It's not going to fall apart. And we'll get your father's new bathroom in shape when we get back. Then we'll figure it out. Day by day. If you want to."

"*We'll* get Dad's bathroom in shape?"

"Yes, we."

"You trying to get into my tool belt?"

She traced his endearing crooked smile with the tip of her unsteady finger. To not have this face...this man in her life...was unthinkable. The thought terrified her more than the threat of West on their heels. "Always, and I'm quite good at getting my way."

He kissed her then, deeply. She kissed him back with every promise she could make. When she pulled back, it was only to tell him, "I'll never feel safer than in your arms."

"I'll never let anyone harm you," he whispered back. "You're all that matters. You're all that will ever matter to me."

* * * * *

# WANT ME

## BY
## JO LEIGH

As always, I owe so many thanks to Debbi and Birgit for being true partners in this crazy writing endeavor.

# 1

THE WEDDING WAS IN FULL swing, "The Irish Rover" was in heavy rotation by the band, beer was flowing and the hundred and fifty friends and family of Theresa O'Brian-Moran were halfway to hangovers.

Shannon Fitzgerald had found a relatively quiet corner. It had taken Shannon the better part of the evening to convince herself to approach her second cousin about joining the small and exclusive St. Marks lunch exchange. But Ariel was perfect, really. At twenty-four, she was three years younger than Shannon, lived in Nolita, worked in Midtown and was still single, as was Shannon. Arial was also very pretty and had attracted a group of red-faced, very happy young men wanting to dance.

Shannon had pulled in her share of slightly older young men, mostly in the twenty-eight-to-thirty-five range, although Angus was hovering and he'd just turned eighty-three. It was like being caught in a swarm of bees. Shannon and Ariel kept swatting them away, but they just circled over to the bar, then came back.

"Trading cards?" Ariel asked, leaning in so she'd be heard above the fiddles and tin whistle of the band and the tipsy pleading of brokenhearted boys. "I thought it was a lunch exchange."

Shannon nodded. "It's both. If you want to do the food part, you bring in frozen lunches for fourteen, then you take home your own fourteen lunches. It saves a ton of money and gives you variety, but the important thing is the trading cards. All of us have friends or exes or coworkers who are eligible single men."

She pushed her cousin Riley a full arm's length away without giving him a glance. His breath. God. "Nice men," Shannon continued. "Men we'd want our best friend to go out with."

Ariel nodded slowly, fussing a little with the bodice of her pink dress, then her eyes lit up. "David Sainsbury at my office. He's off-limits to me, but he's extremely nice and he just broke up with his girlfriend. He'd be a real catch. He's always nice to the temps, and he gets coffee for his assistant every time he gets a cup for himself. He's funny, too."

"There you go," Shannon said, tickled about the addition of David, who sounded like someone she might be interested in.

"How do I do this? Submit his name?"

"You procure a picture of David, a head shot is best, let us see what we're getting. I'll make sure you have a few samples of the cards that are no longer in circulation. Then I put the picture on the front of the trading card."

"Oh, yes. Of course. The printing plant."

Shannon wondered if that was Ariel's first beer. Fitzgerald & Sons was a huge part of the extended family. Ariel's father had worked there for over ten years before he opened his stationery store. But then it was hard to think in all this craziness. "For the back of the card," Shannon said, deciding right then to reiterate all of this information in a follow-up email, "you fill out a short form. It starts with his profession. Then whether he's a marry, date or one-night stand."

Ariel's head tilted as she let the second part sink in. "Ah," she said, when the beauty of that key piece of information hit.

"Exactly. Next, his favorite restaurant. Then his secret passion. Not his career but the thing he loves more than anything. Sports or movies or dancing. Whatever turns him on."

"David is completely into science fiction. He's always got a book nearby."

The wistfulness of Ariel's voice made it clear that Shannon wouldn't be going out with David. She and Ariel were cousins, and she wasn't interested in starting a family feud. "Are you sure he's off-limits?"

"Company policy. He's one of their top attorneys."

"Maybe it'd be worth it to try and find another job," Shannon said, turning briefly to shoo away one of the Wilson twins.

Ariel shook her head. "I've put out feelers. It's murder out there. I'm not risking my job for anything. They have full medical."

"Understood." She took a sip of her white wine, sacrilege in this crowd, but Shannon didn't care. Beer was for the pub. Wine was for weddings. "After his passion comes the bottom line—what it is that makes him special. Why you're recommending him. Then, I put that information on the back of the card, do the printing and, voilà, we have Hot Guys Trading Cards."

"I love this idea," Ariel said. "I really do."

"It works. It's safe, too, because the person who submits the card sets up the date. And no one outside the group knows the cards exist."

"Including the guys?"

"Especially the guys." Shannon made a point of looking Ariel in the eyes. "The whole thing is a secret, very private. No one knows outside the group. Understand?"

Ariel nodded, took a healthy swig of her beer and grinned, showing off her expensive dental work. "It's brilliant."

"I know," Shannon said, not even a little bit embarrassed to say so since the whole concept had been her idea. "We've only been swapping cards for a couple of months, and it's exceeded our expectations. The only problem we haven't solved is how to keep increasing the dating pool while still keeping it a secret. Very tricky."

"Shannon." The deep voice behind her made her look because she couldn't immediately identify who was speaking. It wasn't a cousin, which was astonishing, but he might as well have been. "Hello, Mike."

"I was wondering if you'd like to take a turn with me?" He nodded toward the dance floor.

Mike was a nice man, almost thirty, owned a bookstore that was holding on by a thread, and she felt guilty for not liking him more. They'd tried dating once and there'd been no chemistry whatsoever. Maybe she should put him on a card. He really was sweet. "Oh, sorry. Maybe later? I'm in the middle."

"Sure, sure thing," Mike said, giving her a dejected smile. "I'll be around."

As soon as he was out of earshot, which was a matter of two steps, Ariel leaned in again. "What kind of men are on the cards? Are there any restrictions?"

"Nope. Except that they need to be local. And looking. There've already been some epic matches. Like Charlie Winslow and Bree Kingston."

Ariel's jaw dropped. "That was you?"

Shannon smiled. "It was."

"Holy cow. That's incredible. I'm in."

"Great." Shannon pulled out a tiny little notepad that fit in her tiny bridesmaid's purse that matched her pale green dress perfectly. "I'll give you the address and—"

Ariel was no longer listening. She was staring over Shannon's shoulder. "Is he on a card?"

Shannon looked where Ariel was pointing. "Danny? No. I decided not to put my brothers into the mix. Too complicated. Besides, since when have you been interested in—"

"Not Danny, the guy with Danny."

The guy in question looked kind of familiar. His body, on the other hand...

"What? Who is he? Do you know him?"

"No, I don't think so. I'd remember," she murmured as she checked out his shoulder-to-waist ratio, which looked to be perfect. He was in a white oxford shirt, top button undone, dark tie loosened. His slacks were a great fit, designer, not off-the-rack. The whole package was hot. His dark hair, the way he tilted his head back as he laughed, his smile...

"Oh, my God." Shannon stood up, stuffed the unfinished note back in her bag. "That's Nate Brenner."

"Who?"

"Danny's friend. I haven't seen him in ages."

"Well, go find out if he's single, would you? He's a total babe."

Shannon nodded as she headed his way, staring hard to make sure she was right. Yep. The closer she got, the clearer it became that the boy who'd practically grown up with her family was not a boy anymore. How had that happened? Time, of course, but because she hadn't seen him in so long, he'd continued to be eighteen and skinny and more than a little obnoxious to the thirteen-year-old sister of his best friend. No more obnoxious than her own brothers, though. All four had been insufferable. They'd made fun of her hair, of her desire to be on the stage. It hadn't helped that they'd been forced to come to the various pageants where she'd posed and danced and belted out her off-key songs. She'd made them miss games. The unforgivable sin.

When it came to her four older siblings every topic of conversation was centered on sports. *Every* conversation. Even when the discussion was about, say, books, they were sports books. Movies—sports. Okay, that and car crashes, but those were sports films in a way. Women entered the picture only if they first passed the team test. If they were crazy about Notre Dame football, they were in. The Yankees? In. The only variable was the Boston Celtics. They weren't the favorite, but they were acceptable.

She'd suspected there was more to Nate; he'd been more pensive, more intense than her hooligan brothers, but she'd been young when he disappeared, so she'd stopped wondering.

The transition from teenager to man had been very, very good to Nate, that was for sure. He would be thirty-two now, same as Danny. She'd never once thought of him as being good-looking. Passable, yes, cute, maybe. But hot? Not a chance.

"Hey, Princess," Danny said, as she got within talking distance. "Look who's here."

Nate's eyebrows lifted and his smile widened. "That can't be Shannon."

"It can and it is," she said, and then they were hugging, and it felt weird as hell for a whole list of reasons. His chest, for one thing. Firm, strong, broad. The feel of her breasts against it was sparking things that she had no business even noticing. This was a guy she'd known since she could remember. She'd seen him in his Spider-Man pajamas. They'd been his favorites, although sometimes he'd worn a cape or carried a light saber.

She pulled back to look at him. "Where the *hell* have you been? It's been forever."

"All over the place. It's too long a story to bore you with now. I want to hear what you've been doing." He looked her over then did the vertical version of a double take. "Aside from…you're all grown up."

"That tends to happen," she said. "So are you."

"I'll admit I got older. But I'm not sure about the grown-up part."

"Do you still put cherry bombs in toilets?"

He and Danny cracked up. "No," Nate said. "I'm very proud to say that I stopped doing that."

"It's a start," she said. "Did you come back for the wedding?"

"Coincidence. I've got business. Selling my father's firm. And looking for a town house."

"Selling your father's… Oh, God. I heard about your dad. I'm so sorry." He'd passed away two years ago, and she'd meant to write Nate.

"Thanks," he said as if it were nothing, but then his jaw tensed.

Shannon wouldn't have noticed if she hadn't been staring so rudely. "Did something happen to your house in Gramercy?"

"My mom sold it. She's living in Tel Aviv now. Got remarried. She's working at the university there."

"That's quite a few major changes."

"Not really. You Fitzgeralds are amazingly stable, that's all. What, it's only you and Brady still living in that huge brownstone?"

"And the parents."

"Uh, sorry to interrupt," Danny said. "I'm going to see if I can get Megan to dance with me." He poked Nate in the chest. "You can tell the Princess here all about your adventures. And the good news."

Shannon watched her brother dive into the heart of the crowd.

"So they still call you 'Princess'?"

She looked back at Nate with a sigh. "I've given up trying to make them stop. They're horrible, all of them. I can't imagine why you still like Danny."

Nate touched the back of her arm, and it jolted her like a static charge. "Every one of your brothers would throw themselves on a sword for you."

"When?" she asked.

He laughed, and it was so much deeper than when he'd been eighteen. She looked at him again. "How's your sister?"

"Married. With a kid. A little girl. They live in Montauk."

"Good for her."

Nate looked at the dance floor, his hand still on her arm. "You want to give it a go?"

She hadn't danced yet, and since the set was now modern music instead of traditional Irish dance, she smiled. "I'd love to." Nodding at a beer mug on the closest table, she said, "Your table?"

He slipped her purse from her fingers and put it next

to the mug. "It is now." Then he led her to a corner where they had some chance of not getting an elbow in the ribs.

Shannon liked the song, although she never gave it a thought outside of weddings or elevators, but the beat was good, and she was feeling fine. Happy. She'd recruited Ariel, been completely surprised by Nate and no one had asked her to sing or do any step dancing. It had been part of her repertoire as a young girl, but she'd let it go when she entered high school. Sadly, the family hadn't.

She moved to the music, got her rhythm then smiled at Nate. Ten seconds later, it was all she could do not to burst out laughing.

He was *awful*. The kind of awful that had to be genetic because no one would choose to dance that way. None of his limbs seemed connected to any of his other limbs, and what was he doing with his *head?*

She squeaked as she held her smile in place, and he was grinning right back at her as if he owned the whole dance floor.

Danny and Megan swung close by and Danny, her complete ass of a brother, slugged Nate in the shoulder, laughing so hard he had to stop everything else. "You are the saddest excuse for a white guy I have ever seen on a dance floor. Jesus, Nate, you look like someone stuck a firecracker up your ass."

Nate grinned at Danny and kept on doing…whatever it was he was doing. "I am my own man in every way," he said—no, shouted—then he spun around in an oval. "You don't recognize true artistic expression, you heathen. Be gone." He flapped his hand, although it was pretty much what he was doing already.

She laughed. But not because he was a total dork.

Because he embraced being a dork. Her hand, she noticed, was over her heart, and despite the music and the utter chaos around her, all she could think was that Nate hadn't just grown into a really good-looking man, he'd also become completely adorable.

The music stopped, but only for a second, and the next song was faster, wilder, and she let go. By God, she let herself dance as if she were in her bedroom, as if no one were watching. Like Nate.

His laughter hit her as she spun around, and she couldn't help returning it. They'd earned themselves a nice slice of dance floor, and she couldn't remember the last time she'd felt so free. The song ended too soon, and the two of them fell together to gasp in some much-needed breath.

"That was fantastic," he said.

"It was."

"Not a lot of women appreciate my unique style."

"They're fools and cretins."

"Ah, Shannon. You're too kind."

"Oh, I'm not. I'm really, really not."

Another song started, but this one was a slow tune, a romantic number that made her wonder if she should beg off, or…

He slipped his arms around her waist and started moving. Nothing fabulous, but also nothing uniquely styled. She found it easy to put her hands on his shoulders, to let her heartbeat slow.

"Adventures, huh?"

He shook his head a little. Met her gaze. "Of a sort."

"Danny mentioned you'd gone to help out after the Indonesian tsunami."

Nate nodded. "I did. I had skills, they needed help."

"And now?"

"They still need it. A lot of people do. I work for an organization that sends me where I can do some good."

Someone bumped her from behind, pushing her against Nate's body from knee to chest. Her first instinct was to put space between them, but there was also something else going on that wasn't the crowd and certainly wasn't dancing. There was no way not to look at him, and he was watching her as if they were alone in the room. He'd felt the tension, that was clear. A frisson went through her, and he felt that, too.

Another bump, but this one parted them the way she hadn't been able to.

He swallowed, glanced around at the crowd, then back at her. "I could use a drink after all that self-expression. Do you mind? Our table's open. I can get us drinks."

Thank goodness. She had no idea what the hell was up with those last few moments and she needed some space to get her breath back. "Great. White wine for me, please."

"Rebel."

She grinned. "That's me."

He walked her to the table and her smile faded as she watched him make his way to the bar. If he'd been anyone else, she'd have known what all that sizzle and smoke had been about. Any other guy. Part of her wanted to apologize and assure him she hadn't meant to press against him so intimately. But since she had… No. That wasn't at all what she wanted to tell him. She had no idea what she wanted to say. Mostly because she hadn't been able to read him. For a moment, she'd thought… But that was ridiculous.

He'd been a hellion as a kid. Forever taking risks, talking big. It had gotten him into a lot of messes, and he'd dragged Danny along for most of those, but he'd always been welcome in the Fitzgerald home. Especially since his folks had worked such long hours.

She had to wonder if he were still reckless, ready to jump into crazy situations without a second thought. His work sounded like something to be proud of, but also dangerous. Although she had to consider she'd known only the boy, not the man. Fourteen years was a long time, and she sure wasn't the girl she'd been back then. Or maybe she was. It was sometimes hard to tell.

While he was out of sight, she freshened her lipstick, practically the only thing she'd had room for in her purse aside from the small pen and notepad, a twenty and breath mints. Stupid little thing. At least the bridesmaid's dress was nice. Not great, just a simple sleeveless sheath with a sweetheart neckline. In the past year alone, Shannon had been forced to wear five dresses that would never see the light of day again. At least this time she hadn't been the maid of honor.

She suspected all her friends and relatives asked her because of her connections. Being in charge of sales and marketing for the printing plant meant she was on a first-name basis with almost every vendor from Chelsea all the way down to the Village.

"What's that scowl about?"

Nate put down her glass as well as his big mug of beer, then sat across from her. It caused a stir inside her that was frankly inappropriate. Good grief, she had to get over this. What she should be excited about was putting him on a trading card. A man with his looks, his international lifestyle, his unforgettable dancing needed to be out there. And the good women of St. Marks lunch exchange needed a breath of fresh air.

He'd had a good haircut. Not overstyled, but neat.

Whoever had had him on the chair understood that his high forehead was an asset, and that he could carry a longer sideburn than most.

"You're good-looking," she said. Then froze. She hadn't meant to say that out loud.

Grabbing his beer, he paused. "What's that?"

Oh, what the hell. She was busy, he was busy, after tonight she probably wouldn't see him again for another ten years. "You. I thought you were okay when you were in high school, but now you're actually handsome."

He fought a smile for a long minute. "Thank you?"

"You're welcome. Now, what was the good news you were supposed to tell me?"

"I'm moving in. With you."

## 2

NATE WATCHED HER EXPRESSION change from surprise to greater surprise. He sipped his beer to hide his grin.

"Oh?" she said, sounding as disinterested as a person who absolutely wasn't.

He nodded. "I was staying at Hotel Giraffe, but your mom had a fit, so now I'm moving in tomorrow."

"Danny's, Myles's or Tim's?"

He huffed out a laugh. "You think I'd risk my life in anyone's but Myles's room? Your brothers are savages."

She'd gotten herself under control, which was a pity. At least, her exterior was collected as could be, but he wondered. That dance… Not the first two, because he was under no illusions that he looked anything but preposterous attempting to move to music. Luckily for him, he'd quit worrying. He had other good qualities. Besides, if someone didn't like it they could piss right off.

He was actually thinking of the slow dance, the one where he'd felt her breasts against his chest. The one he'd had to cut short in case she felt his reaction.

There it was. The big deal, the shock, the bewildering new reality. Shannon had grown up to be an absolute stunner. She'd been a gorgeous kid, so why it was such a surprise wasn't clear, but he doubted anyone could have guessed she'd turn into the goddamn Venus on the Half Shell.

It started with her hair. Thick and past her shoulders, it was a lush, fiery red-orange wonder. Especially when she used both hands to sweep it off her neck before letting it fall.

"There's plenty of room at the house these days," she said. "How long will you be in residence?"

They'd been talking. He'd forgotten. "I'm supposed to be back in Bali by the middle of May. But I'm hoping to wrap things up here sooner than that."

"Oh. I thought you were looking to buy a town house."

"I am," he said, keeping his gaze straight ahead so he didn't get derailed again. "Mostly because I need the expenses to offset my capital gains. I'll sublet the place, but first I have to find something, then furnish it." He exhaled, happy that he'd found a topic so boring that his still-too-interested cock would settle in for the night.

Shit, the feeling of her in his arms revisited, and so much for boring capital-gains talk. She'd been a straight-as-a-board kid when he'd moved to his place at New York University, thirteen and a complete drama queen. Every time she spoke it was life or death, where she was the center of the universe, and none of her brothers had much patience. Especially when she kept popping up when he and Danny had convinced girls that they wouldn't be caught sneaking into the house after ten because Mom and Dad Fitzgerald's bedroom was on the third floor and they slept like the dead.

"In Gramercy?"

He had no idea why she'd asked... Oh. "I don't care where it is. Or what. Duplex, town house, row house, apartment. It needs to be in Manhattan, needs to be managed so that I can be gone most of the year without worrying, and it would be nice if it brought in some decent money. If you have any ideas or know of anything, that would be great."

"I'll ask around."

"Thanks." He picked up his beer again, she lifted her wine, and then she turned to look out at the dance floor and his shoulders sagged in relief.

This was Shannon. Little Shannon. He'd known her since he was eight, and she'd been a pest for the next ten years. But now she had curves and legs that went all the way down to the ground, perfect white teeth and deep green eyes. For a natural redhead, she had fewer freckles than he would have imagined, and oh, God, she was a natural redhead, which meant that all her hair was—

"I might know of something in the Flatiron District, come to think of it," she said, and she was looking at him again.

Great. He refused to even acknowledge the jerk in his crotch because he was thirty-two and Shannon had practically been his sister back in the day. "Hey," he said, leaning over the table, focusing, "you were always redecorating your room."

Shannon laughed. "I was a teenage girl. That wasn't decorating, that was illustrating. I was constantly falling madly in love with movie stars or deeply wounded singers."

"Your bedroom always looked nice. Smelled great, too."

"Yes, because I wasn't a savage who left my unwashed gym clothes to stew on the floor for months."

"Oh." Nate leaned back. "That actually makes sense. We were pigs, weren't we?"

She gave him an eye-roll. "I gather you want some assistance with the furnishings?"

He shook his head. "More than that. I need someone to help me find the right place, then furnish it. A woman's touch would be welcome. I've been building basic housing for a long time, living in tents or huts. I don't know the market at all. But I can hire someone if you're too swamped."

"I imagine I can take some time out of my busy schedule for an old friend."

He slapped back the rest of his beer and met her gaze again. He was going to be living in the same house as this newly sexualized Shannon, in the room next to hers. He might as well get this out so he could get on with things. "You're still a beauty," he said, his low voice carrying over a sad Irish love song. "More now than when you were in all those crazy pageants. You must have every man with a heartbeat after you, Princess. Every one."

The blush that blossomed on her cheeks spread like a light show. He used to make her blush as a parlor trick, something that would make her furious and hopefully storm off to her room. Now he found the contrast of her pale skin and the fire of her emotions far too fascinating.

"You're going to cause trouble, aren't you, Nate Brenner?" she asked, just loudly enough for him to hear.

"As much as humanly possible," he admitted. Then he smiled, because what the hell else was there to do about it? "Will you excuse me?"

"Sure," she said, her look suspicious.

Close to the bar he decided beer wasn't going to cut it. He ordered a boilermaker and drank it down right there on the spot.

"Is he?"

Shannon almost dropped her glass at the whisper behind her. It was Ariel, who didn't seem at all sorry for sneaking up on her like a thief. "Is who what?"

"Single." Ariel had to lift her head to see Nate standing with Danny in the midst of the crowd. Midnight, and hardly anyone had left the now stifling room.

"Yes, he is," Shannon said. "But he's not here for long."

"He doesn't have to be. All I'd need is one night."

Shannon frowned at her cousin. She'd been sweating—everyone was—and dark tendrils of hair were stuck to her face and neck. The way Ariel gasped for breath was more a result of the dancing she'd been up to than her interest in Nate… Still, Shannon could be mistaken about that. Ariel looked ready to pounce.

"If I do put him on a card, you'll have to be quick. It's first come, first served."

"Did you see how I caught the bouquet?" she asked. "I hate being single. I honestly do. It's a pity your guy isn't going to be around for the long haul. I like his laugh. That's huge for me. A sense of humor. You can get through most anything if you can find something to laugh about."

"You met him?"

Ariel sighed. "I did. He was great. But he was very involved in a conversation with Danny. Evidently I wasn't enough to distract him."

"Let me guess," Shannon said. "Notre Dame?"

Ariel rolled her eyes. "I swear, I could have stripped

right down to nothing and neither of them would have blinked."

"I doubt that. But I don't think they've seen each other since college. All those games to catch up on."

"At least he was funny."

"Humor's on the top of my list, too," Shannon said. "Along with shared values. And kindness."

"Don't forget great in the sack," Ariel said, still craning her neck to gaze at Nate.

"I can't help you with that one."

"You've never…?"

"No. Nothing remotely like that."

"Pity."

"Not really. He left when I was thirteen."

"God, it's broiling in here. Can't they open some windows?"

"I don't think it'll help. There's a hundred and fifty drunk people dancing like fools."

Ariel grinned at her. "It's wonderful, isn't it? I want my wedding to be just like this. Friendly, open. Plenty of booze and good food. If I ever have a wedding."

"That's what the trading cards are for." Shannon thought about how Rebecca Thorpe and Jake Donnelly were living together now. Part-time in Brooklyn and part-time in the Upper East Side. Shannon had the feeling they'd end up married. They were wildly in love.

"You, too, huh?"

Shannon must have let her envy show. "Yes, I would very much like to be married. So far my dates have been fun. But no magic."

Ariel shook her head. "Sometimes I wonder if magic is too much to hope for."

"Of course it's not," Shannon said. "A little bit of magic is in every good love story. I'm sure of it."

THE BROWNSTONE WAS A RELIC of a New York long gone.
All three stories in the row house belonged to the
Fitzgerald family, and since the third grade it had been
more a home to Nate than his own.

At noon, the taxi pulled away, leaving him with his
suitcase and duffel bag. The traditional wedding hangover lingered, but even so, approaching the red door
on 3rd Avenue in Gramercy Park made him feel like a
kid. The last time he'd been there had been pre-NYU.
Before Danny went to study graphic design in Boston.

He banged on the knocker, the one Mr. Fitz had replaced after the Baseball Incident. Nate liked this one
better. It was in the shape of a shillelagh, and it was
loud.

Mrs. Fitz opened the door and, yeah, he was ten
again, or fourteen, or eight, and all the years in between and around because she looked the same to him.
Her hair was mostly gray now, but for a pale woman
who seemingly had more freckles than skin, he saw
remarkably few signs of the passing years. Then there
was her frown. She wore it most of the time, and it put
some people off. But he knew better. That was Danny's
mom, worrying about her brood. She'd always said life
in her house was most frightening when it got quiet,
and she'd been right.

"Get a move on, Nathan—" and there was a hint of a
brogue even though she'd been born and raised in New
York "—you're letting in all the flies."

He dragged his rolled case and duffel bag across the
threshold into the entry hall, then put the duffel on the
big wooden bench, almost expecting his snow boots to
be underneath on the boot mat. "It's good to be home,"
he said.

When he turned to smile at Mrs. Fitz, she was smiling right back, a rare and wonderful sight. "As long as we live here, boyo."

He wanted to throw his arms around her neck, it was so terrific to see her again. She'd been a major part of his life, and he didn't think of her often enough. But as big as their hearts were, the Fitzgeralds weren't huggers. Except for Shannon apparently.

"I imagine you'll be wanting lunch. You should eat first because Myles and Alice are still in his old room. Everyone slept in after the party, the drunken hooligans."

"Who you calling a hooligan?"

It was Danny, coming down the stairs, looking like a madman with his hair sticking out all over the place, unshaven, wearing some god-awful zombie T-shirt.

"Ah, I see why," Danny said. "We're in for it now."

"You two can set the dining room table." Mrs. Fitz headed toward her kitchen, but she made sure they heard. "My God, there's nine of us. You'll need to bring in chairs."

"So the whole crew stayed over?"

"To be fair," Danny said, scratching his belly as if he was alone in his bedroom, "Shannon and Brady live here. But Tim and me and the married ones, we had to stay. Nobody was taking a train at three in the morning."

Nate slipped off his coat and hung it on one of the wooden pegs that lined the entry hall. "Whatever happened to Gayle?"

Danny's brow furrowed. "Boston Gayle?"

Nate nodded.

"She kicked me out while I was in my boxers. Thought I'd slept with her best friend. Truth was, I had, but we didn't do anything but sleep. Completely innocent. Gayle didn't care, though." He started walking to the kitchen, now scratching his jean-covered butt. "She called me an evil bastard who had no class."

"Go figure." Nate trailed after his buddy, and everywhere his gaze rested he found another piece of his past. He'd fallen against the edge of the massive wooden dining room table, running when there'd been a very strict rule against it. In his defense, Myles had been chasing him, and Myles was six years older and mean.

Nate walked through the kitchen to the pantry door and swung it open. Ignoring the massive amounts of stores Mrs. Fitz kept on hand, enough to feed an army, instead he checked out the marks on the height chart etched on the wall. There was his name, alongside Tim and Myles and Brady and Danny. No Shannon, though. He hadn't remembered that. Still didn't know why.

"Please tell me there's coffee made."

Nate knew it was Shannon behind him, but her voice was as grown-up as the woman herself. Despite his complete and total awareness that she was no longer a child, his memories were in flux. He peeked out from the pantry to see her in her belted robe, her hair hanging over her right shoulder.

It shouldn't have been real, that color, but it was. They'd gone to Coney Island or out to the seashore, and no one ever got lost because all they had to do was look for that firecracker hair in the crowd.

Of course, she'd always gotten sunburned, even after Mrs. Fitz slathered her with goop. Nothing could protect that white skin, not umbrellas, not T-shirts, not the awful zinc on her nose.

"Oh." Her hand went to her hair, then just as quickly lowered. "You're here."

He came out of the pantry. "Just arrived. Currently on table-setting duty."

"My mother's a slave driver."

"I heard that, missy. You'd best get your coffee and get dressed. We have a houseful to feed."

Shannon turned to her mom standing by the stove. "There isn't one person in this house who isn't capable of fixing their own lunch. Not one." She had her hands on her hips, and Nate was taken aback again that she'd developed so many curves. It didn't seem possible. But then, he'd done some changing, too.

"You know your brothers. Left to their own devices, they'll eat nothing but garbage."

"Then that's what they deserve. Garbage." She turned back to Nate. "Don't bother asking who buys the candy and chips and cookies and cake and every horrible, calorie- and fat-laden food in New York."

"I wouldn't think of it."

"Then you learned something hanging around here all those years."

"That your mother is generous and wants her sons to be happy? Yeah, I got that one."

Mrs. Fitz nodded and kept on stirring what smelled like beef stew. Shannon smiled at him, patted his arm and went to the big coffee urn that took up half of the completely inadequate counter.

The house was huge, but that was mostly in height. Eight- and nine-foot ceilings, but small rooms. The old oak table where he'd eaten countless bowls of oatmeal dwarfed the breakfast nook. Even the living room barely fit the furniture. How many games he'd watched on those covered couches and chairs. He couldn't begin to guess. Didn't matter what season, if there was a game on anywhere on television, the Fitzgerald men were glued to it.

And there'd been snacks followed by huge dinners of meat and potatoes and enough cabbage to choke a horse. "That's what's missing," he said.

Danny, who was now pouring his coffee, Shannon, who was drinking hers, and Mrs. Fitz were all staring.

"Cabbage," he said, only then realizing he'd made a strategic error. He couldn't very well announce that he'd missed the stink. "I'm looking forward to some nice corned beef and cabbage soon, Mrs. Fitz. I still think about it all these years later."

"Well, you'll have it as you're staying more than a week," she answered, turning back to the heavy pot. "And since we had the new exhaust put in, it doesn't make the house smell to holy hell."

He grinned and shook his head. This was so much better than a hotel. He should have thought of asking to stay before he'd left Indonesia.

"Danny tells me you work with refugees," Mrs. Fitz said as she wiped her hands on a tea towel.

"Most of the time, yeah." Large white plates were put in his hands, and Danny led him to the table carrying a bunch of silverware. "I work for The International Rescue Committee. They set my agenda."

"Well, don't stop." Mrs. Fitz waved impatiently for him to continue. "Tell us what that means."

"I show up after a natural disaster and help plan and implement redevelopment. We try to recreate villages and towns as much as we can, even if a new design would be better. It's disorienting having everything you know ripped away in a tsunami or an earthquake. So we study old pictures, drawings and blueprints and figure out how to give people back their equilibrium first, then we add a few extras."

Shannon wasn't drinking even though her cup was at her mouth, and she wasn't even standing near her mom and yet he was watching her. He found Mrs. Fitz again. "It's challenging work, but very satisfying."

"I can't imagine."

She couldn't, Nate was sure of it. Not the conditions, not the sweat, the devastation, the utter anguish in every breath.

It was suddenly quiet, a rare thing in the Fitzgerald household, and he wished he hadn't gone into detail. No, it wasn't a pretty picture and better that people understood that not everyone enjoyed a comfortable middle-class life, but Shannon's empathetic expression both pleased him and made him want to kick himself.

Mrs. Fitz finally broke the silence. "Take Nate upstairs, Shannon. He hasn't seen the changes yet."

"Now?" Shannon said.

"You'd rather wait and let the food get cold?"

"Come on," she said to Nate. "I'll give you a tour." One hand had a death grip on her coffee mug, the other was in her robe pocket. "You're going to love what Mom did with Danny's room."

"Hey," Danny said. "He's supposed to be helping me set the table. And my room's a mess."

"You've only been here one night," Mrs. Fitz said. "What have you done?"

"Nothing, Ma. Nothing to worry about."

Nate had no problem leaving Danny to finish the job by himself, and even less of a problem following Shannon up the stairs. He wanted to check out the pictures that had dotted the old ivy wallpaper, but he ended up watching the sway of her hips instead.

SHE'D BEEN ONE OF THOSE kids who loved the limelight, who glowed when she danced and sang and posed. Nate had been roped into attending far too many of her recitals and pageants. He'd been bored out of his gourd, but he'd gone. He and Danny had done their best to cause trouble, and they'd usually succeeded. So it hadn't been all for nothing. But she'd never swayed like that.

Shannon led him to Danny's old room, where Nate had spent the night hundreds of times. She grinned as she pushed the door open, and he peeked before stepping in.

"A sewing room?"

"Not just a sewing room," Shannon said, nudging him forward. "A library, a tea room, a knitting parlor and a quiet room. Mostly a place to escape from the heathens and their games."

"I didn't know your mother sewed. Or knit. Or read."

"She's…expanding her horizons," Shannon said, although there was more to it than that if he correctly read her raised brows.

"Has she retired?"

"Yep, she still does the books for the plant when

I'm swamped, but she decided when Brady took over as manager that she was going to spend time on things that weren't cooking or cleaning."

Speaking of, Danny's clothes were spread over a very comfortable-looking recliner, what probably was a daybed when it wasn't a mess of linens, and even over the doorknob of the closet. "At least one of your brothers hasn't changed."

Shannon leaned toward Nate and lowered her voice, her breath warm and sweet touching his skin. "He's actually doing really well at the advertising firm. Don't tell him I said so, but he's good. He's got a gift."

Too busy inhaling her scent, he almost missed his cue. "Okay, I must be in the wrong house. You? Saying nice things about Danny?"

"It's probably because I don't see him very often. Absence makes my tolerance stronger."

"I don't think that's how that saying's supposed to go."

"It's true, though," she said, eyeing the pile of yarn that had been pushed to the side. "Be warned. You won't leave here without at least a half-dozen new wool scarves."

"I'm working in Indonesia. The average yearly temperature is eighty degrees with ninety-percent humidity."

"As if that'll dissuade her. Oh, and they'll be hideous colors, too."

"I look forward to it."

"No, you don't," she said as she went back to the hallway. "But you can give them away. They are definitely warm."

"What about your room?"

"Mine? It's still too small."

"I'd like to see it," he said.

For a long stretch of barely breathing, Shannon stared at him, her lips parted. Then she moistened them, the tip of her tongue taking a nervous swipe. "Why?" she asked finally.

"Why?" Shit, he felt as if he were twelve again, caught trying to snatch a peek at Mr. Fitz's *Playboy*. "I'm curious about grown-up Shannon's natural habitat."

She shrugged. "Suit yourself. It's two doors down."

"I know." He shoved his hands in his pockets, wondering if crashing here was the right decision. It wasn't as if he couldn't afford to stay in a hotel. Which was probably more convenient. The real problem was Shannon. He hadn't expected her, not this version. "Is this going to be too weird?"

"What?" she asked, widening her eyes, but she didn't fool him for a minute. Her pupils were dilated and the pulse at the side of her neck beat as fast as his own.

"Maybe this isn't a good idea."

"Don't be silly." She laid a hand on his arm, then proved his point by withdrawing a moment too quickly. "We'll practically have the whole floor to ourselves. Brady's room is down the hall but he spends most nights at his girlfriend's place."

He had no business being so pleased about that last fact. No business at all.

FOR EVERYONE'S SAKE SHE HAD to snap out of this case of nerves and act naturally. So he wanted to see her bedroom. Not only was she making too much of it, but it also wasn't as if he hadn't seen it before. Usually with her screaming at him and Danny to get out and stay out, or yelling for her mom, or throwing something that was handy. But it wasn't a little girl's room anymore, and he wasn't that Nate.

He paused as they reached her door. "It occurs to me I should have asked about this first. As in giving you warning, and not just, hey, I want to see your room."

She smiled. "I'm not like the savages. My room is neat enough for surprise visits." She saw the uncertainty flicker in his eyes, and she shrugged. "I think it's going to take us all some time to adjust."

He turned. "You think we'll still like each other?"

"Still? I don't think we ever liked each other," Shannon said. "But then we were kids, and being my brother's best friend, it was your duty to torment me."

"And now?"

She looked into his warm, direct gaze and her body tightened. "Annoy me and I'll short-sheet your bed."

"Ah, so the room comes with maid service." Nate grinned, making him seem more like the boy she remembered and she relaxed a bit.

"Dream on." She moved to her closed door, her hand on the knob. "Go ask Mom about maid service. See what she says."

Nate winced and acted as if he'd been wounded. "You are trying to get rid of me. I don't know why your parents put up with me to begin with."

"Because they're big old softies. They don't even ask for me or Brady to pay rent, and when I started paying them anyway, I discovered they were putting my checks into a savings account for me."

"That's nice."

"My point exactly. With the benefit of hindsight, I believe they thought you needed the security of a big family."

He smiled, but it was more out of pathos than anything else. "My folks tried. They did. They loved us. They didn't have a gift for child rearing."

"Then isn't it good you had a backup plan?"

"Brilliant, even in third grade."

"Now I'm seeing the old Nate." She felt more like herself, as if they'd turned a corner. Not a huge one, but enough to start with. "So, ready for the reveal? God, it's hard to admit I still live here, even though it's becoming common again for people my age, no thanks to the recession."

"I like that you do. You've always been connected to your clan. I envy that."

"Depends on why I do it." She opened her door and stepped back to let him in.

He didn't go far, only a few steps, but she noticed he looked at everything. Her queen bed with the pastel sheets, the hint of lilac on the walls and in the reading chair. She wondered if he remembered the posters of all those boy bands, and Doogie Howser and Jonathan Taylor Thomas. Everything had been pink back then and had ruffles. There'd been a canopy, naturally, and stuffed animals. An entire display case of her tiaras and trophies from being Little Miss Gramercy Park and Little Miss Manhattan, and more than a dozen others. Some were still on display in the living room alongside the boys' sports awards.

"I was right," Nate said.

"About?"

"Your good taste. Although the room's not quite the same without that framed picture of Leonardo Di-Caprio."

"Who was all of fourteen at the time."

He went to one of the pictures on the wall. It wasn't anything fancy. She'd found it at a local art festival, and she'd spent more on the frame than the picture. It was an ordinary bedroom, small and neat, and filled with light. There was an open book on the bedside table, a shawl left draped on a big chair. It was cozy and quiet, not something she'd felt often growing up.

"I don't spend a lot of time in houses anymore," he said. "Or beds. I'm lucky to get a cot sometimes. I've even gotten used to hammocks."

"What drew you away, Nate? Danny said you'd wanted to help after the tsunami, but he never said why."

Nate turned, and he looked so good, so content. He was wearing jeans, a Henley shirt, boots. She could picture him doing errands, getting his hands dirty. But once he'd grown out of his terrible years, before he'd gone away, she remembered him as a reader. He'd liked architecture and didn't seem unhappy that he was expected to follow in his father's footsteps. She'd been surprised at his humanitarian streak.

That sounded kind of awful when she thought about it so bluntly, but she'd never seen him go out of his way much. Admittedly, her perspective had been limited.

"I'm not sure. I don't think I was running to as much as I was running from."

"Was it so bad?"

"No. It's not as if I was abused or mistreated or anything like that. I don't know. I guess I had read too many books about adventures. I wanted some of my own before I settled down."

"From the looks of it you're not done yet."

"Nope. Not yet."

"How will you know?" she asked.

"When, you mean?"

Shannon nodded.

"No idea. I don't think too far into the future, to tell you the truth. Everything is so immediate and real in a way I have a hard time describing. It's interesting to be back here, to shift my perspective." He touched the edge of her bed. "I like your room. It's calm, and it's pretty, but there's still you all over it."

She would have liked to have asked him more about his other life, but she went with the program. "What do you mean, me all over it?"

He walked over to her dresser. "Playbills, perfume, ticket stubs, lectures. I'm surprised you didn't end up on the stage. You loved it so much as a kid."

"Some people would say I've made my life a stage."

"What would you say?"

She waved the comment away with her free hand. "Sales, marketing. It's all just acting, isn't it? Anyway, I imagine Mom is getting antsy. We should go down."

He nodded, but turned to take another sweeping look at her small room. "It's home but it isn't," Nate said softly.

Shannon wasn't sure if he was speaking to her or himself. "What?"

"I'm glad I'm here. I'd forgotten I had memories I wanted to keep."

"About New York?"

"No. This house. This family. You."

"Me? I was the pain-in-the-ass Princess. What would you want to remember about that?"

"You were the prettiest little girl I'd ever known. By the time I was getting ready for NYU, you'd gotten even more beautiful. Now, you're…"

She could feel the blush again and realized it was going to be a problem. "I'm…?"

He inhaled deeply. "We should go eat." He walked past her and out the door.

Shannon touched her cheeks, willing them to cool off, wondering what had just happened.

NATE HAD WOKEN UP BEFORE the alarm. He'd adjusted to the time change, being in the Northern Hemisphere, and the sounds of the city. He hadn't done as well with adjusting to the beds.

At the hotel he'd never found the sweet spot, so those nights had been crappy. Myles's bed was even worse. It sagged in the middle, so no matter where he started, he ended up sinking, his back curving unnaturally. While in the hottest shower he could stand, he'd debated changing rooms after Danny left, but that would be weird seeing as it was now Mrs. Fitz's sanctuary.

So, he'd work in a couple of massages while he was here. The shower had helped get the kinks out, but now he was running late. He finished shaving, then wiped the shaving cream away. Making sure the towel around his waist was secure, he opened the bathroom door and bumped right into Shannon.

He decided to ignore that his startled squeak was almost the same pitch as Shannon's. "Sorry, sorry."

She'd backed up a couple of steps, pulling the top of her robe together. "No, I just didn't expect…"

Her gaze had gone from his face to his chest. And stayed there. He checked. The towel hadn't fallen.

She let go of her robe to gesture at his body, at least from the neck down. "When did all that happen?"

He chuckled. He'd been a skinny kid, but he'd done a great deal of hard manual labor overseas, and when there were lulls, he kept himself ready. He returned her gesture, although his wave was focused more around the breast area. "When did all that happen?"

"Point taken," she said, with an uneasy laugh. "But hey. Nice."

"You, too."

"Now go away. I need to shower." She sounded friendly, unaffected, but he'd seen the telling blush as she pushed past him in a sudden hurry. "You better not have used up the hot water."

"Would I do that to you?"

She turned, her gaze flickering to his chest before meeting his eyes. "Please."

"Yeah, okay. But it wasn't my fault. Have you ever slept in Myles's bed? I kept waking up thinking I was being smothered."

"So, no hot water left?"

"I wouldn't linger if I were you." He couldn't, either. Not without embarrassing himself. Partly her fault, the way she'd looked at him.

Shannon sighed.

He accidentally brushed her arm. "I'm sorry. I'll be more considerate. I will. I haven't had to be for a while."

She stared at the place he'd touched her, and when she looked up again, he knew he was in trouble. She was a very beautiful woman. Not a kid, not a teen. And he'd spent a few hours of sleeplessness thinking about how pale her skin was and if all her hair was as stunningly red. He'd felt weird about that last night, but not now. He wanted her, and he was pretty damn sure she wanted him right back.

She cleared her throat, then hurried into the bathroom and shut the door.

It was a problem. He had no idea what the ground rules were. Except that he had no business being half-hard standing in the hallway. He made it to Myles's room in case Brady hadn't gone to his girlfriend's place last night, but Nate was acutely aware that the next door over was Shannon's bedroom. That she was taking a shower right this minute. Naked. Pale. Her nipples would be pink. Like the color of her blush.

Shit.

"WAIT," SHANNON SAID, pointing at Nate. "Come over here and stand in front of the fireplace."

"Why?" He glanced at his watch.

"It'll only take a second. I need a couple of pictures."

He frowned at her, but he was moving in the right direction. "For what?"

"Neighborhood blog. No big deal, but I edit the damn thing and I need filler."

"Wait a minute. What are you going to say?" He had reached the brick fireplace and placed his hand on the mantel.

She doubted he even realized he was posing, but she brought up her cell phone quickly, clicking as often as she could between flash charges. "You live a very adventurous and heroic life," she said, moving a bit to her right to get another angle. Then she zoomed in even closer. He looked great in his dark suit, no tie, off-white shirt with the top button undone. She wished she could have gotten him in his towel this morning, but then again, she probably wouldn't have been able to keep her hands steady.

She clicked again. "You're a native son. It'll make a great story."

"How many people read this blog of yours?"

"Oh, a lot."

"I'm not sure about this. There are people I don't want to see. I was hoping to keep the visit quiet."

"Oh, well, that's easy to solve. I'll run it after you're gone. And I'll make sure to say great things about your organization. I looked it up. You guys do fantastic work."

"Yeah, we do. And they'll appreciate the mention," he said, then glanced at his watch again. "I've got to go."

"Fine," she said, stealing one last picture.

"But I get to read it, and if I don't like it, you're not going to run it."

She wanted to argue, but it didn't really matter. She could easily skip writing a piece for the blog. This session was about the trading cards. "Deal," she said.

"Okay. See you tonight."

"Maybe Molly's?"

He smiled as he passed her. "Yeah, Molly's sounds great."

She watched him as he walked, still stunned at her reaction to his…to him. The thing was, she hadn't expected the change. He'd been one of those narrow boys, no ass, no chest to speak of. Like most of her brothers. Myles hadn't been that way, though, at least not after puberty hit. He'd gathered a harem when he got on the junior varsity football team, and that hadn't all been due to padding.

But Nate, he'd had an average, if slim, silhouette the last time they'd been to the community swimming pool. He'd been seventeen, she'd been twelve, and she'd threatened to drown him if he continued to splash her with his stupid cannonballs.

He wasn't average anymore. Not a muscle man, either, just, well, sculpted. Defined. Enough chest hair to be enticing instead of daunting, and those guns…who would have guessed?

She'd reacted. As any woman would. But being attracted to Nate seemed every kind of wrong.

She'd make his trading card first thing. Get him out on the market. It probably was good that she hadn't taken a picture of his naked chest. There'd be a riot at St. Marks.

Her mother's call from the kitchen snagged her attention, but a quick look at the clock got her moving. She had a huge day ahead, and now she was going to have to put together Nate's card.

It was possible that would have to wait. The lunch group wouldn't get together for another week. For now, she'd look at the pictures, make sure she had a winner. She hoped so. It would be difficult to come up with another excuse.

"I'll have something at the plant," Shannon said as she got her coat from the peg. "I'll be in and out all day."

"Don't get doughnuts," her mother said, popping up in the dining room. "Your father can't say no."

Shannon opened her mouth to object, then sighed. "How do you do that?"

"I'm your mother. You can't keep secrets from me."

"That's what you think," she said, putting her phone into her purse.

"You and Steven Patterson. Coney Island."

Shannon froze. "What are you talking about?"

Her mother laughed. "Don't try to fool me, missy."

It was time for Shannon to leave before she started thinking about that tattoo and her face gave her mother more ammunition. She opened the door, but only made it halfway out.

"At least the tattoo wasn't a tramp stamp," her mom called out. "That would have been really embarrassing."

Shannon closed the door behind her and blushed all five blocks to the subway.

NATE STOOD BEHIND THE barricade that separated the street from the construction zone. He had no idea how long he'd been standing, but when he sipped his coffee, it was lukewarm, leaning toward cold. The sign on the chain-link fence was as familiar to him as the sound of the cranes and earthmovers. Brenner & Gill. Even after he'd inherited half of the firm, the Brenner referred to his father, not himself. And in about fifteen minutes, he would be meeting with Albert Gill, his father's partner.

Nate had known Albert most of his life. Yet he didn't know Gill well. The basics, yes. His wife was Patty and he had two daughters, Melody and Harper. There had been Christmas dinners, because the Gills celebrated, and a couple of times they'd had Hanukkah dinners instead, even though Nate's family were barely observant. But the families had never been friends. His father hadn't had a gift for friendship, either. It was something of a miracle that he'd gotten married at all, given he preferred to be alone.

That's how they'd found him. Slumped over his drafting table on a Monday morning. He'd died the Friday before sometime between seven and midnight. According to the coroner's office, he'd gone quickly, hadn't felt a thing.

Nate had come back for the funeral, but he hadn't stuck around. It was a quiet business, and he'd been surprised to find that his mother and Leah had sat shivah for the whole week. Nate had worn a yarmulke, although he'd left it in the box by the door when he'd gone back to his hotel. His mother had made sure his old bedroom was left open for him, but he'd felt no need to stay.

And while he'd mourned his father, it wasn't what he'd been led to believe was normal. Frank Brenner had been more of an idea than a dad. He showed up at the important events, paid for most of Nate's college education, but their relationship had been about expectations and conditions. Since Nate had stopped even trying to be his father's ideal son after graduation, there'd been very little left.

Now he would meet with Albert over lunch, and they'd have an awkward half hour when they tried to reminisce. Nate hoped their meal would be delivered quickly. Food would be an essential distraction until they got to the heart of the matter.

Albert wanted out. It was the details Nate didn't know, the considerations. He wanted to read Albert as he spoke, figure out what he could before Nate met with his attorney.

There was a lot of money at stake. Building commercial crap paid well. The firm had a great reputation. But it wasn't going to be close to a handshake deal. Albert had run the business. He'd made the deals, set the terms, got the financing. Nate's father had designed the buildings, coordinated the construction plans. Albert had many, many friends. He was good with people and he was smart. No doubt he wanted a sizable amount.

What he'd get was his fair share. Nate headed to the restaurant, four blocks from the construction site, prepared to be read in return. He was up for it. He wasn't afraid of much these days. Too much time spent facing reality.

He had to admit, though, he was looking forward to the game. He'd always liked chess.

# 4

DESPITE THE HORRIBLE DAY, as Shannon reached the entrance to Molly's Pub, her pulse and breathing quickened. Nate was there already. He'd texted her ten minutes ago, which was a good thing, as she'd been so caught up in looking at the receivables she'd lost track of time.

He'd said not to worry, he was relaxing with a pint. She glanced at the window that announced with green lettering that this was Molly's Shebeen before she opened the heavy wooden door.

It took a moment for her eyes to adjust, and there was Nate, sitting three booths from the wood-burning fireplace that was fed and stoked all winter. She hung up her coat, then went toward him, her excitement mounting.

It would be fun to talk to him, was all. She wasn't even thinking about how he'd looked in that towel this morning. Okay, she was thinking a little about that, but she wasn't dwelling. That would be wrong. Foolish. The minute she started truly contemplating Nate as more than a friend, things got uncomfortable. He was family, and while it wasn't technically inappropriate, it was close enough to make her squirm.

His grin, however, made her light up. "Finally. I'm starving to death."

"Why didn't you order something, then?" she asked as she slid into the seat across from him.

"Because I'm polite."

"Don't be ridiculous. You're only polite when you want something. Is Danny coming?"

"Nope." Nate took a swallow from his half-empty Guinness. "It's just you and me."

She picked up the menu although she didn't need to look at it. Molly's was literally just down the street from her house, and she'd been coming here long before she'd been legal. Not that they'd let her sit with the customers. She'd been escorted to the back room, where she'd been fed and given cold milk with her dinner, and no matter how she'd explained that in Ireland even kids got to drink beer, she was denied the pleasure until she'd hit her twenty-first birthday. Or so she'd have her family believe.

"How was your day?" she asked, content to listen to Nate all evening.

"Interesting." He pulled out the *New York Times* classified section where he'd circled a bunch of listings. "It's never not going to be insanely expensive to live in this city."

"You're right," she said as she noticed Ellen coming over with two beers on a tray.

"How are you, Shannon?"

"Good, thanks."

Ellen put a perfectly chilled and poured Guinness in front of her, then gave Nate another. "You two want food?"

"God, yes," Nate said. "Cheeseburger with blue for me."

Shannon started to order her regular spinach salad, but said, "The same for me, please," instead.

Nate's brow rose first, then Ellen's.

"I've had a bad day. I'm hungry. So you can both be quiet."

Ellen left, and Nate leaned forward, elbows on the table. "What happened?"

"Don't want to talk about it. Tell me what you've found in the paper."

"Ah," he said, frowning at the real-estate section. "Everyone told me this is the best time to buy, because everything's going for rock-bottom prices. Rock bottom of what? I can't find a decent two-bedroom town house with an on-site manager for less than a million and a half."

"It's still Manhattan," she said. "People keep coming, and they keep paying."

"Crazy is what it is." He looked up at her with wide eyes, and even in the dim amber light, she could feel his interest. In the conversation, of course. "Your house has got to be worth many millions. You could sell that sucker and retire tomorrow, all of you. Move somewhere, pretty much anywhere but London or Paris, and live like kings for the rest of your life. And if you sold the plant, too?"

"Yeah, well, that's not going to happen. The house has been with us for generations. We're not about to let it go. Not the plant, either, dammit."

His open mouth closed and his excited gaze turned to concern. "I didn't mean anything by that," he said. "I wasn't serious."

She drank some so she could get her equilibrium

back. After she patted the foam off her upper lip, she smiled at him. "I know. I shouldn't have snapped at you. As I said, bad day."

"Did you eat lunch?"

Shannon blinked at him. "Uh, yeah. Why?"

"You used to get cr—out of sorts when you waited too long to eat. When we were kids."

"I admit, I did get cranky years ago, and all right, yes, I probably should have eaten more today. How did you even remember that?"

"Funny, huh, what sticks?" He tapped his temple. "Let's just say I have a lot of blackmail material stored away up here."

She feigned covering her mouth for a cough that didn't do much to hide her saying, "Underoos."

"Ouch," he said. "Although, I seem to recall a My Little Pony phase that went on for an incredibly long time."

"Those were adorable. And very appropriate for a child my age."

"I wasn't wearing Underoos to high school, you know."

"No, I didn't," Ellen said, and Shannon and Nate looked over at the grinning waitress. She put their silverware down and patted Nate on the head. "It's good to have you back for a visit," she said, then wandered off.

"I never realized how much the sawdust dampens sound," Nate said.

"I imagine everyone in the bar will be talking about your underwear in the next couple of days."

"And people wonder why I stay overseas."

Shannon reached for a napkin. She did wonder why he'd stayed away. And why he was so keen on selling

Brenner & Gill. But she didn't want serious tonight. She wanted to relax with her...friend.

NATE WANTED TO PUT HIS ARM around Shannon as they walked back to the house. It was close to midnight, stupidly cold, and he was so drawn to her it was a bad joke. Instead, he kept his hands in his pockets and tried to stop watching her long enough to prevent walking straight into a streetlight pole.

"I shouldn't have had that last beer," Shannon said.

"No, you probably shouldn't have."

She slowed her step and bumped his shoulder with hers. "You had more to drink than I did."

"We weren't talking about me. I should have stopped after my second Guinness. But come on. Guinness. At Molly's Shebeen. How am I supposed to resist that, hmm?"

"You're right," she said. "You were perfectly justified. I, on the other hand, was reckless and foolish. I should be ashamed."

"Well, hell. If you're going to waste shame on something like having an extra beer, you should give up right now."

Her laughter warmed him like a hot toddy. "What, you want me to rob a bank? Steal a car? Have an illicit affair?"

"Those are all legitimately shame-worthy, yes. Although I never said that shame had to come along with a prison sentence. You still need to have good judgment. So that leaves illicit affairs."

"I don't have anyone to be illicit with."

"No?"

She grabbed his arm and pulled him close. There wasn't enough beer in Molly's to slow down his heart.

"You almost walked into that pole," she said as she released him.

"Damn, I thought—"

"What?" she asked, and he shook his head. "You thought what?"

"Nope."

She studied him for a second. "Coward."

"Yep."

She laughed. "I could get it out of you if I wanted."

"Hey, go for it. I welcome the challenge." Suppressing a smile, he kept walking. She hated a dare, and he doubted that had changed.

"You have some nerve bringing up good judgment," she muttered. "I'd like to know where you got your measuring stick."

He had a totally juvenile remark at the tip of his tongue, which only proved how deeply irresponsible he'd been about the beer. Though the pole—that had nothing to do with drinking and everything to do with the illicit-affair remark. "Experience has taught me not to sweat the small stuff."

This time Shannon stopped completely. "You must be drunk if you're throwing that old clunker at me. How do you know what the small stuff is? One extra drink could be devastating."

"But you're not driving or operating heavy machinery. You're walking a block to your home, and you're safely accompanied by a man who knows how to kick the crap out of anyone who might try anything untoward. Therefore, you having a third beer isn't a big deal."

"What do you mean you know how to kick the crap out of anyone?"

"I have skills."

He couldn't see her smile in the shadow between streetlights, but he would swear on his life he could feel it.

"Would those be mad skills?" she asked in the most smart-ass, taunting voice he could imagine.

"They would," he said, realizing that with every word he was digging himself a deeper hole.

"Of the martial-arts variety?"

"And if I said yes?"

She poked him in the chest with her index finger. "You still have every single comic you ever bought, don't you?" Poke. "You store them in airtight containers and don't let other humans touch them." Poke. "You don't have to rent your costume for Halloween. Ever."

He grabbed her poking hand and walked her toward a streetlight until he was sure they could see each other well. "I do have a hell of a comic collection, which is worth a great deal, by the way. I do store some of them in a temperature- and humidity-controlled storage facility because of their value. I do not have costumes in my wardrobe, however. But I've been known to go to comic conventions and I keep up with the industry. I like comics. I like graphic novels. And someday, if you agree not be bitchy about it, I would like to show you why."

There was a moment of silence. Not just from Shannon, but from the street, from the city. A fleeting lull in the traffic, the subway vibrations, the chatter of pedestrians. He heard her inhale, sharp and startled, as if the last thing in the world she'd expected was his little speech.

He was surprised himself, so that seemed fair. He'd had no preparation, though, for how she was looking at him. As if he was someone unexpected. Someone interesting in a way he shouldn't be.

Good. That's what he'd wanted. And if he hadn't had the extra beer, he'd lean over right this second and kiss her until she cried uncle. But he was tipsy enough to know that he was treading on thin ice, illustrated perfectly by his use of the word *tipsy*.

Both of them having inappropriate thoughts didn't mean the thoughts were no longer inappropriate. He had one place he considered home in this world, and to risk that, he'd have to be sober as a judge and twice as sure.

"I'd like that," she said, her voice a breathless whisper in the quiet. "A lot."

"Yeah?"

Her nod was slow but it still made that gorgeous hair of hers move forward on her shoulder. He raised his hand, but the last vestiges of good sense stopped him from carrying out the gesture. He was going to be at the Fitzgeralds' for several weeks. There would be time to figure things out. Time to see where the lines were drawn.

The last thing on earth he wanted was to be ashamed about anything to do with Shannon. So tonight, he'd walk her home and he'd sleep it off.

Tomorrow he might curse himself for letting this chance go by, but better safe than sorry when there was so much at stake.

Dammit, he was going to wake up to his second hangover in two days. The sooner he got back to his real life the better off he'd be. He looked again at Shannon as they reached the steps of the brownstone. Then again, as long as he had to be here, he might as well enjoy the visit.

Shannon hadn't seen Nate at breakfast, and she was almost late because she'd dawdled, hoping. Then she'd castigated herself the whole way to the plant. Last night hadn't been a date. She wasn't sure precisely what it had been, but not a date.

Despite the extra beer, she'd stayed up far too late. Her brain wouldn't stop. Thoughts of his voice, his scent, how he looked in a suit were only the beginning. She imagined vividly his friendly touch on the small of her back sliding past her waist until his palm slowly brushed over the curve of her behind.

A smile, then as his gaze hit her lips, the heat of his breath, the brush of a tentative kiss.

An innocent look turned smoldering, unmistakable want.

By the time she'd entered her office, she knew her first order of business wasn't going to be a call to the deputy commissioner in charge of Union Square Park. That and everything else on her list would wait while she turned her total attention to creating Nate's trading card. Maybe then she could stop obsessing.

He was going to be staying at the house for several weeks at least, and wouldn't it be nice and smart to hook him up with one of her friends from the lunch exchange? He'd be otherwise occupied while she pulled a new card or two for herself. The next lunch exchange meeting was coming up soon, and she had six new trading cards to prepare including Nate's.

She decided to do the copy first. After locking her office door, she opened a blank trading card template and started by typing.

His profession was easy: architect and urban planner. No need to talk about his humanitarian efforts on the

card. That information would be much more dramatic
coming out when she talked him up.

Marry, Date or One-Night Stand, another simple
answer: Date. Only, wait. She deleted that and entered
One-Night Stand. Then she deleted that. He certainly
wasn't Marry. Come on, she'd know if he wanted to get
married. He wouldn't be rushing back to Bali as quickly
as he could if that were the case. Or would he?

He hadn't said anything about a woman. Did that
mean there wasn't one? Or was she someone exotic and
adventurous, a woman who would steer clear of anything to do with New York. Who lived on the edge.
Maybe a doctor from the World Health Organization,
someone who put herself at risk to save lives in regions
fraught with danger.

That made sense. Nate had changed so much, and
wasn't there always a woman behind that kind of trans-
formation? She should have known there was more to it.
He'd probably gone to Indonesia full of the best intentions. But then he'd met her, probably saving a small village cut off from civilization, and he'd helped her, both
of them hot and sweaty, sleeping in bits and snatches as
they slowly patched together the survivors. They were
bound to be hyperaware of each other, especially when
he heard her accent. French, had to be French. She'd be
beautiful, naturally.

Shannon sighed as she realized she'd typed a long
line of *B*s all the way across her document.

Okay, she would go with One Night Stand and move
on.

His Favorite Restaurant was easy. It was undoubtedly
something in Paris or Hong Kong or Monaco but screw
that, she was going with Molly's Pub. He was certainly
comfortable there. He'd laughed a lot. He'd made her

laugh. His stories were preposterous and creative. She could thank his comic books for that, she was sure.

That tale he'd told last night about pirates? Seriously, pirates? Yes, she'd read about Somali pirates in the paper, and yes, the frequency and brutality of their attacks on ships had made the waters of the Indian Ocean extremely dangerous, but Nate Brenner, fighting off armed bandits with a cricket bat and a tin gas can? He'd painted quite a picture, even though she knew the pirates he'd been talking about had nothing in common with broadswords and buried treasure.

She scratched out Molly's Pub. That wouldn't work. She went there too much herself, and the prospect of having to watch him with a date made her stomach feel a little off. Which was stupid. She'd be the one setting him up with the date so she'd know the woman, and wasn't that the whole point of the trading cards? Making sure the matches were suitable and safe?

Oh, hell, she'd have to come back to favorite restaurant.

Anyway, next was his Secret Passion. Shannon exhaled loudly, thought about putting down comic books, but she didn't type the words. Instead, she went to the break room, nodding at the people on the floor. They were doing two very large textbook runs for a university press, which was good, and all but one of the other presses were busy with baseball trading cards. It looked as though the company was standing on a solid foundation. Only she knew the depth of the corrosion of customers slipping away, and how precarious their situation was for the long haul.

No, that wasn't quite true. Every walk through the plant was full of evidence to the contrary. The long looks, the fear in their employees' eyes. They knew.

They were on the front lines, after all. Especially painful was the change in her relationships with two of her press operators, Daphne and Melissa. The three of them had been close. Now they avoided her gaze and talked about her behind her back.

It was Shannon's parents who didn't quite get the dire picture. The two of them weren't involved in the nitty-gritty of the plant any longer, and she was glad of it. If things went Shannon's way, they would never know. Because she would fix it. She had a battle plan. At least some of the new customers she'd been working on were bound to come through.

She couldn't think about it now. She got her coffee, put on a smile and returned to her office. She would finish the cards and scan the photos. Tonight, after hours, she'd do the typesetting and the printing. She'd complete the job early tomorrow, and that would be that. She'd be ready for the lunch exchange, she'd stop thinking of Nate as anything other than family and she'd get on with her job.

Someone had to save Fitzgerald & Sons.

After stopping to answer yet another surly question from Melissa, Shannon entered her office not feeling any better from the break.

She woke up her computer monitor, trading the screen saver for Nate's card, and almost dropped her coffee. Her heart slammed in her chest at the picture on the screen.

It was a photograph of an obviously abandoned printing plant. No caption, but then none was needed.

A wave of anxiety swept through her, forcing her to turn away from the computer. A press of the intercom brought a quick response from Brady. "What's up?"

"Can you come to my office, please?" Her voice had wobbled, dammit.

"Shannon? What's wrong?"

"Just come, Brady. Now." She disconnected the intercom and took several deep breaths. She wanted to get rid of the image, but her brother needed to see it. This wasn't the first incident of what—vandalism? protest?—although it was the most brazen. She'd been in the break room for all of five minutes. Enough time to pour, to stir in milk and a sugar substitute. Her conversation with Melissa had been uncomfortable, but brief. Whoever had done this had raced.

Brady had raced, too, because he was at her door amazingly quickly. "What happened?"

She nodded toward the computer.

His sigh held so much of her own frustration. "What do they think this will accomplish?"

She turned to her older brother. He was a redhead, but not like her. His hair was dark and so were his eyebrows. He was also a hell of a decent guy. Of all the brothers, he was the most down-to-earth. He liked running the plant, knew the machines as if they were his own creations. Nothing was too complex for Brady except the human capacity to be cruel.

"They're scared. They feel impotent and terrified."

He gesticulated wildly even before speaking, which only happened when he was extremely riled up. "They think this will help save the shop? Save their jobs?"

"That's just it. They don't know what to do."

"But you've told them the truth. You've been there to help them when they needed it. Just last week you gave Terrance an advance on his wages. Again. At this rate, he'll never pay us back."

"It's for medical bills. Taking away the health plan

was a horrible blow." She inhaled deeply. Brady wasn't totally on the mark. It wasn't so much that she'd told the whole truth as she hadn't lied.

"Would they rather we closed down? Would that be better?"

She shook her head. There weren't words. She was doing everything in her power, but it wasn't enough. Never enough.

All she could do was keep trying. So she sat, and she got rid of the picture on her screen, found where it had been loaded on her desktop and deleted it. She'd have to lock her door now, whenever she left, even to go to the bathroom.

This wasn't how it was supposed to be. This was a good company. A conscientious company. She wished she could understand how things had spun so far out of control.

She saved Nate's trading card in her private folder and clicked out of that program. There was no time for frivolous matters. She had to get new customers before it all went to hell.

# 5

"YOU'RE UP EARLY."

Nate jumped at Shannon's voice, although he covered it quickly with a cough. It was 6:30 a.m. and it wasn't as if he hadn't expected someone to be in the kitchen—the light was on, coffee made—but he hadn't seen her sitting at the table in the breakfast nook. For reasons that only made sense when they'd been nine, he and Danny used to sit underneath that table for breakfast every morning until they did something horrible and messy and had to report to the big table in the dining room, where the first and last meals of the day had been family affairs, complete with table settings and lessons in manners.

It was yet another adjustment to find Shannon in the nook, half in shadow, in the now familiar pink robe. "I'm house hunting," he said, bringing down a large mug from the cupboard.

He'd missed her the past few days. According to Mr. Fitz, she'd been staying late at work, and Nate and Danny had been catching up with friends at old haunts. He'd looked for Shannon, though, each morning. Each night. Hoping he hadn't spooked her on their walk home from Molly's. He didn't think so, he'd shown restraint, but seeing her smile now he knew for certain things were okay between them. And up to him to keep it that way.

"Where are you looking?" Sleep still clung to her voice, lowering the pitch and giving her a sexy rasp he had no business thinking about.

Great. His resolve had lasted all of two seconds. "Starting in the East Village. Then Greenwich and SoHo if there's time."

"All town houses?"

"The Realtor convinced me not to be so set on a specific type of building. She's basing her suggestions on the maintenance companies."

"That makes sense," Shannon said, "considering you won't be around if something bad happens."

The scent of the coffee was enough to kick him into the next phase of waking up. He hadn't showered, hadn't done anything but put on his robe. It was damn cold to be barefoot, but he hadn't brought slippers and hadn't thought to put on socks. The chill hurried him to the bench across from Shannon's. "You should come with me."

She coughed, having just sipped some of her own coffee. "Just come with you, huh? Blow off my whole day?"

"I'll buy you a good lunch. And you can say rude things about people's decorating choices."

"Why would I want to do that?"

He gave her a look that told her she wasn't dealing with an amateur. "You couldn't have changed that much."

"It's not rude if it's constructive criticism."

"Like hell."

She smiled at him behind her Gramercy Park mug. Her skin stopped him, his own cup an inch off the table. She looked as if she were made of cream and silk. Something that couldn't possibly exist in nature. Like the ads in the magazines that made every flaw disappear with the magic of airbrushing. But he was close, and she was as real as anything. He ached to touch her, not just on her cheek, although that's where he'd start. He could barely imagine the feel of her inner thigh, what it would be like to rest his cheek on her tummy, right below her belly button.

"Okay, that's pretty creepy," Shannon said.

He put his cup down. "What?" He knew he'd been staring. So why was he playing dumb?

"You do that a lot," she said. "There's a pattern. Am I that different from who you remember?"

"Yes," he said, and he should have hesitated there. For a few seconds at least.

"Okay."

She sipped more coffee and, ahh, there it was. The blush. He wanted to watch it evolve in all its heated glory, but he'd already crossed the polite behavioral line.

What he didn't understand was the reason for the blush. Yes, he'd stared too long, and that was rude, but was she blushing because she was embarrassed at the attention? If he'd been anyone else, would she have blushed or would she have walked away from the situation? Was she reacting to the stare itself, or had she sussed that he was thinking about her sexually?

"Did you and Danny go out and cause havoc last night?"

A change in the subject was probably a good thing,

and he'd roll with it. "Well, I wouldn't go so far as to say havoc."

"Let me be the judge," she said. "But first, I need another coffee. You want a refill while I'm up?"

"I've barely touched mine, thanks."

He didn't hesitate to watch her cross the short distance to the giant coffee urn. The timer switch had to have been set at some ungodly hour for it to finish perking so early. So like Mrs. Fitz.

The thought of her mother vanished as his gaze ran down the back of Shannon in her belted robe. The curves killed him. She'd been so straight for so long. Now, he couldn't stop thinking of his hands on her waist. Shit, the desire to have her naked had become more and more acute with every passing night. He was the one blushing now, and he never did. He got too much enjoyment from crossing social boundaries. Blushing was for people who cared if they were offensive.

But wanting Shannon…he hadn't been able to talk his way around that issue. This new mind-set should've been squashed each time he went upstairs and was regaled with pictures of little Princess Shannon, the Shannon he'd known best. In her tiaras and her tutus, she was the essence of innocence. Not like those kids they put on parade today. She hadn't been made to look like a miniature centerfold. In fact, she hadn't been sexualized at all, thank God. She looked like a fairy, like a Disney character come to life.

Except she wasn't that child any longer. She was twenty-seven and she was single and only one thin wall separated their bedrooms at night.

He turned his head, stared hard at the refrigerator, which frankly wasn't that interesting, but he didn't want her to see his face at the moment. He wasn't a very good actor, and his want felt bigger than his ability to pretend.

If for no other reason than out of respect for Mr. and Mrs. Fitz, Shannon should be out-of-bounds. Maybe he needed to go back to staying at the hotel. He could make up some lie that wouldn't hurt any feelings. Anything would be easier than being so close when he had to keep his distance.

THE TOTE BAG FULL OF FROZEN Irish stew servings banged against Shannon's thigh as she walked down the path to the St. Marks basement door. For the first time since she'd joined the lunch exchange, Shannon wasn't looking forward to the gathering. She had new cards ready, as always in a box so she could pour them out in a cascade of eligible men; all the drama she could fit into a dreary kitchen basement. She'd go through the motions—it was expected, after all—but her heart wouldn't be in it.

Work had been eating Shannon alive. Aside from the Easter preparations, the baseball team shirts, posters and calendars and the regular day-to-day pressings and bindings, she hadn't gone a day without making cold calls, without visiting at least one new potential client, without placing at least a dozen business cards in likely and unlikely venues.

In between, every spare second, she'd been consumed with thoughts of Nate, then feel guilty, talk herself out of that, then start the cycle over again. Midnight after midnight found her wide-awake, coming up with new approaches to get clients, or, more frequently, remembering every detail of Nate in a towel, Nate at the bar, Nate in the hallway, Nate, Nate, Nate.

She was doing all she could to increase business at the plant, and today she'd make a stand in her madness over Nate. While she couldn't ask him to leave the house, she could send him on a date. Hopefully more than one. And, despite her insane schedule, she would go out on dates of her own. Every night, if necessary.

The thought of which made her feel sick.

It was the stress. So much of it, and so few opportunities to vent. Brady had enough of his own troubles, so she couldn't whine to him, and she didn't want to tell the other brothers because they couldn't be trusted not to blurt out something in front of her parents. Thank goodness for all those years of practicing to smile and acting cheerful at pageants.

As she opened the basement door she put one of those smiles in place, ratcheted up her enthusiasm and went inside. The sound of her friends helped make both smile and attitude more true, and by the time she was in the kitchen, she felt better.

Everyone stopped. It had been one of her favorite parts of the trading cards. The expectant hush, the anticipation, the possibilities. Her, center stage. It was Christmas every couple of weeks. No, she hadn't found her perfect man yet, but there were so many success stories. She'd done that. Not alone, but the idea had been hers, and why couldn't she find something equally wonderful that would bring business to Fitzgerald & Sons?

"Shannon? You all right?"

Ariel was at her side, looking concerned. Shannon had forgotten she'd be there despite the fact they'd spoken two days ago. Shannon wasn't surprised to see that her cousin had gone all out for her first meeting. She'd worn her hair down, swept into a Lauren Bacall bob that looked slinky and sophisticated. Her jacket was of a theme—big shoulders, fitted waist—as was her pencil skirt and five-inch heels. It worked.

"Shannon?"

"I'm fine," she said. "No problem finding the place?"

"None. And everyone's already been nice, although there's no chance I'll remember the names."

"I'll take you around. After." She held up the box of new cards. There weren't many brand-new ones, but there were a number of men for the taking. Some hadn't been chosen at all, though very few. Most had come back to the pile because that elusive piece of magic had been missing. Shannon had returned several cards of her own.

The room was relatively warm, no thanks to the inadequate radiator. They were lucky, though, that the church let them use the place to hold their exchange and in some cases cook their meals.

Long, rectangular tables had been set up in a circle of sorts, every participant had fourteen frozen containers stacked and ready to be distributed, waiting for the bagging portion of the afternoon.

For now, though, the women who were still seeking their special someone were gathered in front of Shannon's table. She put the box down as well as her heavy tote. "This is Ariel, everyone. I know she's met some of you, and in no time at all she'll be one of the regulars. She's a paralegal, smart as a whip and gorgeous, but you'll like her anyway. She's my cousin and she understands that we don't discuss the trading cards with outsiders. Lucky for us she's contributed a very attractive lawyer."

Her friends were smiling and shuffling closer, and she wondered if they could tell she wasn't herself. Part of her wished someone would take her aside, get her to spill all her woes. But while it was true she did consider most of these women true friends, they weren't like the girls she'd been close to in high school and college. Completely her fault. There had been ovations, invitations, phone calls. But for years now, the plant had been her life. The plant and her family.

Shannon began the ritual. She lifted the box of cards high, and the energy of the room expanded, a palpable spark. The box tilted and the cards fell into a gorgeous pile while the women dove in.

Only one pick was allowed each session. Only returned if there was no hope, or a one-night stand. How lucky were those guys? If they only knew. But sometimes the date turned into a relationship, and the one-night stand became a series of dates. In the two most famous cases, those one-night stands had turned into life-changing, living-together, monogamous relationships.

There they were, standing back by the kitchen itself, Bree Kingston and Rebecca Thorpe. They had become very close friends in the last two months. Bree was living with Charlie Winslow, owner and editor of the Naked New York media empire. Rebecca was responsible for that match because Charlie was her cousin. Then Rebecca had been rewarded with Jake.

Fairy-tale romances, both of them. The outcome every woman in the room prayed for.

And Shannon had forgotten to look for another card and now the pile had dwindled considerably. She sighed, not surprised. Things weren't going her way lately, so why should the trading cards be any different.

"I got him!" Ariel said, her voice an octave higher than normal.

"Who?" Shannon asked, her cousin's excitement infectious and fun.

"Nate. Your friend Nate. I had to fight for him, though. There were three of us who grabbed for the card but I was fastest. I told you I'd get him."

Shannon had to struggle to keep her smile, her composure. Ariel was going to go out with Nate. If he accepted… But of course he'd accept, why wouldn't he, especially because Shannon herself was going to set the date up.

"I can't wait to find out what he's got under that suit," Ariel said.

Shannon knew Ariel would be pleased. From the way the towel had draped, there was every reason to think Nate was fantastic all over.

Why had she thought this was a good idea? What kind of moron was she, thinking this would be the solution to her problem? As much as she liked Ariel, Shannon was seconds away from ripping the card from her hand and running for the hills.

*He was hers, dammit.*

Her breath stilled as a shudder ran down her back. He was hers? *Really?*

"Shannon? Something is wrong. You look terrible." Ariel put her hand on Shannon's arm. "I think you should sit down. Have some water."

Everyone hustled to make sure she was seated, that she had a fresh bottle of water, that she wasn't too warm or too cold. At least five palms pressed against her forehead. Which was sweet, it truly was.

What mattered most, though, was that she didn't cry. She wouldn't, because that's not what she did, not in front of people. Not because of a man she shouldn't be thinking about, not like *that*. She was tired, that's all. No breaks, no sleep, no answers.

Bree, pretty as a picture in her weird purple-and-orange dress, crouched down beside her. "Do you want me to call a taxi? Get you home?"

"No, thanks. I'm just tired. Insomnia. It's a bitch, but I'll get over it. I need to sit for a little while. Sip some water. Do you think you can get everyone back on track?"

"Absolutely. But I'll check with you again later, all right?"

"Thanks."

Bree squeezed her shoulder and Shannon relaxed as much as she could in the awful plastic chair, letting the commotion wash over her like a wave.

She'd set up the date between Nate and Ariel, she would. Just not right now.

THE SIXTH PROPERTY HAD seemed so good on paper, standing in the actual living room of the duplex made Nate's chest hurt. He'd been dreaming if he thought he could get a two-bedroom place for even a million. He turned to his Realtor, Aiko, and shook his head. "I know you warned me. Sorry I've wasted your time."

"It's no problem, Mr. Brennan. You needed to see what's happening for yourself. If you can believe it, this condo would have sold for twice what they're asking before the bubble burst."

"That's a terrifying thought." It wasn't as if it were filthy or had active rat colonies. The problem was the size. He'd lived in New York most of his life, and he'd thought he understood what that meant. But he'd been spoiled. His family home had been a relic, like the Fitzgeralds', only not as many floors. And not as much warmth, and the windows had been small even after the remodel. This condo looked as if they'd taken a moderately sized one-bedroom and split it into doll-sized rooms. He doubted either bedroom could hold more than a double bed, and that's with no other furniture included.

"Okay, so, what's next?"

Aiko smiled cheerfully, even though she had to be exhausted, hauling him all over hell and back looking at inappropriate buildings. "There's a nice condo in the Lower East Side you might really like."

"From now on, you lead the way." He glanced at his watch, surprised that it was after five. "I had no idea it was so late. We can reschedule."

"It's not a problem for me, if it's not a problem for you."

"Won't the building manager have an issue?"

"If I wanted to look at anything in this city at midnight, I wouldn't have a problem. But it's completely up to you."

He had a meeting with his attorney tomorrow, but not until eleven. There was one thing that he could do with, though. "One sec," he said, as he pulled out his cell.

Shannon answered on the first ring. "Hey," she said.

"Are you still at work?"

"Not at work, but working."

"Thinking of quitting anytime soon?"

"You read my thoughts," she said, sounding tired.

"I have a proposition. Meet me at a condo in the Lower East Side and I'll take you to dinner after. What do you think?"

She was quiet for so long he figured she'd beg off,

but then she said, "Where? I'm in Little Italy. If it's going to take me forever—"

"Hold on. I'm putting you on with Aiko. She has the address."

The women spoke as Nate rocked on his heels, anxious now to get to the new condo. Or maybe he was just anxious to see Shannon. He wanted her opinion. Her eyes. Hell, he wanted her.

# 6

SHANNON MET NATE AND AIKO in the lobby of a twenty-story building. The maintenance of the grounds, grass, shrubbery and trees was impressive, as was the location itself.

The Realtor, a pretty Asian woman in her early forties, was dressed impeccably and sensibly in heels that would merely hurt after a long day, not maim.

Nate looked wonderful. Very Euro in those crazy slim trousers that did wonders for his butt. Although, come to think of it, it was probably the other way around. A dark plum shirt tight enough that it stretched a tiny bit at the buttons. His black jacket was equally tailored and fit him like a glove. Oh, this had been such a bad idea.

"It's on the third floor," Aiko said, leading them to the elevator. After a quick ride they went to the farthest corner unit and she took them inside.

For its location alone, Shannon could see straight away that the unit was worth considering. It had low ceilings, standard in high-rise buildings that weren't off-the-charts expensive, as were the smallish rooms, but at least the living room would comfortably hold a couch and a couple of decent club chairs, and there was a fireplace. Gas, but ah, well.

"This is much better," Nate said.

Aiko then led them into the kitchen. It was a typical New York nightmare, everything crammed into the size of Shannon's mother's pantry. But the cabinetry wasn't bad, and neither was the flooring. Stainless-steel appliances. No task lighting, though. She'd seen professional chefs deal with less.

Aiko told them about the security, the gym, the laundry room, which was all fine, but the bedrooms had terrible closets, neither bathroom had a tub and, again, most of the lighting sucked. Still, there was natural light from two sides, which was a big deal. Depending on the price, he could do worse.

"It's seen some interest, but it's only been on the market for five days," Aiko said when they returned to the living room. "Why don't you think about it, and give me a call tomorrow. If you want to see more, we'll set up times then."

Nate smiled, put his hand on the small of Shannon's back and escorted both women to the door.

Shannon was absolutely, completely certain that he had not only felt the electrical jolt that had scorched through her at his touch, but could also sense the full-body blush that was going to set her on fire if he continued to let his thumb make little circles on her blouse.

She didn't breathe much on the way down, letting out a loud gush of air as Nate stepped away to shake hands with Aiko.

"It was nice meeting you," she said.

Shannon made some sort of sound, cleared her throat and somehow managed to say, "You, too. Have a good evening."

Nate turned to Shannon and narrowed his eyes. "I was thinking Katz's."

"Katz's sounds great."

He held the door open for her, but didn't touch her as they left the building. She would tell him about Ariel the moment they sat down at the deli. He'd be delighted. Why wouldn't he be delighted? Ariel was great. Pretty. Shannon had a picture of her on her cell so she could show him. It would be done in a flash, then she'd have the matzo ball soup, and they'd talk real estate. She knew a lot about real estate.

"I'll warn you right now, I'm ordering all the stuff I can't get in Indonesia. A knish, latkes, kishke, the works." He grinned.

They walked to the curb, where they waited to get a cab, as several, occupied, drove by. It was dinner hour and it would be nuts at the deli, but that was okay, because she was going to set up the date with Ariel first thing, then it would become easy. Simple. Eating good things, talking square footage and hardwood floors.

Finally, an empty cab stopped in front of them. Nate opened the door, and she jumped inside, grabbing the door handle in a panic. "You know what, I forgot. I'm supposed to be... I'm sorry, I have to... I'll see you at the— Sorry." Then she slammed the door shut and pretty much screamed her address at the cabby.

"WHAT THE HELL WAS THAT?" Nate said, to no one in particular. Stunned, he watched the taxi weave into the bumper-to-bumper traffic as he tried to interpret the past few minutes.

He was certain she hadn't forgotten anything. Unless the thing she'd forgotten was hugely embarrassing, but that seemed unlikely.

Had he said something out of line before the deli talk? He reran the evening as nearly as he could remember and nothing jumped out at him. Nothing even whispered vaguely. Everything had been fine, then whoosh, she was out of there like a shot, and her cheeks had burned pink, and he was utterly bewildered.

He debated going after her, but he doubted she wanted to be chased. So he raised his arm and flagged down another cab, too dazed to care about how long it took.

The wait at the deli was even longer. He tried to think about the condo, then about tomorrow's meeting with the attorney, but each thought was hijacked by Shannon. He gave in and picked up one of the free papers at the door and turned to the classified section. It wasn't very big, and most of it was for rentals and rent shares.

It kept him occupied for a couple of minutes while he stood in line, but then thoughts of Shannon returned to bedevil him. He wasn't dim about women. He had enough empirical evidence to prove it. He was perfectly capable of picking up signals, and ever since the wedding, he and Shannon had definitely been signaling. Which was complicated because—

"Oh," he said aloud, gaining the attention of the older woman in front of him. He smiled briefly, then went back to his revelation.

She'd left because of the signals. The heat between them.

No, wait, that wasn't quite right. She'd run because of the complications that came along with the heat between them. Now everything was falling into place. He sighed, and it must have been a hell of a sigh because the same older woman put her hand on the back of her hair, turned and gave him a very disgruntled glare.

He smiled again, dismissed the notion of apologizing and went back to his theory. Luckily, the unhappy woman and her group were led to a table, and a few minutes later he was sitting in a small booth underneath a wall of framed celebrity photographs, staring at a large menu.

Since he already knew what he was having, he waited impatiently for someone to take his order, asking preemptively for take-out containers, then, with his Dr. Brown's Cream Soda crackling over ice, he pulled out his cell phone.

He turned it so he could text, then thought for a moment before he decided to keep things light and easy. No reason to stir the pot yet.

I can order an extra knish if you want. Maybe some chopped liver?

Nate smiled at that. Shannon hated liver in any guise. As the seconds ticked by, his smile faded. He probably shouldn't have texted her. She'd left because she was uncomfortable, and he could only guess at the why. That whole signal thing? Was that just wishful thinking on his part? He got all hot and bothered when he touched her, or saw her, or thought of her, but she might not feel a thing.

Maybe *he* was making her uncomfortable, not the complications. She'd come to see the condo tonight because she felt obligated. He was Danny's best friend, practically part of their family. Of course she'd agree to come help him find a place. She wanted him out of the house. Her house. Jesus, what had he—

His phone beeped, notifying him of an incoming text. He clicked it so fast he almost dropped the phone.

Thanks, but that's ok. Sorry I ran off.

Don't worry about it. Stuff happens.

It was rude. I wanted to ask you something.

I'm all ears. Or eyes, I suppose.

Nate tensed. He felt it from his neck to his calves. It didn't make a lot of sense, considering she was probably going to ask him something completely innocuous.

U interested in dating while you're in town?

Dating? She was asking him on a date? On the cell phone? So he'd been right. It was about the signals. He'd known it, dammit. Things didn't get that hot between two people without both of them knowing. Especially when one of them had worn nothing but a towel and a rising hard-on. But he still had to play it cool. It would be a damn shame to scare her off now.

Sure. What did u have in mind?

He sipped his soda as he waited. And waited. It must be one hell of a long text because she was taking her sweet time. His food came, and he kept watching the phone as the waitress arranged the big plates on the small table. Finally, another ding.

He was back to tense in a second, only this time it was with eager anticipation.

My cousin Ariel met u at the wedding. She'd like to meet u for drinks tmrow nite at Molly's. She's great. Pretty. You'll like her.

The breath he'd been holding rushed out of him, smothering the spark starting to flame. He didn't remember meeting anyone named Ariel at the wedding. He had no interest in going for drinks with Shannon's cousin. How the hell had he gotten things so screwed up?

Sure. Send me her #. I'll call.

His typing was slow, each word a punch to his gut. It wasn't easy to press Send, but he did.

The pause that followed gave him enough time to realize the containers the waitress had brought weren't going to be sufficient. His hunger had vanished, and while he wanted to walk out and leave it all behind, he wasn't going to. That would be ridiculous. Shannon wasn't intentionally hurting him. There was nothing between them, couldn't be anything between them. Any interest he'd experienced had been one-sided. It happened. Not to him, not before now, and that was why he was caught off guard. Hell, he was just her brother's friend, that's all.

In fact, what she was doing was something friends did. It was nice of her to set him up. A few dates would keep him from getting bored as he waited to get back to his real home.

The beep sounded, and he hoped it wasn't her saying goodbye.

It was.

SHANNON KNEW HE WAS HOME. Not because she'd heard him—the one thing this old brownstone had was excellent soundproofing as long as there weren't connecting walls. No, for some reason she couldn't fathom, Danny had knocked on her damn door and announced Nate's arrival. At least her brother hadn't opened the door. He knew better. But she especially didn't want Nate to see her like this. In her flannel nightgown, scrunched under her covers, TV on some show she didn't care about, her laptop open on some website on marketing she hadn't bothered to read and a big bowl of Kraft's blue box of macaroni and cheese in her hands, the alarmingly orange pasta being devoured as quickly as she could shove the spoonfuls in her mouth.

She hummed a bar of "I Feel Pretty" then sagged against her pillows. How had her life come to this? And why, *why* was the nonstarter with Nate the thing that was crushing her chest?

It must be transference. Better to obsess about a guy than the very real fear that she couldn't save the plant. That no matter how many times she thought things would be okay, that the family would move on, that the struggle to hold on to a building and a brownstone when they were worth enough that her whole family could be secure for the rest of their lives was idiotic....

Yes, better to think about a guy, when the truth was, she couldn't let the business go. Everything in her believed in holding on. That what her family had was precious and worth keeping, and that money—even barrels of money—was no replacement for the legacy, the lessons, the heart and soul generations had dedicated to this life.

Maybe her crush—and was there ever a more appropriate word?—on Nate was another way to cling to her past. It probably had nothing to do with the man he was now. But what he represented. Continuity. Treasured memories.

She put the almost empty bowl on her nightstand, wanting to weep. She should never have taken those psychology classes at City College.

Finding the remote, she clicked off the TV, then logged off her computer and slipped it under her bed. One click and the room fell dark, except for the alarm clock that mocked her with it's big red 8:30. She'd never fall asleep this early. Or at all. It was ludicrous to try, but she shut her eyes anyway.

She had no idea what she was going to do tomorrow. How she was going to face Nate. She was a decent actress, but no one was that good. He'd see too much if he got a look at her. Pain, lust, jealousy, sadness. Or maybe that had just been her when she'd looked in the mirror before climbing into bed.

Ariel was a nice person. Nate was, too. And if they slept together, Shannon would shatter like spun glass rolling off a table.

It didn't matter that he'd never be hers, that wanting him made no sense at all, that she was being ridiculous. She didn't even know him well enough to like him this much.

Hmm. Maybe she'd gotten it backward, and it would be easier to think about the business closing down. At least that sadness made some sense.

A SPLASH OF LIGHT ACROSS her eyes woke Shannon with a start. She was shocked she'd fallen asleep at all, let alone 'til morning. But there was no denying the very loud buzzing of her alarm, which she ended as quickly as she could.

Her eyes felt gummy and her mouth awful. Ah, she hadn't brushed her teeth. She never went to sleep without brushing her teeth. And, if the evidence were to be believed, she'd wept.

She ought to have remembered that part, no? Given the state of her bed, there'd been lots of tossing and turning. Regardless, it was past 6:00 a.m. and she wanted to make it out of the shower in record time. She planned on grabbing a bite to eat on the way to work, and if the coffee wasn't ready, she'd buy a cup, too, even though it was a terrible waste of money.

What mattered was leaving the house before she had to face Nate. She should stay, show him Ariel's picture, talk her cousin up, smile, act like the friend she was pretending to be. But not with puffy eyes. Not this early. She'd send him the photo. That's what cell phones were made for. Sort of.

Didn't matter, she was out of bed, had her clothing ready to go, her robe on, and she practically ran to the bathroom. The lock clicking into place was a very welcome sound, and the hot water pouring over her eased some of the tension that had become a regular part of her life. At this rate, she'd have an ulcer by thirty.

She didn't waste another moment, though, and went through her routine double time. She was glad the mirror was fogged, because she needed to prepare to face herself. Maybe she wouldn't turn on the lights on her bedroom vanity. No, that wouldn't work. She needed the makeup too much.

As soon as she made it back to her room, she got dressed, got her iPod out and set it to shuffle. Then she turned that sucker up loud. She planned on listening all the way to the plant and only when her workday began would she let herself think a single thought.

It was an extremely effective technique up until the moment she bumped into Nate in the kitchen.

"Sorry," he said.

She didn't hear him say it but even she could read those lips. Tempted to throw up her hands and run, after a moment's thought, she put the idea aside. She'd have to face him sooner or later, so why not now? The silence when she turned off the music was profound.

"You okay?"

She made a small production of taking out the earbuds. "Didn't know you were here."

"So I imagine. You must be pretty serious about your musicals to listen that loud."

"Musicals are important."

"So's your hearing."

"Thank you, Doctor, I'll take it under advisement."

He raised a sardonic brow. "I was getting some coffee."

The empty mug in his hand had clued her in, but her snarky comeback stalled in her throat as she got a load of him in his pajamas. Spider-Man had been replaced by out-and-out elegance. They were glen plaid, with blue piping, covered by a plush white robe, like something she'd expect to see in the movies, not in their brownstone. The sartorial splendor was damn near dazzling. T-shirts and boxers were the ongoing trend with her brothers, and her father was a flannel man all the way. Nate looked sharp. Sexy.

Shannon went for the cupboard with the mugs before things got out of control. More out of control.

"You gonna take a lunch to work?" Nate asked.

"I hadn't thought about it," she said, busy, very, very busy with her to-go cup.

"I could put something together, if you want. I was

kidding about the chopped liver. I wouldn't do that to you."

She tried to laugh, but had to switch to a cough midway. "Nice of you to remember."

"Nice of you to set me up with your friend."

"Cousin."

"Right. Cousin. Ariel, is it?"

"Yep." She kept her voice peppy. Making sure to smile as she said the word. That really did work.

"I've tried, but I don't remember her from the wedding."

"There were so many people there." Shannon filled her cup from the big old urn, then focused on stirring.

"I stopped noticing after I saw you."

Her spoon stilled. Her heart raced. She didn't dare look up. If she looked at him, she was going to fold. She would confess to everything, even if she didn't know what she was confessing about. One look, and she would get herself into a mess she wouldn't be able to get out of.

Instead she laughed. The smile trick worked with laughter, too. Well enough, at least. "You were just surprised I wasn't wearing a tiara." She kept her head down as she went to the sink. "I've got to dash, but—"

Shannon glanced up. It was a mistake, a reflex, but Nate was standing right there, directly in her line of sight, and the way he was looking at her stopped her midsentence.

She felt a punch to her heart, an ache of need and want and *please*. But only for a second. "I'll send you her picture," she said, turning away, pulling down the curtain. "You guys will have a great time, I know it."

But she got the hell out of the kitchen. Fast. She put on her coat, grabbed her purse and her briefcase and she was out the door. It occurred to her as she reached the subway that it would have looked more natural if she'd said goodbye.

No matter. She'd let down her guard for only an instant. He'd probably thought she'd been making a face about her coffee.

# 7

At two-thirty, Nate caught a cab and told the driver to take him to Fitzgerald & Sons. He hadn't been there since high school, but that didn't matter, he knew the address. It was a huge building, half a block long, and the smell of it—hot-melt glue and the emulsion they used for the lithography—was unforgettable. The noise was crippling, and he and Danny had been under a mandatory earplug rule.

As the cab inched its way through the omnipresent traffic, he made a couple of phone calls, then spun the phone around for texting.

Where are U?

She might not answer him. She'd know the text was his, and she could just not reply and he'd never know if she had turned her cell off for a meeting, or left it in her desk, or if she'd glanced at his name and thought nothing of putting the phone away. But he stared at his screen anyway.

Three very long, slow blocks later, the phone beeped.

At the plant. Why?

U real busy?

Just the usual...

Mind if I stop by?

Anytime. I'll be here.

Nate clicked out of his phone and put it in his coat pocket. He'd have been in trouble if she'd told him she wasn't busy. That hadn't been likely, though. According to Danny, according to everyone who knew Shannon, she was in perpetual motion, if not working on marketing for the plant, then putting together some special event at the church or at a park or coordinating a fundraiser for something or other.

Everyone who lived between Midtown and SoHo knew Shannon Fitzgerald. It wasn't a surprise she edited the online Gramercy newsletter. She wasn't involved with the kid pageants anymore, but she did help out with an amateur theater group and a dance studio. Danny hadn't told him that. Mrs. Fitz had. In fact, Mrs. Fitz had a hell of a lot to say about her only daughter.

None of it had been unkind. Shannon was a blessing to the family, but she was working too hard, doing too much, and for what? Mrs. Fitz had sprayed cabbage soup across the kitchen counter as she waved her spoon during that discourse. Nate had picked up a sponge and followed her around, nodding when appropriate and smiling at how Mrs. Fitz hadn't changed a bit.

Shannon had, though. He couldn't think of her anymore as that child he'd known. The pictures of her back then had been replaced by current images, mental snap-shots he'd collected since the wedding.

The best part of New York so far? Mornings over coffee, when Shannon was there. Molly's, with her laughter high and sweet over the noise of the crowd.

He'd spent today with attorneys, nitpicking their way through a contract so complicated it made his head spin. He'd had enough of maneuvering and tricky language. Ever since Shannon had bowled him backward with that look this morning, he'd had a low-grade fever that needed attention. He'd felt as if he'd seen her naked. Want had been clear as day in her eyes, and her heat had singed him from across the room.

She was at the plant. Being four blocks away, if the traffic didn't ease up, he was gonna get out of the cab and walk. Because he needed to know what the hell. That's all. Just what the hell.

SHANNON LOOKED UP AT BRADY, who'd stopped talking. Shouting, actually, as they were on the floor of the plant and the noise was ridiculous with three of their biggest machines running. He wasn't even looking at her, and he seemed surprised.

She turned, expecting to see Nate, but not the effect he'd have on her.

Her whole body reacted. Heat raced up her neck and into her cheeks, her heart could have jump-started a stalled car, and even the small hairs at her nape stood as pure adrenaline replaced all the blood in her veins.

He knew. He knew that she wanted him, that it was killing her to give him to Ariel. He'd seen it this morn-ing, maybe before this morning. He knew she wanted him, and that she thought of him naked, and that she'd masturbated twice while she'd pictured him, and oh,

God, maybe she'd blurted out something in her sleep and he'd heard her because the wall was so thin, and now he was coming to tell her to stop. To leave him alone. To quit thinking of him as anything but a friend of the family; for God's sake, what was she, some kind of animal who couldn't control herself?

Even the pounding of the pressrun and the offset rollers couldn't compete with the hammering in her heart as Nate approached. He nodded at Brady, then caught her eye.

She knew she should smile. It was only polite. She managed a delayed blink instead.

He pointed to the offices—to her office—and she stumbled forward, got her feet steady and led him, squeezing her hands into tight fists until she held her door open, waiting for him.

As he passed, his hand brushed the back of hers, the clenching hand flexing open, reaching, but for only a second. She closed the door, automatically pulling out her earplugs and dropping them in the small ceramic bowl she used only for that purpose.

Nate slipped his coat off, hung it on the hook on the back of the door. She used the time to move behind her desk. When he turned to face her, he seemed disconcerted that she'd crossed the room so quickly.

"You know, I think I recognized a couple of people out there," he said. "Discounting Brady. But it's been years since my last visit. I was in high school, I think, working that summer before I went to NYU."

"That makes sense. Some of our employees have been with us over twenty years."

"I seem to remember there were more of them."

She wet her bottom lip, wished she had a bottle of water in the office as her throat felt parched. "We've had to downsize. Like most of the businesses around here. It's tough out there these days."

He took a couple of steps, but didn't head for a chair.

She wasn't sure if he was waiting for her to sit first or— "What are you doing here?"

He got that startled look again. Eyes widened, lips parted, a tiny little jerk of his head. Then he smiled, and he went back to looking like regular Nate. Calm, confident, as if he knew something she didn't. "I was hoping to talk for a few minutes, if that's okay with you."

All she had to do was say no. That she was due in a meeting, that it wasn't a good time. Then she remembered his text, and her response.

"Well, it depends what you need because I'm not off-the-clock yet. But I did think that condo was a good deal."

"I'm not here about real estate," he said, taking yet another step.

She pulled her office chair closer, as if the desk weren't enough of a barrier. "I don't understand."

"I've canceled my date with Ariel," he said. "I thought you should know."

Shannon hadn't expected that. Not even a little. "Why?"

Nate grinned again. "I hope it doesn't make things uncomfortable between the two of you. It was nothing to do with her. I told her that, and I think she was fine. It wasn't as if there was much for her to be disappointed about."

"What are you talking about?" Shannon stepped away from the chair and rounded her desk. "You're great looking, you work for Architects Without Borders or whatever, but the bottom line is you're a hero who is helping all kinds of people who've just gone through the worst thing living can throw at them, and you're funny. Not how you used to be—you and Danny, God, you were awful when you were kids with all that bathroom humor—but now there's wit there which I wish I could say about my brother. So don't go saying you're not much, because that's not true at all. She'd be lucky to go out with you."

Nate's stare was a mix of wonder and bewilderment, at least that's what it looked like from her end. She had gotten carried away a little, but it was because she was nervous, and when she got nervous things got jumbled if she didn't have a script or a routine or prepared answers to questions she'd been asked a hundred times.

"I meant," he said carefully, "because we didn't know each other. Me and Ariel. For all she knew I could be the worst date in New York. I don't think I am, but that's pretty subjective."

She inhaled. Exhaled. Stared at his hazel eyes, at the gentleness of his smile. He had great teeth, just great. White and even, and his lips, they were exactly the right size for his face. He was really good-looking, but in a nonthreatening way. He didn't beat you over the head with it. In fact, he made her relax, when she wasn't being an idiot and thinking about what his body looked like under that suit. "Well, okay, then. Thanks for telling me." She turned, walked back around the desk and pulled the chair in front of her once more.

NATE BURST OUT LAUGHING, BUT caught it fast with a quick fake cough covered by his hand. But damn, it was hard not to just let go. His head had been spinning since the minute he'd seen Shannon's face when he'd walked into the plant. She'd seemed paralyzed and frantic at the same time. He couldn't hear shit, but maybe that had made him notice the way her eyes got huge and her breathing quickened, and how she looked like she was waiting for the starting gun to go off.

The fists had made him doubt the wisdom in coming to see her. He never wanted to make her anxious, and if clenching her hands so tightly her knuckles paled wasn't a sign of anxiety, he didn't know what was.

The big giant question was what she wanted to run from. Him? Had he said something horrendous and not known it? Did something happen between the condo and the taxicab that had fundamentally changed her attitude toward him? Maybe it was a memory, an awful thing he'd done as a kid that she'd repressed until the moment he'd mentioned knishes.

But if she suddenly had realized he was someone to run from, what the hell was all that about his being a hero, and how he was great looking—

She thought he was great looking. That was cool. It wasn't what he lived for, but it was nice to hear, especially when she was such a knockout.

It didn't matter. Because knockout or not, he couldn't do anything about it until he understood what her deal was. He waited until she was looking at him again, and when their gazes met, he said, "What's going on, Shannon?"

She froze again. "What do you mean?"

"The cab yesterday. This morning. Have I done something? Said something to offend you?"

"No!" she said, way too loudly for the room. About an octave too high, as well. "No, don't be silly." Her cheeks had started to get pink and as she kept looking at anything but him, plucking at the top of her chair, moving sideways, away, a quarter-inch at a time— "Of course not."

Nate turned his head, looked behind him, expecting a person, a camera, something that would explain this completely insane sketch-comedy routine of hers. As far as he could tell, it was the two of them, alone, and she'd gone off her rocker.

"Did you want coffee?" she asked, brightly. "I think we have doughnuts left, but they won't be the good ones. Nothing cream-filled or glazed. Everyone goes for those first."

"Nope, I'm good," he said.

"So no coffee?"

"No, thanks."

She continued to pluck at the back of her chair. Gave him a disarming smile when the time had stretched past the awkward stage. "Tea?"

"Shannon. Please? You're my…" He hesitated, uncertain what to call her. "I admit we weren't very close when we were kids, but we're not kids anymore, and I've enjoyed talking to you. Getting to know you now. As a friend." He stepped a little closer, afraid if he moved too far too fast, he'd spook her and she really would make a run for it. "As a woman. The other night at Molly's, that was a good time, wasn't it? And in the mornings when we've had coffee? I mean, you came to the rescue yesterday about the condo, and then, I don't even know what happened. I must have upset you somehow, and if I did, I'm sorry. It wasn't intentional."

"You didn't."

Her voice was so low he wasn't completely sure he'd heard right. "What?"

"You didn't. Upset me."

"Then why am I making you so nervous? I don't understand."

She looked so uncomfortable, it made him want to

do whatever it took to relax her. But he had no jokes at the ready, nothing, in fact, that would change things. Except to leave, and he wasn't going to do that. It would drive him insane for this to continue, to not know. If it truly was his interest in her that was at the heart of things, he'd stop. He wasn't sure how, but he would. He wouldn't let himself linger over thoughts of her, would turn away when all he wanted to do was drink her in like champagne.

"It's not you," she said, and then it seemed as if she were going to explain everything. But she didn't. Instead she lowered her head a fraction. "It's work. There are so many people doing their own printing now, and we've had to make adjustments. The employees are having a difficult time. We've had to end the medical plan here, which is a blow to everyone. But it was bleeding us dry. I'm going to get new customers, though. Before you know it, we'll be right back to full capacity. In fact, I'm meeting with a rep from Carnation foods. Printing can labels is a very lucrative market that we never pursued. And then there's print-on-demand for novels, that's a whole new field."

He didn't believe her. Not that the plant was having financial difficulties, that was to be expected. But what was going on between the two of them had nothing to do with her job. "And that's what freaked you out on the street? When you jumped in the cab? Right that minute, you realized things were hard at work?"

The pink in her cheeks remained steady, but Shannon turned her body to the right, as if she were going to move to the big filing cabinet that stood in the corner. "No, not right that second."

"Shannon? I…"

Her shoulders rose then fell, and she turned to face

him, her smile not nearly reaching her eyes. "I should really get back to work."

"Right," he said. He wanted to kick the chair he hadn't taken. He'd never been in a situation like this before. But he couldn't see how he could force her into telling him the truth. Then a thought hit him, and he grew concerned. "You're all right? You're not sick or anything?"

"No. I'm fine. There's nothing wrong, Nate. I'm sorry my behavior seems erratic, but I've always been weird. I've heard you call me that enough times."

"That was different. You and your tiaras."

"I was a little kid," she said. "With four big brothers who liked nothing more than tormenting me and making my life a living hell. And you were no better."

"I'm sorry about that. Princess."

"Hey," she said, and for the first time since last night she smiled at him for real. "It was more my mother's idea than mine."

"You loved it, though. Being on stage, doing all that twirling around. Singing and posing."

She nodded. "I did."

"By the time I was old enough to appreciate your talents, I was too busy going through puberty to pay attention. I'm sorry about that, too."

"You didn't miss all that much."

"I think I missed a great deal," he said, and his voice had gone low and rough as he moved right next to her massive wooden desk.

There it was again. The look from this morning. Raw and real and there was no way he was getting this wrong. He rounded the desk and shoved her damn chair right back into the wall. Her head tilted up, and her pink lips parted.

He took hold of her arms and pulled her into a kiss that blocked out every single thing but the taste, the feel and the scent of Shannon Fitzgerald.

# 8

SHANNON STOPPED. STOPPED breathing, moving, thinking. His lips. Her lips. Together. Kissing. *Oh.*

Then his tongue, the tip of his tongue, slipped over her bottom lip, and sparks shot through her like fireworks, and she gave up, gave in. Her hands went to his hips, under his jacket, and she steadied herself as she touched him, as she parted her lips and took what he offered.

Thinking would come later. Now was for goose bumps and heat. She'd wanted this so much, and even if she had to stop, because at some point they'd have to, she wouldn't have to give this back.

Nothing between them could go beyond the press of his mouth and the slide of her tongue, but she could have the memory and that was something.

She felt him pull back, and maybe it was just to breathe, or to change his angle, but what if it wasn't? She followed him, leaning forward, chasing him. It couldn't be over, not yet, not when they may not ever…

His breath on her lips and her chin, the loss, made her open her eyes. He was still close, still gripping her arms, but he looked startled, as if he weren't sure how he'd ended up in this kiss. Not sorry, though. Smiling. As if he might laugh or shout, and it wasn't at all a surprise when he looked around the office for a second or two, because she needed to get her bearings, too.

He came back to her, though. His smile settled down, his eyes darkened, and he stared at her. His right hand floated near her face before his fingertips brushed the path of her blush up her cheek to her temple. "You're so beautiful," he said, then winced slightly. "More than beautiful. How did that happen? When?"

"You went away."

"And you became a gorgeous woman."

She doubted she could blush harder. "You came back better, too."

"Older, at least." His fingers moved through her hair, carefully, slowly. "Hopefully wiser."

"Definitely better," she said, momentarily panicked that wiser meant he knew they shouldn't be doing this.

"I don't want to stop."

She stepped closer to him, letting more of her body press against his. "No one's asking you to."

"But—"

"Not yet," she whispered as her eyes were closing. "Please."

"No, not yet," he repeated before he kissed her again.

It didn't seem possible, but the second kiss was better. She could feel how she affected him, and not only by the passion of his kiss, the slide of his tongue, but also by the pressure on her hip from his burgeoning arousal.

"Shannon," he whispered as he pulled back, then his mouth was on hers again, as if that tiny distance had been too much to handle.

His hands had grown as possessive as his lips, running over her shoulders, her back, the curve of her bottom.

She smiled against his mouth, right in the middle of the kiss. Then she pushed her hips forward. Nothing major, not a bump or a grind, just a yes, permission to move again, to keep stealing her breath with his desire.

How she wished there weren't all these clothes between them. She had been aching to touch his bare chest since that moment in the—

A knock on her door made her gasp and jump back as if it had been a gunshot.

Somehow Nate was a good foot away from her, his eyes panicked. She had the feeling she appeared as guilty as he did. Fortunately for her, she didn't have an obvious erection to worry about. "Sit down," she said.

He nodded, went around her desk. Sitting wasn't enough, he had to cross his legs.

She pulled her chair back, then ran her hands down her blazer and slacks. She exhaled, hoping like hell she wasn't as red as a beet as she opened the door.

Brady barely glanced at her. "I could use your help," he said, then turned and headed back to the floor.

Shannon closed the door, leaned her head against it and tried to catch her breath.

"I'll go in a minute," Nate said.

"Okay," she said. "Thanks for…"

He cleared his throat. "I'll see you later."

She left her office, remembering at the last second to take her earplugs with her.

All she could think was that she'd just made the biggest mistake ever. How was it possible to feel like this after one kiss?

Two hours later Nate still couldn't stop thinking about the kiss. He hadn't planned it. If he had it wouldn't have happened in her office with dozens of people around. But then maybe that had been a good thing. Or else he doubted he could've stopped. They both sure as hell had some thinking to do.

He came up on an old haunt of his and Danny's—the basketball court three blocks down from the Fitzgeralds'—amazed that at this time of day it wasn't jammed with kids. He couldn't remember ever finding the place empty. It didn't make sense, until he climbed over the fence and almost broke his neck landing on a crack in the asphalt.

The court was situated in a corner field belonging to a family who owned a bunch of drugstores. They'd turned it into a basketball court, put in lights for night games, built risers, made it nice. There'd been neverending graffiti on the two walls, and the big fence had gone up when Nate had been fourteen. But everyone in the neighborhood played there. Kept things civil.

Guess the goodwill had run out. Or maybe a basketball court didn't mean all that much when people were having trouble feeding their families. It still made him sad, and he debated chucking it in and going to Molly's for a beer instead.

What the hell. It was a Friday at four-thirty, so maybe he'd shoot some hoops, see if he could get a game of one-on-one. If not, he'd still burn up some energy. He'd always done his best thinking while sweating.

He tossed his jacket on a low riser, grateful he'd brought the basketball he'd found in Myles's room. Dribbling took on a whole new dimension as he zigzagged to miss the cracks and gouges. At least the hoop was still in play, even if the backboard was half-gone.

He stood where he imagined the free-throw line was, shot and missed. That wasn't a big surprise. He hadn't played in a long time.

In Bali, where he stayed between jobs, he did a lot of kayaking and swimming, and the gym he belonged to didn't have a court. He got more practice shooting pool than hoops, which was a shame. He loved the game even though he wasn't that great at it.

With hardly any backboard left, he had to run after every other shot, and even though the temperature was cool he worked up a sweat pretty quickly. But as time passed he began to hit a little more often than he missed.

Although he couldn't afford not to pay attention to where he was running, he still had enough concentration left over to think about Shannon.

Damn, he hoped things didn't get weird between them.

He had no idea what he'd expected. To take her right there on her big old desk? That they would rush back to her parents' home and go at it in her bedroom with Mr. and Mrs. Fitz downstairs and the TV blaring from the family room?

None of the reasons that being with Shannon was a bad idea had disappeared. He was a guest in the family home. He supposed he could move back to the hotel, but he hated that idea.

He had to really think this through. Yeah, he wanted her something fierce, but he wasn't going to be in New York for long. Shannon didn't strike him as a casual sex kind of woman. Besides, he wasn't feeling particularly casual about her. Casual meant that each of them were mostly out for themselves. Not a bad thing when it was mutual, but Nate cared about the possible fallout.

Danny had mentioned that Shannon was looking for something real, for something that would last. She wasn't sitting in an ivory tower waiting, but she was particular about her choices.

He wouldn't be anyone's choice, especially someone like Shannon. She'd never want his kind of life. He couldn't picture her in Bali, not the Bali he knew. He wasn't living with the expats or hanging out with the spa retreat crowd. He lived on the cheap, in a shack near the beach. The electricity was spotty at best, the plumbing wasn't much better, and he slept in the raw under a mosquito net.

A friend of his, an expat from England into real estate, kept a room for him in his South Bali cliffside villa, which was where Nate stored his clothing and anything of value, but as he spent so much time in inhospitable areas where the only shoes he needed were flip-flops or his heavy work boots, he didn't visit it often.

Shannon was a villa woman all the way.

She was also someone he liked a great deal, and sex complicated things. He might not want to live in Manhattan, but when he did come to visit, there was no place he'd rather be welcomed than the Fitzgeralds'. He'd hate it if he messed things up with her, with them.

Weirdly, though, he wasn't interested in anyone else. It didn't seem to matter that sleeping with Shannon was off the table, he'd rather spend his evenings with her than any other woman in New York.

Good thing he was well versed in the single palm arts.

He threw the basketball entirely too hard. It flew back to the shadowy section of the court. He hadn't noticed it was getting so late. Time flew when a guy was realizing he wasn't going to get laid for at least a month.

Wiping his face with his T-shirt, he headed for the

ball, and when he bent to get it, he heard a very distinctive voice.

"My ma says you better get home right this minute, Nate Brenner. She didn't slave all day over corned beef and cabbage so that you could be out here playing with yourself."

He grinned through his wince. The speech had been almost verbatim from back in the day. Only he'd been out here with Danny, and Shannon had never said that last bit. He was glad she had now. Guess things wouldn't be weird between them.

"Tell her to keep her shirt on," he said, which was something Danny had shouted more often than not. "I'm coming." Nate stood, and there she was, outside the gate. She had her hands stuffed in her coat pockets, and the last rays of the sun were showing off in her hair, making her look like something created by magic. As he walked toward her, his grin got bigger with each step.

"How'd you know I was here?" he asked.

"Mom saw you leave with the basketball."

"I didn't see her."

"She's good at that."

"Stealth Mom."

"I think it comes with the territory. Especially with four boys."

"What," he said, standing inches away, watching her through the wire fence, relieved there was no awkwardness, no averting of gazes, "you don't think she had to keep her eye on you?"

Shannon shook her head. "I was the Princess, remember? I got off on being perfect."

"Sounds excruciating."

"It was. Certainly no fun."

"There's still time to make up for that," he said. "Catch." He tossed the ball over the fence and she caught it easily. After grabbing his jacket, he started climbing, jumping down on the other side a little too soon. He jarred his neck and cursed his vanity.

"I'm not good at getting into trouble. Not enough practice." She slid him a look he couldn't interpret, but something about it got his cock's attention.

"Good thing you're friends with a master, then," he said, studying her reaction.

"A master, huh?"

He slipped on his jacket, his mind racing. So neither of them was bringing up the kiss. Not overtly, anyway. Trouble was he had no idea what that meant. That they were going to pretend it never happened? Or pick up where they left off as soon as humanly possible? His body emphatically voted for the latter, but his head warned him to watch his step.

"You coming?" she asked. She'd taken a few steps toward home and he hadn't noticed.

He decided to test the water. Put a toe in, nothing too drastic. He caught up with her. "After dinner, you want to do something?"

She looked at him, eyes narrowed, and if he had to guess he would say that she was testing the water, as well. "What did you have in mind?"

"It's obvious you've missed out on a large part of your education. It's a moral imperative that I corrupt you to make up for the lack. We could start with stealing a candy bar at the Duane Reade."

"No." She laughed the word more than said it. "I'm not going to steal things from the drugstore. Jeez."

"Ah," he said, as they walked very slowly, "a challenge. Which is fine. I'd be disappointed if you made this too easy."

"And there'll be no cherry bombs in toilets, or toilet paper wrapped around trees, or crank phone calls, either."

"Those are classics for a reason." Her laughter made him ridiculously happy. "You don't have to work tomorrow, right?"

"I don't have to, but I'm going to. I have to make a million Easter baskets."

"A million?"

"Give or take."

"Okay, so that means I can get you drunk, but not epically hungover."

A big man walking a tiny little dog shared their sidewalk for a moment, forcing Shannon's right side against Nate's left. When the coast was clear, they didn't shift back. "I don't like being drunk," she said.

"I'm beginning to see why you aren't very good at getting into trouble."

"I don't think you were drunk every time you got sent to the principal's office."

"Not *every* time, no." He turned to find her grinning up at him.

"I don't like to be drunk because I don't like to miss things," she said. "Especially not wonderful things. I want to be where I am and remember what I've done."

"You think getting into trouble with me would be wonderful?"

"Not a doubt in my mind."

They had slowed down so much they were barely walking. They'd reached the steps of the house, cars continued to zoom past, the night had finally come to stay. She stood in a pool of lamplight, and he couldn't hold off any longer.

He had to kiss her.

SHANNON KEPT HER GRIP ON the stupid ball under her arm, even though she wanted to pull Nate closer. She'd wanted to kiss him again, but it had seemed like a bad idea. She'd been right. They were standing in front of her house, for goodness' sakes. He was a master at getting in trouble.

Unencumbered by basketballs or good sense, Nate found the perfect angle, and his lips warmed quickly in the night air. Actual breathing was thrown out in favor of not stopping at all, just learning new ways to make the parts that mattered light up with sensation and need.

A honk blew it straight to hell. She jerked back, he tried to push her behind him in some kind of caveman-ish gesture of protection, and the kids honked again, shouting lewd things out the window of their car.

"Well, that sucked," Nate said.

Shannon shoved the ball at him until he took it. "I'll see you at the dinner table." She didn't even glance at him as she ran up the stairs. It probably would have been more polite to hold the door for him, but she let it slam in back of her instead, then made a beeline for the stairs to the second floor, to her room, where she locked herself in.

She leaned her head against the door, struggling to catch her breath. Nate was going to be here for another month. The situation was already untenable. What was she supposed to do now?

Obviously, the kiss in her office had been an error in judgment. So what had they done within five minutes of seeing each other again? Kissed. Awesome.

But that wasn't the real issue anyway.

He was here for a short while. He would be gone soon for a very long time. The way she liked him wasn't appropriate for a short-term fling. That was the core of the problem, and it wasn't negotiable. Feelings weren't.

Why she had to care this much about this man, she had no idea. There was no vote, no thoughts with pros and cons and doubts. Boom, she'd been punched in the heart and the head. If there had been a choice, she'd have nipped this business in the bud. But he'd kissed her, and she'd kissed him back. Twice. It was unrealistic to think things would get easier.

She pushed off from the door and took off her coat. She was still wearing her work clothes—black wool trousers, black blazer and a deep blueberry silk blouse. It was one of her favorite outfits, which she saved for special meetings or events. She'd had none of those things today.

All week she'd been dressing to impress him, on the off chance that she would see him, or more accurately, that he'd see her. Idiotic female behavior. As was the extra care she'd taken with her makeup, the time she'd spent last night over her pedicure, the gloss she'd put on her hair.

There had to be something she could do. Leaving wasn't an option. She hadn't heard the final word from Carnation yet, but she had a feeling she was going to have to start smaller if she wanted to compete in the label game. But she had gotten one new client. A small chain of automotive parts suppliers wanted Fitzgerald & Sons to do their catalogs. It was a good account, and their financial stability was rock-solid. It wasn't a game changer, though.

So that meant that Nate needed to be the one to leave.

She couldn't ask him to go back to Bali. But she could help him find a town house, then make sure he moved there for the duration of his stay.

How? She had no idea. She really didn't have time to go house hunting, let alone decorate a two-bedroom place for sublet. But this was an emergency, and she'd have to make time.

First thing? A call chain. She had five women she could always count on to phone at least five other women each when there was something that had to be done yesterday. She could get a few of them to take over the Easter basket duties. God, her mom could gather up a crowd in no time for that. So Shannon wouldn't supervise every last bit of candy placement. No one ever noticed the details anyway. More importantly, she'd put out the word for condos, town houses, duplexes, brownstones, whatever.

What was the use of doing favors for half the people from Little Italy to Midtown if she couldn't tap them for real-estate tips?

She'd include Nate's Realtor, get her excited. But before that she had to find out if Nate had made a decision on the condo they'd already seen. She doubted it. He would have said something.

Shannon changed into jeans and a sweater, then went downstairs for dinner. After that, the plan would go into motion, and she'd feel a hundred times better knowing she was taking action instead of simply sitting back, letting her hormones run her life.

She might not have a choice about who she fell for, but she was completely in charge of what she did once the die was cast.

"Has anybody done anything about it?" Nate asked.

Shannon hadn't rounded the corner to the dining

room yet, so she had no idea what Nate was talking about or to whom. That didn't seem to matter to her libido. His voice alone was enough to stir things that had no business being stirred as she was about to sit down for the family meal.

"What's there to do?"

It was Danny's voice, and Shannon hadn't realized he was coming by. That probably meant he expected to go prowling with Nate. So why was she disappointed? Problem solved. She wouldn't have to make an excuse about not doing something with him.

"It's private property, and they don't have the money to fix the court. They don't want to sell, either."

"Then the community should pay for it."

"Pay for what?" Shannon joined Nate, Danny and her father, who were all seated at the table.

"The basketball court." Nate frowned. "You saw what a mess it is. No wonder there were no kids playing. Somebody's got to be interested in fixing it up."

"What about your company?" she asked, looking at Nate as she tried to act as if everything was completely normal. "Brenner & Gill must do playgrounds and things when they build apartment complexes."

Nate stared at her for longer than would be acceptable in mixed company, but it wasn't her aura of glamour keeping him riveted. His eyes weren't even focused. He was thinking. When he snapped out of it, he shook his head. "It's not my company. Not mine alone, and there's no way Albert's going to want to donate our services, much less spring for materials and labor when he's on his way out. He never would have gone for it even when the company was rolling in contracts."

"He doesn't believe in contributing to the community?"

"No, nothing like that. He donates, but he's careful about where and how much, and what the company gets in return."

"That's a shame," she said. "I know how much that court meant to you two growing up."

Shannon's mom poked her head out from the kitchen. "If you think I'm waiting on you like this is the bloody Ritz, you've got another think coming."

Nate grinned, and Shannon returned it as Brady walked in to join them. "Head right to the kitchen, Brady," Nate said. "Your ma's on a tear."

Everyone pitched in to bring the big meal to the table, and Mr. Fitz did the carving of the corned beef. The beers came out, but Shannon passed, having water instead. The boys got to talking about fantasy leagues, and the food was delicious as always. Shannon watched as she ate, listened to how Nate spoke differently to Danny than he did to Brady. He was respectful, always, to her parents, but he had learned where he could tease and what he should ignore, and that compliments to Ma were always a good idea.

He was part of this family, there was no getting around it. He had listened to fights, gotten into fights, interrupted fights. He'd wept, he'd laughed and he'd bled at this very table.

But he wasn't her brother. He wasn't even the kid she'd grown up with. What he *was* made all her scattered wants and needs and likes and dislikes fall into place. He was the man she'd been looking for.

Who was only passing through.

# 9

NATE COULDN'T BELIEVE HOW many prime two-bedroom homes his Realtor had lined up for him. Or that Shannon had been free to come along for the viewings. That took some of the sting out of being hijacked by Danny last night. But she was here now and it was a good thing Aiko was completely professional and easygoing, because Shannon was not just on her game, but on fire.

Her eye for detail impressed him, but not as much as her practical sensibilities. She hadn't been swayed by inconsequential trappings, not at any of the five properties they'd been to this morning, and she was also quick to find the bottom line.

He couldn't help but imagine what she'd be like in a crisis. She was such a natural leader, she'd calm people instantly and she'd make practical decisions that would save lives. That was an incredible gift, one he hadn't really understood she possessed until today.

She'd be an asset anywhere. Now he got how that monstrous old printing plant was still in business, despite the antiquated equipment. Shannon wouldn't have it any other way. They'd have to move into digital printing soon. Or get a whole lot of new clients.

It wasn't a kind thought, not considering his loyalty to the family at large, but she was wasted at the plant. On the other hand, what did he know? He'd never had a family that valued loyalty or togetherness. Since he'd been in the States, he'd spoken to his sister twice and met her for a quick lunch. He liked his sister, he did, but they weren't connected the way Shannon and her brothers were.

She tugged on his sleeve. "You coming?"

"Yeah," he said. "Where are we going?"

"Are we boring you with finding your new home?"

He grabbed her hand and brought it to his lips for a kiss. "You're distracting," he said. "It's hard to look at storage space and dishwashers when you're so much more captivating."

She rewarded him with a blush, but she pulled her hand away. That was a shame because he hadn't lied. Touching Shannon in any capacity was his new obsession, and he wasn't a man known for getting carried away.

All his rules seemed to crumble in her wake. He'd been determined not to kiss her, yet he fully intended to do it again at the next opportunity. He knew that taking her to bed was an enormously stupid thing to do, and if he hadn't believed she'd regret it, he'd have gone after that, too.

He'd built his life around not being beholden to anyone. He was fond of his family, but he'd never made an adult decision about his life that took their wishes into consideration. Many people didn't understand that, especially not someone like Shannon, but that's who he was. Who he would continue to be.

"Well, come on," Shannon said, standing by a door that led…somewhere. He dutifully followed her, noticing how her slacks hugged her body, want for her riding low and hot in his body.

Ah, the master bedroom. Which was really big and nice. He was instantly drawn to the motorized blackout drapes.

"Just a toy," Shannon said. "You can write them in but don't let that influence you."

"A good toy, though," he said. "The bed's probably got a mattress that doesn't try to swallow me every night."

"I told you to switch rooms."

He almost said exactly where he'd prefer to sleep.

"The management company here charges a slightly higher fee than most," Aiko said, "but they have a sterling reputation. They screen everyone who works for them. Drug test, checkup on past employers. They're worth it."

"I like the layout," Shannon said, opening the closet door. It was huge for New York. You could actually walk inside the thing, although you couldn't walk far.

"If the bathrooms are as well-done as the kitchen, this place is a real contender." She walked into the bath, and he could tell by her sigh that it had passed the test.

He joined her at the door and nodded when he saw where she was staring. "Whirlpool bath."

"Look at the shower," she said. Then she walked into the glass-enclosed stall and turned on the water.

"What are you doing?"

"Checking the pressure. We're twelve floors up."

"You'll get soaked."

Undaunted, she rolled up the sleeve of her white blouse and stuck her hand under the stream. "Oh, yeah. I like this one."

"Aiko, are they getting action?"

"It only went on the market this morning. I was told we'd be the first to see it. I'm still not sure how she found out about it."

"She?"

Aiko nodded at Shannon.

Nate was puzzled. "You found it?"

"I told you at the wedding I'd ask around."

"Huh," he said. "That doesn't happen very often. I thought it was like 'Have a nice day' or 'Welcome to Walmart.'"

Shannon laughed, drying her hand with one of the guest towels. The town house had been staged for sale, which was smart. It was easier for him to get a feel for the place with furniture in situ. In fact... "Can we see about buying it as is? I like the way it's decorated."

"I can ask," Aiko said.

"Also," Shannon said, stepping closer to the pedestal sink, "can you see if they're amenable to a fast escrow?"

Aiko looked at the sheet she'd picked up from the seller earlier that morning. "Nate's prequalified, so I don't think they'll object. But it all depends on what kind of offer you want to make."

"Why don't we adjourn for lunch," Nate suggested. "We can discuss offers over food."

Both women nodded, and he escorted them out of the building. He would make sure to sit across from Aiko at lunch so he could focus on the business at hand. He wanted it over with so he could make plans with Shannon about the night ahead.

SHANNON SLIPPED OFF HER shoes and curled her toes into her bedroom rug. Today had gone more smoothly than she'd ever expected, which worried the hell out of her. The Easter baskets had been finished, all hundred of them, by her mother's book group. Shannon had thought it was hysterical when she'd heard the books they discussed were cookbooks, but then she'd been invited to a meeting and the lunch had been outrageously good. Her mom hadn't let her forget it.

Nate's offer had been submitted on that fantastic Bleeker Court co-op apartment. Her phone tree had come through in spades, and she owed Bree Kingston for that tip. Or maybe it was Bree's boyfriend, Charlie, who'd gotten the inside scoop.

Shannon opened her purse and took out Nate's trading card. She'd gotten it back from Ariel, who had been very disappointed. The pain hadn't run too deep, though, seeing as how she'd talked nonstop about her lawyer friend David during lunch. They hadn't gone out yet, but they had been meeting up after work for drinks. Other lawyers were there as well so it wasn't too suspicious. Shannon gave it two weeks at the most before they broke down and did the deed. They were only human, and Ariel was clearly over the moon about this guy.

Shannon knew what that felt like. But at least David and Ariel lived in the same country.

It didn't seem very fair that she'd finally found her perfect trading card man and she couldn't have him. A cosmic joke on her, she supposed. She'd put her heart and soul into the trading cards, not to mention her skills, and while she was happy for everyone who had met their match, she felt cheated.

After Nate went back to Indonesia, she'd start dating again. Maybe now that she knew what she wanted she'd be able to find someone like Nate. Probably not as funny, though. Or as sweet.

She put the card away, then changed into her favorite pair of worn jeans and a cozy sweater she'd had for ages. Her folks were out for the evening at a play. Her father had grumbled, but every once in a while he just had to suck it up and take his wife someplace nice to eat before a Broadway show.

Brady was staying at his girlfriend Paula's, as usual, and Danny had a work function so she knew he wouldn't be popping in unexpectedly. Which left her and Nate alone for the evening. He'd wanted to take her out, to thank her for the day, but she was tired, and she hadn't had a night to chill in a long while. They were going to order in Chinese food, then watch a movie.

It sounded great, but she wasn't at all sure if she'd be better off locking herself in her bedroom right now. Being alone with Nate was a huge risk. She wanted to believe she wasn't going to give in to her baser urges. After all, they were both adults. Responsible adults.

On the other hand, they probably wouldn't be alone again before Nate had to leave the country, and who knew when or if the sale would go through, so maybe one time wouldn't be all that terrible?

*Oh. Damn.*

NATE WASN'T USED TO THE house being so quiet. So empty. It had been the worst idea ever to stay in.

Now that they'd finished their dinner and were running through the pay-per-view movies, all he could think of was curling Shannon into his arms on the couch and making out like a couple of teenagers. As usual, his cock wasn't looking at the bigger picture, but for tonight making out would be fantastic. Dangerous beyond words. Still, fantastic.

"I don't want to see anything depressing," Shannon said, from all the way at the other end of the couch.

"Definitely not. Hate depressing."

She had her gaze on the LED TV above the fireplace, and her hand on the remote, clicking and clicking. She had socks on. Multicolored fuzzy socks. Under jeans that had been designed specifically to make her bottom look like the most gorgeous thing he'd ever seen. The sweater, however, was just mean. It was probably warm as all get-out, but it hid way too much. He could picture what was underneath, yes, but that wasn't a good idea. His imagination was already going crazy without trying to guess the exact pink of her nipples.

He bit back a groan and shifted on his section of the couch, stealthily adjusting his jeans. "Sure you don't want to take a walk over to Molly's?"

"It's karaoke night." The look she gave him expressed her feelings about amateur vocalists quite succinctly.

"We could sit far away from the speakers."

"We are sitting far away from the speakers."

She had a point. His point kept pressing harder against his fly. "All right, how about we go to Café Lalo and get some dessert? I've heard they have over a hundred kinds of cakes. Jazz, too. Coffee and chocolate cake, huh? Yeah?"

"Oh, God, after eating all that lo mein? I'd burst."

There had to be something in Manhattan that would convince Shannon to get up and go out, because he couldn't take this much longer. Sitting close, but not close enough. The memory of their kiss was the elephant in the room. A very large, very insistent elephant.

"This is supposed to be funny," she said.

He looked up at the TV. He'd seen the movie, hadn't liked it. "Saw it." Was she really that indifferent to their last kiss that she could flip through channels as if any movie on there was more interesting than the fact that the two of them were alone in the house? Frankly, it was kind of pissing him off.

"Okay, then you choose," she said, as she kept on clicking. Each time she paused, Nate said, "Saw it."

When she cleared her throat, he looked up from where he'd been staring at the area of her breasts beneath the Evil Sweater of Shattered Dreams. He smiled as benignly as he could.

"So Bali has a ton of multiplexes? Because I thought you said you didn't have a TV so you couldn't have cable or satellite, right?"

He nodded. "Tons of multiplexes. Practically on every street corner."

"For a man who travels the world and has seen countless amazing and wonderful things, you're a ridiculously bad liar."

"What do my travels have to do with it?"

She turned off the TV. "You don't want to be here. With me. You don't want to be here alone with me."

He exhaled loudly. "No. I don't."

"Okay, then," she said as she put down the remote. "I'll just leave you here to spend the evening however you like."

"Fine," he said, but then she stood up. "Wait, wait. That's not why. I *want* to be with you. I do. Come on, you didn't think I meant I didn't want to be with you."

She grinned at him. "No. I understood exactly what you were implying." She continued to smile as she walked toward him. But the closer she got, the more uncertain she appeared. Still, she kept on coming. "We could sit here and make out until someone comes home," she said, and then she flicked her gorgeous hair back behind her shoulder.

His breathing was becoming problematic. "Okay. I can do that. I can do the hell out of that."

She stopped slightly out of his reach. "But that's it. Just kissing. Because doing more than that would be a huge mistake. A giant, horrifying mistake."

"Horrifying?"

"No, I didn't mean it that way. It wouldn't be horrifying at all. Never. I'm so sorry. It wouldn't even be a mistake. Certainly not a huge mistake, because you're great. You're really...really great."

He took her hand. "And you're amazing. Now stop talking so we can start kissing."

She nodded. "Excellent advice." Shannon sat down next to him and put her hand on his thigh. "Think we can do this without getting ourselves in trouble?"

Shit. He wasn't about to lie. Besides, they both knew the answer to that question.

"There could be consequences." Her voice was low and serious, but her hand had moved up his thigh. Not far enough up his thigh.

"Like going to your bedroom?" he asked. "Because no one else is home? And we have the house to ourselves? Alone?"

She grinned at him. "You must be smoother than this. It's impossible for you to have lived your incredible life and been this dorky with women. Look at the way you dress."

"You're not just any woman."

Her breath caught and he watched the beauty of her blush blossom across her pale, pale skin. He stared into eyes that had grown dark with want. He was hoping as hard as he'd ever hoped that she'd want to use that bed of hers right now. He had a condom...well, two condoms…in his wallet. And he wanted to take off her sweater more than he wanted to breathe.

"I'm pretty sure we're about to make that mistake we were talking about," she whispered as her hand moved one last inch.

HE LED HER UPSTAIRS, AND Shannon could hear his harsh breathing, but that wasn't caused by the climb. Neither was her own thundering heartbeat. They were going up to her room, and she was being stupid, stupid, so stupid that it broke records for being stupid. Not that she cared. Because she wanted him, and this might be it. Her one chance.

Honestly, it wasn't that much of a mistake. She was already going to go through hell when he left. At least now she'd have a sexy memory to keep her warm at night. Until she got over him, which she most definitely would.

They reached the second floor, and he walked so fast she was practically running to keep up with him. She liked that a lot. He pulled her inside her bedroom, then slammed the door so hard she jumped, and then he locked it. The next second she was in his arms and his mouth covered hers.

He slid his hands under her sweater and the first touch on her warm skin was electric. He moved quickly up to her bra and surprised her by passing right by her breasts.

"Off," he whispered against her lips. "Off now."

Ah. She stepped back and let him tug up the sweater and toss it away. Good thing she'd decided to wear one of her pretty bras and matching blue panties.

He stared, wide-eyed with wonder, as if he'd never seen such fabulous lingerie, which she knew couldn't be true. If he liked the undergarment so much, she wondered what he'd look like when she reached behind and undid the clasp.

She stretched out the moment, the performer in her loving the standing ovation in his pants. When she finally let the bra fall to the floor, his lips parted and he slowly blinked.

"Pink," he said.

"Pink?"

He nodded. "Perfect and pink. God."

She wouldn't have guessed she'd be this nervous, not with Nate, but the way he was staring at her...wow. With unsteady fingers she undid her jeans and let them drop, then toed off her socks.

He was unbuttoning his shirt so fast she thought he'd pop a button. She'd already seen his chest, but it was a welcome sight especially since she would get to touch it this time.

He ripped his wallet out of his pocket, took out two condoms and put them on the nightstand. Then he shook off his jeans the same way he danced. Adorably. Next it was shoes and socks, and he didn't even try to pretend that he wasn't hot and aching for her. When he stood up after slipping off his boxers, he was so hard his erection pressed against his stomach.

She swallowed thickly at the heat that filled her from the inside out. He was stunning, and, oh, the way he wanted her.

# 10

NATE TOOK HER HANDS AND pulled her back with him until he sat down on her bed. Her breasts were a most incredible sight, but not nearly enough.

He put his fingers underneath the edge of her panties and pushed them down, laying kisses on the soft, sweet, pale skin all the way down to the top of her red, red triangle. "Oh, God," he said as her panties dropped and he sat back, needing some distance to see the total picture and also to slow down. It would be a shame to hurry through this. "You're…"

"Thank you."

He looked up at her. "You are."

"So are you."

He reached behind her, his large hands on her waist, and he drew her closer. He breathed in the scent of her as he bent to that incredible patch of brilliant red hair and he kissed her right there before he moved down. He nuzzled against her until his lips found her soft folds.

She gasped above him, her fingers snaking through his hair.

"Spread your legs," he whispered.

Either the words or his breath did something for

her, if her shiver was anything to go by. She parted her thighs, and he moaned as he kissed her, savoring her taste as he explored with his tongue.

He wasn't able to reach everything, not in the position he was in, but that would be all right. He got far enough to make her squirm, to make her tug at his hair as he became more and more focused. God, she tasted so good, and his hands had moved down to her lush, round buttocks. He squeezed them none too gently. Her moan said she had no complaints.

He'd felt her tense. Her body had grown rigid, and dammit, he couldn't stand the angle so he pushed her back until he could drop to his knees.

Now it was both hands on his head, and she quivered in his arms. He had that little nub of hers held between his lips and he sucked hard before he used his tongue once more.

Shannon cried out above him. She pulsed her hips forward, pressing herself down on his tongue, and then she froze, just froze as he felt her body spasm in release.

He didn't stop until she made him. When he stood, they were both panting, and her cheeks were as pink as her nipples. He kissed her, threw back the sheets and finally got them both horizontal.

The feel of her trembling from knee to chest was a full body rush. His hand went to her shoulder, then down. At the first hint of the curve of her breast, he paused, rolled over to grab a condom and sheath himself. When he came back to her, it was with a heartfelt sigh. "I want more," he said. "I want everything."

"Yes," she whispered, her voice more breath than sound. She ran her palm down his chest, right to his nipple, which she proceeded to rub and tug between two of her fingers.

He moaned, and when he cupped her breast at last, she whispered, "Now, please."

He moved his legs between her thighs, took hold of himself and entered her. Nothing in his life had ever felt better than that slow slide.

SHANNON TREMBLED ONCE he was flush inside her. Her head fell back on the pillow as she groaned her pleasure. He was made for her body, exactly the right everything that made her feel wonderful and wicked.

She'd already known his kisses fit her to a T, but she hadn't known what his body would feel like as it rubbed against hers, and she hadn't imagined how his hands would thrill her.

He rolled his tongue over her beaded nipple and she arched her back, pushing her breast into his mouth.

He caught her legs and pulled them around his hips, then ran his hand up the bottom of her thigh. Pushing with his palm, he encouraged her to bring her knees closer to her chest.

Nate moved in tighter, deeper. "Look at me," he said, his voice as low as she'd ever heard it.

She hadn't realized she'd closed her eyes. Staring into his gaze while they were so incredibly connected exaggerated every sensation. Not just the flush that was the beginning of yet another orgasm, but how his hard chest rubbed against her nipples and his breath brushed across her lips. Shuddering, she reached up to touch his face but she had no strength in her arm and it fell back against the sheets. He bent his head and kissed her right knee, his gaze never wavering from hers.

With a small controlled thrust, he drove in deeper, rocking against her, so deep, the pressure so unbearable that she gasped and jerked. Instinctively she clenched her muscles, squeezing him, and he tensed.

"Oh, God, no, no, I can't be this close yet," he said, his expression tortured as he held himself completely still.

Wet and slippery with longing, she bucked, trying to get him to move again. He slipped his fingers between them, knowing exactly where and how to touch, and way sooner than she'd have ever guessed a second jolt of heat shot through her body and she spasmed around him, knocking his hand loose and letting out a startled cry.

He started to withdraw, but before she could object, he drove in deeper and after two thrusts he cried out her name as he stilled, as the muscles of his body tightened.

By the time her legs fell to the bed and he rolled to her side, she had relearned how to breathe. She looked at him, all sweaty and gorgeous, lying on her pillow. "That was…"

"Amazing," he said, his voice ragged. "Incredible.

Shannon grinned, feeling like she'd had too much to drink, or hadn't had enough oxygen or some other crazy thing that made the world spin faster. She found his hand by her thigh and she folded her fingers between his. "You have to be back in Bali when?"

"Not for a while."

"So you're not leaving tonight."

He smiled. "Nope. Why? You have something in mind for later?"

"It's possible." She smiled.

He brought their joined hands up to his lips so he could kiss her fingers. A different kind of pleasure shimmered through her.

She closed her eyes, letting her heartbeat slow as she rubbed her foot up his calf. He made contented sounds, and soon he was gently rubbing her from belly to chest. Sensual and slow, a perfect interlude.

When he moved, it was to kiss her tummy before he sat up. "Did I tell you how terrific you were at the property showings?"

She laughed. It was unexpected, but then he'd surprised her at every turn. "No, you didn't."

"I'm serious. You should run for office or something. You'd straighten this city out in six months. They wouldn't know what to do with someone as clever as you."

She looked up at him to find him looking back. He was completely serious. "Stop. I've already got too much of an ego."

"I think you're wonderful and I'm not about to stop saying so."

"Well, thanks."

He squeezed her hand before he let it go. "I'm going to make a run to the bathroom, then I'm going to get my robe, then I'm coming back here to ravish you again. But first—" he stood and pulled the comforter and sheet up across her chest "—I'm going to kiss you."

It felt odd and sexy when he bent over her to capture her lips, him being naked when she was covered up. When that ended, which wasn't for several long, delicious minutes, he disappeared out her door, and she stretched like a cat under the sheet. She closed her eyes and pushed her fingers through her hair and it was very quiet. No footsteps from the floor above, no music from Brady's room. Just the sound of her breathing.

Her brain, the one that had convinced her that this was the best idea ever, was starting to back down a bit, and the voice of real life was becoming more than a whisper. She'd known—how could she not have known?—that everything she'd felt about Nate before would be nothing compared to what she felt now. She wasn't sorry. Given a chance to do it again, she would. But she'd better prepare herself for a hell of a blow when he left. It was going to take some serious time to get over him. She hadn't considered the memory of his skin, of how they fit together, of what he looked like when his eyes were dark with want and, God, how he said her name.

Yeah. It was gonna be a bitch. Because while she had no doubt how very much he wanted her, she also knew he didn't want her for very long.

NATE SLIPPED ON HIS BATHROBE as quietly as he could, not wanting to wake Shannon. The light was on beside the bed, but that hadn't stopped her from falling asleep. He wished he could succumb himself, but he had to get back to Myles's room. It wasn't likely that anyone would come knocking, but he wasn't going to take the risk.

Leaving should have been easy. So much about Shannon was. Conversation, laughter, touching. He'd never had sex with someone who'd been a longtime friend before, and now he saw the appeal, although they hadn't actually been friends. She'd been a presence in his life, and he in hers, the only thing they'd had in common was the rest of the family. In all the years he'd come to her home, they'd never sat down and had a private conversation.

They had grown accustomed to each other, nonetheless. Since first seeing her in her green bridesmaid's dress, he'd felt drawn to her. He'd never have imagined he would know what she looked like when she came undone. That giving her pleasure would be right up there in the sexiest things he'd ever experienced

"What are you doing?" Shannon hadn't opened her eyes and her voice was mumbles and exhaustion.

"Go back to sleep."

"Don't leave. It's the middle of the night."

He leaned over and brushed some hair away from her cheek. "I know. That's why I'm leaving."

She sniffed and rubbed her head into her pillow, shaking loose the silky hairs he'd pushed back. "Don't leave," she said again.

Was he going to break every rule? There was no reason to think anyone would come looking for either of them on a Sunday morning, but the chance existed. He kissed her gently, then whispered, "Sleep well."

Shannon didn't stir.

Nate went back to the bed from hell and tried to get comfortable. The sheets were cold, the mattress continued to suck, and instead of his usual après-sex relief at being alone, he felt…something else. He could imagine so clearly what it would have been like to curl up in back of Shannon, tuck in his knees, circle her waist and breathe her in as he drifted to sleep.

It would have been nice to watch her wake up. He had this image in his head that she was one of those people who went from sleep directly to alert. When he'd run into her after his shower, she'd had none of the somnambulist haze about her.

But he couldn't be sure. She could wake up drowsy and tousled and blinking, and Christ, how was his cock even thinking of getting hard? They'd wrung each other out. He'd come twice, while she'd come at least three times, maybe more. He wasn't good enough at reading her yet to be sure.

Now, there was a project worth tackling. He'd begun, but only in the most fundamental ways. Her nipples were moderately sensitive, which was rare, but the little spot behind her ear drove her crazy. She had a thing for being somewhat constricted. Twice, he'd held her wrists up above her head as he'd done wicked things to her body, and it was like plugging her into a socket.

He'd loved how responsive she'd been when he'd hunkered down between her thighs. God, she'd smelled incredible. His head still ached from where she'd tugged his hair a little too enthusiastically. Not that he'd minded.

But there was still much to learn. More to taste, to touch, to try. Problem was, how…and when? Far more problematically, where? She was incredibly busy with work and her side projects. He'd been astonished that she'd come out with him to look at the properties, and it wasn't likely they'd have another night where they'd be alone in the house.

He should hear quickly about the offer on the co-op. Since the owners were out of the city Aiko had given them forty-eight hours to respond. He'd offered just under the asking price, so he figured he had a good shot. The furniture was already out, so he hoped they'd be willing to close quickly. And if not, he simply had to move back into the hotel. Yeah, he liked staying here with the Fitzes, but it was pretty clear that it had become more about staying close to Shannon.

IT WAS LATE MORNING BY THE time she awoke. Still, she wasn't anxious to hop out of bed right away. Nate's scent was all over the pillows and the sheets, and she lazily rolled over, her body aching but in a good way. She buried her face in his pillow and inhaled deeply, the memory of him inside her still so vivid a frisson of excitement raced through her.

She'd stay there for an hour if she could, reliving every moment, basking in satisfaction, but she had to go to work for a few hours. There was payroll to do, and signs to be printed up for the Easter egg hunt. Then she needed to look over the baskets, check out the condition of the back room where her mother and friends had worked so hard.

Thinking of her mother propelled Shannon into her robe and into the bathroom. Best of all worlds, she would be gone by the time her parents returned from mass, but that was unlikely. Her mother would want to know what had kept Shannon up so late that she'd slept in. Mothers didn't care how old their daughters were when it came to Sundays. Her mother in particular would poke at Shannon until she coughed up some kind of excuse.

If asked for details, Shannon would deftly change the subject to the payroll, and that would be that. It was an underhanded thing to do, given her mother's guilt at leaving the accounting to Shannon, but all was fair in…

Not love or war. Just evasion, plain and simple.

It really was time for her to move out of the house. As much as she loved her family and this house, she yearned for the freedom. Yes, she would resent paying rent to live in a strange apartment, especially knowing how exorbitant rents were in the city, but last night had shown her how impossible it was that she still lived with her parents. It had nothing to do with Nate. She wasn't fooling herself in any way. He would leave at some point, she knew that.

She turned on the water in the shower, then stripped and stood under the spray. It was foolish to start worrying about moving out yet. There would be plenty of time for that when Nate was out of the country, out of her life. Then there would be the inevitable fall....

Okay, she was not going down that path. Nate wasn't gone. He was here right now. There would be time enough for regrets later. Today, she would be happy to see him. If she were lucky, they would be able to spend time together tonight. If not tonight, then soon.

She couldn't afford to let this fling take over her life. First came the job, the very important business of getting new clients. Everything else came in at a distant second, including her sex life.

If there was one thing she'd mastered, it was how to prioritize. As much as she liked Nate, he wasn't at the top of the list. Even if she wanted him to be.

# *11*

DANNY SPRAWLED AGAINST the booth back at Molly's, his second beer nearly gone and his gaze meandering over a couple of girls who didn't look old enough to drive, let alone drink. Nate glanced at his watch, wondering when Shannon was going to get there. He hadn't seen her since yesterday morning except in passing. It hadn't been intentional, just bad timing. But he'd thought about her. Too often.

"Yeah, no, the work is good," Danny said. "I mean, it's decent for an ad firm. There's only gonna be so much freedom in an environment like Madison Avenue. But I'm starting to put together a portfolio of my own stuff, you know? On the internet."

"That must be easier than getting a gallery showing."

"Yeah, but it's easier for everyone else, too, so you still need to get the showings. Maybe now more than ever. I'm getting there, though. I've had a few private commissions."

"Yeah? Why haven't I seen any of your work?"

Danny grunted. "Because you're a selfish pig who never asked."

"Yeah, I love you, too, bro. Seriously, what's it under? Your name?"

"Yeah." Danny sat up straighter and pulled out what looked like a baseball card from his back pocket and flicked it over to Nate.

"This is yours?"

"No, I'm showing you my aunt Martha's artwork. Of course it's mine."

The picture on the cover of the trading card was striking as hell. Like some of the best graphic-novel work he'd seen, right up there with Alan Moore and Dave Gibbons. "You're kidding me with this, right?" he asked.

"What?"

Nate stared at him. "You're an illustrator? These commissions, have they been for comics?"

Danny smiled at him. "Not yet. I know I should have told you before now what I was doing, but I wanted to… Anyway, I'm getting my stuff out there. I've had a few calls, had a few encouraging rejections. In the meantime the day job is great, if a person has to have a day job."

"You were always drawing something, mostly where you weren't supposed to. But not stuff like this. You were into street art. Like Banksy or something." Nate grinned. "Remember that wall behind the supermarket?"

Danny nodded as he laughed. "I thought for sure we were going to jail."

"You and me both. How long were we stuck under that crate?"

"Three hours?"

"It felt like three years." Nate turned over the card. Read the short bio and the contact info, and admired the two other small images. "This is clever," he said, holding up the card. "You did this at your plant, huh?"

Danny nodded. "Lots of artists do trading cards. It's a thing now."

"Huh. Can I keep this?"

"What do you think?" Danny asked, then signaled Peggy the waitress. "The pisser is I'd be able to quit the day job and concentrate all my energy on illustration if it weren't for the Princess."

Nate put down the card. "What do you mean?"

Danny sighed. "She's determined to keep the old bucket of a printing plant running. Man, she kills herself over it and my folks won't let anyone tell her she's wasting her time."

"Wasting her time?"

"You have any idea how much money the folks are sitting on with that place? They want to retire. My father says Ireland, and Ma just laughs and gets secret brochures from Florida. Brady's been offered a couple of great jobs that he can't take because the Princess isn't supposed to know that trading cards aren't ever going to be enough, although to be fair, he wouldn't mind staying at the plant forever. But the truth is we're losing textbook contracts and catalogues. The land is worth so much more than the business, it's not even funny. The whole situation is the stupidest thing I've ever heard of. We're talking millions of dollars. That's not even counting selling off the equipment. And then if we sold the house? Shit."

"The business has been in your family for generations. And the house? No way your parents would let go of the house," Nate said, even though the thought had crossed his mind. Yeah, he'd said something about it to Shannon, but he hadn't been serious.

"Wanna bet?"

Nate took a drink of his Guinness as the new data sunk in. "And everyone knows this but Shannon?"

"The neighbors know, the mailman knows. Unfortunately, the employees aren't idiots and they're just waiting for the shoe to fall. They're upset especially since the benefits aren't what they used to be. Everyone's surly, and it's only a matter of time before someone manufactures an accident so they can sue. The plant is outdated, my old man won't upgrade 'cause he doesn't want to refinance and get stuck. It's a losing situation from every angle, all because no one wants to hurt Shannon's feelings."

"She'll be crushed."

"I know. We all know. It's gonna tear her up." Danny shook his head. "That's where you come in."

"What?"

Danny sat up, leaned over the table, his beer forgotten. "You and Shannon, you've been getting along really well. She likes you, and you're practically family. And you're good with hard stuff. I mean, you're used to helping people who've lost everything. Believe me, she's not going to lose anything. She'll walk away not having to worry about money to get herself situated, figure out what she wants to do."

"You want me to tell her?"

Danny stared at him. "Yeah. Not straight-out, not mean or anything. Maybe let her know you overheard Ma talking about Florida. About Brady's job offers. You're dealing with real estate right now—you could mention how much the land is worth."

Nate felt as if he'd been punched in the gut. He almost admitted that he'd already made a passing comment but that was before the other night. Before he and Shannon had… "For God's sake, Danny."

"It's a hell of a lot to ask. And we all know we're going to have to talk. As a family. But maybe you could just think about it, huh? You'd be good with her. You can kind of pave the way to the big showdown. We all need to move on, including her."

"Man. She's been fighting so hard for the family. For a legacy."

"You don't have to, buddy. We'll come up with another idea. I don't mean to get you caught up in our mess."

The waitress came by with a couple more drinks and Danny flirted with her a bit, his discomfort with the topic of conversation obvious. Nate couldn't give him an answer, not until he thought long and hard about what Danny wanted him to do. Particularly now.

"You all set, honey?"

Nate smiled at Peggy, but his heart wasn't in it. Shannon would be devastated. It was a damn shame, too, because she was incredibly talented and would be an asset anywhere. If he thought he had a chance, he'd try to get her to come work for The International Rescue Committee. But he wouldn't even try. Gramercy was woven into the fabric of her life and he'd never dream of taking her away. She should run for city council. She'd see to it that corner basketball courts weren't left to rot and ruin.

But that was the long view. In the short term, discovering her family wanted a separate future more than they cared about their collective past was going to cripple her.

"Speak of the devil," Danny said, leaning back in his seat again. "The Princess hath arrived."

"Don't call her that anymore. She doesn't like it." A wave of anger at his friend made his gut tense. It wasn't logical. Danny was right. She was tilting at windmills. The business had been going downhill for a long time, but he hated like hell that he'd been asked to be the messenger.

She came up to the table and smiled at Nate in a way that made him want to whisk her to Bali and help her forget all about New York and family ties. "Shove over," she said. "I'm tired, thirsty and I have really exciting news. But first, did you hear back from Aiko?"

"Not yet." Nate moved, but not much. He wanted to be able to touch her. "What's so exciting?"

"Who's Aiko?" Danny asked. "You holding out on me?"

"The Realtor" was all Nate said. He'd already told Danny about the back-and-forth countering that was driving Nate nuts. Right now he wanted to know about Shannon.

She gave him a dazzling smile, then turned to search out the waitress. "Give me a minute." She put her purse on the outside of the booth, then let her head drop forward. Her hair cascaded into a fiery pool on the tabletop, until she sat up straight again when Peggy came to take their order.

"I'll have the chicken Caesar salad, dressing on the side."

"Screw that," Danny said. "I want the potpie, but first I want the calamari."

Nate wasn't very hungry anymore, but he still said, "I'll have the grilled salmon, please."

"'Please'?" Peggy said, sounding confused. "What's that word mean again?" Then she looked at Shannon. "Your regular?"

Shannon frowned. "Water, thanks."

Danny's brows went up. "What's with all the dressing-on-the-side business? You hate that."

"I have to look my best," she said, then grinned like she'd just won Miss Congeniality. "Because the camera adds ten pounds."

"TV?" Nate smiled back at her, even knowing what he knew. She looked so damn happy. "They're doing a reality show about your life?"

She waved him away as if he'd been joking, but now that he thought about it, she'd be great at that. "I'm being interviewed by WNYC. About Easter at the park. They've asked me to come in on Thursday. It'll be live, on *Local Happenings with Grant and Lisa*."

Nate took her hand and squeezed it. "That's terrific. What's the station?"

"It's not a big affiliate or anything," she said. "A local independent that broadcasts in Manhattan and some parts of New Jersey. But everyone watches it. They talk about what's going on in town, and sometimes they do exposés on petty local scandals and profile pieces on charities and people who are making a difference. But mostly they announce book fairs and library programs, stuff like that."

"The Easter thing is where you raise money for the church renovations?" Danny asked.

"Nope. That's our Christmas program. This benefits outreach programs for feeding the homeless. But in each of the gift baskets there are cards from Fitzgerald and Sons, and we're handing out trading cards to everyone who comes to the park. Two of the food trucks are letting me put up big banners. You know I'm going to talk about the printing plant when I'm interviewed."

"There's not a doubt in my mind," her brother said, then shot a glance at Nate.

Shannon glowed as she went on about her plans, and as she talked, Nate thought about what Danny had asked him to do. An interview about Easter baskets wasn't going to save the day. In fact, it made things worse. Getting her hopes up. Putting that look in her eyes.

He didn't want to think about it, but after the interview was over, someone was going to have to tell her that the rest of the family wasn't on board with her plans.

It made horrible sense that it should be him. He owed the Fitzgeralds so much, and he couldn't picture any of them breaking the news to her. Theoretically he was part of the family, for good and bad, and this was not going to be good. But he would be careful. As careful as he'd ever been in his life. He'd try and take as much of the sting away as possible.

And he sure wasn't going to bring it up before she had her last hurrah.

"You're tired," he said, his voice low, close to her ear.

"I am," she agreed, letting her thumb run over the back of his hand as they walked slowly in the direction of home. She should probably be concerned about someone spotting them, but she wasn't. "It's a good tired."

"Probably don't want some crazy man sneaking into your boudoir later."

"Depends," she said, smiling in the dark. "How much later?"

"Fifteen minutes?"

She laughed. "Is that starting now, or when we cross the threshold?"

"Fine. We'll wait. The basketball game's over, though.

It's past your mother's bedtime. So it's only your dad, right? Or will Brady be home?"

"No, he's not there, and Dad likes to be in bed for the eleven o'clock news."

"There you go. So, fifteen minutes after the start of the news."

"Fine. Jeez. So impatient."

He pulled her to a stop between streetlamps. "Damn right I'm impatient. I've never slept with a TV star before."

"Well, whoever she is, you can tell her to get in line. I've got you booked for the night."

He pulled her in as if they'd been dancing, her coat billowing behind her as she stepped into his arms. His kiss made an excellent day perfect. He tasted of beer, while she, being the most considerate person ever, tasted like peppermint. But she wasn't complaining. Every kiss she got from Nate was another memory she'd store away.

There was another one, a quick brush of lips, but still sweet, three doors down, and then she was at the big red door, her key at the ready. Nate's hand touched hers, stilling the turn. "I forgot something," he said. "I'll be back in half an hour."

"What?"

"Condoms. I meant to—"

"Top shelf, medicine cabinet. Big old box. Probably Brady's but he shouldn't miss them. Grab a handful."

Nate's eyes opened very wide.

"Not all for tonight. For God's sake, I've got work in the morning."

He laughed and followed her inside, where the downstairs was quiet, and the evening was about to get juicy. After hanging up their coats, they hurried to the second floor. Luckily, Brady's room was dark just like the rest of the hall. As if it were some kind of spy mission, Nate gave her a nod before he peeled off to Myles's room. She hurried to her own and got undressed as quickly as she could.

Her thoughts were tripping over themselves, first about Nate, then about the interview, then back to Nate. She made a quick trip to the bathroom, and when she closed the bedroom door behind her, she let all her thoughts of Easter eggs and interviews go in favor of picturing how she wanted to look when Nate came in.

Robe off or on? Her first thought was off, but naked on the bed seemed so normal. Although he really liked her hair. Maybe she could arrange it so that it covered certain bits....

Nate wouldn't care at all. It wasn't a show, and she wasn't trying to dazzle him. He liked her. She liked him. They were good together. For now.

Her robe slid off her shoulders, and she pushed the comforter back on the bed. He would be here in a moment, and her heart was already beating faster, her nipples getting hard. He'd been so happy for her. Cheering her on.

The line she straddled was thin. Too much optimism and she feared the eventual crash would smash her beyond help. Too much pragmatism and why bother?

Two quick taps came seconds before he slipped inside and locked the door. It still felt like a spy novel, and that was good. The element of drama was important in this fragile game.

"You take my breath," he said, walking slowly toward her. He was James Bond sexy in his robe. All he was missing was the martini. It helped that he'd run his hand through his hair, that his eyes were already dark with arousal.

"I'll give it back before you leave." She reached for his belt, then pushed the robe off, and the press of his skin on hers made everything fuzzy. He kissed her long and slow as they maneuvered between the sheets, breaking only when absolutely necessary. Finally, though, their heads were on pillows and his knee was between her thighs.

"I almost came here last night."

"Why didn't you?" She smiled at the feathery swirls he idly traced on her belly.

"I had a very long conversation with myself. I was completely unreasonable for the most part." He pressed a warm, moist kiss to the side of her jaw, then trailed his lips to her ear. "God, I can be an idiot."

Her eyes briefly drifted closed. "How so?"

"I'd almost convinced myself that it would be in both our best interests for me to wake you at one-thirty in the morning when you had to be up at six o'clock."

"That's not idiotic."

He lifted his head, moving the breath that had been warming the back of her ear to her cheek. "I ended up being noble. What did I get wrong?"

"It would have been okay, that's all. If you'd come."

"It was one-thirty."

"I know. I'd have let you in." She slid her palm across the contours of his chest. He felt so damn good. So solid and safe. So Nate. "Turns out I like you."

He kissed her, smiling. She felt his grin, then matched it with her own. When he pulled back, his gaze grew serious and the smile faded. "I wish you didn't have to go to work tomorrow. You could reacquaint me with your city."

"You lived here most of your life."

A single finger trailed down her neck, then lower, all the way to her breast. "That's true, but I never lived in your city. Mine was crowded and noisy and selfish. You love yours so much it has to be something special."

It was an odd thing for him to say, even his voice sounded a bit strained. She searched his face, but if something was wrong, his expression gave nothing away. "It's New York," she said. "Of course it's special. It's the best city in the world."

One hand was holding up his head, while the other continued to play with her body. It felt delicious and intimate for all its unconsciousness, so she settled down and dismissed her initial reaction as her own weirdness.

He'd switched from the single digit to all the fingers and sometimes the palm as he traced her, mapped her. Everywhere he went left a trail of sparks, and it was difficult to split her attention between the sensation and his words. But she wanted both. It was important to fit in everything she could while she had the chance.

"How many big cities have you been to?" he asked. "Paris? Florence? Sydney?"

She shook her head, shifting to her side a little more so she could get in on the touching action. She ran her hand up his hip and kept on going. "The only foreign city I've been to is Toronto. Which was wonderful, but it wasn't New York."

"Too bad you haven't visited Europe. It's not a bad plane ride from here."

"Nope. When I was young, my parents were always at the plant. Now I'm always at the plant. It's the curse of a family-run business."

"That's crazy."

"That's real life."

"Well, see," he murmured, "now the best is yet to come." He kissed her nose, then her lips, and that was the end of talking. That hand of his got serious. When he slipped between her thighs, stroking lightly on the tender flesh, she tipped onto her back, thrusting up with her hips to show him she wanted more.

Two fingers pushed inside her and before she could grab hold of any part of him, he was down the bed. He licked her all over and around where his fingers were before he settled in with pointed tongue.

Her knees went up and her heels dug into the mattress as he kept thrusting inside her, kept circling her clit with ever increasing pressure and speed.

Shannon's back arched with exquisite tension, her hands fisted the sheets, and she could already feel the beginning of her orgasm starting low and deep.

"Now," she said. She lifted her head and tried to focus. "Now, please, Nate, now."

He looked at her from where he sucked her nub between his lips, and she could see he didn't want to stop, but she did. As wonderful as it was, she wanted him inside her.

"Please."

He let her go, his fingers as reluctant as his mouth.

She had enough sanity left to grab one of the condoms on the night table, but he had to take it from there. Even though he wasn't touching her, except for his knees against her inner thighs, she was still close, still trembling, still moving her body as if his cock were already buried to the base.

Seconds later, he was there, he was sliding in and groaning as if it were the best feeling he'd ever had in his life.

The way he filled her made her writhe, made her

crazy, and when she tasted herself on his tongue as he kissed her, she made noises she'd never heard before.

She came from his thrusting. He didn't use his fingers again, and neither did she. But she came and the sensation was so strong she nearly bucked him off.

"Jesus, Shannon," he said, holding her hips as if he'd never let her go. "I can't…"

He came while she was still shuddering with aftershocks. There wasn't enough air in the world to fill her lungs, and her heart was beating itself out of her chest, and oh, God, it was unbelievable.

"I've never…" she said between deep gasps. "I've never had that happen before."

Nate had pulled out, flopped next to her. "What?"

"I've never come from intercourse alone."

He looked at her and grinned. Smugly. "No kidding."

"It's true. You do have mad skills."

"I'm inspired. You're amazing. Everything about you gives me such pleasure."

She curled into his side and brushed her hand across his chest. "I know. You, too."

He petted her arm for a while. "Where would you go?" he asked. "If you could go anywhere at all?"

"Um, I'm not sure. Paris. London. I've always wanted to go there. Rome, Florence, Switzerland, India, a safari in Africa, Machu Picchu, the Netherlands, Australia, New Zealand, Banff—"

His laughter made her head bounce on his chest.

"What?"

"You surprise me. I was starting to think you'd evolved into a typical stagnant New Yorker."

"Hey."

"Don't get me wrong. That's a lot of dreams and I'm glad you have them," he said.

She sniffed. "That's all they are. Dreams."

"Don't say that."

"It's true, but it's not as if I'm trapped in some urban tragedy. It's my family we're talking about. Everything we've built for generations. I'm doing my part, is all. Times are tough, but the plant will—"

He squeezed her arm. "I don't want to talk about the plant. In fact, I want you to pretend that you don't have anything standing in your way. You've got the time, the money, the freedom to go wherever you want. Where would you go first?"

"No responsibilities, huh?"

"Exactly."

"I don't think my imagination is that good."

"Sure it is. It's just pretend. You can go anywhere on earth. Where would it be? The first place?"

She sighed and let the reality float away, let herself imagine a life that couldn't be. "An island, I think," she said. "Somewhere exotic and quiet and mystical."

"Ah, now you're talking my language." He brushed her skin with the tips of his fingers. "That's Bali. It's a magical place. The mountains, the caves. The people are so generous, and you can lose yourself in the green jungles or in the water with coral reefs and brilliant fish all around you. Take a whole day and wander the beaches, or go to the temple where the monkeys are sacred. The scent of incense mixed with the smells of the earth, the water, the sky. It's so beautiful there, Shannon, I don't have enough words. It's paradise."

Shannon's eyes were closed and she tried to picture herself on his island, but the passion he had for his true home overshadowed his descriptions. "It sounds perfect."

"It is."

She smiled and kissed his chest. Promised herself she'd be brave and not choke on the words. "And you can't wait to get back there."

He stilled beneath her. Not even breathing.

# 12

NATE PURPOSELY LEFT FOR his noon lunch at ten. The meeting was at Eleven Madison Park, in the Flatiron District, and he wanted to walk. It was a beautiful day, he hadn't even worn a coat, just his suit jacket. He headed north on 3rd Avenue, thinking about everything that had happened since his conversation with Danny at the pub.

There were a lot of things he'd had to do in his life that were unpleasant, even painful. He'd witnessed the devastation caused by tsunamis and earthquakes on people's lives and their communities. But he'd been there to help people recover and rebuild. Now he was being asked to rip apart the foundations of Shannon's life, and it was burning a hole in his gut.

All that travel talk had been illuminating. He'd wanted to get a feel for how much of her dedication was something she chose versus something she hadn't been able to avoid. Naturally, he'd hoped her choices had been limited, and that letting the plant go would be liberating, but that wasn't what he'd heard. Yes, it was hard and she'd sacrificed a lot, but she hadn't been forced. At least not on a conscious level.

He'd wondered when he saw that big sign outside Fitzgerald & Sons how Shannon had felt about being overlooked. She'd been a surprise to the family, five years after they'd stopped trying for a girl, but still, she must have felt like an outsider from time to time. She wasn't one of the boys in other ways, as well. She'd been a show pony to their workhorses. That they still called her Princess said so much.

Finding out the truth wouldn't kill her, but it would be a close thing. At least for a while. Her emotional investment was so complete he doubted she gave herself any room to imagine a different kind of life. She'd have to start from the ground up. It wouldn't be a quick transition, that's for sure.

So basically, he was going to yank the rug right out from under her, then disappear, leaving her to find her way alone.

That sucked. That sucked so hard he wanted to smash something. He slowed his pace, surprised that he'd been speed walking. Escaping? He was on Lexington, at East 26th, at the Armory in Kips Bay, and he had barely any recollection of how he'd gotten there. The building was a beautiful example of Beaux-Arts architecture, one of his personal favorites. But then a lot of buildings in the city were his favorites.

The Flatiron. The neo-Gothic New York Life Insurance Company, the marble courthouse on East 25th. Hell, the fantastic houses all around Gramercy Park were where he'd head when he needed to be on his own. Somehow, he'd always end up in one of the small green corners that weren't exactly private, but not precisely parks. Or the basketball courts. There'd been so many when he was a kid, and had he passed a single one on his way up here?

He might have been walking in a daze, but he'd have stopped if there'd been an inviting court. Didn't matter where he was in the world, he would always be lured by the call of a pickup game even if all he could do was watch.

It was a shame. There were schools and Union Square Park and Madison Square Park, but those weren't places where he and Danny had hung out. They liked the little places, the neighborhood games.

He guessed that was one more thing that had vanished in the age of the internet. Too many kids spending their time online, playing video games, watching hundreds of channels on TV. Such a damn shame.

If he could get Shannon to put her talent to work on the neighborhood, she could transform the whole district. No one whipped up enthusiasm like she did. More importantly, she would love it. He was certain of that. She'd been born to do great things, and while keeping the family together was a fine goal, it only worked if the family wanted to be held together.

He wished, though, that he could be there for her. To encourage her, to make sure she knew every day that she could do anything she set her mind to.

Leaving behind the armory, he headed toward Park Avenue, trying to imagine some clever turn of phrase to tell her she'd been fighting for nothing. That her efforts had been wasted.

Nope, there was no nice way to say any of that. She would be crushed, and he'd be the one to deliver the blow.

SHANNON HAD NO BUSINESS whatsoever meeting Rebecca and Bree for lunch at Brasserie 8½ in Midtown West, but she couldn't stand having so much to say and so few people to say it to.

They'd just finished ordering, and she faced both of her friends from across the booth. "So," she asked, as casual as she could possibly be, "what's new?"

Bree put her hand up in front of her mouth, trying to hide her grin, while Rebecca didn't even bother faking it. She just laughed.

"Please. You're bursting with whatever it is you've got going on." Rebecca Thorpe, who was still in the honeymoon phase of her relationship with her ex-cop, had no compunction about poking Shannon's arm with the back end of her knife. "I have one hour for lunch, and I can't even cheat a little bit. So talk."

"I'm going to be on *WNYC News at Ten* on Thursday night."

Bree and Rebecca both grinned like maniacs. "How come?" Bree asked.

"I'm being interviewed about the Easter egg hunt that my company sponsors in Union Square Park. Well, we're not the only ones who sponsor the festivities, lots of local businesses do, but Fitzgerald and Sons coordinates the event and we put it all together."

"Which means you put it all together," Rebecca said. "But congratulations. This is thrilling. I'm not only going to watch it, I'm going to DVR the whole half hour, then call the station to tell them how impressed I was with the interview. And could I have the name of the beautiful redhead who was in charge?"

"Really?" Shannon asked. Rebecca wasn't just a Thorpe, she was also a Winslow, which in this town meant huge money and incredible influence. Rebecca herself ran the Winslow Foundation, which raised millions for international aid. Huh. She should arrange a dinner with Nate while he was in town. They'd have a lot to talk about.

"Of course, really."

"Why didn't you say something before?" Bree asked. "I didn't know a thing about an Easter egg hunt. How fun. Charlie can put something about the interview in his blog, and then we can do an ad for the event, if that would help."

Shannon took a breath. Then another. She'd never asked her friends to go out of their way for her, even when it was tempting. Charlie, Bree's boyfriend, wasn't an ordinary blogger. He was Charlie Winslow, Rebecca's cousin, and his blog was *Naked New York,* the single most talked-about social-media column in Manhattan.

"That's going way, way above and beyond. I appreciate it so much, but please ask Charlie first. The proceeds all go to feed the homeless and I can send him the information about the charity and how it's run. I don't want either of you to feel obligated."

"We're friends," Rebecca said, leaning over to clasp her hand. "And besides, you deserve everything good for coming up with the trading cards. We both owe you for that."

Shannon held up her water glass, then put it down because the waiter came with the bottle of wine they'd ordered. After he left, she made a proper toast. "To friends and lovers and trading cards."

"And to TV interviews," Rebecca added.

Shannon sipped the very delicious chardonnay and couldn't help but smile. There were wonderful things happening in her life, not the least of which was Nate. The trick there was not thinking too much about how soon he'd be gone.

She felt her mood falter and switched back to focusing on the interview, which with Bree and Rebecca's help she could imagine actually having a big audience. She'd have to be smart, though. Not so self-promoting that she looked as if she didn't care about Easter or the little kids who would be hunting for eggs.

"Oh, God. I'm going to be on TV. With people watching."

"Yes," Bree said. "That's the point."

"Okay. I know it's been done a million times, but I'm going to wear green because it does look best on camera with my hair."

"You look fantastic in green," Bree said. "I have this great tartan skirt that would go so well with that hunter-green blouse that you wore that time when we went for sushi."

"One of your skirts would fit on one of my thighs, but thanks for the offer."

"You always look gorgeous anyway," Rebecca said, just as the waiter brought out their food.

It took a few minutes to deliver the three salads, but soon they were alone. Again Shannon's thoughts returned to Nate and what he would say when she told him the news about Charlie's blog and Rebecca's support. He'd be thrilled for her.

"You know," Rebecca said, turning to Bree, "while the news about the interview is wonderful, why do I have the feeling that our friend Shannon buried the lead?"

"Hmm," Bree said, nodding, ignoring Shannon completely. "I have to agree. The glow? The pink cheeks? The way she's shifting around like she can't sit still?"

"I'd lay odds it's a guy."

"The toast was a dead giveaway," Bree said. "Not just a guy. A trading card guy."

Shannon held up a hand. "Stop. Yes. You're right. I wasn't burying the lead. I was saving the best for last."

Bree shook her head. "I'd say he's one hell of a guy, but that's only because you're blushing so hot you're about to set the tablecloth on fire."

Shannon leaned forward. "His name is Nate Brenner, and he's an architect and urban planner who works in international relief. He's really good-looking, but more importantly he's wonderful. You guys would like him so much. I bet he knows all about the Winslow Foundation, Rebecca."

She smiled. "You mean you haven't spent your nights talking about me and my foundation?" Her friend grinned, put her fork down and held out her hand. "Come on. Out with it."

"What?"

Rebecca sighed. "You know very well exactly what. His card. Let's see it."

Shannon wasn't proud of the fact that she'd stolen his card from the group. Not that she'd change one single thing, but she was still not proud. She opened her purse and took the card out. God, he was gorgeous.

She handed it over to Rebecca, and she could feel her blush intensify.

"Holy cow, he's a hottie," Bree said, as she practically laid over her friend to get a look. "No wonder you kept him to yourself. Look at that smile."

"What organization does he work for?" Rebecca asked.

"The International Rescue Committee."

"That's one of the highest-rated charities in the

world. They do phenomenal work. You say he's an architect?"

"He rebuilds infrastructure in places that have been hit by earthquakes and tsunamis. Mostly in Indonesia and Asia but he thinks that might be changing soon. His home base is in Bali."

Rebecca handed the card to Bree. "Oh, you have got to go see him in Bali," Rebecca said. "Seriously. You'd love it there. It's one of my favorite places on earth."

"He loves it there, too. But there's no way I can go," Shannon said. "Everything at the plant is so tenuous. We're short-staffed as it is. I can't leave the country. I shouldn't even be here."

"It's been like that since I met you," Rebecca said. "There has to be a way you can steal some time for yourself. I'm sure your family would understand."

"I don't know much about what you do," Bree said, not even looking up from his card.

"Run everything but the printing machines, basically. Payroll, taxes. The usual. But most of my time these days is spent on finding new clients."

"It's just your family running the whole thing?"

"We have forty-seven employees. For a couple of years now it's just my father, my brother Brady and me in charge. My mom and my other brothers jumped ship."

"Well, you should figure out a way to take some time off," Bree said, meeting her gaze. "Did you know that when you talk about Nate, your whole face lights up? You really do glow."

"I do?" She put her palms on her heated cheeks. "I've known him all my life. Since we were kids. He's my brother Danny's best friend. But then Nate went away after college and came back all grown up. Gorgeous.

Sweet. Obviously, he's got a tremendous heart. He could be earning buckets running his father's architectural firm, but he doesn't want to live in New York. Or do traditional building."

"How come it says he's a one-night stand?"

"He's leaving as soon as he finishes his business here."

"But his passion is making a difference," Bree said, showing the back of the card to Rebecca, who snatched it up.

"And the bottom line is that he's a sweetheart." Rebecca held up the card as if it was a flag. "A *sweetheart*."

"He is. He's just not going to be my sweetheart," Shannon said, "at least not forever." She straightened, really hating how her voice had dropped off.

"Ah," the two women across from her said in sync.

"No, it's not like that. I've known all along he's leaving, so it's not a big deal." She sipped her wine, avoiding eye contact.

"You've simply got to go to Bali to visit him," Rebecca said, her voice brooking no arguments. "You owe it to him, and to yourself." She gave the card back, but she'd made her point.

Shannon stared down at his picture, his smile, and she shivered as she remembered the feel of his body so intimately tangled with her own. There was no way in hell she could take the time off to go to Bali.

But she was beginning to think she might not have a choice.

NATE WAS ON THE PHONE WITH George, his direct boss, and the man who was in charge of all projects, excluding fundraising and marketing. George told them all where to go, those who were on the payroll, who were few, and those who consulted or volunteered, who were the real backbone of the IRC. He was also an incredibly nice guy, whom Nate had known since NYU. The man had been responsible for helping Nate find out where he belonged.

"Sumatra is still an issue," Nate said. "They lost so many of their construction people, it's going to be hard for them to pick up the ball and run with it."

"You're going to have to deal with it," George said. "Find someone who can communicate well and we'll make sure you can interface. You've got four more months, Nate, and then we'll need you in Africa."

"No, fine. That's fine. I know we've exceeded our mandate. It's hard to let go."

"I know. The refugee situation has to be dealt with, and all we keep doing is shuffling people from tent city to tent city. These people need something they can call their own. They need to work for themselves and see their labor turn into something real."

"Of course. I'll be wherever you need me." Nate put down his coffee and looked back at the kitchen table, where Shannon was on her laptop doing something that kept her clicking her mouse. She looked so pretty in the morning light, in that pink bathrobe he was going to miss.

"Let me know when you're heading back, yes?"

"I will. Take care, and have Alex send me all the data on where I'll be headed. I need to start planning." Nate disconnected, then went to sit next to Shannon. "What are you so busy working on?"

She turned the laptop so he could see the screen. It was a picture of him surrounded by villagers. He was standing in the middle of a town square, an open air market to his right, a row of sturdy buildings around the perimeter of a small park, with infant trees planted in the general shape of a *Rafflesia arnoldii* flower, the largest flower in the world. That day they had opened the market with great ceremony. It had been scorchingly hot, as wet as the ocean itself, and a day he'd never forget.

"You look so happy," she said. "And so tan."

"Yeah, we didn't have a lot of sunscreen at our disposal. And I was happy. That was a big day."

"But you're not staying there?"

He shrugged. "I go wherever they need me. Which right now is Africa."

"How do you do that? It must be so hard to pick up your life and move it at someone else's whim."

"I don't have a home like you do," he said. "I never did, but I've pared way down. I can carry everything I need in a couple of duffel bags. And everywhere I go, I'm welcome and I'm needed."

"I can see how much you love it."

He almost said, "Just like you love your home," but the thought hurt, the thought of how she didn't know what she was about to be hit with.

Instead he leaned over and kissed her. Long, slow strokes of his tongue, tasting her beneath her coffee, wanting to walk her back upstairs to her bed.

She pulled away first, checking behind him as if they were criminals. It made him want her even more. When her gaze came back to his, she softened, her concern gone knowing they were alone. "I want to hear more about what you do," she said. "I can't now because I have to get ready for work, but I would like to listen. My only frame of reference is 9/11, and how the word *fear* stopped being adequate. How our illusion of safety had been stolen. But there was also the high of coming together. All of New York had been a family, even if it was temporary. You go to those places all the time, and it must be so, so hard, and yet unbelievably satisfying to be part of the solution."

Nate's chest tightened. "It is," he said. "There are horrors and miracles around every corner. Each one breaks my heart. In between is where it gets tricky. I've talked to other relief workers and we all have that sense of disconnect from the ordinary world. We're like soldiers in that respect. It's a limited reality, and it's truly indescribable."

Shannon closed her eyes for a long moment. Took a deep breath. When she opened them again, she smiled. "I've got to go. Busy day ahead. If you're free around three o'clock I've got to go to the park to take some photos. Maybe you'd like to come with?"

"Yeah, sure. Sounds great. I should hear about the offer on the co-op today."

"Oh, exciting. I'm betting it's a yes all the way around." She shut down the laptop and put it under her arm, carrying her coffee in her free hand. He didn't want her to leave, not yet. But she disappeared in a whirl, leaving him to the realization that for all his experience in the face of earthshaking events, he still had absolutely no idea how to help Shannon while still telling her the truth.

# *13*

SHANNON HAD TRIED ON SO many clothes the night before her room now resembled a messy change room at Filene's Basement. It was tempting to call Bree to come help, but in the end she went with her original plan: green blouse that fit her well, slim black skirt, black heels. Tomorrow evening's interview was scarily close, the reality made more terrifying when she'd gotten an email from WNYC about where to go at what time.

The idea that it was live television scared the crap out of her, so she tried not to think about it. But different nightmare scenarios kept popping up: burping in the middle of a sentence, spilling coffee, throwing up, nervously giggling like an idiot. The spectrum of humiliations was huge and varied, but she'd been on stage plenty of times and the butterflies always disappeared the moment she was in the spotlight. Television should be no different.

She got dressed, wishing she had time to put her things in order, but she really did have a packed agenda. She would be sending a massive group email to everyone in her database, asking them to watch the show. She wasn't discriminating about the names, either. Whether they be work related, folks from the church, the St. Marks lunch-exchange crew, family, friends of friends. It was such a large list that she had to break it down into units, or she'd be considered a spammer. Which she supposed she was. But it was for a good cause, so she could live with that.

She also had a meeting with a potential new client this afternoon. Nothing huge, not a lifesaver, but the income would help, and the work was simple. Brochures. Lots and lots of brochures.

Oh, she had to check out *Naked New York* as soon as she got to the office. That would be exciting. She'd send a thank-you card to Charlie and Bree, handwritten, on a card.

The list went on in her head as she did a quick makeup-and-hair check, then she was racing down the stairs. As she turned the corner on the first floor, she bumped into the console table on her way to the coatrack. A file folder fell, spreading a stack of brochures all across the wood floor.

Cursing under her breath, Shannon crouched down and picked up several. They weren't brochures the plant had printed, but rather all about various locales in Florida—Tampa, Orlando, Miami. The file folder wasn't marked, but there was a phone number in the corner written in her mother's hand.

Shannon hadn't realized her folks were thinking about taking a vacation. She should tell them about Bali. It would be good for them to get away. They never went far. They hardly ever took time off at all. An occasional trip to Atlantic City. A weekend at the beach. Good for them for thinking about Florida.

She finished putting everything back, wondering about the brochure for a senior community. She went to open it, noticed the time and shoved everything inside the folder. Then she was off like a shot.

THE SECOND AFTER NATE disconnected with Aiko, he pressed Shannon's speed dial.

"Nate."

"Are you at the plant?"

"Yep. Not for long, though. What's up?"

"I'll come get you, and we can go to the park together."

"Okay," she said, and he could hear the smile in the single word. "Give me ten minutes."

"'Bye."

He put his cell in his pocket and raised his arm out to catch a cab. He hit pay dirt a few minutes later and gave the driver the address. It was a short ride from Murray Hill, where he'd been with his accountant since their lunch meeting at noon. The negotiations on the firm were moving at a snail's pace, which wasn't shocking considering the kind of money they were dealing with.

He hated all this crap, but the whole reason he'd come to New York was to get his financial life squared away. He needed enough in his coffers to live without the burden of a traditional job or family. He loved his work, but if he got burned out, which happened with great frequency on the front lines, he wanted to be able to stand on his own. To have insurance, to be able to live where he wanted. He also needed to make sure he was building a future. Maybe someday he'd find someone who fit, who he'd want to settle down with.

Of course he thought of Shannon, but by the time he'd be ready to give up his life, she'd be taken. He was pretty damn stunned she wasn't taken already.

Children weren't in the plans, although, if he thought

he could have a couple of girls with that fantastic red hair... He shook his head. He hadn't wanted children ever, but he did care about a safe retirement. So if it took the lawyers and the moneymen time to work out the deal, so be it.

He was very grateful that his parents had always been smart with money. His mother was set, as was his sister, Leah. The purchase of a co-op apartment had been his accountant's idea, and so far, she'd been an excellent combination of conservative and sufficiently forward-thinking to take reasonable risks.

Shannon would be in good shape, too. In the end. Financially. How she'd be emotionally was a huge unknown. The only thing he knew for sure was that she wouldn't be settled into her new way of life by the middle of May when he had to leave.

The cab turned onto 10th Avenue. He paid the driver, then went inside the building. Shannon was in her office, searching through a stack of papers. She looked up at him and how glad she was to see him was a jolt of adrenaline.

He shut the door. He hadn't seen her since the kitchen. She looked beautiful, as always, but today she'd put her hair up in a smooth ponytail. There should have been another name for the hairstyle because on her it was sleek, elegant and sophisticated. There weren't many women who could carry off that look, but Shannon did.

"Did you hear?"

He blinked at her, trying to figure out— "Oh, yeah. They accepted the offer. Two weeks from Friday on the escrow. The sellers are eager, therefore accommodating."

She dropped the stack in her hands onto her desk

and came to him, her long orange-red ponytail swinging behind her as she walked. Her arms went around him in a tight hug, and it was all he could do not to kiss the daylights out of her. But he didn't know where her dad or Brady were, so...

"I'm thrilled. It won't give you much time to furnish the rest of the— They did agree to include the furniture?"

"Actually, no. It didn't belong to them. So I have to shop from the ground up." The delight on her face made him laugh. "And yes, I'd be very pleased if you could help me with that."

"I've always wanted to do an entire house. This is the best, this is...I can't even start to think about it until next week."

"It'll wait. But we can go back to take measurements, if that helps."

"Yes, yes, of course, it does. What about finding people to sublet? I never asked, did you have someone in mind?"

"Nope, the management company will take care of that."

She kissed him, but only on the chin. Then she stepped back. "We should go. I need to catch the light for the pictures I'm taking. I'm doing a before-and-after of the space for an event bible. So that if I'm not able to coordinate things for any reason, someone can just pick up the book and carry on."

"You are a very smart cookie, have I mentioned that lately?"

"Not nearly often enough, if you ask me."

He nodded. "Noted. You have to do anything, tell anyone before we go?"

"Nope. We're clear."

"You mind if we cab it to 16th and walk the rest of the way?"

"No. Why?"

"I've been in an office or a cab all day. If you're tired, though, it's no big deal."

"I'd love to. My day's been chock-full of stress. A walk will do me good. It's been ages since I've been to the gym."

"You don't need a gym," he murmured. "I'll give you a workout."

Shaking her head in mock disapproval, she led him out to the street, and they walked to 9th Avenue, where they caught a taxi. He held her hand on the ride to West 16th, but they were both quiet—the good kind. They kept sneaking glances at each other, which was silly, but okay, too. He was thirty-two and this thing with Shannon felt like a high-school romance. All the sneaking around. Her parents on the top floor. He didn't mind, although if he had been planning to stay in New York, they would have ended the game by now.

He didn't think her parents would object to him in the long run, but they'd need adjustment time. So would Danny, when it came down to that.

"What's that look?"

He had her hand in his, and they set an easy pace, which made quite a few people tsk at them as if they were tourists. "Trying to imagine what Danny would say if he knew we were together. In the biblical sense."

She gave him a startled look, and he realized that might not have been the right word to use. "He'd have a heart attack, then he'd want you to get your head examined."

"Sounds about right. Although big brothers are supposed to be kind of stupid about their little sisters from what I've heard."

"Mine fit the bill. I'll keel over myself the day they stop calling me Princess."

"It took me a while to realize how very grown-up you are."

"You'd been gone for years. The last memory you had of me was at thirteen. They were here. They were at my graduation. I was a Phi Beta Kappa. That should count for something."

"Why didn't I know that?" he asked.

She shrugged. "I thought Mom let everyone on earth know, but if you'd only been talking to Danny it wasn't the World Series or the Stanley Cup finals, so it wasn't important."

Slipping his arm around the back of her shoulders, he pulled her close. "He can be an idiot, that's for sure. But congratulations. That's an incredible achievement."

"Thank you."

They walked past an empty lot overgrown with weeds, an old dilapidated fence with a fading Keep Out sign doing nothing to prevent a group of tattooed and pierced kids from squatting on junk furniture and makeshift seats. A sight endemic to all big cities, as much a part of New York as the skyline, but it still bothered Nate. Danny accused him regularly of being a bleeding-heart hippie, and Nate had a hard time disagreeing.

"You should bring your IRC crew out here," Shannon said. "Let them take a whack at Manhattan, see what they could do to rebuild and renew."

"The IRC does work out here, but the mandate is different. We help refugees get on their feet, find work and safety."

"That's good," she said. "Important."

He stared as they kept on walking, then turned back to Shannon. "You should seriously consider running for city council."

"In my copious free time?"

"You could do so much good. You're brilliant at organizing, at galvanizing. The Easter thing is a perfect example. I know without a doubt that it's going to bring in tons of money for the homeless, that everyone involved is going to come away from the event happy and that you won't get nearly enough credit for all you've done. See? You're practically a full-fledged council member already."

She squeezed him closer, her hand around his waist. "I've got enough on my plate," she said. "Let me get a few more deep-pocket clients for the plant, then I can relax a little."

He nodded, even as he called himself every kind of coward. But he wasn't going to bring up the family business until after her TV interview. He wouldn't do that to anyone, let alone someone he cared so much about.

They kept walking, slowly, as close as they could be without tripping. "I missed you last night," Shannon said.

"We agreed."

Shannon sighed. "In retrospect, it would have been better if you'd come."

"Tonight, then?"

She nodded, then rested her cheek on his shoulder. "I can't guarantee sexy times. Would that bother you?"

"I'd take sleeping next to you over anything else, hands down. Although I won't be upset if sexy times occur."

They were at the last intersection before the park, and she tugged him around so they faced each other. "This won't take long. The only shots I need are of one area, where the tables and booths will be set up. Then, maybe we could grab a quick dinner. When I get home, I want to go over my bullet list for the interview, get my clothes ready. Nothing very exciting. I plan to be in bed by ten."

He kissed her, a quickie, as there were people in every direction, some very close. "I'll meet you there. Now, if you point me in the right direction, I'll take pictures, too. Anything you need."

She kissed him back, and despite the pedestrians and the traffic, she put her cool palm on the back of his neck to hold him steady as she slipped her tongue between his lips.

She'd just hung up the last of her clothes, the outfit for tomorrow night covered in a dry-cleaner bag. She'd wear the same shoes as she did for work, but her accessories were in a velvet bag in her purse.

It was so much like the old days when she'd lived for being on center stage. The real princess stage of her life had been the pageants, which were only slightly embarrassing. By the time she'd reached her teens she had given up her quest for tiaras and gone after the applause of strangers. She'd been in many school plays, right through her first year of college. She'd have continued for the pure joy of it, but by then she'd accepted that she would join the family business, and she'd focused on her studies.

It was ten o'clock and she needed to get ready for bed. For Nate. As exciting as the interview was, as pressing as the needs of the printing plant were, she'd found herself thinking about Bali or Africa or wherever Nate was going to be. Now that she knew her parents were going to take some time off, she felt less guilty about wanting some for herself.

For ten minutes this afternoon, she'd looked at pictures of Bali. The internet was a wonderful thing, bringing the world to her in her little office. But for once she wanted to go to the world. Despite her best intentions she hadn't been able to stop her traitorous practical mind from taking her to the end of the line. She wished she hadn't seen that picture of him in Sumatra. Before, she'd had vague images in her head about where he lived and worked. Now she couldn't pretend he was anything but temporary, and rightly so.

He was a great man doing great work. A real-life hero. Even in her daydreams she couldn't compete with that. No wonder he thought of her in terms of doing bigger things, like running for city council. Because that's where he lived, in a world where he had a direct impact on the lives of hundreds if not thousands. She had her family and forty-seven employees to take care of. No contest.

She went down the hall to the bathroom, took off her robe and pinned up her hair before she stepped under the shower. The heat and pressure of the water felt incredible, and for a long while she dipped her head, closed her eyes and let her body relax. Tensions had been so high at the office lately that she felt as if it were more of a war zone than a business.

Every effort she made toward easing the stress—bringing doughnuts, making fresh pots of coffee whenever she was there, saying hello, attempting to talk the way they all used to—was met with indifference if she were lucky, barely suppressed antagonism when she wasn't.

Daphne had literally run away from her yesterday. Run, as if to look at Shannon was too painful. Daphne was a few years older than Shannon, and she, along with Melissa, had been really good friends before the cutbacks. They'd often had lunch together, talked about guys and dating and clothes. Before the economy tanked and the layoffs started, she'd invited them to the lunch exchange. Daphne had seemed interested. Now Shannon was the bad guy, the one responsible for everything that had gone wrong at the plant, including the shrinking client base. Shannon had stopped trying to fix what was broken relationship-wise, but she hadn't given up hope that an influx of customers, the type of big clients they used to have, would change everything.

The interview wasn't a guarantee of new business, neither was the Easter egg hunt or the banners or the cold calls or the personal meetings. But there was a chance that it could turn into something major. She was due, dammit, and yes, she understood that was magical thinking. Nevertheless, she would continue to hold on to good thoughts. Positive energy and action combined with a quality product and a track record to be proud of would prove that this was only a temporary downswing. Fitzgerald & Sons had too much history to lose now. She wouldn't let that happen, not under her watch.

She put bodywash on her sponge, her senses filling with lilac and spice, and let all her troubling thoughts run down the drain. In a very short time she would open her door and her bed to the man she wanted more than anything else in the world.

For tonight, she was the luckiest person ever. She couldn't wait until his arms were around her, until she could run her hands down his strong back, feel his breath on her neck, taste him and hear him gasp out her name.

Spurred on by excitement and the ache between her thighs, she rinsed quickly, dried off, brushed her teeth and grinned as she hurried back to her bedroom

She turned on the bedside light, but as a surprise, she'd bought a beautiful pink scarf that she draped over the shade. The room looked exotic and almost as sexy as she felt crawling naked between the sheets.

When he tapped on her door, she tugged down the top sheet so the first thing he saw was her hair spread out on the pillow and her very erect bared nipples. So much for skipping the sexy times.

# 14

Nate had gone back to his room at two that morning, still careful not to upset the applecart, especially today. He'd set his alarm for 5:45 a.m., and after his shower, he'd been glad of it.

Shannon would be down at six-thirty and he wanted her to have more than coffee for breakfast. He'd put on a pair of jeans and a T-shirt and prepared to make the best damn pancakes in all of New York.

The light was already on in the kitchen, which meant Shannon hadn't slept well. He didn't care that his surprise was screwed up as much as the fact that she was starting the day out nervous. Only it wasn't Shannon in the kitchen, but Mrs. Fitz.

"What are you doing up so early, boyo?"

He walked in to the scent of freshly brewed coffee and butter melting on a grill pan. "I came to make pancakes for the TV star."

Mrs. Fitz grinned. "That was very nice of you."

"And you," he said, as he got his mug down from the cupboard.

"She's so excited. She'd tried to get every station in New York to advertise the fundraiser, and no one's ever taken notice. It's a fine thing, her efforts paying off so well."

"Yeah," he said. "She works hard for the church. For everything she loves."

Mrs. Fitz put a ladle's worth of batter on the griddle, bringing vanilla and cinnamon into the delicious mix of aromas. "I know what Danny's asked you to do."

He stirred his coffee, then went to the table. "I wasn't sure."

"We're in a terrible position," she said. "We've done it to ourselves, and now we're asking you to fix it. Shameful. I'd speak to her myself if I had the courage God gave a ten-year-old. She's my little girl, and this situation is breaking my heart."

"I understand," Nate said. "But she's got to know the truth. It'll work out, I'm sure of it, but it's not going to be easy for any of you. I can't say I'm glad to help, but I'm the right person for the job."

Mrs. Fitz, still in bathrobe and slippers, had poured out four cakes, and she was watching them for the first of the bubbles. Syrup, the real kind, was at the ready, and there were four place settings on the table. "It's kind of you, Nate. We've all noticed how you two are thick as thieves. That's good. That's wonderful. You're family, and she can use the company. She works too hard, that one. I hope…"

"What?"

She flipped all four pancakes, then glanced at him before facing the stove once more. "I hope she lands on her feet. That's what frightens me the most. She's so talented and bright, but it never seemed to matter how often we told her she could do anything at all, chase any dream, she was convinced that the business came first. That we all lived and died for the bloody printing plant.

I'm grateful for it, God knows, it's kept us in food and clothing and our home for all these years, but if I never set foot in that place again, it'll be too soon.

"Mr. Fitz is deaf in one ear, did you know that? And the hearing in the other ear isn't good. He's tired, and he's ready for a full retirement without the worry. We all are. Shannon deserves her own life, cut off from any obligations, real or imagined. I want her to be happy, Nathan. I want her to be free."

He stared at his coffee, wishing he could skip the painful part, the part where Shannon would be crushed by the betrayal. But he couldn't. "You'll need to tell her that in a while," he said. "You'll need to say it many times, I think. She won't believe it at first. She'll just be angry. Worse, she'll feel like a fool."

Mrs. Fitz filled his plate and brought it over to the table. After setting it down, she placed her hand on his shoulder. "I'm sorry to bring you into this," she said. "But we're all grateful for you being there to help us through it."

He covered her hand with his. "We're family," he said. "I love you guys."

"Shannon'll be down in a minute. Eat up. You're far too thin."

Today was going to be wonderful for Shannon. She deserved the spotlight, the attention. She deserved the best he had to offer.

THE DAY WENT BY IN FITS and starts. Shannon's butterflies would swoop around and she'd fixate on the potential for failure, then some bit of work would catch her notice. Rinse. Repeat. It was only two o'clock. She was due at the studio at eight. She'd decided to eat her lunch at midafternoon, because she didn't want to have a blood-sugar crash, but she also had to account for the nerves. She'd brought soup, crusty bread, a banana.

Now she wanted chai tea, which they had only in the big break room. She left the quiet of her office, putting in her earplugs as she walked. Across the floor, she saw Melissa, Greg and Patrice huddled around someone in a chair. Shannon raced over to find out what was going on.

There were accidents from time to time; it was a big plant with lots of machinery, but it had been a while since anyone had been injured. Brady ran a tight ship, and there were frequent enough breaks so that no one would get too drowsy at the controls. Oh, God, she could see now that it was Daphne, and she had her face buried in her hands, shaking, crying. What the hell?

Patrice saw Shannon first and the expression on her face, such incredible contempt, made her flush. It was awful being the object of scorn, of mistrust. She was hated and no amount of explanations seemed to change anyone's mind.

Greg and Melissa were staring at her now, and they backed away from Daphne, who continued to weep. Shannon crouched in front of Daphne's chair, touched her knee. Daphne glanced up, her mouth opened as if gasping, and she rose so swiftly she almost knocked Shannon on her ass.

Daphne darted past her coworkers, heading toward the back of the shop, Shannon right on her tail. There was no way she could ignore this or even send Brady to investigate. She didn't know if Daphne had been injured or if something else was tearing her apart.

Daphne rushed into the ladies' room. By the time Shannon went inside, her ex-friend was shutting a cubicle door behind her. Shannon's right hand pressed back, and she yanked out her earplugs with her left. "Daphne, wait."

"Go away."

"I can't. Please. Tell me if you're hurt."

"No. I'm fine. Just go away."

"You're not fine," Shannon said. "I hate this. Please, let's just talk. I know it's been rocky between us, but—"

The pressure on Daphne's side of the door vanished, and Shannon stumbled forward, barely able to stop herself before she plowed into Daphne. Straightening quickly, Shannon took several steps back.

Daphne didn't seem to have noticed either the stumbling or Shannon's attempt to give her some breathing room. "Rocky?" she repeated, as if Shannon had spit the word at her. "Things have been rocky? Do you know what the insurance company wants to charge for catastrophic illness coverage? More than my monthly paycheck, that's what. Because I was born with diabetes. I've stopped sleeping, I'm going to lose my apartment, and then what? All I know how to do is work the printing machines, and there are no jobs out there. None."

She took a step toward Shannon, her face blotchy and her eyes red. She pointed her finger like a weapon as she shouted, "Why don't you just do it already. You think we're stupid? That we don't know?"

"Do what? Know what?"

Daphne's face twisted into such an ugly mask it made Shannon feel sick. "Yeah, you do think we're idiots. Working twice as hard for less money. Doing the job of three and four people. No insurance, and your father is all about planning his retirement so he can go sit on a beach somewhere and have fancy drinks. Brady's got a drawer full of brochures about new and better places to work. We know that guy that came by last week with your dad was a buyer. You all are going to walk away millionaires, and we'll be shit out of luck without a nickel."

"What are you talking about?" Shannon had to grip the sink behind her. The tirade was insane, it made no sense. "My father's not retiring. We're not trying to sell anything. I'm doing everything in the world I can to bring us more clients. Why do you think I've been working so hard on this Easter project? I'm trolling for customers. I spend half my day making cold calls. Would I do that if we were trying to sell the plant?"

Daphne wiped her nose with a tissue, then crossed her arms defensively. "Fine. Great. And I was feeling all guilty, but now I— You'll just keep feeding us this bullshit until we're all so desperate, we quit, and you won't have to pay severance."

"What? No. That's not true."

Daphne looked over Shannon's shoulder, and Shannon followed her gaze. The entrance to the ladies' room was filled with the other employees, and it was clear they hadn't believed a word she said.

"I've never lied to you." Shannon stood up straight, rallied her dignity. "It's been a struggle for everyone. All I've been working toward is keeping the plant going. Getting back on our feet so we can rehire a full crew. The decision to cut the insurance came down to the wire. It was that, or close the doors for good. You know that. I told you that. I give you my word, we're not trying to sell the building. Why would we? It's been in our family for generations."

Daphne laughed. "You know what? I don't feel so good. I think I'll take a paid sick day." She put her hand in front of her mouth. "Oh, wait. Those were cut down to two days every six months. I don't have any left."

Shannon opened her mouth to keep trying, but Daphne shut the cubicle door. The staff didn't leave, but they did part to let her through. It was torturous, walking that gauntlet of mistrust and anger. She wasn't everyone's favorite person, but she'd never been hated before. Not even for things that she had done wrong.

Why did they all think she was lying? The confrontation had been a nightmare, her worst fears shouted in her face.

It had to be terrifying to have a chronic illness and not have insurance. Scary to have no real job security. But that was how it was now, not just at Fitzgerald & Sons. At least they had jobs. The plant had never missed a single payroll, not once. Shannon knew other companies were eliminating sick pay altogether.

She went back to her office, staring straight ahead. She wanted to leave, to find Nate, to fall into his arms and have him tell her that things couldn't have gotten this messed up.

She locked her door, closed the blinds. Tears threatened, but she wouldn't give in, not today. Not when she was busting her ass to keep all the employees. Daphne wasn't the only one who wasn't sleeping.

Her screensaver mocked her with pictures of happier times in the plant. Birthday parties, potlucks, costumes on Halloween. This had always been a great place to work, and it could be again. If only the staff were willing to have a little faith. But they weren't. After all these years, all the effort and the stress. They obviously hadn't bothered to think about the family's side of the equation.

She sniffed, opened her purse to get out her face powder, but took out Nate's trading card instead. She smiled at him and at the fact that she still carried his card around with her. She thought of calling, but he was in meetings until this evening when he was going to watch her interview along with half the neighborhood at Molly's.

That was the good side of living someplace forever. With the obvious exception of their employees, the Fitzgeralds meant something in Gramercy. They were honorable people. Her family had taught her to tell the truth, to value a job well done, to treat people with respect.

Time to focus again on Nate and let his picture bring her blood pressure down. It was coming on three o'clock. She had work to do, as always. Cold calls, mostly, but some filing, emails to answer. There was very little chance those things would be accomplished if she didn't lift herself out of this funk. So she'd take her lunch, a whole damn hour, and she'd go for a walk. Walking always helped. Then she'd come back to the office, and she'd do her job.

Tonight she'd put on her favorite outfit, brush her hair, freshen her lipstick and she'd smile when she got on camera. She'd talk about the fun they would have on Easter Sunday after mass. How each donation would help people who were truly in need. She refused to be in a bad mood when she had no power to change the outcome. She was doing her best. Working as hard as she knew how.

She was not a failure, and she wasn't going to act like one.

THE BUILDING WAS STEEL AND glass, and it didn't look like a television studio lived inside, but she'd never been to one before, so that made little sense. It had taken Shannon over an hour on the subway to arrive at the studio in Yonkers. She'd used the time to gear herself up, to let the earlier part of the day go as she focused not on the opportunity to promote Fitzgerald & Sons, but on the altruistic purpose of the Easter egg hunt itself.

Inside she was given a badge, and an escort, a harried young woman named Felicity, took her into a tiny little makeup area where someone who barely acknowledged Shannon powdered her face within an inch of its life. Felicity then took her to the green room, which wasn't green and didn't smell nice, either. The monitor that would have let her watch the broadcast was down, needing to be replaced, so Felicity pointed out a stack of old magazines. Shannon would be the only in-studio guest for the evening.

As soon as she was alone, she brought out her phone and called Nate.

"Hey," he said, his voice as comforting as a hug. "How you doing?"

"Fine," she said. "Nervous."

"You're a natural. They'll probably ask you to be their next anchor."

She laughed a bit, a first for the day, and debated telling him about what had happened at work. The decision was made a second later as she really couldn't afford to get caught up in any drama. It was disappointing, though, to realize that her pep talk had given her only a veneer of equilibrium.

"Tell me about your meetings," she said.

"They were about as dull as meetings get."

"I don't care. I don't want to think about being on camera. So you need to entertain me. You're at Molly's, right?"

"I am. It's packed. Everyone's here. Even people I

used to know. Mrs. Gailbraith from four doors down is here."

"What? She never goes out. Did you thank her for all those candy bars?"

"I did. Told her she was the best Halloween house on the whole block. She seemed pleased."

"What about the family?"

"Myles and Alice are here, so are Brady and Paula. Danny's come with a very beautiful girl who's far too good for him— Ow."

Shannon was smiling now for real. She knew instantly that Nate had made that last crack within hearing range of Danny, who had proceeded to exact immediate revenge.

"Princess!" It was Danny himself on the phone now. "Ow. Jesus, Nate, take my shoulder off, why don't you." Danny added a muttered expletive. "Hey," he said into the phone. "Is it true you don't want to be called Princess anymore?"

"Yes." She let out a happy sigh. Nate would get a bonus tonight for that. "Who's your friend?"

"She's a gorgeous woman of discriminating taste, and you'll meet her when you come back to visit the little people."

She shook her head. "As always, Danny, you're a riot. Is Tim there?"

"Yeah. He and Brady are arm wrestling. For money."

"Don't let Ma catch them."

"She's already made ten bucks, are you kidding?"

"Give me back to Nate, you hooligan."

It took a moment for the phone to get into Nate's hand, and then he told her to hang on. When he spoke again, the background was much quieter. "I'm back. It's a madhouse out here."

"Watch, I'll probably do something horribly embarrassing. Get the hiccups or something."

"No, you won't. And even if you did, we'd love you just the same."

She knew he was talking about the family, about love in the broadest sense, but that didn't stop the flurry that kicked up inside her. "I'm going to splurge after this and take a cab home."

"Good. I was about to suggest that. I was worried about you on the subway."

She wished he was there with her, not at Molly's. "I can take care of myself, but I'm tired, and I want to be at home."

"Tonight's going to be rough," he said, his voice lower, a little harder to hear. "The gang's all staying over."

"I figured. Maybe you can sneak in when everyone's asleep."

"Or maybe I could steal you away, and we could spend the weekend at a hotel."

She sighed. "That sounds—"

Felicity opened the door. "You're up."

"I've got to go," Shannon said, as the butterflies in her stomach suddenly grew teeth.

"Break a leg," he said.

"Thanks. 'Bye."

Felicity barely glanced at her as she led her through corridors, over great big cables that were strewn about on the floor. There were flashing red Silence signs all along the way, and as they got closer to where the action seemed to be, the signs changed to On Air.

There were cameras, two of them, and the cohosts' desks. The set itself seemed incredibly smaller than it looked on television. She recognized Lisa Jenner at one desk, a very large picture of the New York skyline behind her, talking to the camera, reading from a Tele-PrompTer. She seemed relaxed and pretty, never once looking down at the papers that were in front of her.

Grant Yost was at the second desk, the one Shannon was escorted to. It had a swirled blue backdrop with the station's call letters in white. To his right, out of camera range, Shannon saw herself and Grant in a very large monitor. Her hair looked okay, but she should have gone with the matte lipstick. She was seated in a chair that had a low back. Since Lisa was still speaking, no one gave her any instructions, but she assumed that would come in a moment.

Sure enough, the red light on the camera went off, and before Shannon could introduce herself to Grant, Felicity got her attention. As she fit Shannon with a tiny clip-on microphone, she said, "Look at Grant, not the camera. Seriously, looking at the camera ends up being creepy."

Shannon took out the flyer for the Easter egg hunt. "Who should I give this to?"

Felicity looked at the paper blankly, then said, "I'll take care of it. You'll be on in five."

Five didn't mean minutes, but seconds. Grant still hadn't looked at her when he faced the camera. "Tonight's guest is Shannon Fitzgerald of Fitzgerald and Sons Printing. They're famous for making trading cards for the New York Yankees and the New York Mets, to name two famous franchises. They also print textbooks and catalogues and even children's books. What WNYC has recently discovered, however, is that Fitzgerald and Sons also prints a different type of trading card."

A picture replaced the live shot of her and Grant. Shannon stared in mute horror at Nate's trading card, surrounded by five other cards, all the men from the last batch she'd taken to the St. Marks lunch exchange.

"These cards aren't keepsakes. They're solicitations. Traded among a prominent group of women including, it appears, Rebecca Winslow Thorpe, CEO of the venerable philanthropic Winslow Foundation."

A video of Rebecca, Bree and Katy came up in the nightmarish slide show, walking into the church, with Rebecca looking behind her as if she were doing something illegal. Shannon's mouth opened. Inside her head she screamed for Yost to stop but she couldn't seem to make a sound.

"The men on these cards," Grant continued, "have no idea they're being traded like so much chattel."

Grant shifted his attention to Shannon. "Ms. Fitzgerald, I understand you were the person who came up with this trading scheme several months ago, and since then, over a hundred unsuspecting New Yorkers have been up for auction in the basement of St. Marks Church. Is it true that a percentage of each sale goes directly into your pocket?"

# 15

SHANNON COULDN'T BREATHE. The room spun and she had to grab on to the desk to keep herself upright. "I don't understand," she said. "What about the Easter egg hunt?"

"Please, Ms. Fitzgerald. Explain to us how this trading card system works. How you've managed to keep the scheme quiet for so long. I was told there's a strict confidentiality agreement among the women who sign up to be involved with the auction?"

"There's no auction. It's not like that. We're friends. It's for fun, and for connections between friends."

"If it were for fun, then why weren't the men who are being traded asked if they wanted to participate? If it were as innocent as you claim, why would so many of the men on the back be marketed as One Night Stands?"

Nate's picture was still on the backdrop, but next to it now was the picture of the back of his card. One Night Stand written in bold.

Shannon felt as if she were going to be sick. "There's no auction, no money. It was meant as something nice. Something good."

"Tell that to the men you've been swapping."

She knew she had to explain, get him to listen and stop making horrible accusations. But Nate was watching this show. Her family and everyone she knew were watching this show, and she hadn't asked. She'd used Nate, and all the other men, and she hadn't asked. How could she have not seen how intrusive…?

"None of this was done maliciously or for profit," she said, trying with all her heart to be as professional as she could. The humiliation was strangling her, but she had to keep on. "We're all friends. We share lunches. And we talk about dating and how hard it is in New York—"

"So you saw an opportunity and you ran with it. Using the printing plant. Did your family know you were printing trading cards with such personal information? One card we saw said, and I quote, 'He's so hot, you'll need a fire extinguisher.'"

"You're taking everything out of context. That's how girls talk about potential dates. It's not wrong." Her voice caught, and she knew her face was red, which made her want to double over and die.

"I think you'll find the men on these cards, and we have yet to quantify exactly how many that is, will have something to say about whether it was wrong to use their pictures, their personal information, to barter them without their express permission." Grant turned to the camera, and Shannon caught sight of the monitor. Nate was center stage, as if he represented all kinds of horrible and salacious things done in secret basement meetings.

"We'll have more on this story in the coming weeks as we uncover how many men have been secretly shared among this group of women under the guise of trading lunches. We'll return in a moment."

The red light on the camera turned off, and Grant calmly removed the microphone hidden under his tie. He didn't look at her. Not once. He got out of his seat and walked over to some woman standing by the exit.

Shannon forced herself out of her seat. She took the microphone she'd been given, dropped it on the floor and stepped on it as hard as she could as she followed signs out of the building. Someone called her name, a man, whom she ignored.

Where had they gotten their information? She trusted every last woman at the lunch group. No one would have blabbed. Not only were they all trustworthy, but publicizing the cards ruined everything for everyone. So who...?

"Oh, God." She braced a hand on the wall. She knew...she knew...

The day she'd been working on Nate's card, she'd gone for coffee and when she'd come back, the picture of the abandoned printing plant had been on her screen. That's when someone had downloaded the batch of cards.

She knew who that someone was, and that hurt almost as much as the blinding humiliation. Daphne. Shannon pressed a hand to her stomach.

Daphne had been to Shannon's home. She knew her family. The two of them had shared more stories about dates than Shannon ever had with any member of the exchange. Daphne had been her friend.

Then again, Shannon was Nate's friend, and what had that gotten him?

NATE WAS STILL STARING AT THE big television behind the bar at Molly's. The packed room had gone silent, the TV muted. He was squeezing his beer glass so hard, either it would shatter or his fingers would break. *Shannon.*

It had been a shock to see his picture on the screen. Trading cards? He'd always dreamed about being on a card, practically every boy he'd known had wanted that, but for sports. For being famous. Nate had no idea what to make of the card he was on. One thing he knew for certain was that Shannon hadn't done anything wrong. That two-bit hack of a news anchor had been full of it.

The other thing he was sure about was that Shannon had been eviscerated. Tricked, shanghaied, humiliated, three days before her charity Easter egg hunt. Nate wasn't a violent man, but he would personally strangle whomever had planted that story.

He would also call his old buddy Brent first thing in the morning. Brent was one of the best litigators in the country.

"What the hell was that?"

At Danny's bewildered question, Nate jerked out of revenge mode. He didn't answer, but it did get him pressing her speed dial number. Her cell rang and rang, until it went to voice mail. "Shannon. I'll call you back. Pick up, honey. Please. It'll be okay, but I need to know where you are."

He hung up, hit redial. Got the same result. She hadn't turned off the phone, then, but she wasn't answering. The next three times he called, the number was busy. So he wasn't the only one calling. He hoped it was friends, but for all he knew, there could be other news media trying to get in on the story. Rebecca Thorpe was involved, and that was big news. Very big.

"I can't get through," Mrs. Fitz said.

"Me, neither," Nate said, swallowing hard.

Mrs. Fitz looked wild-eyed. "She's all the way in

Yonkers. She'll be beside herself. We have to go get her."

"She told me she was going to take a cab home," Nate said. He would have hugged Mrs. Fitz himself if Mr. Fitz wasn't already holding her.

Every person Nate saw looked shell-shocked. He felt the same. The accusations that bastard had flung about had been disgusting. To blindside Shannon without giving her the chance to defend herself was the worst kind of sensationalism with no regard for the truth. He didn't give a damn if his picture ended up on every news show in America, he would not have Shannon treated like that.

He was shaking in his rage, with his worry. She was out there, an hour away at least, and if she didn't pick up the phone, he didn't know what he was going to do.

She had been so frightened of things going wrong. The hiccups. Jesus. The bar was too hot, too crowded, and he thrust his way out.

The night was supposedly the coldest in weeks, but he didn't feel it. Adrenaline made his heart pound, made him want to jump in the next cab and race to her side. He had no idea how to find her. Someone could probably trace the GPS in her phone, but not anyone he knew.

"Shit," he said, and he said it again because he could. He was going to find out where that prick Grant lived and make him sorry he was ever born. Nate dialed again, and when he got the busy signal he almost threw the cell as far as he could launch it. With an effort, he held back. Barely. He didn't know what to do with himself. Except worry. And think the worst.

SHANNON WAS ON THE SUBWAY. She wasn't sure which train or where it was headed. She'd just used her MetroCard and climbed aboard the first open door she saw.

She'd shredded a number of tissues and stuffed the remains in her purse. There were two clean ones left. She might have to buy more because she wasn't getting off this train. Ever.

She was sitting on a side bench, holding on to a pole, staring out the window as the tunnel flashed by. Oddly, she felt as if she'd left herself on a chair in a TV studio where the world she used to know had been crushed out of existence. She had no idea who was riding this near-empty subway car.

Thankfully, it was after eleven. Not too many people out and about at this time, not like rush hour. Still, New York never really shut down, so she wouldn't be alone no matter what. Too bad.

She closed her eyes and just as quickly opened them again. It was the fourth time she'd tried and she wouldn't try again. Closing her eyes didn't provide enough distractions. Behind closed eyes she would remember not any particular word, but a tone, the way it felt when she realized exactly what he was accusing her of.

All her work, all the struggle, the effort, the calls, the nights she couldn't sleep worrying about Fitzgerald & Sons—all of it was for nothing. They were a joke now. It didn't matter how the story ended. Even if by some miracle the reporter apologized for his misinformation on the air, it wouldn't be enough. People's memories were short, and with a shocking story like this one, that's all they'd need.

No one would think of Fitzgerald & Sons without the association of Shannon Fitzgerald running some underground man swap. She didn't even know what that meant, except that it was salacious and filthy. That's all her customers would think. As they canceled their orders.

How could she ever make another cold call? How could she assure the potential customers who were on the brink of signing? Credibility, gone. Self-respect, none. And they'd used Nate as the symbol of her disgrace.

Damn, now she was down to one tissue. She had money. Credit cards. She supposed she could get out at the next stop, find herself a place to hide for the night.

No, no, not a hotel. She would never sleep. At least here there were people coming and people going. All of them looked as if their world hadn't been shredded.

God, they'd shown Rebecca. How many times had they sat outside St. Marks shooting footage, trolling, hoping to find the right person or shot? How long would it take for someone to recognize Bree as Charlie Winslow's girlfriend then make their connection to the cards? Shannon couldn't even imagine the backpedaling they'd have to do.

She bent over, holding her stomach, biting her lip to keep from moaning out loud. Charlie had no idea about the cards. Rebecca's boyfriend, Jake, had been wounded in the line of duty in the NYPD, and now he'd be a laughingstock, and it was all Shannon's fault.

At least Nate was leaving New York. Not soon enough to outrun the ridicule that would come at him from all corners. Shannon had used every weapon in her arsenal to make sure the interview was watched by everyone who had even a tangential relationship to the Fitzgerald family or the business. She'd even figured out when affiliates of the tiny independent station would rerun the piece, and had sent alternative times and channels to all her address books.

God, with every stop and start of the subway a new horror came to haunt her. The repercussions to the lunch exchange women! Their families, their coworkers, all the men they'd ever dated. The circle kept growing and growing. How was her mother ever going to walk into church again? The Easter egg hunt!

Shannon sat up, but she was breathing too fast, and if she didn't get herself under control she was going to hyperventilate and pass out, and wouldn't that make a lovely picture for the *Post*.

It took two transfers and a dozen or more stops to finally reach Grand Central. Shannon could get tissues. Could find a train to anywhere. She'd heard rumors that people lived underground, in the station in abandoned train tunnels. That might not be so bad. Although she'd need a toothbrush. And more practical shoes.

The doors whooshed open and she stepped out. She walked. The four-faced clock was straight ahead. Shannon looked up and smiled. At last, something that made sense. The sky was backward on this ceiling. She'd come here with her fifth-grade class, and her teacher, Mr. Thomas, had made a very big deal of the backward ceiling. He'd said it was supposed to be the sky as God would see it.

According to all four faces of the clock, it was very late. She'd been riding the trains for hours, and somehow it had become 2:00 a.m.

She found her last tissue and kept on walking.

NATE SAT ON THE FITZGERALDS' porch steps, leaning against a post, freezing cold. They'd left the outside light on for when Shannon came home. If Shannon came home.

In all the places he'd been across the globe where

people had been desperate to find loved ones, Nate's role had been to be calm, supportive, gentle. He'd been the person they'd turned to for comfort.

Tonight he was the desperate soul, the one panicked beyond reason. The truth was the comfort he'd offered overseas had been useless. The hot coffee or the blankets had been all that mattered. His calm support had only helped him, not them.

He didn't know how to find her. Shannon was out there, and anything could have happened. He'd run through a hundred scenarios, all of them ending in tragedy. It was torture. For hours, every moment that went by was the moment before she would appear. When Molly's had emptied, only staff and Shannon's family remaining, he'd been certain she'd left a message on the machine at the house, only to have Mrs. Fitz remind him that Brady and his girlfriend had gone home hours before, just in case.

Nate had paced and dialed her cell until her voice mail had no more room. Now, as he sat in the cold, gripping his cell phone so tightly he bruised his hand, he was bargaining. If she came home, he'd never say a word to her about how she'd turned him into a trading card.

He would have preferred that the story hadn't already gone viral on the internet. Evidently, the Winslow family was big news everywhere. One of them was running for senator. Danny had shown Nate the story on Yahoo. A quick Google search had links to everything from the Winslow wiki to the history of trading cards, male prostitution, which had been a body blow, and the entire interview on YouTube.

But he didn't care. He wouldn't say a word because he knew she hadn't meant to hurt any of them. He'd only really gotten to know her in the past couple of weeks, but he was absolutely certain that this trading card thing was her attempt to help her friends find love. That's all. Because that's what Shannon did. She helped people—strangers, friends, family, community. The gorgeous redhead didn't have a malicious bone in her body, and God only knew how she was dealing with this avalanche of lies and blame.

He'd give up pretty much everything so that she wouldn't have to go through this pain, and that was a body shock of a different kind.

He hadn't realized until this morning, until he was alone waiting on the steps, that things had gone way beyond friends who have sex. He'd been convinced for years now that he wouldn't have to worry about the consequences of love. Wrong. So wrong. And with, of all people, the Princess.

He thought about going inside. He wouldn't go to bed, that was out of the question, but he could use something hot to drink. It was after 3:00 a.m., and his panic had been cycling for so long it felt as if he'd never relax again.

Then he heard footsteps. The click of heels on the sidewalk. He didn't move, didn't dare breathe in case he jinxed it or scared her off. If it was her.

It had to be her.

More steps, steps slowing down. It was Shannon. The relief hit him so hard he nearly passed out. Then he saw her face as she looked up at her home. His chest seized at the sorrow. At her hopelessness. Her pain and her guilt were written in her skin. Her eyes… Jesus. This was a woman gutted.

She shook her head, pressed the heels of her palms

against her eyes, then turned away, took a step to leave again.

Nate was on his feet in a second. "Don't."

Shannon gasped as her hand went to her chest.

"Don't you walk away," he said, running down the few stairs until he could grip her by the shoulders, hold her in place. He didn't even care that his cell phone was still in his hand, he was not letting go. "Do you have any idea how worried I've been? How worried we've all been? Your mother's beside herself. You didn't answer your phone. It's goddamn three in the morning, and anything could have happened to you. Anything."

She opened her mouth, but all that came out was a squeak.

"You can't do that to me again, you hear me?"

"Why?" she said finally, her voice high and lost. "How can you even look at me? I've done everything wrong. I made a laughingstock of you. Of the plant. I've ruined *everything*."

"You're remarkable, but not even you could ruin everything."

Shannon pushed at him weakly. "There's nothing funny about this. I'm a disgrace and Fitzgerald and Sons is going to pay for it. That terrible anchorman used your picture, and I lied to you about that. I didn't put your picture in the Gramercy newsletter, I used it to get you dates, and then I stole the card so no one could date you but me, but I never asked you, and that was horrible. You have every reason to hate me for it. And now I've dragged Rebecca into the mud, and she didn't do anything wrong. All my friends, they were just playing along with me, but the trading cards were my idea. My fault. And I made sure everyone kept it a secret. I had to have known it was wrong or I wouldn't have cared that it was a secret." She took in a deep breath, and when she let it out her whole body sagged.

He pulled her close, right up against his chest.

"I'm so sorry," she said, and he felt her body tremble, her shoulders shake with her weeping. "I'm so sorry."

Nate closed his eyes and rocked her, using his free hand to gently stroke her hair, giving her as much comfort as he could. But all he kept thinking was how grateful he was that she was alive. That she was here. That he could hold her.

That he loved her.

# 16

"YOU READY?" HE ASKED, as he lifted her chin.

Shannon shook her head. "As soon as they realize I'm not dead, they'll remember what I've done."

"You haven't done anything. Your family needs to know you're all right. I can't imagine even one of them is sleeping."

"No."

"Yeah, and trust me. Every moment is torture, so buck up."

She couldn't believe she'd have to face them when she was this tired and fragile. But since her feet had brought her home without her permission, she supposed it was inevitable. People didn't actually die from shame. They just wished they had. "All right. Let's go."

He had his arm around her shoulders, and she slipped hers around his waist. Nate's effort got them up the stairs. He put his hand on the doorknob, but kissed her temple before he used it. "It'll be okay," he said, as he took her inside.

There were lights on in the living room and the kitchen, and the moment the front door closed, Shannon heard her mother cry out. Then it was bedlam.

Her mother and father, hurrying from the kitchen, her mom holding an empty cup. Brady, Danny, Myles, Alice and Tim all came thundering from the living room and upstairs. Finally Paula, whom Shannon had met only twice, came stumbling down, tying her robe around her middle.

"Where have you been?" her mother asked. "We've been frantic. God in heaven." She pulled Shannon away from Nate and into her arms. "Never do that again, young lady. You aged us ten years with that disappearing act. Never again."

When Shannon was released, it was for only a second, and then her father took her up in a bear hug. He'd never been the type for hugs, and it was weird to feel him shaking, to feel the strength of his emotion. "Jesus Christ," he said. "You scared the life out of us."

The brothers just stared at her, for which she was more than grateful. When her father let go, she stepped back until she felt Nate at her side. "I'm sorry I made you all worry," she said. "And I'm sorry for the incredible mess I've gotten us all into. I never meant any harm. I don't know why they thought I was taking money or doing anything unsavory with the cards, but that's not the point. The fact is, I did use the printing plant for my own reasons. To make trading cards for my friends at the lunch exchange. I never did ask any of the men for their permission. That was wrong, and I'll apologize to each and every one.

"Mostly, I'm sorry for the damage I've done to Fitzgerald and Sons. I've humiliated us all. I don't know what's going to happen. People are bound to believe what they've heard on the news, even if it is just WNYC. I've tried so hard to keep our good name in front of the public, and now we're a joke, an embarrassment, and that's all my fault."

"It's…a little more than WNYC," Danny said.

"What? What's happened now?"

"I'm sorry, Prin—Shannon," Danny corrected himself and smiled, and that alone almost made her start crying again. "But the internet got wind. Because of Rebecca Thorpe. The story's out there."

Nate's arm went around Shannon's shoulders again, and he gave her a squeeze. "There are things we can do after we've all had some sleep. A retraction, for one thing. That son of a bitch Grant Yost is looking at a hell of a slander suit, and that's just from my attorney. I can't imagine what Rebecca Thorpe's going to do to him."

"But I didn't get permission."

"If you think that there's a single straight man out there who wouldn't agree to being on one of your trading cards, then you need to get out more."

Shannon blinked up at him. "But—"

"Am I on a card?" Danny asked.

"No," she said, not understanding his tone. He should have been outraged at the thought.

"Why not? What, I'm not good enough for your lunch exchange?"

She stared at her brother, wondering if she were hallucinating. "You'd want me to put you on a card?"

"Hell, yeah. Especially one of those one-night-stand numbers. Wouldn't that make life easier. Everything right out in the open."

"I'd get in on that action," Tim said. "You know all these women, right? There are no scary ones? I met this woman through an online dating service, and she turned out to be a stalker. She wanted to get married on our second date."

"That doesn't make her a stalker," Myles said.

Danny poked Tim with his elbow. "That makes her crazy. Wanting an ugly idiot like you."

"Hey, you're one to talk."

"Hold it," Nate said, his voice carrying over the room. "It's late. Tomorrow we can talk about everything. Sleep is the next order of business."

Shannon's mom turned to face her boys. "You all go on. Get to your rooms. Myles and Alice, don't worry about Nate. He's going to be bunking elsewhere."

"Where's that?" Nate asked, taking a step away from Shannon.

Her mother looked Nate in the eyes. "Your choice. The couch in the living room is comfortable. But you might as well go on and be with Shannon. Mr. Fitz and I appreciate your consideration, but given the circumstances, we're prepared to keep on pretending we don't know a thing."

NATE GRABBED HIS STUFF from Myles's room, then hurried to Shannon's. He thought about getting his bathroom business out of the way, but he didn't want to leave her on her own until she was safely in bed.

Good thing he came back because while she'd managed to get her shoes off, she was having trouble with her blouse. Her exhaustion ran so deep she could barely control her fingers enough to undo the top button.

Nate stepped in to help. Her hands dropped to her sides the second he touched her. Her eyes kept closing and opening until the blouse was undone and pulled out of her skirt. It was like undressing a wobbly mannequin. He'd raise her arm, and it would sink back down before the sleeve was off. He ached with how woozy and pale she was. Eventually he removed her blouse and quickly slipped off her bra. Taking off her panties was faster, and he felt as if he'd won something when she was finally naked.

God. She fell against him, and he held her, knowing he should help her lie down. He ran his hand down her back instead, so incredibly grateful she was in his arms, that she hadn't been lost to him forever.

It was easiest to lift her, bridal style, and put her down on the bed. He hadn't taken down the covers, but he managed to tuck her safely inside after a bit of maneuvering.

He watched her the whole time he undressed. She was out, completely still, even her breathing hidden below the comforter. But a single strand of her hair had broken free from the rest, and with every exhale, it quivered, making it hard to look anywhere else. It was proof enough until he could feel her again.

He didn't bother with shorts or pajama bottoms. He wanted to feel every part of her he could. When he climbed in to join her, he turned off the light, then pulled her close. Her head rested on his chest, her hand on his stomach. He wanted to kiss her, but she needed to sleep. So did he.

Just before he nodded off, she snuggled closer, one of her legs curling over his. He breathed easy for the first time since the ten o'clock news.

WHEN SHANNON OPENED HER eyes, the room was so full of light she had to squint. She was plastered against Nate, which was wonderful until the next second when she remembered what had happened at the TV studio. Her whole body seized in a clench and she closed her eyes so tightly she saw stars, but it didn't help. There was no magic that could change the past. She couldn't even hide in bed. The world had kept turning. They'd all been up so late. Had Brady opened up the plant? The company still had orders to fill. The employees still had jobs. All of them, including Daphne.

Shannon couldn't think about her, not yet. Nate was asleep. She moved carefully, trying not to wake him as she got out of bed. She didn't remember getting undressed. She donned her robe, her glance catching the clock. It was past noon. God, what havoc was waiting for her downstairs? In the real world.

She hurried in the bathroom so she could get back to Nate. She remembered him surprising her in front of the house, remembered his words and hoped like she'd never hoped that he meant them.

She brushed a lock of hair from his forehead, her heart aching for what she'd done, how she'd messed up so thoroughly. No one was that forgiving, not in the light of day. He'd been all over the news, and if last night hadn't been a horrible nightmare, his picture was now on the internet, as well. She doubted his bosses would be very thrilled about his notoriety.

She turned to get dressed but gasped as her wrist was caught by a strong hand.

"Where are you going?" he asked, his voice filled with sleep.

"To put on clothes. The second-worst day of my life begins."

He shook his head. "No. You're coming back to bed."

"I already thought of that, but I can't stay there forever. I'll have to face the music eventually."

"The music will wait for an hour." He let her go in order to sit up, but his gaze kept her right where she stood. "Please. I'm going down the hall for two minutes. Please be back in bed when I return."

"Nate—"

"For me."

She couldn't say no. In truth, she didn't want to. "Hurry," she said.

He was up more quickly than she'd have thought possible, his robe thrown on, and he was out the door. She was left in her too-bright room, the room of her childhood. The safest place on earth for most of her life. There would be no more procrastinating. She would find a place to move and leave this house. No matter what happened out there, whatever price she had to pay, she needed to step away from this cocoon. Maybe she'd have thought twice about her actions if she hadn't felt so protected all the time.

For now, though, she'd take the comfort. She let her robe drop where she was and crawled back under the sheets. She pulled her pillow close and breathed in the scent of Nate, so masculine and so him. She knew why his specific odor made her clench and shudder. She'd bonded with him. His scent would continue to please her for as long as they were together. Which wouldn't be long at all.

She inhaled again, not foolish enough to waste the good things she had. Not naive enough to believe she would get over him, not now. He would be the one man, the lost love. She would miss him forever, and even if eventually she did find someone else, Nate would remain the true love of her life.

She didn't mind. He was worth it.

It dawned on her that she was assuming that he'd wanted her to stay in bed to comfort her. It was equally likely he wanted the time to ask her what she'd been thinking. Why she'd lied. Why she'd ever thought it was all right to pass him around like a toy.

The door opened, and she tried to see it in his face, what he thought, what he wanted. His reason.

He dropped his robe, climbed in next to her and wrapped himself around her, kissing her as if it were the most important thing he'd ever do.

*Thank God.*

He tasted too much like mint, but that was okay. The bad things were coming, they were, but not while Nate kissed her. While he ran his hand down her back and up her arm, when he moved his thigh between her legs just hard enough to make her gasp. He kept surprising her. He should be angry. Maybe he was angry, but it didn't feel like that. His touch was too tender and his body too warm.

She didn't exactly trust her judgment, however, and this was important. "I know I told you this last night," she said, her lips an inch from his. She wasn't allowed to touch them again until she found out the score. Until she told him again. "But I need to say it one more time. A hundred times. I'm sorry. I'm so sorry that I used you, that my actions caused you to be embarrassed."

"Who says I'm embarrassed?"

"You're on a trading card. A trading card that trades men."

"I've always wanted to be on a trading card. I think I looked pretty good. Besides, you stole my card. I'm not sure, but I'm guessing you broke all kinds of trading card rules by your thievery. You need to apologize to the other ladies."

She laughed. She could hardly believe it was possible to laugh, or to feel this way about anyone. Ever. She'd had no idea what love was like, and now she did. Nothing else like it in the world. It felt as if…but no, her actual beating heart was changed because she loved

Nate Brenner. To love him with all her heart was a re-ality, not a poem. She wanted to tell him, she did, but because she loved him in such a real way, she wouldn't. He was leaving. He had another life, a world away. It wouldn't be fair, and he'd feel badly about it, and she would never want that for the man she loved.

"I'm glad you're not angry," she said.

He kissed her, a small kiss, just lips on lips, then pulled back far enough so that she could see his expres-sion. "It would have been better to have asked because there might be men on the cards who would mind. I can't imagine it, but it's possible. But I'm not angry. I know you would never do anything to purposefully hurt anyone, especially not someone you care about. I know that you wanted your friends to be happy. To have fairy-tale lives and bigger-than-life love stories. How could I be angry about that?"

She was glad she'd been able to watch him through that speech. He meant every word. She didn't have to worry about Nate. Not a bit. "Okay," she said.

"You do know the rest is all going to work out, don't you?"

"Eventually."

"Sooner than you think," he said, right before he captured her mouth in another searing kiss. His hands went to the sides of her face to hold her steady as their kiss went from hot to torrid.

She wouldn't have minded if that's all they'd done. Yes, she was aching with want, and yes, every time he rubbed his chest against hers it sent shivers all through her body. She pressed against his thigh, riding him, and it was almost as good as being filled, of being as close as they could possibly be. And then it wasn't enough.

"More," she whispered. "Please."

Tearing himself away, he rolled over, grabbed a condom and was back before she finished her exhale. "More. Yes. Everything. God, I want you." His hiss told her he was ready, and she grabbed the pillow she wasn't using, placing it in the general area of her hips before she lay back.

He moaned as he followed her, kissing whatever part of her he could—the inside of her elbow, her nipple, the side of her neck. Random sizzling sparks all over, everywhere his lips and tongue landed.

When he was above her, braced on his arms, she could see his desire for her in his dark eyes. Even when the lights had been on at night, she'd never seen so much of him. The crazy sleep hair that made him look adorable. He'd shaved, of course she'd known that somewhere because she hadn't felt his beard, but he'd had to have shaved *fast* because he hadn't been gone long. Lucky thing he hadn't cut himself. She touched his jaw, his chin, making sure. All she felt was smooth, warm skin. When he dipped down and captured her finger in his mouth, she gasped again. He was so good at that.

She spread her legs for him. "Please," she said again. "Come inside me. Fill me up. Make me forget about everything but you."

He pushed into her slowly, his gaze unwavering. "Oh, Christ, how you scared me. When I thought I'd never see you again, I couldn't think what to do." His eyes clenched as he seated himself all the way. Both of them were breathing harder now, faster, their chests rising and falling in perfect synchrony. "Promise me you'll never run like that again." He pulled out and pushed back in. "Promise."

She wanted to tell him she wasn't the one who was

running away. Instead she ran her hands down his back and looked him straight in the eyes. "I promise I will never run from you. Ever."

# *17*

NATE STARED AS STRANDS OF Shannon's silky hair slipped through his fingers to fall on the pillow. She was dozing, still tired after such a grueling night, and then they'd made love. His gaze went from her hair to her face. Her eyelashes were red. Red. He should have noticed that by now. Maybe she wore dark mascara on them, because how could he have missed the wonder of her red lashes?

He didn't know what to do. She'd suffered last night, and even if everyone in the city told her she was forgiven, he doubted she would believe it. Not until she'd made the amends she felt she must. After that? She was sensible, she'd go on with her life, but the memory would always hurt her.

He couldn't add to that. He didn't want to be part of anything that would always hurt Shannon. That was unacceptable, and even though it would be turning his back on the family who'd loved him best, he had to tell them that he wouldn't help. He'd rather cut off his own arm.

The air slipped out of his lungs as reality hit him anew. He had fallen in love. The impossible thing had happened. He was no longer the same man. Shannon had changed everything.

He got out of bed, and when he heard her squeak as she stretched, he smiled at her. "I was going to go shower. But I can wait if you'd like to go first."

When she shook her head, she looked at him as if nothing were wrong, as if last night had never happened. "Go ahead. But you'd better not use all the hot water."

He tightened his robe, then kissed her softly. "I won't be long."

"Good."

As he walked down the hall, the ripples of his new awareness started expanding. At the center was Shannon. Everything flowed from there. He had decisions to make.

SHANNON HAD DRESSED FOR work, although she doubted she would make it to the plant. It was almost two o'clock, and she was about to face her family.

Nate was right behind her as she walked down the stairs. They both stopped at the living room entrance. "You're all here."

"Brady's at the plant," her dad said. "Paula and Alice have gone to work."

She wasn't sure what it meant, that they'd stayed. Support? An intervention? "I hope there's some coffee."

"Danny, go get them some coffee," her mother said.

Danny didn't even make a fuss.

Shannon was growing more concerned by the moment. Her mom was wearing one of her company dresses. Not going-out-to-the-theater nice, but a cut above the norm.

"There's been a number of phone calls this morning," her father said.

Shannon winced. "Sorry. I'll certainly be saying that a lot today."

Danny came back with two mugs and put them on the coffee table. Coincidentally, there were two seats open on the couch. Shannon and Nate went to sit down, although her stomach was so tense she couldn't even think of drinking at the moment.

"I don't see why you should have to apologize," her mom said. "On the other hand, that reporter fellow needs to be tarred and feathered."

Nate threaded his fingers between hers where they lay on the couch.

"Well, I think what happened last night was a good thing," Danny said. "We all needed a little shaking up."

"What?" Shannon asked, appalled. "What part of that horror show was good?"

"For one thing, Fitzgerald and Sons is getting a lot of publicity."

"That's not the sort of publicity we want."

"Depends on what the objective is, doesn't it?" Danny gave her a lopsided smile.

Shannon leaned forward, wondering if she were still asleep and having one hell of a weird dream. "What are you talking about?"

Looks were exchanged. None of them with her. Nate scooted closer to her.

"First of all," her mother said, "we love you, and we have no quarrels with you using the plant for your own projects. It's your company, too."

"And?" Shannon said, her voice quivering.

"And we all agree you've done a wonderful job at the

plant. We would have closed a long time ago if it wasn't for your efforts."

"We appreciate that," her dad said. "I'm being a hundred-percent honest here. Every one of us knows you've worked yourself to the bone keeping us in business."

"But," Myles said, "we think that the days of Fitzgerald and Sons are over."

Shannon felt as though she'd been punched in the gut. If it wasn't for Nate's steady arm slipping around her, she'd have crumpled into a tiny ball. "Oh, God. I've ruined everything. I knew it was bad. I didn't think—"

"Wait, wait. You didn't ruin anything." Her mother came closer, sat down across from Shannon. "Sweetheart, listen to me. This isn't your doing. The truth is your father and I are getting on in years. We're tired of worrying about that old plant. We've been talking about retiring."

"In Florida," Danny said. "Tell her, Ma."

"That's right. We're also very tired of the snow. If I never see another flake…"

"You've been talking about it?" Shannon asked. "For how long?"

Her mother took in a deep breath. "For a while, Shannon. A while."

"The land's worth a fortune," Danny added, and damn him, he sounded excited. "That's prime territory. We're talking millions."

She could barely believe what she was hearing. They wanted to sell the plant. Move to Florida. Retire. She looked at every single member of her family, and each one was looking more abashed then the next. Except for Danny, of course. "Why didn't you say anything?"

"Because you were working so hard," her mother

said. "Although, to give us some credit, you do realize I've been telling you for years that you should find your own dreams."

"I thought you were talking about a husband."

The doorbell rang, and her brothers all made a dash out of the room as if it were a fire drill.

Shannon turned to look at Nate, and he seemed just as disconcerted as her folks. "Did you know about this?"

He nodded.

She pulled her hand free, feeling gut-shot. "How could you…?"

"I didn't want to tell you even though you needed to know. I'm sorry. I thought I was doing you a favor waiting until you'd had your interview."

"But why did you know before me?"

He winced, then took hold of her hand again. "Because your family loves you, and no one wanted to hurt you. They thought it would be kinder coming from me."

"I see."

"They didn't know I couldn't go through with it. I couldn't. I also know that you deserve a chance to find out who you want to be. You're amazing, Shannon. You can be anything you want."

"I thought I wanted to keep my family together," she said.

"Sweetheart," her mother said, looking right into her eyes, "we're still going to be a family. That will never change. No matter where we live, or where we work."

"Shannon." Tim motioned with his chin. "You've got some people here."

Dizzy with too much information, she rose on shaky feet. Nate got up, too, and together they went toward the foyer.

Shannon stopped when she saw Rebecca and Bree, along with Katy and her cousin Ariel standing inside the door. As if she hadn't had enough battering for the day. "I was going to call all of you," she said. "I'm so, so sorry."

"For what?" Rebecca asked.

"For putting you in such a horrible position. Everyone from the lunch exchange."

The women approached, none of them looking as if they'd been crying, or even upset. "There's been a lot of explaining," Bree said. "But no one's mad."

"Jake said he was flattered as hell. Grateful to you for getting us together."

"We've been on the phone all morning," Katy said. "Letting the cat out of the bag, so to speak. So far, everyone's been cool about it."

Shannon turned to Bree. "Charlie?"

"He's fine." Bree shrugged. "Quite amused, in fact."

"He's more than fine," Rebecca said. "Between his attorneys and mine, we will own that TV station. There's going to be a press conference tomorrow morning where Grant Yost is going to make a very public apology. You're going to be famous, but for all the right reasons. The trading cards are brilliant. Whether the men are in on the game or not."

Danny popped up between Nate and Ariel. "Brady's on the phone," he said, speaking to Shannon. "He needs to speak to you. Now."

She took the phone, wondering what bombshell Brady was going to drop.

"Shannon?"

"What's going on?"

"The phones are going crazy. I haven't had a second to do anything else. People are insane."

"What people?"

"Women. Men. From all over the damn country. First it was local, then it started spreading west."

"Excuse me?"

"They want the trading cards. Women want to start their own clubs and men want to be on the cards. It's nuts."

Shannon pulled the phone away from her ear and looked at it, sure there must be something wrong with it. "He says people are calling. To do their own trading cards. Women. Men."

Nate helped her bring the phone back to her ear. Brady was saying something she didn't catch. "What was that?"

"Not just the trading cards," he said. "But that literary publishing house in SoHo?"

"Yeah?"

"They want us to be their printer."

"I called them weeks ago."

"They're not the only ones. We've had three new orders placed, all from your cold calls."

It was too much. Shannon couldn't take in anymore. She handed the phone to Nate as tears filled her eyes. That wouldn't have been so bad if she weren't having so much trouble breathing.

"Shannon." Ariel came over and hugged her. "What's wrong? This is good news, isn't it? That everyone can see what a great idea you had? How many people you've made happy?"

Shannon nodded, but she couldn't speak. She couldn't stop crying, either. Then she was being shifted from one pair of arms to another—to the right pair. Nate held her close and tight, rocking her gently. "It's going to be okay, sweetie. You'll see. It's just overwhelming right now. Breathe, okay?"

"The only thing is," Rebecca said, "we can't figure out how WNYC found out about the trading cards. No one in the group would want this. We were all enjoying it too much."

Shannon sniffed, wiped at her face as she stepped away from Nate. "It wasn't anyone in the group. I'm pretty sure it was someone at the plant."

"Who?" Danny's eyes blazed.

"Never mind that," she said. "I'll take care of it."

"I hope whoever it is will be happy on unemployment."

"Danny, you don't know the situation. You're always so quick on the trigger."

"You okay?" Nate asked.

"I will be. Once I sort things out. I don't understand half of what's going on."

"Right. Executive decision." He looked at the women in front of him and the family behind. "I'm taking Shannon away for the night. For two nights, in fact. We're going to pack her a bag, and then we're leaving. She needs time to think, and so do you all. We'll see you again at the Easter egg hunt, where I expect all of you to donate as much as possible."

Shannon stared up at him. "But—"

"We need to talk. I have some calls to make, which I'll do while you're packing your bag. Make sure you've got your Sunday things with you. Now go on upstairs. I'll be with you as soon as I can."

She sniffed again and smiled. "Sounds like a plan."

Then he kissed her. Right in front of everybody.

THE FIRST THING HE DID WHEN he got Shannon inside their room at the Gramercy Park Hotel was order dinner. Nate knew she'd barely eaten a thing, and that the past twenty-four hours had turned her world upside down.

He also knew he was going to be adding yet another layer of improbable to the mix.

They'd ordered nothing more extravagant than pasta and salad with a good bottle of red wine. He liked the idea that they were staying at the hotel where they'd first danced together. That so much had happened since that wedding was difficult to believe, but he was used to that. It was a wild ride, this life, and things happened at breakneck speed. The trick was to be holding on to the reins, not the tail.

His poor Shannon wasn't quite in saddle yet. She hadn't spoken much, but he could see by her eyes that she was sorting and sifting and working hard to get her bearings. He was ready to help, but he needed her more stable before he got to the main event.

Luckily, room service had believed him about the extra tip, and he made good on his promise when the food arrived. The waiter set them up on the table in the room, the pasta steaming hot, the salad crisp and the wine excellent.

For the first ten minutes or so, there was just eating. Getting the hunger under control had been vital, and now that they were both slowing down, he felt ready to begin.

"So, I've made a couple of changes to my itinerary," he said.

"Don't tell me you have to leave sooner than you'd planned."

He shouldn't have started off so glibly. Shannon looked as though one more blow would do her in. "No, I'm not. In fact, I'm not leaving at all."

Her fork clattered on her plate. "What? What does that mean?"

He reached over and put his hand on top of hers. "It

means I'm not going back to Bali. Or going to Africa. Well, okay, I'll have to go to Bali to get my things, but I'm hoping you'll come with me, because you really need a vacation after this week."

Shannon stared at him, her lips parted, her eyebrows raised in a perfect picture of shocked surprise. "That makes no sense."

"Why not?"

"You love your job. Your work is everything to you."

"Not…quite," he said. Then he picked up his glass of wine and held it as if in a toast. "Turns out, you're everything to me."

That didn't make her any less shocked. In fact, he wondered if she should be worried about how pale she looked. "Shannon?"

"Did you just say…?"

"Yeah. I'm staying here, in New York. In the co-op I just bought. And I'm hoping you'll consider moving into that co-op with me. When we've finished furnishing the place."

"What about…everything?"

"I've decided there's my kind of work to be done right here in the city. I'm going to buy out Albert Gill's half of the business. We're still going to make fast-food franchise buildings and ugly strip malls, but I'm also going to repurpose our business plan to include restoration and rebuilding of community areas, starting with a certain corner basketball court. If the owners let us, that is. Anyway, I'm an urban planner and architect, and New York needs my kind of people. So I'm staying."

Shannon's mouth opened, then closed. Then she leaned forward. "You mentioned living together?"

"Right. That's kind of key to the whole deal. See, I've fallen in love with you. I didn't expect to, but you are just the most remarkable woman I've ever met, and the idea of leaving you doesn't work for me anymore. I want to start a new life here, Shannon. With you. I'd like for you to consider working on the nonprofit side of the new firm. Only if you want to. I still think you'd be fantastic on the city council, but more than that, you should find out what you want. I hope that what you want includes me."

"You've fallen in love with me."

He hadn't seen her blink in a while. "Yeah. Pretty hard, to be honest."

"Oh. I…"

"Shannon? You okay?"

She blinked. And then she smiled. And it was one hell of a smile. "I've fallen in love with you, too."

"Thank God." He put his wine down, then went over to where Shannon was sitting. He leaned over and kissed her. Then he kissed her again. "This is a whole new beginning."

"We can start our own legacy," she whispered, her eyes moist and sparkling.

He brushed the back of his fingers across her pale cheek. "It's going to be fantastic. Even the scary parts."

She laughed. Then she stood up, and they kissed some more.

BY THE TIME THEY GOT TO THE park on Sunday, Shannon had gotten a lot of things straightened out in her head. She had personal apologies yet to make, and no matter how many of her friends from the lunch exchange said it wasn't necessary, she would be in touch with every single trading card man.

She'd gotten on a speaker call with the family, who'd made a few decisions of their own. They weren't going to sell the plant after all. Brady wanted to stay, and there were so many new orders and so much interest in the trading cards that they were going to hold off. See what happened. But they were going to have to find themselves a new Shannon. Because after she'd helped train whomever they hired, she was going to be busy.

Moving out of the brownstone was going to be a huge undertaking. For everyone. Her parents would be heading off to sunny Florida. Brady was moving in with Paula. And she was heading to a brand-new life with Nate.

The booths were all set up, the Easter baskets looked terrific on the beautiful April day and her whole clan was already in position. Little kids were arriving in their Sunday best, Easter bonnets were everywhere and the sound of laughter rippled in the breeze.

When Shannon tried to get behind the counter to take donations, she was summarily dismissed by one of her mother's book-club friends. In fact, Shannon wasn't needed anywhere. Friends from the lunch exchange, from the neighborhood, the church, business contacts… it felt as if everyone she'd ever met was in the park that afternoon, and they all wanted to speak to her about the trading cards, about that horrible Grant Yost and how he was so apologetic on the news. And on the internet. And on every other local New York TV station.

It was all pretty glorious. But the best part was the man with his arm around her shoulders. The man she'd fallen head over heels in love with.

The man whose trading card was still in her purse.

\* \* \* \* \*

# MILLS & BOON®

## Why shop at millsandboon.co.uk?

Each year, thousands of romance readers find their perfect read at millsandboon.co.uk. That's because we're passionate about bringing you the very best romantic fiction. Here are some of the advantages of shopping at www.millsandboon.co.uk:

* **Get new books first**—you'll be able to buy your favourite books one month before they hit the shops

* **Get exclusive discounts**—you'll also be able to buy our specially created monthly collections, with up to 50% off the RRP

* **Find your favourite authors**—latest news, interviews and new releases for all your favourite authors and series on our website, plus ideas for what to try next

* **Join in**—once you've bought your favourite books, don't forget to register with us to rate, review and join in the discussions

Visit **www.millsandboon.co.uk**
for all this and more today!

# MILLS & BOON®

## Helen Bianchin v Regency Collection!

Discover our Helen Bianchin v Regency Collection, a blend of sexy and regal romances. Don't miss this great offer - buy one collection to get a free book but buy both collections to receive 40% off! This fabulous 10 book collection features stories from some of our talented writers.

Visit **www.millsandboon.co.uk** to order yours!